AN EMBARRASSMENT OF RICHES

AN EMBARRASSMENT OF RICHES

A Novel

Gerald Hansen

iUniverse, Inc.
New York Lincoln Shanghai

AN EMBARRASSMENT OF RICHES

iUniverse books may be ordered through booksellers or by contacting:

iUniverse
2021 Pine Lake Road, Suite 100
Lincoln, NE 68512
www.iuniverse.com
1-800-Authors (1-800-288-4677)

Because of the dynamic nature of the Internet, any Web addresses or links contained in this book may have changed since publication and may no longer be valid.

This is a work of fiction. All of the characters, names, incidents, organizations, and dialogue in this novel are either the products of the author's imagination or are used fictitiously.

ISBN: 978-0-595-44759-6 (pbk)
ISBN: 978-0-595-69083-1 (cloth)
ISBN: 978-0-595-89080-4 (ebk)

Printed in the United States of America

For Mom and Dad, with love.

"The best lack all conviction, while the worst
Are full of passionate intensity."

—W.B. Yeats, *The Second Coming*

Acknowledgments

Thanks to the brilliant people of Derry, without whom this book wouldn't exist.

Gosia, eternal gratitude for all those Thursday nights at the R-Bar plowing through reams of paper (and thanks to the R-Bar staff for putting up with us at "the round table"). Erin, what would I have done without you …?! Thanks for your editing while camping, scrutinizing the manuscript with a flashlight in a sleeping bag. Wes, Jack and Steve, thanks so much for not tossing the manuscript back in my face! Stacey and Shaun, thanks for your support and input. Mark, what would I have done without those hour-long phone calls? Brianne, you know how you helped me! Special thanks to Swan Park, for the excellent cover illustration, and to Brian Appio, photographer extraordinaire, for taking the brilliant author photo. Thanks as well to all my students and, of course, to everyone at the Olive Tree Café in the heart of Greenwich Village, NYC!

From *Guide to the Emerald Isle*:

"Gateway to the lush green pastures of Ireland's Northwest, Derry City is a priceless historical treasure, which today is as famous for its confident modern outlook as it is for the sparkle in the friendly eye of its inhabitants. Second in size after Belfast, this bustling city of 84,000 sits proudly astride the fast-flowing River Foyle and is a marvel of two communities (Catholic on the west bank and the Protestant on the east), three names (Derry for Catholics, Londonderry for Protestants and London/Derry for the confused) and countless nights of *craic* (pronounced "crack" and the local word for a good time). Visitors uneasy about the city's recent violent past have nothing to fear; there is little to suggest the dark days of the Troubles save an army watchtower or two. The splendor of modern Derry cannot be excluded from any thinking person's itinerary. Step into the Bogside, scene of Bloody Sunday and once a no-go area for even the British forces, meander through the bustling cobblestoned streets of the only Walled City in the British Isles, hearken to the echoes of 1450 years of history, and marvel at the ever-changing skyline of a city which is constant only in the warmth of its welcome. Here you are assured many a smile of greeting from people who are known the world over for their hospitality and charm."

From the mouth of a lager-fuelled indigenous person:
"Outta wer way, ye feckin eejit, or ye're gonny get a screwdriver in yer flimmin eye!"

From the *Derry-Speak Dictionary*:

wer: our
eejit: idiot
flimmin: expletive to express anger, disgust, annoyance, etc. (see also: piggin, bloody, bleedin, effin, flippin, et al)

JULY, 2000

She thought she would want for nothing after that bloody win. She'd clearly been deranged. In the dock of Her Majesty's Magistrate's Court, Ursula Barnett gripped the railing, her eggplant-hued bob a shambles, a woman on the wrong side of both fifty and, if her family had their say, a row of prison bars. She withered under the rows of glinting eyes in the public gallery.

Attempted manslaughter of a minor? Reckless endangerment? Whichever verdict was arrived at, those creatures heaved into the benches would be her moral judges, if not her legal jury.

Her husband Jed was the only solace, giving a watery thumbs up and a weary smile. These were cut short as the usher barked at him to remove his cowboy hat. Ursula loved Jed dearly and appreciated his support, but the sound of his muttered apologies in that Wisconsin accent made her cringe. She suddenly hated his faded goatee, his frail body in that checkered polyester blazer, his Buddy Holly specs and, most of all, she hated him for picking those damn lottery numbers six months earlier.

The courtroom door clattered open, and Ursula flinched as in Fionnuala and Paddy tramped, a pair of hardened hooligans in bargain bin rags. They claimed their place in the public seats, settling themselves with grand self-importance and eyes bleary from the previous night's drink, their looks letting Ursula know there would be hell to pay. The door burst open again and an unruly mob of wanes—as children were called in that part of the land—trawled in after their parents, sniggering as they took their seats and opening packs of sweets they had smuggled in past the security guard.

"Merciful Jesus," Ursula muttered.

She could hold her tongue no longer. She tapped her solicitor on the back. Ms. Murphy turned and glared.

"What in the name of God," Ursula hissed, "is them wanes doing parading into the courtroom? I thought wanes wasn't allowed?"

Ms. Murphy started. Surely her client knew the Northern Irish made rules only to break them?

"Technically, yes," Ms. Murphy admitted.

"What's that meant to mean, for the love of Christ?"

"I can ask the clerk to remove them from the court, if you feel they will affect your testimony, if their presence is intimidating or threatening in any way."

Her tone implied she thought this unlikely; a woman of Ursula's worldly experience terrified of wee creatures aged six, eight, and eleven.

"That wane there is me accuser, but!" Ursula said, nodding to Padraig, who was beaming like a superstar and scoffing down Jelly Babies.

The eyes of the court usher warned them to be still. Ms. Murphy nodded in his direction, and her look appealed to Ursula's sense of compassion.

Ursula leaned back into the dock, spiraling into helplessness and frustration. All the rules were being bent, except those to which she herself were being held. The whole ridiculous world had gone mad, and she and her handbag were expected to be answerable for everything.

Three justices of the peace filed in. A trio of Orange Protestants, no doubt, shipped over from Manchester. As they took their places behind the raised bench, Ursula could only hope their privileged Proddy educations would allow them to see sense: she was the injured party in all of this.

"Hear ye, hear ye, all rise, the court is now in session," the clerk called out. "This is case number 30251, Flood Vs. Barnett, the honorable Magistrates Sterling, Hope and Caldwell presiding."

Ursula tensed at the snickering from the public gallery. It was all passing before her in a blur—the magistrates settling and silent, their eyes passing judgment; the solicitor for that pack of hooligans droning on; the whine of her own solicitor piercing the air in response; Mrs. Feeney swanning up to the stand, face hardened, wooly cardigan buttoned; the Holy Book placed before her; the raising of her right hand; Do you affirm that the evidence you are about to give ...

Ursula struggled to comprehend how she had arrived at this crucifixion. She had been cast out of the family, a disgrace, after that shameful business with the IRA in 1973, it was true, but hadn't a lifetime spent clawing back their trust and affection been penance enough?

"*That* heartless bitch," Mrs. Feeney growled, a finger singling Ursula out, "has a lot to answer for!"

Apparently not. When it came to love or money, money won out every time.

"Crime of malice!" Mrs. Feeney roared.

The magistrates, the multitude of faces in the public hall, all regarded her with contempt. Ursula gripped the handrail of the dock and braced herself for the worst.

THE LOAN
THREE MONTHS EARLIER

1

The officer in charge of the Magilligan Prison visits room flinched at the unsightly creature clomping towards him, resentment etched proudly on her brow. Mutton dressed as lamb, he saw, his eyes slipping from her bleached pigtails, past her alarming overbite and resting on the low-cut leopard print top, skimpy skirt, and the chain-link belt cutting into her groaning middle-aged spread.

Fionnuala Flood still believed her waist had snapped back into shape after popping out seven wanes in a row decades earlier. She tossed the bag of freshly laundered football jerseys and jeans at the officer, waved hello to her cousin Maggie already at a table with her youngest—in for a joyriding manslaughter—and galloped over to where her pride and joy, the eldest of her seven, waited impatiently.

"Right, Lorcan," she said, leaning over the chipped table, lips puckered. Their mouths met, and her tongue flickered between his teeth. She slipped the polythene bag of Vicodin into his mouth, maternal duty done, and smiled mechanically. Her foxlike eyes darted around the hooligans and thugs that blathered on around them, searching for what she had come looking for.

"Ach, ma, am gasping for a fag," Lorcan pleaded.

Fionnuala flicked open a packet of unfiltered Rothman's cigarettes, and Lorcan was soon sucking down.

"What about ye, son?" she asked as they were shrouded in smoke, and the baggy was transferred by sleight of hand from his mouth into his pocket. "Ye've not been interfered with, I hope?"

"God bless us, naw! I'd clatter seven shades of shite outta any fecking poofter trying for a go at me arse!"

A hard, Bogside man was what she had raised. Fionnuala settled back into her chair with a confident nod. Better a hardened criminal at twenty than a nancy boy, she thought. She was proud of the Grievous Bodily Harm which had Lorcan sent down, hammering the crap out of some simpleton in the Craglooner pub who had spilled Lorcan's pint. Everybody knew drink was very costly.

"Any bars, hi?" Lorcan asked. *Any news?* he was wondering.

Fionnuala took a deep breath and leaned forward.

"Would ye believe that bitch Ursula has only gone and snatched 5 Murphy Crescent from under wer noses! The years yer granny struggled to keep up them house payments, and then in swans the lady of leisure Ursula, handbag bulging, and snatches up the family home. You know we've always had an eye on 5 Murphy, planning to get at a bargain rate from the city council."

Lorcan struggled to recall a time his mother had ever mentioned wanting to get her hands on 5 Murphy Crescent. He was too much his mother's son to mention that it wasn't even his mother's family home; that was a dilapidated ruin amongst the landscape of torched phone boxes and discarded mattresses that was the Creggan Heights Housing Estate. Her house was peopled by the Heggartys, a terrifying herd of bruisers. He cleared his throat through the fag smog to reply, "You were gonny buy it yerselves, then?"

Fionnuala spat, "Ach, don't be daft! We've not two pennies to rub togeller. Yer faller and me is working all the hours God sends, and even with all them double shifts at the Sav-U-Mor, I've still been reduced to taking on anoller job to put a dent in wer debt. Scrubbing the mingin loos of all the pubs down the town, I am now, and wan word outta you and ye'll be getting a smack in the gob!"

Lorcan fought to suppress a snigger at the thought of his mother on her hands and knees cleaning the filthy bar toilets.

"Does wer Moira not send her check from Malta every week to help ye out?" he asked.

"Am after getting a letter from her telling me she kyanny afford it this month as she's moving into a new flat. A pure waste of a postage stamp, so it was! She's herself a new ... flatmate. Selfish bean flicker bitch!"

Bean flicker: Fionnuala was mortified to have spawned a lesbian. The disgust flashed briefly in her eyes, then she rattled on.

"We've had yer sister Dymphna handing over a wee bit from her pay packet from the meat and cheese counter to help us out. Thank merciful Christ she got that job at the Top-Yer-Trolly down the town." The superstore in Derry's city center which proudly boasted "Our Prices Are Always Less Than Right!" and stocked everything from porridge to curling tongs.

"And wer Eoin?"

"Legless with drink he staggers home from that Craglooner every night. I haven't a clue where he finds the funds to be always blootered. That pub must have some drink special for them that kyanny find work. I've half a mind that he's—"

The warden hovered above them. She shifted herself and a brightness affixed itself to her voice.

"I had the headmistress of the school ringing me up the oller day saying wer Siofra was caught flinging rocks at Una Murphy in the playground. Silly wee gack hadn't the presence of mind to duck when she saw them flying through the air at her. Sure, it's not wer Siofra's fault Mrs. Murphy's wane is a simple-ton. And, never fear, I let the headmistress know that and all! So we've Ursula giving Siofra communion instruction every week, to rein her in, like."

Lorcan stared, and Fionnuala nodded.

"Aye, I must have been outta me mind with drink to allow yer faller to let yer auntie Ursula less than ten yards from Siofra."

Fionnuala looked around shiftily before leaning in towards her son's sallow face.

"What am here for, actually, son, is … Have ye no mates that's up for release soon? Am looking for some dead hard rowdies."

"Why, fer feck's sake?"

"To follow that shameless cunt round the town and frighten the merciful Jesus outta her."

"Outta wer Siofra?" Lorcan asked, taken aback. His wee sister was only eight.

"Outta that hateful bitch Ursula!"

"I can help ye there, Mammy. Ye see themmuns over in the corner?"

Fionnuala stole a glance at two thugs in track suits, swallow tattoos on their necks, surrounded by a selection of hardened mothers and sisters and pregnant girlfriends. Her heart went out the poor souls, incarcerated in the prime of their youth.

"I do indeed, aye. What about them?"

"Do ye mind that touristy bastard from South Africa that was beaten sense-less with lager bottles and a lead pipe down the Strand a few months back?"

"I do mind, aye," Fionnuala said, nodding eagerly. How could she ever for-get? It had been a particularly heinous crime. The victim had been shipped back to Johannesburg in a wheelchair, his knees done and his head battered in.

"Themmuns is the perpetrators. Liam and Finbar, they're called, inside for malicious fires and all. Themmuns is to be released in three months, and they owe me. Do ye maybe want Ursula caused some bodily harm and all? Liam and Finbar is sure to be up for it."

Fionnuala grazed on her lip for a bit, brain cells trundling, but reluctantly shook her head in the end. She didn't want the police rung up.

"Naw, we don't want the peelers involved; am only wanting the fear of the Lord put into her. Do ye think themmuns can contain themselves with a wee bit of threatening and menacing behavior, just?"

Lorcan shrugged.

"We can but hope," he said.

They shared a laugh, then Fionnuala sighed and clutched his hand.

"Ach, it's a terrible sin sending themmuns after yer auntie Ursula, and ye must think am a hard-faced cunt, son, doing this to her. She always puts on a show she's the Lord's right hand woman, what with her singing in the choir and volunteering as an OsteoCare provider and all. If ye only had the slightest clue, but, how she made us all feel, staring down her nose at us after she paid off wer mortgage, and never shutting her mouth up about it. Am heart-scared she's gonny toss us all out on the street. I know she's always been yer favorite—"

"No worries there, mam," Lorcan said with a shake of his head. "I've learned me lesson. She's as quare as a bottle of chips, that wan."

A lunatic, in other words. And he said this although Ursula had always been first at their door with gifts on birthdays, had phoned him and even visited him there in Magilligan once.

Fionnuala was grateful; Lorcan might be saddled with the Flood surname, but his loyalty lay with the Heggartys.

He smiled. Fionnuala leaned back and memorized him until even that bored her and was grateful when the bell finally rang.

"Ach, that's me away off," Fionnuala said, affecting a pout.

She kissed him on the cheek and promptly snatched her remaining smokes.

"Cheerio, then, mam," Lorcan said. "Till next month. You'll tell the ollers I was asking after em?"

"Right ye are, son."

Lorcan was escorted out. At the other end of visits room, Fionnuala received another bag of his dirty laundry.

Sending hooligans with such a pedigree of violence to terrorize her sister-in-law was a mortal sin, and three months was such a long time to wait, but

Fionnuala had the satisfied smile of a day's hard work completed. This had little to do with putting the hit out on Ursula, more the £5 she had passed her workmate Magella to punch her timecard in and out at the Sav-U-Mor.

£ £ £ £

The numbers of his demise were 7, 9, 12, 20, 24, 29 and Bonus 36.

The day after the lotto win, they had bought matching Lexuses. Ursula's still smelled of new Coach leather; Jed's reeked of Marlboros and stale booze.

Jed Barnett swerved past the British Army watchtower in his new Lexus and barreled down towards the Bogside, a maze of terraced pebbledashed houses piled atop one another with staunch Catholics heaved inside. He fought a shiver of claustrophobia. He was an American, dammit, used to the huge lawns and sprawling back gardens of his home county.

He passed the lone wall announcing *You Are Now Entering Free Derry*. The house the wall used to prop up had long since disappeared. Bombed by British soldiers? Set ablaze during a common street riot? Jed didn't have a clue, nor did he care.

He steered past huge murals, memorials of the Troubles: kids in gas masks, working class Catholics racing from clouds of tear gas let loose by Protestant paratroopers, the victims of Bloody Sunday. Driving through the massive stone walls that had surrounded the city center for 400 years, he had never felt so trapped.

He jumped out of the car and headed toward the bookies and salvation.

Seven years earlier, Jed had found himself stepping off the plane at Belfast International Airport, alone with his shrew of a wife and her misery-stricken working class family in that war-torn afterthought of a rain-drenched town on the edge of a decaying British Empire. Now Jed had to get the hell out of Derry City. Permanently.

Flopsy Dun, a horse currently at only 50/1 odds but certain to win amongst those in the know, was running the Wolverhampton 2:40 race and was his ticket out. Literally. If the horse won, he could finally afford that flight back to Wisconsin. The ticket would be one-way.

For months Jed had been plotting to abandon Ursula. Not that he wanted to, but she refused to leave her family. So what else could he do?

During thirty-odd years of marriage, it had been a trial putting up with a woman who expected more out of her life, and lately it was becoming impossible to love one claiming the upmarket life she thought she deserved. When the £500,000 had landed in their bank account six months earlier, it recast her as the lady of the manor. If only in her mind.

Now she and the family were at each other's throats like rabid ferrets, and Jed was in the middle with a silly grin plastered on his face.

Even after his lotto win and taking out the second mortgage on the house behind his wife's back, he still couldn't afford the plane fare back to his hometown in Wisconsin, let alone the lump sum he would have to leave Ursula to tide her over before he could send her a portion of his retirement checks.

He opened the door of the bookies and darted inside before anyone he knew saw him. He pushed past the swallow tattoos, glazed eyes and soiled clothing of the drunks within. All around him, breath struggled to escape congested lungs. Jed sidled up to the counter and, with a mixture of embarrassment and desperation, whispered his horse and race.

"To place, aye?" the bookie asked.

"To win," Jed said.

The bookmaker glanced down at the huge wad of cash, and his eyes never met Jed's again. *Another soul lost,* the bookie thought.

Jed left the alkies and druggies, skirted past a pile of vomit on the curb and made to steal back to his Lexus, hungrily clutching the betting slip. He would listen to the race on the radio in his car. He bleeped the locks open and tugged at the door handle to plunge inside.

"Ye right there, Jed?"

He froze and forced his lips into a smile. He stuffed the betting slip into his pocket, well-hidden. It was Paddy, Urusla's brother and the only thing he had resembling a friend in that town. Paddy was with his mates from the fish-packing plant—a hoard of men thirty and beyond who still thought they were teenage delinquents. Trailing behind them was Paddy's youngest, Seamus. What a five-year-old was doing with his drunk father, Jed didn't wonder about anymore.

They descended upon him, stinking of fish in their overalls covered with innards and scales, and the usual strange greetings and Derry accent spewing from their mouths:

"What about ye, hi?"

"Any bars, mucker?"

"What's the craic?"

Jed couldn't reveal he had just squandered more money on a horserace than any of them earned in a week of hauling dead fish into crates.

"I'm going to try out that new café over there," he said, motioning vaguely and knowing they would be in the mood for lager, not food, so they wouldn't want to join him.

"Ach, catch yerself on! That Magella who works there is a right scaldy gee-bag."

"Aye, dead narky and crabbit, so she is!"

Had he just stepped off the plane, Jed would have stared at them with a cocked head and a quizzical smile, but he had been observing the Derry dialect and slang over the years, at first with a wry detachment, but lately with slight unease.

One of the few reasons, and there were very few, why Jed had tolerated life with Ursula in Derry was the people. He had found them a never-ending wonder, their wit sharp and their passion all-consuming, and this came through in their language. Recently, however, Ursula's family had begun circling the wagons, and his wife was finding herself the target of their acid tongues and exhausting obsession.

Just as every punch in that town was dealt with a disarming smile, so the delightful upward inflection of their tone meant an insult or threat could be delivered with such charm that a tourist would be smiling right as the fist was heading toward his face. As an objective observer, Jed had found this fascinating. Now he found it worrying.

"Go on and join us for a pint," Paddy said.

Jed motioned helplessly to his stomach and the café.

"Ach, ye daft gack," Paddy said. "Right ye are. See ye in the Bogside Inn the morrow for a game of darts."

Off they staggered, Seamus squealing as his heels scraped against the cobblestones. Jed scampered into the car and flicked on the radio, hoping he hadn't missed the race. The race was in full swing.

"Flopsy Dun," howled the commentator, "breaking from the back and coming on ever so strongly on the outside ..."

Jed stared in excitement at the radio dial. He couldn't believe his good luck. He wrenched open the glove compartment and scrabbled around for a flask of Jim Beam to celebrate.

"... Flopsy Dun starts to kick on, up two or three lengths, and Flopsy Dun is away!"

Shoving aside messily folded maps and Ursula's lipsticks, he grappled the flask and tugged it out. Two tattered pieces of paper, photocopied and stapled together, covered with ketchup stains, fluttered to the floor of the car. As the Jim Beam burned down his throat, Jed bent and picked the papers up.

"Holiday Man in second place three lengths behind, Sunshine Sam falling off, In the Wind neck and neck with Holiday Man ..."

As the excitement welled, he unfolded the paper and almost burst out laughing. It was the dictionary of Derry-speak that an old American friend had handed him when he first arrived in the city. How Jed had pored over the two pieces of paper, memorizing every word. He would take it with him on the plane and burn it with great glee when he touched down in Wisconsin.

DERRY-SPEAK DICTIONARY

A
afeared: afraid
affronted: embarrassed
am: I am ("Am affronted.")
and all: also
anoller: another
anyroad: anyway
arse: butt
arse bandit: gay male
arsified: drunk
away in the head: crazy
aul: old (an aul wan ... an old one)

B
bangers: Ecstasy
bars: news ("Any bars, hi?")
beanflicker: lesbian
bleedin: damn
bog: toilet
boggin: filthy
blootered: drunk
boller: bother
broller: brother

C
carry-on: commotion
catch yerself on: wise up
civil: polite
clarty: filthy
crabbit: crabby
craic: fun
cuppa: cup of tea

D
drawing the brew: collecting unemployment
dole: unemployment
dote: sweet child

E
E's: Ecstasy
eejit: idiot
eff-off: f*ck off
effin: f*ckin

F
fancy man: sexual partner
fear-hearted: scared
Fenian: supporter of the Cause
Filth: police
flash: showy
flimmin: damn
flippin: damn
frock: dress

G
gack: idiot
gacky: stupid
gaspin: thirsty
geebag: annoying person
git: idiot
gobshite: contemptible person
grabby: greedy
grotty: vile
Green: Catholic

H
hard man: headbin: lunatic
headcase: lunatic
heart-scared: scared
hi: you. Used in many greetings

J
jacks: toilets
jumped-up: pretentious

K
kyanny: can't

L
legless: drunk
(to) lift: steal
loo: toilet

M
magic: fanstastic
manky: filthy
(to) mind: remember (I do mind, aye ... I do remember)
mingin: filthy
minger: slut
moller: mother
mucker: friend

N
wee nadger: small child
nancy boy: gay male
narked: annoyed
narky: irritable
nick: prison
(to) nick: steal

O
(it's no) odds: it doesn't matter
oller: other
Orange: Protestant

P
paladic: drunk
palaver: commotion
pansy: gay male
peelers: cops
piggin: damn
(to) pinch: steal
poofter: gay male
Proddy: Protestant

Q
quare: very
quids: £.

R
raging: angry
right: alright ("Are ye
right there, hi?")
rowdie: thug

S
sarky: sarcastic
sausingers: sausages
scabby: vile/greedy
scullery: kitchen
skint: broke
slapper: slut
(to have a) slash: to uri-
nate

sleekit: crafy/sly
spastic: idiot
stoke: scumbag (origi-
nally gypsy/traveller)
stroppy: brattish

T
terrible: very
themmuns: those peo-
ple over there
tip: filthy place
toerag: annoying person
tole: told
trainers: tennis shoes

W
wan: one
wance: once
wane: child
weemin: women
wer: our
wile: wild = very
wingers: Ecstasy

Y
yer man/woman: that
person over there
youse: y'all

"... Flopsy Dun's the one to catch," the announcer blared, "with In the Wind rallying on the inside as they continue their journey towards the end line ..."

Fists strangling the steering wheel, Jed willed the stupid beast's snout to clear the finish line.

"Flopsy Dun, Holiday Man and In the Wind will go for the line together, flying home now and ..."

Jed could feel the ticket in his hand ... smell the kielbasa ...

"—*Oh!* What an upset! Flopsy Dun is down, colliding into the gate and—*Oh!* Taking In The Wind and Holiday Man down with him! What a palaver just five lengths from the finish line!"

Jed deflated against the steering wheel, and a sob rose.

"Jubilee Years rallies strongly form the outside, past the pileup, and ... *takes it for England!*"

A hoard of hooded rowdies erupted from the pub next to the bookies and glowered over at the shiny Lexus.

"With Sunshine Sam coming in second, and it looks like Half Hodds will be third!" the announcer said.

A hubcap clattered from the force of a well-aimed kick.

"Mingin aul git!" snarled one of the rowdies into the window. *Filthy old fool!*

Jed wept.

£ £ £ £

"... *Infinite thy vast domain, everlasting is thy reign ...!*"

The saints smiled down at them from the stained glass installed after the cathedral had been bombed in 1979. Ursula gamely tackled the key change near the end of the first verse of "Holy God, We Praise Thy Name" and peered over the top of her songbook. Choir practice in the pomp and granite of St. Eugene's was the only solace she had in her empty coalbin of a life.

In the nave sat Ursula's mother Eda, the Flood matriarch's fluffy head beaming and her foot tapping along to a hymn of her own making. At eighty-five, she had a mind that wandered and ears that needed frequent syringing.

"*Hark! The loud celestial hymn, angel choirs above are raising ...!*"

Ursula was at one with the choir members, good Catholic women in their twilight years, untrained voices raising as one, throats straining in a great effort at harmony for the sake of the Lord. The other week Ursula had taken them all to her new dream house over in Gleneagles, the swanky section of town, and they had marveled at Ursula's Neo-Gothic lounge with its row of gargoyles, the Gaggenau fridge with the filtered water tap in the scullery with heated tiles, and the ensuite in the master bedroom with the two headed shower so strong the water fairly took the flesh off of you. *Wile grand, wile lovely*, they had cooed, pressing her hands and praising her good fortune as Ursula poured the tea.

"*Cherubim and seraphim, in unceasing chorus praising ...!*"

Ursula smiled over at them now, but there was a question in her smile. Her choir sisters all seemed to be wedged against the far side of the choir stall, their hymnals bunched together. Ursula wondered if she had forgotten her deodorant that morning. She warbled along as she mulled this latest confusion and tried to sniff her armpit.

"... *Fill the heavens with sweet accord, holy holy holy Lord ...!*"

Earlier that morning, she had visited the ATM and taken a long, hard look at the screen which revealed the state of her account. The interest of the lotto money account was meant to be transferred monthly into her housekeeping account, but lately her balance had been shrinking at an alarming speed that even Ursula's tenuous grasp on finances found unbelievable.

The ladies of the choir struggled through "Glory Be To God On High," and "Palms Of Glory," and finally the chapel was still.

"Brilliant, girls!" cooed Mr. Ming in his sagging black cardigan. "I think that's it for the night."

They chatted and laughed quietly as they placed their hymnals in their handbags and reached for their plastic raincaps. Nobody was uttering a word to Ursula, nor even passing her a glance. Ursula tapped Mrs. Gee on the shoulder.

"Are ye up for a cappuccino at that new café down Shipquay Street?" Ursula asked.

Mrs. Gee's head trundled around on its neck, and her look excluded Ursula.

"Them coffees is wile dear," she sniffed.

"Ach, am paying, sure," Ursula said. She made to peer into the old woman's eyes, certain she had seen *guilt* glinting there, but she found herself already staring at Mrs. Gee's scraggy shoulder blades.

Mr. Ming patted his palms together with sudden excitement.

"Girls! Girls! Silence, now, girls!" he squealed in tones of glee.

They looked over at him expectantly, their arms half in their sleeves. He took a deep breath.

"I've a wile important announcement to make," he said with a dramatic flourish. "It saddens me heart to say we're gonny be losing wan of wer best singers, transferring to St. Moluag's Chapel down in the Bogside, so she is. A terrible wile loss."

Ursula looked at the group in surprised sorrow, feeling a pang at losing any one of them; they were a team singing together, just like the Von Trapps. She wondered which one was leaving. She didn't envy whoever it was, banished to that hardened church which squat in the squalid Catholic ghetto, where Fionnuala and her brood tramped in weekly, snorting at the sermons, their trainers up on the pews and why in God's name were the choir ladies aligning themselves into a primitive horseshoe a meter around her?

"We'd like to thank ye for all the help ye've given us over the years," the choirmaster said. "We'll all miss ye terribly."

They were beaming strangely. At her. Ursula felt a flicker of alarm as they shuffled closer, the horseshoe shrinking, a thank-you card materializing from a pocket and a scone with a candle appearing from behind a back.

"Sorry to see ye go, like," Mrs. Murphy said.

"A terrible wile loss, sure."

"Aye, ye're dead sound, Ursula."

They grinned up at her until she finally found her voice.

"Me?" Ursula gasped wildly, staring down at the envelope and flickering flame inching closer and closer. "Off to St. Moluag's?"

She turned to Mrs. Gee to share a snort, but the pew beside her was empty.

"There's some mistake, surely!" Ursula cried.

She looked to her mammy for understanding. Eda had slipped out to the street for a fag. The choirmaster's smile faltered.

"Faller Hogan tole me ye were to leave!" he gasped, wringing his hands.

When hell froze over!

"Am piggin sure!" Ursula snorted, smacking the gifts to the transept floor.

They all inspected her in curious shock, and Ursula's anger quickly veered to anguish.

"Where's the Faller?" she demanded.

"He's hearing confessions," Mr. Ming said with a nod at the end of the nave. "Ye kyanny barge into the confessional, but!"

"Faller Hogan hadn't a hand in it!" Mrs. Gee announced with a soupçon of glee.

Ursula stared, struggling to make sense of it all.

"But … But youse is me …"

She thought she had seen the faces of friends, but she gazed down now upon sharp lips and glinty eyes, necks stretched with hatred, cheeks scorched with scorn.

"Ach, we're sick to wer stomachs of singing songs of praise to the almighty Ursula!" Mrs. Gee called out.

"If I hear wan more word about them flimmin Jamie Oliver roasting pans of hers, am gonny spew, so am are!"

"Them airs and graces!"

"That'll be the lotto win going to her head, sure."

Mrs. McCracken turned to Mrs. O'Hara.

"Her husband, mind …"

"Ach, sure, Jed's a decent spud, him."

"Aye, Lord love him. The stench of drink off of him would fairly turn yer stomach, but!"

"It is any wonder he's blootered every hour God sends, the persecution yer woman there's putting him through?"

With a tortured wail, Ursula turned and fled through the rows of pews, the waterworks spewing down her face.

£ £ £ £

Fresh from three hours of slopping bleach down pub loos, Fionnuala slammed shut the hot press door, balanced the empty laundry basket on her hip, and headed downstairs for another load. Her face hung in its perpetual state of exhaustion. The tired stairs moaned and creaked under her heavy steps. How she hated the poky little rooms of their attached hovel in the Bogside, the cramped depths of which were dank, damp and slightly rank from the stench of crusty socks.

In the front hall, she glared at the post which had just slipped through the letterbox. Another round of effin bills, as sure as Mary was a virgin, and a final notice for the gas and electric, if she wasn't mistaken. Which reminded her … She punched Dymphna's mobile number into the phone.

"Mammy? I kyanny speak—" her 18-year-old daughter said over the whirr of the meat slicer.

"Mind ye steal enough saugingers for the tea the night," Fionnuala instructed. "Skinless pork, like. A dozen'll do grand."

"Mammy, but—"

"Youse'll be feeding on leftover rhubarb cake again if ye don't lift some food. See if ye kyanny shove a black pudding into that handbag of yours and all."

Fionnuala slammed down the phone. Glancing warily at the clock in the scullery—if she was late for her double shift at the Sav-U-Mor, they'd dock her wages £10—she dug into the pocket of Siofra's pink hip huggers and pulled out two mini Pokemon action figures … Pikachu and Wurmple, if she wasn't mistaken. Her face was black with sudden anger.

"Siofra!" she bellowed up the landing, over the dancey Europop of S Club 7 pulsating from the girls' bedroom.

Siofra skulked into the scullery, her porcelain skin and pale blue eyes deceptive; jet black hair revealing the tone of her eight-year-old heart. She started, defensive, at the sight of the toys in her mother's hand.

"Where," Fionnuala asked, "did ye get themmuns from? Ye've not been battering the shite out of that wee girl from yer class again? Pinching her toys in the playground?"

Siofra flinched under her mother's outstretched hand.

"Naw, Mammy! I never!"

"Don't come the innocent with me, wane! Themmuns cost more than ye can afford. If ye've been thieving pound coins from me handbag again, I swear by almighty God, I'll clatter the living—"

"Me auntie Ursula gave em to me," Siofra blurted.

"Yer auntie!" Fionnuala's eyes flashed. "I might've known! When did ye see her?"

"She gave me anoller of them First Holy Communion lessons, and we went shopping down the town after."

Fionnuala flung the grimy jeans into the basket.

"She's meant to be teaching ye about the body and blood of Christ, not how to be a grabby wee bitch!"

Siofra's hand shot out for the toys, but Fionnuala's was quicker.

"Me life's a bleeding misery!" Siofra wailed. "You and me da never have any money in this house for nothing. What am I meant to play with? Me shoe-laces?!"

"Ach, catch yerself on, wane! Ye've a bleedin room up there bursting at the seams with toys ye never lay a finger on!"

"Aye, a black and white Gameboy and a Bob the Builder with no head!"

"When I was yer age, ye know what wer playthings was?"

"The rusty mufflers and hubcaps from the barricade of burnt-out cars at the end of yer street," Siofra recited.

"Yer auntie's stuffing sweeties down yer bake, filling yer head with poison! She's only trying to buy yer affection, that wan!"

Siofra stamped a tiny foot.

"And am bored stiff every week with them piggin communion lessons, but she can buy me affection all she wants if it gets me Pokemons!"

"Ye're not to go near that woman again, ye hear me, wane? Now get you up them stairs and play with that Bob the Builder before I shove it up yer arse, ye jumped-up wee cunt, ye!"

Siofra turned and fled out of the scullery and up the stairs, her tearful wails echoing through the house.

Fionnuala went to the sitting room and attacked a cigarette with trembling, nail-bitten fingers.

She simmered once again with resentment against Ursula and Jed's wind-fall. If those Barrett's hadn't won the lotto six months earlier, Fionnuala and Paddy would've never gone on such an outlandish shopping spree. The bills in the front hall were the legacy of those weeks of madness, and the interest and fees and late charges were piling up quicker than their fingers could toil. If she didn't get her claws on some cash soon, the electricity and gas would be disconnected.

She suddenly saw it all clearly in her mind's eye: the washer groaning to a halt, the picture disappearing from the telly screen into a tiny pinpoint of light, and the house plunging into darkness and silence for a second before the wanes started roaring out of them.

There was only one person in Derry who had plenty of cash to throw around. Fionnuala squirmed on the settee and set her lips, suddenly decided.

"Siofra?" she called out.

After a while, the rheumy-eyed child shuffled into the sitting room. She inspected the two Pokemon figures her mother had placed on the coffee table.

"A-aye?" she asked.

"Forget you what am after saying," Fionnuala said with a nod at the figures. "Take you them toys back up to yer room and play with em to yer heart's content. And yer auntie Ursula has me blessing to teach ye about yer communion and all."

Siofra eyed first the toys then her mother with suspicion. Was her mammy stark raving mad?

"But—"

"She can read ye the flimmin Bible from cover to cover for all I care!"

Siofra snatched the toys and scuttled off.

Fionnuala stubbed out her cigarette, reached for her handbag and headed for the door. A smile played on her lips as she screwed her heel into the mound of bills. If Ursula was so desperate for companionship she had to steal an eight-year-old away from the family home, the bitch would have to pay for the pleasure. And if it made Siofra's life a misery, even better. Fionnuala would approach Ursula for the lend of £400. And if the tight-fisted toerag refused, there would be hell to pay.

There had been great fanfare in Derry when a branch of the multinational chain superstore Top-Yer-Trolly finally opened in the city center, even though there did seem to be something less than right about their 4-for-the-price-of-5 weekly specials.

While her co-worker Fidelma was stocking the Utterly Butterly beside the cheese triangles, Dymphna slipped twelve Doherty's special sausages into the pocket of her work smock. The meat and cheese counter was low on black pudding that day, so her mother would just have to do without. Dymphna ran her fingers over her smock, adjusted the badge on her lapel which demanded *Ask me now about our less than right prices!* and sighed. She had to get the sausages into her staff locker before they congealed.

She should be helping stock but couldn't be bothered. Plus, she was three weeks late with her period and had to avoid the strain. She hadn't a notion who the father of her unborn wane was likely to be.

Tall and shapely, with a bosom that could breastfeed an entire maternity ward, and a reckless throng of ginger corkscrew curls framing her bonny face, Dymphna was never without a fit young lad at the end of a night of boozing, her eggs, seemingly, poised. Three weeks earlier had been February, so it was maybe the fella from the bookies, your man from the fish and chip shop down the Strand, or perhaps her ex-boyfriend Liam.

"Am gasping for a fag," she said to Fidelma. "Am away off to the break room. Ye'll cover for us if that aul poof O'Toole minces by, sure?"

Fidelma's eyes flickered with disapproval, surveying the break schedule on the clipboard next to the meat slicer.

"What am I meant to tell him?" she wondered. "I don't want any boller with him, Dymphna. Not after last time. Sure, ye know what yer man's like, like."

Dymphna knew only too well what your man was like. Nancy boy Henry O'Toole: the bane of her youthful existence. His lapels were too wide and his trousers too tight for a man his—or any?—age. With his blow-dried hair and eyes piercing hungrily at the arses of every male employee of the Derry branch of Top-Yer-Trolly, Dymphna could well understand why the Church forbade homosexuality.

"Ach, wise up, you," Dymphna said. "He's over in Belfast the day for a meeting, sure."

"Hi, you, Dymphna Flood!"

She whipped around as Rory Riddell cleared the display of Spaghetti Hoops and swaggered up to the counter. Three of his mates stood by the stacked tins, nudging and smirking.

"What about ye, Dymphna?" Rory said.

"Rory," Dymphna acknowledged coolly, hating his upmarket Proddy gear that nobody from the Bogside could afford, shooting a foul look at his mates and—realizing with terrifying clarity there was fourth candidate who might be the father of her unborn wane. How could she have forgotten that night in her granny's spare bedroom?

A fat disgrace of a woman with piggish eyes pushed past Rory to the counter with her tartan shopping cart. Rory gave the woman a curt nod; there were no strangers in Derry, so she was either a relative or an acquaintance. Dymphna knew her as a right hard bitch from the Health Clinic but greeted her with an unfamiliar speed and smile.

"Right there, Missus Bryant?"

Rory had seemed like such a god of sexual prowess after six pints of lager when Dymphna had been gagging for a shag. How she had squealed for more as her granny snored away in the room next door. Under the fluorescent lights of the Top-Yer-Trolly, however, he was a walking disappointment: skinny, spotty, even slightly smelly.

"Am here for something for wer tea the night," Nurse Bryant said.

Even worse, Dymphna realized with a plunging heart, Rory was from the *Waterside*, and everybody knew what *that* meant! One of those who called the city Londonderry instead of Derry City. A rich, smug Orange Protestant bastard! From the green, white and orange of the tricolor of the Irish flag, the Protestant majority of the country had appropriated orange as their color, and the Catholic minority green. Neither side seemed interested in claiming the white as their own.

Nurse Bryant peered through the counter, a bloated finger poking at the glass.

"Give us six of them ham rolls, and a black pudding, three kilos of lunch tongue and, ach, them pork pies with egg look wile lovely. Give us six of them and all."

"Right ye are," Dymphna said.

The sausages in her apron threatened to seep through the nylon as she wrapped the cold pig flesh as quickly as she could.

Being an unwed mother was disgrace enough, but to admit she had been at it with a *Proddy?* That her unborn child might be tainted with bastard Orange blood? Her mammy would beat seven shades of shite out of her! Especially as Fionnuala's great-uncle was a bishop!

"Here ye are now, missus," Dymphna said, hauling the load over the counter.

"Ta, love," Nurse Bryant heaved.

"Ach, sure, not at all," Dymphna mechanically replied.

Nurse Bryant shot the sniggering trio at the Spaghetti Hoops a disapproving glance as she struggled off towards the check-out lines. Rory's smirk blossomed into a sneer as he slouched closer to the counter.

"What's the craic, hi?" he asked.

Dymphna shrugged, confused by the sneer.

"Me mates was just wondering, like ..." Rory said. He struggled to suppress either tears or laughter.

"What?" she asked, feeling Fidelma's eyes boring into the strings of her smock. The remnants of her well-gnawed fingernails tapped uncertainly atop the blood-stained countertop.

"Ye were wan bleedin deadly shag the oller week," Rory said.

"Aye, and?" Dymphna said, lips taut and blood seeping into her face. Her hand shot to her hip, eyes all defiance and Spice Girls girl power. Their songs no longer debuted at number one on the pop charts, but sex was still power, as their videos had taught her.

"Ye wouldn't mind spreading yer legs for me mates the night, sure?" he said.

She leaned over the greasy glass and hissed into his face: "I'll kick ye in yer fecking bollacks, ye hateful gobshite! Shaggin you was like rolling around in a bag of sick!"

She grabbed a thick pork sausage and shoved it under his nose. "This is what I was hoping for, ye see."

She flung the sausage into the deep freeze and grabbed a cocktail frank. "This is what I got, but!"

"Aye, and I've a serious dose of knob rot from the manky cunt butter of yer filthy greaseflaps!"

"Clear on off out of here now before I give ye a swipe in the snotter box and call the security on ye, ye mingin manky cunt ye!"

"Mingin swamp donkey slapper!"

Rory and his hooligans raced through the aisles, brays of laughter and scattered tins in their wake. Fidelma teleported to her side from the convenience cheeses.

"Ye must be mortified," Fidelma said. "Bleedin Orange scum!"

"Ach, go on and *feck yerself*, ye clarty wee gee-bag! Am away off to the break room!"

Off she stomped and flung herself into the break room, where she wrenched open her locker and shoved the sausages into her handbag. She delved into her hip pocket and tugged out a packet of unfiltered Rothman's.

She puffed away, wondering if she were pregnant and, more importantly, if Rory were the father. But somehow she knew he was the one, the way a young woman does. To make it official, she would have to get one of those pregnancy tests. She knew exactly where they were, aisle 7A, bottom shelf. She had browsed that aisle during many a break for precisely this eventuality, feigning interest in the foot creams. She stabbed out her fag and headed out of the break room.

Shirley from the Youth Center was at the first cash register, and old Mrs. Heffernan from across the road was at the second. Too proud for shame, there was nothing else for it: Dymphna would just have to shoplift the pregnancy test.

She sidled down the book aisle where nobody, but nobody, ever shopped, slipped the kit into her smock, turned quickly—

And jumped at the sight of her Auntie Ursula staring at her from the birthday card rack, the idiot's jaw sagging with disbelief. Dymphna's granny Eda stood at Ursula's side, staring intently at nothing. Dymphna swiftly pulled herself up to her full five feet ten inches, rearranged her soiled smock and the smirk she always reserved for the scabby toerag ever since those balls had clattered from their cage.

"Ursula," she said with a dismissive nod.

"Dymphna," Ursula said weakly.

Dymphna gave her granny an affectionate press of the arm, then flicked her curls and marched off towards the meat and cheese counter. Ursula stared after her, resisting an uneasy glance at the *New Arrivals* rack.

"Am away off for me dinner break," Dymphna announced over the counter to a startled Fidelma.

"Ye're only after coming back from yer fag break, sure!"

"Am away off, I've said."

Dymphna glared menacingly. Fidelma shrank against the cheddar slices.

"The schedule, but ..." Fidelma managed weakly.

"Ye can shove that bleedin schedule up yer arse!" Dymphna announced and whipped down the aisle. She just couldn't do the test in the staff loos of Top-Yer-Trolly. Even she wasn't that tacky.

2

The toilet door shuddered.

"Outta that loo now, you!" Eoin barked from the landing.

Dymphna pulled the chain and shoved the pregnancy kit into the pocket of her work smock. She patted the bulge quickly, then tugged open the door and glared into her 17-year-old brother's face, which looked, as usual lately, ravaged from drink.

"Ye kyanny wait two bloody seconds, ye narky cunt, ye?" she seethed, clattering him around the head.

"Eff off, you," Eoin said, his shock of ginger hair and praying mantis limbs slipping into the bog.

The door slammed behind him.

"The shite's fairly falling from me after them manky sausingers of yers last night," he yelled from inside.

"After too many pints of beer, more like," she hollered back.

Brow creased with worry, Dymphna thudded down the stairs. In the sitting room, she stared unseeing at the telly screen. Her lips tugged in desperation on a fag. She ran her fingers slowly over her as-yet-still taut stomach. A wee baby, a wane, was growing there. A wane with Orange bastard blood flowing through its tiny veins.

Eoin swaggered into the room, his sallow eyes bright with malice. Dymphna placed a throw pillow over her stomach and clenched it with apprehension. Did Eoin somehow know of her predicament? Impossible.

"Any bars, hi?" He flopped beside her on the settee, reaching over and teasing her curls.

"Get off of me, you!"

She snapped his hand away from her pink barrettes.

"How's Liam, hi?"

Dymphna stiffened at the mention of her ex-fella's name, and a chill of unease crept up her spine; it was as if somehow Eoin *knew*.

"Ach, sure I mind now," Eoin said with mock innocence. "Ye caught him with his hand down that slapper Siobhan Feeney's knickers in the car park of the Top-Yer-Trolly, so ye did. So maybe ye've got yerself anoller fella, like?"

"Are ye simple, you? Shut yer cake-hole!"

He reached into the pocket of his jeans, pulled out the pregnancy test instructions and brandished the paper with a flourish and a taunt. "Look what am after finding in the bin of the loo. Looks like somewan in the house's been getting her hole filled."

Dymphna gaped down in horror, her heart plummeting.

"Give it to me now!" she begged, snatching at the paper.

Eoin leapt from the settee and bounced up and down behind their daddy's armchair, flapping the damning document and roaring with cruel glee. He ducked as the zapper whizzed by his ear.

"Eoin! Don't tell me mammy!" Dymphna implored, tears abruptly erupting from her eyes and lashing down her cheeks.

She shot across the sitting room and grabbed at his jersey, missed, and wound her fingers in desperation through his belt loop.

"Give it to me! Give it to me!"

She dragged his guffawing body across the carpeting. Eoin tugged away, jumping up and waving the paper towards the ceiling.

"Teenaged mum! Pregnant slapper!"

Dymphna's free hand scrabbled up his arm. She grunted as her fingers scratched again and again for the paper. She scuffled and he shoved, they spilled over the coffee table. Something clattered to the floor. Eoin fell on his back and Dymphna pounced with a snarl, pinning him to the floor, screaming into his laughing face and tearing the paper free. Eoin threw her off.

"Ye hateful pig, ye!" Dymphna sobbed, ripping the instructions into tiny pieces and—

—staring down at a sea of pills scattered all over the carpeting. Pink and blue, round and heart-shaped, each with a logo stamped into them, anchors and dolphins, shamrocks and doves. Eoin choked on his own laughter and scrabbled after them.

Well! This explained how he could afford to get blootered every hour God sent. And his new trainers. And mobile phone. *Wingers!* Or *bangers!* In other words ...

"Eoin! Ye've not been dealing bloody *Ecstasy?!*"

"Eff off, ye slapper," he scowled. But there was fear in his eyes.

He scooped up all the tablets and shoved them back into the baggy, slipping it into his pocket with a reddening face.

Dymphna eyed him with a mixture of victory and contempt and, most of all, disappointment. Eoin couldn't meet her eyes.

"Ye were a fecking altar boy three years ago, you! What in the name of feck are ye up to?"

"Dymphna, ye kyanny tell a soul, so ye kyanny," he said. "Am dead serious. Them McDaid brollers who is me suppliers is a right hard pack of stokes."

"The McDaids!"

Dymphna stared in horror. The trio of drug-supplying brothers from Creggan Heights were even worse than her mother's lot, the Heggartys! "Them McDaids is ex-Provos, ex-IRA members, who would sooner tar and fealler ye than have a pint down the pub with ye, and afterwards would put yer kneecaps out just for the craic of it. Ye're a right bloody headbin!"

"Not a bleeding word of this to anywan, ye hear?" he begged.

"How long have ye been at it?"

"Three weeks now."

Her older brother Lorcan had always been a headcase, a lunatic. Dymphna thought the sentence at Her Majesty's Magilligan Prison suited him. Eoin, however, had always been the meek, mild one with the soft voice and altar boy history. The sensible one. She couldn't fathom what turn of events, what desperation, had led him to such stupidity. Well, she was one to talk … She placed a hand on his shoulder.

"Eoin, if ye—"

He shook her off.

"I don't wanny talk about it," he snapped. "Just don't you be telling wer daddy about me drugs, and I won't be telling wer moller about yer wane. Deal?"

"Aye, deal," Dymphna said reluctantly.

She left the house to finish her shift at the Top-Yer-Trolly, dazed and terribly alone, scouring the streets for suitable places to dump an unwanted wane.

£ £ £ £

"What does God be?" Ursula asked, giving Siofra a critical once over. *Honestly, the way Fionnuala dressed the poor wee critter!*

"God's a spirit," Siofra recited like an automaton. "He hasn't a body like oller men."

"And where does He live?"

Decked out like a right wee slapper, hem up to her navel, tarty halter top of pink and purple!

"Everywhere."

It was no wonder her sister was nicking pregnancy tests.

"Can ye see Him?"

Siofra stared at the row of gargoyles.

"Naw, I kyanny, but He can always see me."

Siofra wriggled on the settee. She didn't know why she was sat here, prisoner in Ursula's perplexing new house.

"Does God know all things?"

The sitting room had no carpeting, and those drapes hanging from the ceiling were terrible daft!

"Aye, He's terrible clever; nothing can be hidden from Him. Auntie Ursula?"

Ursula clicked her tongue impatiently.

"What is it, wee girl?"

"What's all this palaver to do with me first communion? I already learned it in school, sure."

Ursula looked down, clearly at a loss herself.

"Let's have a wee look at the frocks," she decided, pulling out a catalog of First Holy Communion gowns and spreading it open on the refectory crate that the interior designer had insisted would be a perfect addition to the Neo-Gothic-style of the front room and had cost more than Ursula now cared to admit.

At the first sight of the flowing tresses, Siofra clambered up eagerly, bright eyes drinking in the fairy tale finery, bypassing the pound signs and the alarming numbers that followed them.

"Ach, they're lovely, sure," Siofra gasped. "Effin class! I want this wan … and this wan … Are you gonny get wan for me, Ursula?"

Ursula had told Jed she was going to buy her goddaughter's gown, but Jed had swiftly put an end to that expense. Ursula had exploded, but now the sight of the girl beaming up, the glint of her mother's pound-grabbing greed in her eyes, made her think she had been too hard on him.

"Sure, that's yer mammy and daddy's job, so it is."

Ursula slipped the catalog away.

"Now we're gonny practice yer First Communion," Ursula said breezily. "That'll be a right wee laugh, aye?"

"Are ye to be the priest, Ursula?" her goddaughter asked, giggling into her little hand. "Faller Ursula? Bleeding deadly!"

"Aye," Ursula said with a grim smile.

She reached into the carrier bag, avoiding the box of Cadbury's chocolate Roses which she had bought for her hairdresser Molly's birthday, and pulled out a package of Jelly Babies. Siofra's eyes lit up. How she loved these baby-shaped gummy sweeties!

"These Jelly Babies is gonny be the communion wafers," Ursula said. "Ye kyanny forget, but, that the body of Christ is terrible delicate and terrible holy. Yer wee mouth has never had something as important inside it before. Do ye understand me, wee girl?"

Siofra looked up.

"Under no circumstances," Ursula warned, "is it to get anywhere near yer teeth. That's why we're meant to practice."

"Why, auntie Ursula? What's to happen if the body of Christ gets near me teeth?"

"Then," Ursula explained gravely, "ye'll spend all eternity in Hell."

Siofra suddenly felt as if her mouth were overflowing with teeth. Her lower lip trembled.

"How am I meant to chew em, but, without the use of me teeth?"

Ursula felt a throbbing in her skull. She attempted a patient smile.

"The wafers won't be real Jelly Babies. They're more like ... thin biscuits, like ... papadum. Ye'll have no need to chew them."

"I need me teeth to eat papadum as well, but!" The tears started to well. "I don't wanny go to Hell, Ursula."

"No need to worry, wee girl," Ursula said in slight alarm. "Wance ye receive the Lord, ye'll understand what I mean. Ye sort of ... let it melt on yer tongue, like. It disappears as you be's walking back to yer place in the pew, praying."

"What am I to pray for, Ursula? For it to not touch me teeth?"

Ursula ran a harried hand through her bob and frowned down at the simpering wane. She was relieved to hear the phone ring and scuttled into the foyer, lunging for the receiver.

"Ursula?"

"Aye?"

"Roisin here."

Ursula tensed. Why would her older sister be phoning from her Yank husband's beach house in Hawaii?

"Aye?" Ursula asked.

"Am just ringing to let ye know am gonny be in Derry in three days."

"Oh."

Ursula reeled, while in the lounge a secret smile played on Siofra's lips. She would have a right wee laugh with Dymphna about it after. Terrified of her teeth touching communion wafers? *As if!* It was a quare aul craic, winding Auntie Ursula up!

"I've not been home for ages," Roisin was saying, "and it's about time I checked out me pension and seen how much money them Brits owe me."

"Well, ye're gonny stay with us," Ursula decided.

"Ach, naw, I'll be grand at me mammy's at 5 Murphy, sure."

"Catch yerself on, Roisin," Ursula snorted. "Ye'll put yer back out tossing and turning on that lumpy aul bed in the back room. Sure, the springs is fairly shooting out of the mattress. We've a grand new Queen-sized bed in wer Blue Room, so we do. Never been slept in."

"… yer *Blue Room*?" Roisin snorted.

"Ye've not yet seen wer new house," Ursula explained. Siofra fidgeted on the settee and heaved impatient sighs. "Up in Gleneagles. It's grand and lovely, so it is, a sight for sore eyes. All mod cons. Not like that damp and dingy 5 Murphy."

"Naw," Roisin announced flatly.

"And we're right next to the shopping down the town," Ursula tried to explain, watching as Siofra delved into the sweetie bag and *chewed* with wild abandon.

"No need to put yerself out, Ursula," Roisin insisted. "I wanny go back to the Derry I know, the Bogside I love, and watch the telly in the sitting room where I grew up, sure."

"Ye're quare and soft," Ursula said with a tsk of contempt. "Ye'd need a microscope to see that manky aul telly in that boggin sitting room, so ye would."

"So me moller's house is damp, the beds is all lumpy, the sitting room boggin and the telly too wee?"

"Aye, aye, aye!" Ursula said eagerly. Precisely why Roisin should stay with her!

"And all that didn't stop ye from racing down to the city council to snatch the house from under wer noses the second ye won the lotto, ye hateful bitch!"

Ursula paused, stunned. She looked swiftly over at her goddaughter, then inched out of the foyer into the scullery.

"What are ye on about?" she hissed in a sharp whisper down the receiver.

"Ye think we're all daft, do ye? Ye think we all don't know what ye're playing at, Ursula? Ye think now yer handbag is bulging with pounds, ye own the whole effin world. Ye've always been desperate to get wan over on the rest of us yer entire miserable life. Now ye're letting on yer helping the family, when all the while me poor aul mammy's yer sitting tenant!"

"Nobody tole me they wanted that flimmin house!"

"Ach, ye're fairly turning me stomach, you!"

Siofra's head peeped around the doorjamb and Ursula waved it back into the lounge with a glare.

"Ye ran screaming from Derry the second ye got yer mitts on a passport," Ursula said. "You was itching to marry the first Yank fool enough to have you, leaving me mammy and daddy in the lurch with the bombs exploding around them, and nowan to look after them in their twilight years!"

"There is things I've done that am terrible ashamed of," Roisin said loftily. "Abandoning me mammy and daddy is wan of em, aye. You've a bold faced nerve, but, Ursula, to be pointing a bloody finger at me! I wasn't the wan who—At least I never—"

Ursula gasped, her fingers strangling the receiver, praying into the wee holes that were meant for talking, silently urging *Please dear Lord, naw, not 1973, not '73, not '73 ...*

"Roisin, naw ...!" Ursula begged, the pleading caught in her throat.

But even Roisin couldn't bring herself to mention it.

"We're gonny have a few words when I get meself to Derry," Roisin finally said.

Ursula deflated with relief and hung up, grateful that her sister had dredged up somewhere within herself a heart. She walked into the lounge on unsteady feet, still reeling from the unspoken family shame that had almost reared its unsightly head. Siofra grinned innocently up at her.

"Who was that after ringing ye just now, Ursula?"

"Am late for me wash and set," Ursula decided, passing her goddaughter the catalog, gathering up her handbag and shoving the bag of Jelly Babies into Siofra's hand. That was all the greedy wee bitch was interested in anyway.

£ £ £ £

1973

The rubber bullet had pierced the bay window, ricocheted against the bald-patched carpeting around a fireplace spitting sparks and now stood proudly on the mantelpiece, the Flood's new knickknack. Five Murphy Crescent still reeked from the tear gas. Ursula stared at the boarded window. Why had she been dancing around her handbag at the Yank base nightclub when the street riot had broken out? Her wanes could've been killed.

They were now on their way home from school, rags and jars of vinegar tucked in their satchels in case the occupying British paratroopers let loose with more canisters of tear gas. That morning she had ripped into Vaughn and Egbert for pelting rocks at the armored cars, but secretly she had been proud. Now she was wracked with guilt. If Jed had to get a leave of duty from Vietnam because his wee sons had been gunned down in the street like common animals …

Ursula picked up her purple velour handbag and rummaged through the cough drops and bobby pins until she found the slip of paper. She read the five numbers scrawled on it, thinking carefully.

If you disregarded the pram searches outside the shops, the rubber bullets, bombs and CS gas, life in Derry was deathly dull: marking off the days until Jed came back from Vietnam, attending mass every Sunday, confession every Wednesday, gossiping with her mate Francine and trying to poison her brother Paddy against his current fancy woman Fionnuala Heggarty. What did Ursula have to look forward to when her husband finally rescued her eleven months hence?

Endless years of dusting and darning socks in a whirlwind of godforsaken military outposts, uprooted every two or three years, terminating tenuous friendships, greeted by another selection of strange faces in a new base in a stranger land, over and over again, amen. The only constant would be Jed and the wanes, the dusting and the socks.

The letterbox clattered in the hallway.

"Mammy! Let me in!"

Gretchen, safely home from school. Ursula was slightly fearful of being in her daughter's presence, but then remembered her daddy had doused the wanes' heads with medicated shampoo the day before, so they were free of head lice for a week. She slipped the telephone number into the side pocket of her beige and brown maxi-skirt with a flash of irritation. Vaughn and Egbert would soon follow their younger sister, flooding the five tiny rooms with their shrieking and stomping and their bottomless pits of stomachs.

"Any boller with the soldiers on yer way home from school?" Ursula asked.

Gretchen shrugged her little shoulders.

"Naw," she said, racing into the sitting room and flicking on the telly. "Them Brit bastards is crawling everywhere through the streets, but. Siobhan Healy tole me her broller was picked up last night for flinging rocks at em, so he was. Fecking Proddy bastards!"

Ursula stared down in alarm at her child, now crawling onto the settee.

"If ye utter them words again, ye're to get a bar of soap in yer mouth. Understand?"

"Aye, Mammy," Gretchen said with a roll of her eyes.

As the telly blared out, Ursula walked into the scullery, deep in thought.

In Arizona two years earlier, her children had babbled on about Etch-A-Sketch, Kool-Aid and Barney and Betty Rubble. Ursula leaned against the larder door for a second and thought of what they talked about since they had arrived in Derry: confiscate, internment, hunger strike, armored car. And then, of course, there was bleedin, feckin, Proddy and bastard. Her children were changing, and she didn't like the direction they were heading. When she and Jed had been deciding where she and the children might best stay during his tour of duty in Vietnam, Ursula had envisioned the gentle lush Derry of her own childhood, not this gritty everyday brutality.

If her beloved hometown hadn't been invaded by British soldiers, there would be no need for "fecking bastards" in either their vocabulary or their life. Not just her wanes' lives were in danger, their minds were as well. Ursula was suddenly decided. She raced into the hallway and flung her coat over her shoulders.

"Am just away off to the O'Malleys to make a call," she called into the sitting room.

The one telephone on the block belonged to the next door neighbors. With phones so rare, there was usually nobody to call, so Ursula was making quite an announcement, but Gretchen just shrugged again.

Ursula opened the door and passed the green picket fence, the gate clattering behind her. She turned and took a quick glance at the bottom of the street. Vaughn and Egbert were frolicking on the barricade of hijacked, burnt-out cars the IRA had erected a few months previously under the cloak of night to help make the Bogside a no-go zone for the Brit troops. She had beaten her boys senseless for playing amongst the singed shock absorbers and jagged windscreen sills the week before.

Ursula set her face in anger, then swiftly turned away. She could deal with them later. After her phone call, there would be no barricades left for any Bogside wane to risk their lives on. With every step of pavement, she realized she was making the right choice, for her beleaguered country, for the safety of her wanes, and, most of all, for herself. She knocked on the O'Malley's front door.

Mrs. O'Malley, fag hanging, opened the door to the dreary depths which stank of soot. A filthy infant gnawing on a leaky pen straddled her hip. From upstairs came the shrieking of a baffling amount of children. The whole street wondered how the O'Malleys could afford the luxury of a phone. There were whispers of Proddy bastards in their family tree, or maybe a second cousin who was an informer for the IRA.

Had they one of them swanky new refrigerators hidden away in their house as well? Ursula wondered.

"Right, Mrs. O'Malley," Ursula said, tuppence in hand. "Am here for the use of the phone."

"Right ye are," she said with a nod and disappeared.

Ursula slipped the coin in the wooden box on the phone stand and dialed nervously, staring at the peeling primroses of the hallway wallpaper to avoid the disapproving glare from the framed portrait of the Bleeding Heart of Jesus towering above her on the wall.

"Aye?" came a voice through the crackles.

"Aye, Tommy? Am ..." Ursula glanced around to be sure nobody was in sight. "... Gracie. Am the wan ye gave yer number to the oller week down the Bogside, after me taxi ride."

"Ach, aye. The lovely-looking girl with the Yank husband in Vietnam, aye? Have ye given me offer some thought?"

"I have, aye."

"And?"

Ursula took a deep breath, heart racing.

"Am in."

"Grand! Good on ye."

"I've a girlfriend that's willing to help and all. Ye mind yer woman with us ye dropped off at the Lecky Road?"

"Aye, I mind."

Ursula searched her mind for a suitable name for her best mate Francine. "... Una."

"That's grand," he said again. "We're gonny meet in person and discuss this the three of us. Next Wednesday at five in front of what's left of the Guildhall?"

"Right ye are," Ursula agreed.

"Fair play to ye. Ye're not gonny regret this, Gracie," Tommy said.

"Cheerio, then."

The receiver clattered as Ursula's trembling hands sought the cradle.

She took a step to the threshold of the sitting room, clutched the door frame and poked her head inside. It was a fright, with dirty diapers and half-eaten sandwiches and toys scattered everywhere. But in the corner stood a telly twice the size of the one in 5 Murphy Crescent, and that one Ursula had only been able to afford with the money Jed sent from his immense Yank wages. Ursula would have bet on her granny's grave that the O'Malleys' telly was color too.

"Mrs. O'Malley?" she called into the filth.

The lucky bitch shuffled out of the darkness, a different wane clutching her hip, this one gnawing on a raw potato.

"Am wile parched," Ursula said. "Could ye give us a wee drink of water?"

"Right ye are," Mrs. O'Malley said, giving Ursula an odd look and turning back towards the scullery.

Ursula quickly followed and spied a glistening new white fridge under a sink overflowing with grotty dishes.

"Ach, sure, no need now," Ursula said. "I was just wile faint-headed there for a wee bit."

Ursula raced back to the hallway.

"Thanks for the use of the phone, anyroad," she called.

"Ach, sure, it's no boller at all," Mrs. O'Malley said with a frown.

But Ursula was already halfway down the street to clobber Vaughn and Egbert.

£ £ £ £

The rain spat down and the cannons towered overhead from the city walls. Fionnuala propelled herself down Shipquay Street towards an alarmed Ursula. Derry's main shopping street was on an incline so steep it caught the unfamiliar unaware, reaching the summit gasping for breath. Fionnuala skidded to a stop.

"Right, Ursula!" Fionnuala panted, carrier bags heavy with tinned budget mushy peas, hollow eyes glistening with sudden opportunity.

Ursula managed a smile.

"Right, Fionnuala. Am late for the hairdressers," she said, giving a glance at her wristwatch and a tsk of disappointment.

"Ye know Roisin's to be in town the day after the morrow?"

Ursula stiffened.

"She's after ringing me, aye."

"Is she to be staying with you and Jed up in Gleneagles? I know you've all them new guest rooms in that grand house of yers, like."

Ursula's ears were on the alert for a note of sarcasm, and were surprised to detect none. Desperate as she suddenly was for a kind word from the family, Ursula was grateful to Fionnuala for once. She clutched a nearby railing for support.

"Naw," she said, eyes averted. "She wants to stay at me moller's down the Bogside."

"Ach, right around the corner from us, then? That's grand, so it is! We'll have to get togeller, the three of us, for a right wee knees-up."

Ursula forced a leery nod and grin and turned to leave.

"And I hear ye're after giving Siofra anoller of them lessons?" Fionnuala said.

Ursula stopped in mid-turn. Word certainly traveled fast in Derry. The Jelly Babies were still fresh in Siofra's digestive system.

"A-aye," Ursula said.

"Ach, she loves em so, highlight of her week, them."

As Ursula stared at her blankly, Fionnuala clucked impatiently.

"C'mere a wee moment," she finally said.

Ursula gave a helpless second nod to her watch. Fionnuala grabbed her elbow, for effect or to stop a headlong plunge down the street, Ursula didn't know.

"Would ye give us a lend of 400 quid?" Fionnuala blurted out.

Ursula wasn't sure what to reply, nor even where to look, her bank account and balance suddenly threatened. She gently shook Fionnuala's claw from her slicker.

"Four hundred …?"

"We've the rates due, ye see, and Paddy won't get his pay until next week, and me wages isn't due for anoller fortnight. And, am affronted to say it, but am after getting an advance for them wages and all," Fionnuala explained in a breathless rush, the color rising in her face. "We kyanny have wer electricity turned off, so we kyanny, not with wanes in the house."

"Well, I really couldn't say if—"

"Ye know we're good for it, Ursula," Fionnuala said, hoping her sister-in-law had the good grace not to mention they were anything but.

"Ach, sure, that I know," Ursula said, the smile glued on her face as the rain lashed around them. "The only problem is, well, Jed takes care of the finances now, so I really kyanny say …"

She trailed off, seemingly uncertain yet hopeful. *And I don't mind wan word of thanks when we paid off yer mortgage after wer lotto win, ye ungrateful cow, ye,* Ursula might have said, but Roisin's scornful tones down the line still lingered in her ear.

"Ye've been wile good to us over the years, Ursula," Fionnuala barreled on, shameless in her quest for cold hard cash. "Too good. I mind that time ye baked them scones for wer Dymphna's birthday, like. And you always give such grand gifts to the wanes every Christmas. We were happy enough to make ye Siofra's godmoller, so we were."

Fionnuala stopped just short of wringing Ursula's hands, and it was at that moment, wobbling there on the slope of Shipquay Street with the Saturday shoppers coming at them from odd angles and their two umbrellas weighing their balance, that Fionnuala realized how old Ursula was looking. It had been such a long time since she had looked at her and actually seen her. Fionnuala feared she was confronting her own future.

She had been feeling the passage of time on her own body as she grimly approached her fiftieth birthday, a life of giving birth and sucking down sixty fags a day, dodging bombs, and grasping every minute of overtime she could. The helplessness, the sense of rotting away into a dottering old aged pensioner struggling on a fixed income, the destiny of them all.

She and Ursula had spent a lifetime together. A lifetime bickering, certainly, but a lifetime nevertheless. They were a team, growing old together.

This moment of sudden clarity didn't make her loathe Ursula any less of course. In fact, she was even more disgusted that—at this late stage of her life—she was forced to rely on the generosity of a tight-fisted cunt like her sister-in-law. Ursula deserved each bold-faced lie that came from her lips.

"Even when you and Jed were having them money troubles of yer own," Fionnuala continued, "when ye first moved back to Derry and the dollar was so weak against the pound, mind, ye always had something to spare when we were on wer last legs. That's why I feel I can rely on ye, Ursula ... love."

Ursula managed to get out, "Am gonny have a wee word with Jed and see what we can do."

"*When?!* We're bleeding desperate, so we are!"

"I'll let ye know the morrow."

Then, attempting to throw back her helmet of an aubergine bob in bright-eyed buoyancy, she turned and made her escape, scurrying as quickly as she could manage down the slippery slope of Shipquay Street. Every hair remained stubbornly in place.

Under her umbrella, Fionnuala grappled a pole and deflated with relief, the £400 already a fait accompli. She started mentally subtracting all the payments she would be able to make. The milkman, the gas, the electric, *thank feck!* Perhaps she would even have enough left over from Ursula's misguided generosity to purchase that new pair of tights.

£ £ £ £

Padraig Flood and his mate Declan McDaid teetered on the railing opposite the newsagent's, an arsenal of rocks between them, on the lookout for old aged pensioners shuffling by. Their limbs were gangly from an eternal diet of spuds, fish sauce, and beans on toast, yet they were the picture of youthful menace with their cropped black scalps and the red and white stripes of their Derry Football Club jerseys.

In the 1970s, the Shops in Creggan Estate had been a row of frugal points of purchase in the wilderness of the frontline of sectarian violence, the concrete of the newsagent and butchers and hair salon festooned with barbed wire and bullet holes. Today they were a streamlined gallery of brightly-lit chain stores. The only nod to the past was a drab convenience store called the Sav-U-Mor, which was tucked apologetically off to one side and was where Padraig's mother worked long hours for little pay because no other place would have her.

"Here comes wan now," Declan giggled.

Mr. Murphy dragged himself towards the newsagent door, squinting through his lopsided spectacles at them.

"Ye blind aul git!" Declan yelled.

Padraig pelted a pebble at his foot. Declan fired a rock at his head. Mr. Murphy's shoulders tensed, and he scuttled into the safety of the shop. The young rowdies doubled over with the force of their laughter.

"Ach, sure, this is a quare aul craic!" Padraig squealed.

Padraig had recently graduated from rocks to paint bombs thanks to Declan. His best mate had learned everything a ten-year-old schoolboy needed to know about malicious diversions from his older brothers. Caoilte, Fergal and Eamonn McDaid had been in and out of Magilligan Prison as if a revolving door had been installed for their personal use and were now the city's main Ecstasy dealers.

Old Mrs. Feeney, in a perm long past its prime, rounded the corner, a face on her like a bulldog's licking piss off a nettle. Declan reached for the broken brick, but Mr. Murphy teetered out of the newsagent's, puny fist shaking.

"Fecking rowdie bastards!" he croaked.

"Ach, go and shite, you!" Declan hollered.

Declan tossed the brick inches from his elbow, Padraig took aim at his tattered shoes.

"Clear on off out of here, youse!" Mrs. Feeney called out.

She trembled up at them on the railing, the triteness of her age overpowered by rage, her eyes able to drive rats from a barn. Mrs. Feeney hadn't suffered a lifetime of civil war, sons gunned down in their prime, to be victimized in the relative calm of the peace process. The Brit paratroopers had departed, and the need for senseless violence was gone, but that didn't mean it had departed her beloved city.

"Ach, piss off, ye crabbit aul slapper," Declan snorted as Mr. Murphy shuffled gratefully around the corner, leaving Mrs. Feeney to fend for herself.

"That aul wan there could be yer own grandda. If youse is so desperate to have it out with somewan, have it out with me!"

Padraig and Declan howled with laughter. Mrs. Feeney pointed a shuddering digit at Padraig.

"I know ye, wee boy. Yer auntie Ursula's me caretaker for OsteoCare. She's up in me house every Thursday, and I'll be on to her about ye, so I will! Ye're a bad wee brute! Ye kyanny help it, like, as yer moller's wan of them rowdy Heggartys! Yer auntie Ursula's the only wan in the flimmin pack of ye that's got a decent Christian bone in her body. That wan's never outta the church, always has a smile for everywan she sees—"

"Shut yer bake and clear on off outta here, or ye'll get a rock in yer skull!" Declan roared.

An enraged Dymphna, clutching a video of *Pretty Woman*, rounded the corner of the parade and stormed up to them through the panorama of broken glass and dog shite.

"Padraig!" she hollered. "What in the name of feck do ye think ye're playing at? Away from that aul wan now!"

"Ach, eff off, you!" Declan sneered into her face.

"Roaring abuse at elderly wans nine times yer age!" she barked.

Padraig hung his head. Dymphna turned to Mrs. Feeney.

"C'mon you away now, love," she urged, gently ushering the pensioner further down the pavement. "I'll take care of them rowdies."

Her hand caressed the old one's tartan-clad elbow.

"I can take care of meself," Mrs. Feeney spat, heaving herself free and dealing Dymphna a feeble kick in the shin. "Ye Heggarty bitch, ye!"

Declan doubled over with snickers. Padraig looked sharply at him. Mrs. Feeney shuffled towards Boots the Chemist, turned and flipped Dymphna off. "Nine times his age, me hole, ye daft cunt, ye!"

She disappeared into the store as Dymphna exploded.

"Ye see what ye're doing to the family name? Showing us up like that! Am mortified, so am are!"

She turned to Declan. "Ye're leading me broller down the path to Hell."

"Ach, feck off, ye slapper. Padraig and me is best mates. Aye?"

Dymphna gave a disgusted shake of the head and left them, racing to the video store. Another five minutes and she'd have to pay the late fee.

"What yer sister needs is a head job," Declan snorted.

Padraig blinked, knowing, as every Derry schoolchild did, that a 'head job' was IRA parlance for a hood over the head and a bullet through it.

"We've no gun," Padraig said.

"More's the pity. We can still make the cunt's life pure misery. Let's bomb her."

"With paint?" Padraig asked, relieved.

Declan snorted.

"Paint bombs is for wanes! I've something grander in mind."

Padraig shifted uncomfortably. He knew well enough what generally followed paint bombs in the list of malicious crimes of diversion.

"She's me sister," he said weakly.

"Aye, and a right narky bitch to boot! Yer hateful sister's to be the target of wer very first petrol bomb!"

Padraig looked up at the darkening sky with a dramatic scowl.

"I kyanny be late for wer tea. Ye know what me mammy's like, like."

Declan snorted.

"I never woulda taken ye for a feardy custard," he said.

Padraig tensed. Being called a feardy custard, a coward, was an insult on par with arse bandit or nancy boy.

"If ye kyanny discuss wer plans like a hard man ... Feardy custard! Feardy custard!" Declan trailed off his chant with a baited sneer, eyebrow raised in a taunt.

"Naw, naw," Padraig said quickly. "Let's get us a petrol bomb and toss it in her geebag face!"

£ £ £ £

Ursula glanced up at her hairdresser, Molly, who was twittering around her with a gratitude that was unnatural and becoming increasingly irritating.

Why was your woman making such a grand carry-on over a box of flimmin chocolates? Well, it was obvious Ursula had shown up the staff, as she couldn't see amongst the shelves of crimpers and conditioners any cards on display, or obvious gifts they might have given.

Outside on the cobblestones stood Dymphna, who knew, as everybody in the city seemed to, that Ursula had her hair done at Xpressions every Wednesday at two. She peered through the window and paused at the door, hating herself, before pushing it open and poking her head inside.

Ursula caught sight of Dymphna and tensed, the enemy invading her camp, the slapper's hand clutching a McDonald's bag. Ursula noted the receipt crumpled in her niece's fingers with slight surprise; she hadn't thought that her niece with the shifty fingers ever paid for anything.

"Am here for Ursula," Dymphna announced.

The junior stylists parted to let her through. As Dymphna stomped over, Ursula shirked slightly. Dymphna attempted a pleasant smile.

"C'mere now, Ursula," she whispered. "A wee word in yer ear?"

Dymphna motioned to the front door with a jerk of the head.

Ursula hesitated. Dymphna might well have a gang of mates outside, waiting to hurl insults or rocks at her the moment she stepped out the door. She wouldn't put anything past her hardened stoke of a niece. Steeling herself, Ursula nodded and followed with heavy steps. The staff and clientele all watched her go.

Dymphna flicked open the door and bounded to the pavement. Ursula lingered in the doorway.

"What?" she asked flatly.

Dymphna looked around the crowded street, then learned forward like a best mate with gossip to spread.

"I know ye saw me nicking that pregnancy test the oller day in the Top-Yer-Trolly."

"Aye, and?" Ursula asked, hand still on the door. She glared down at this brazen trollop, affronted to call her family, and was shocked when Dymphna burst into tears.

"Am pregnant," she admitted, delving her hand into the McDonald's bag and pulling out a napkin to daub her watery eyes. "I took the test the oller day, and I know it's true."

Somewhere in the depths of her heart, Ursula felt a softening, an empathy she hadn't addressed in decades, seeing a desperate wane caught in the hopeless situation of single motherhood. And, just as suddenly, her eyes flickered with suspicion as she realized the only reason Dymphna could possibly be confiding in her. She was, quite frankly, flabbergasted.

They were attacking her from all angles, those Floods, greedy palms outstretched, demanding free payouts. She wouldn't even have put it past the scheming bitch Dymphna to have orchestrated the entire scenario, lurking in the aisles next to the foot creams until she caught old pushover auntie Ursula shopping in the Top-Yer-Trolly, and lying about being up the scoot just so she could wheedle some spending cash for a few pop CDs of the day and a bright frilly frock from Warehouse. Ursula's voice and face grew hard.

"And just what do ye want me to do about it?" she asked stiffly. "I expect ye'll be wanting me to pay for the termination? All you and yer family ever wants me for is that flimmin lotto money, sure. Well, ye're off yer head if ye think me check book's gonny be pulled out for this occasion."

She turned to go inside, suddenly cold and impatient and full of hatred. Dymphna stared, genuinely startled, at Ursula's mention of an abortion. Her tears contracted to sniffles.

"Naw," she sniffled, touching Ursula's elbow. Dymphna felt her tense. "A termination's the furthest thing from me mind. It's against the law, sure."

Ursula felt the pangs of resentment growing as they stood there on the pavement with the shoppers bumping into them, tears rolling down her niece's face as if she had caused them, the stench of American fries escaping from the bag in her hand.

Sure, her life was misery enough, Ursula thought, and this shameless tart stood before her able to afford flash Yank fast food was part of that misery. She turned back to Dymphna

"What do ye want from me, then?"

"Just don't go telling me mammy and daddy," Dymphna implored with an approximation of desperation. "Am gonny tell em meself. Sure, I won't be able to hide it soon enough, like, so they're gonny have to know. I wanny wait until am ready, but."

Ursula searched her niece's face for a trace of craftiness and was almost disappointed she couldn't find any.

"It would take a sight more than a pregnant wane for me to race to yer moller for a session of hot gossip. I've other things to do with me life, ye know," Ursula said with a bitter laugh. "Is that it, then?"

Dymphna nodded with slight uncertainty.

"Grand," Ursula said. "Then this discussion between us is over. Ye've me word yer parents won't hear of yer foolishness from me own lips, at any rate. God luck to ye."

"Ach, sure that's wile civil of ye, Ur—"

Ursula slammed the hairdresser's door as she went back inside.

"Wile sorry about the delay, Molly," Ursula said, more out of convention than apology.

But with a box of chocolates and a wee card, how could Molly have the heart to be narked? *Themmuns is me favorites, sure,* Molly was thinking, *Cadbury's Rose's. And wile dear! But how in the name of feck did Ursula get it into her head that the day was me birthday? It doesn't be till November, sure, miles away!*

Dymphna flounced down the pavement in a rage.

How the flimmin feck did that aul bitch catch me out? she wondered. How had Ursula immediately known she wanted a loan of her endless cash reserves to flush that Orange bastard out of her system? She now knew her faith had been misguided, and her mammy and daddy were right after all: Ursula Barnett was nothing but a scabby, scaldy tight-fisted cunt!

£ £ £ £

Slouching into the scullery, Fionnuala glowered in sudden fury at the sight of a plate wrapped in aluminum foil languishing beside the dripping sink. Two sausages and some turnips, the leftovers of the family's tea the night before, were to have been Eda's sustenance that afternoon. Before she had left for her round of pub loo scrubbing, she had told Padraig to take it around the corner to his granny's house.

Hearing a sudden unhinged giggle from the four square feet of concrete and crabgrass that was their back garden, Fionnuala looked out the scullery window. She peered past the sopping bed sheets weeping in a damp breeze on the wash line, and her eyes rounded, incensed. The window rattled with the fury of her fist.

Declan and Padraig glanced up in alarm, just in time to witness Fionnuala's apoplectic face disappear from between the faded daisies of the curtains.

"Fecking shite!" Padraig hissed. "Me mammy!"

The back door to the house flew open. Padraig scrambled to hide the canisters and petrol, the fizzy lemonade bottles and rags. Declan just sat on his haunches on the grass, a smug look on his face. Fionnuala barreled towards them, housekeeping smock flying and toilet roll trailing from her left shoe.

"What in the name of merciful Christ is youse wanes playing at now? Paint bombs *again*? Ye never pay me wan blind bit of notice, do ye?"

She grabbed Declan's left earlobe and hauled the child to his feet.

"Outta me back garden, you, or am ringing yer moller!"

Her eyes widened abruptly.

"Jaysismaryandjoseph and a wee donkey! That's not fecking *petrol* ye have there, ye fecking simple eejit wanes?"

Declan roared in anguish as her fingernails gouged his flesh.

"Are youse away in the head?" Fionnuala demanded.

"Get offa me, ye bleedin gacky sleekit geebag toerag, ye!" Declan snarled, delving into his repertoire of abusive terms for annoying people. His arms flailed for a crack at Fionnuala's skull. She snatched his wrists and tugged his face to her own. Declan struggled free, his hand whipping once again towards her face.

"Ye see if ye grab hold of me again—" he warned.

She grabbed his wrists a second time and dared with a hiss into his face: "Aye, you just try it, son. I'll be marching yer hateful wee body down to the cop shop, and they can batter the living shite outta ye with their truncheons. That's after I've finished clattering ye meself!"

She threw the child to the yellow crabgrass. Declan struggled to his feet, shuddering with rage, and scurried off, flipping Fionnuala off.

"Eff off you, ye crabbit aul crone!" he called with a sudden squeal of brazen laughter. He disappeared through the back gate.

"He's a bad wee brute, him," Fionnuala panted. "His moller's a right sarky slapper and all."

"Mammy!" Padraig wailed. "Am mortified! Ye've showed me up in front of me mate!"

"I'll show ye up in the intensive care unit of Altnagelvin hospital, so I will!" Fionnuala seethed. "Mortified me effin hole! What in the name of feck do ye think ye're playing at, wee boy, hanging around with rowdies like that Declan? Ye wanny end up in the nick, in prison, like yer broller, like?"

A teary silence greeted her. She grabbed a petrol-filled bottle and thrust it under his nose. Padraig whimpered against the concrete of the garden shed, trapped. The rim of the bottle grazed his nostrils.

"Am after asking ye a question, ye bloody eejit! And I want an effin answer now! Ye think yer broller's a hard man, locked up in his cell, sent down to Magilligan for Grievous Bodily bloody Harm, do ye? Do ye know what goes on in them fecking cells? No sunshine, no Internet, no bloody fecking freedom! Perishing in the dead cold as they march his flippin body up and down the courtyard for hours on end, nancy boys and poofters grabbing at his arse at all hours of the day and night!"

Fionnuala threw the bottle to the grass.

"Ye want yer life to be a dead loss? Have ye given it a moment's thought? Naw, ye haven't, because ye're a simple wee gack, kyanny think more than seven minutes into the future. Clear that lot up now, or I swear by almighty God they'll be queuing up for that young arse of yers down at Magilligan! And I tole ye to take them sausingers round to yer granny's hours ago. The aul pensioner's probably perishing with hunger now!"

Padraig simpered up at her.

"Me granny makes me fear-hearted. She's off her head, always muttering to herself, and that house's boggin, fairly reeking of piss."

Whack! Whack! Whack!

Fionnuala dealt him three sharp smacks across the face.

"Ye were a right hard man two seconds ago when yer mate was here!" she bellowed. "And now ye're letting on you be's afeared of yer dottering aul granny?! She's a thorn in the side of us all, a lunatic headbin, right enough, that don't mean she kyanny shovel down the food, but!"

She grabbed his hands and seemed on the verge of another tirade, thought the better of it, and flung his hands down.

"And them hands is absolutely mingin and all," she said. "I want them washed after ye clear off that lot, and before ye touch that plate of yer granny's!"

She turned to march back into the house, and it was then that Declan came at her with the poker.

£ £ £ £

"I kyanny fathom it!" Ursula wailed, angrily rumpling Jed's sweatshirt into something resembling a fold.

Jed shifted uncomfortably before the football game blazing from the massive flat screen televison and slipped the scratch card under his butt-stuffed ashtray. Ursula glared at the glass of white zinfandel at his side and resented his good spirits. She wrenched up a shirt and folded with a terse hand.

"Me sister Roisin had the bloody cheek to waste a long distance call from Hawaii just to accuse me of snatching away that mingin tip of 5 Murphy from the family. Nobody ever wanted to lay a finger on them crumbling bricks and mortar, never gave that house a moment's thought until, she's now after telling me, I decided to take it off the city council's hands."

Jed slipped a scratch card out from under the ashtray, pretending to rearrange his cigarette butts. He discreetly scratched a pence piece against one of the six silver circles. *Win.*

"She probably just wants to stay in the house of your childhood," Jed said. "It's only natural."

Only five more wins, and £5000 would be his. More than enough for that damn ticket.

"Wer childhood!" Ursula exploded. "When we was wanes, they was bleedin desperate to escape that flippin firetrap of a house! Couldn't wait for the day they'd be free from them rotting floorboards!"

Scratch, scratch. *Win!*

"So many of us was shoved into them four walls, wanes sitting atop each oller in the front room, sleeping three to a bed, wer fannys and arses pressed up against wan oller, sweltering in the summer, starving in the winter, infested with lice more months than not ..."

Jed sat in shock. Three weeks earlier, against a backdrop of outraged uproar from her entire family combined, Ursula had forced him to purchase that "mingin tip" with the remnants of their lotto winnings, against his better judgment and at the expense of the fishing boat he had wanted.

"Maybe they all wanted to buy it but realized they'd never have the cash," he said slowly. Scratch, scratch, scratch. *Win!*

Ursula heaved a sigh as she tossed a sock onto a pile.

"They want it purely as it's mines."

She snatched a pink ankle sock and searched desperately for the match. Scratch, scratch. *Win!*

"Well, it's done now anyway. For some foolish, gacky reason, Roisin's her heart set on staying at me mammy's, so that's where she'll stay. I can only imagine the persecution she'll be putting me through when she swans into Derry, but."

Ursula hauled out the ironing board, flung it open and began attacking the clothes.

Win! Jed chose that impasse to heave silent breaths of excitement as he stole glances down at the five *Win*s. The pence piece hovered ...

Ursula ironed with wrath for a few minutes. Gradually the strokes softened, and finally she cleared her throat.

"Speaking of money, Jed," Ursula said almost apologetically, turning off the iron. "I know am just after roaring abuse about me family and how all they want is to get their filthy mitts on some of wer lotto cash ..."

She paused, iron aloft.

"Not that we've much left, like. But Fionnuala cornered me down the town the day and asked us for the lend of 400 quid. They kyanny afford to pay—"

"Don't start that crap!" Jed cut her off, the penny almost flying from his fingers. "You just said it yourself, for Chrissake! We paid off that stupid mortgage for them, and they took that money as if it was their God-given right. And look at how they're treating you now. They've got it into their heads that you can spew out money like an ATM! Stick your card in, out pops the money. Stick a compliment in your ear, out spits the dough! I know they're your family, Ursula, but, really! They act like the lotto winners of the world united owe them a living. I can't believe she had the *nerve* ...!"

He was one scratch away from the fare for his escape and wasn't about to hand it all over to her family.

Ursula nodded slowly in agreement and folded up the ironing board.

"I was only thinking, but—" she began, then stopped herself. She placed the ironing board back in the cupboard.

Ursula wandered into the scullery and paused by the island unit with the green granite worktop. She contemplated her thoroughly modern fitted scullery. There was something soothing about the flat, clean lines, something welcoming about the warm cherry wood of the cupboards that reached to the ceiling.

Ursula had given great thought, effort and care to making that room appealing, because she hoped, against all evidence, that the lotto win would transform her into a lady of leisure, a charming hostess to endless cocktail parties.

She had clearly been out of her mind. The only items in the scullery which got any regular use were the kettle and the microwave. She crossed into the dining room that sat unused. She settled herself on a chair and wondered why for the love of God she had made the decision to buy a dining table that sat eight.

She chewed her lip in frustration. Nobody in Derry held Roisin's opulence against her; why did everyone hold the lotto win against Ursula?

She didn't relish breaking the news to Fionnuala. Although the sight of her sister-in-law made her sick, and the money was much safer in a bank account collecting interest rather than being poured down Paddy's throat and pissed down the drain, something didn't sit right with Ursula. There were the blameless Flood children to think of, searching for their bedrooms under a cloak of darkness, bathing in cold dirty water. And refusing the loan, with Roisin's visit looming, would hardly endear her to anyone. Well, she supposed with a grimace, the Floods could share their sorrows with their nice new visitor from Hawaii lodging around the corner at 5 Murphy if they wanted. And maybe Roisin would lend them the money. Ursula continued sitting, wondering why that scenario made her even more angry than herself loaning Fionnuala the money would have.

She had just about enough in her own bank account, didn't she? It would be tight, but she could just about afford to loan a struggling family £400, couldn't she?

Ursula came back to reality with a thump. Gone were the heady post-lotto days, when she most certainly would not have been doing the ironing herself. The housekeeping account was perilously close to zero. Running two foreign, petrol-gobbling cars, property taxes, and the like ensured that she and Jed were barely able to keep their heads above water themselves.

Unless . . .

There were always those national savings bonds Jed had bought right after the lotto win. Five thousand pounds' worth, if she recalled, in denominations of £500 each. Where had he stored them away again?

Ursula strode back into the scullery, opened the Gaggenau fridge and slipped a hand into the individually regulated wine cooler. She pulled out the bottle Jed had already guzzled from.

She wondered if Jed would look up in alarm, thinking she was going to crack it over his skull. But—

"Let me pour ye anoller glass," Ursula would say.

He would stare in shock as the wine splashed into his glass. But she needed him passed out in a paladic stupor that night so that she could sneak into that old tackle box he kept under the bed. She had made her decision with sudden conviction: she would get her hands on one of those savings bonds to loan Fionnuala the money. And she wouldn't even be resentful when her sister-in-law never paid her back.

Ursula marched purposefully into the lounge and stared in shock at the empty Laz-E-Boy, a cigarette butt still smoldering in the ashtray. Her shock turned to anger, and just as quickly dissolved into relief. She didn't trust herself to run upstairs and rustle through his tackle box right then. The off-license—the only place he might have raced off to—was right around the corner, so he wouldn't be long. When he came back, however, she would keep refilling that glass for as long as it took.

£ £ £ £

Pushing through a fog of John Player Special, Dymphna stepped grimly into the ambience of sharpened screwdrivers and Euro dancepop that was the Cra-glooner pub. Vandals' heads swiveled for a quick inspection, and she was treated to leery stares from punch-hungry rowdies and glares of disapproval from packs of girls less lovely than herself. She paused at the mirror, wincing at the stench of sick from the corner, and peered through the graffiti to be sure the pregnancy couldn't be seen on her face.

Heaving herself into the churning horde, Dymphna searched for her girl-friends while she considered her two options: an abortion, or bearing a Protestant bastard.

She caught sight of her brother Eoin in a sordid corner thronged by a pile of skeletal teens and seething alcoholics. Bridie eyed her and waved frenetically through the smog.

Dymphna tossed Eoin a frosty glare and stumbled through a field of elbows and cleavage, tripping over handbags and rolling lager bottles. Her mates were all perched on barstools around a pillar: Bridie from the ChipKebab fast food joint, Marie from the bookies down the Strand, Ailish from Pricecutters, and Moire from that swanky new café on Shipquay Street. They were all eye-shadow and slashes of red lipstick and cascading curl hairdos and acne and clusters of cold sores, some festering.

"Right, Dymphna!" hollered a boozy Bridie over the disco strains of Spiller's "Groovejet" and shrieks of unbridled laughter.

"Right, girls!" Dymphna said.

She noticed with dismay the dregs of lager in each of their pint glasses.

"Right ye are, Dymphna," said Moire, shifting her arse on a stool and allowing Dymphna to perch next to it.

"What's the craic, hi?" Ailish asked.

"It's fairly black in here the night!" Dymphna said as she settled and motioned to the crowd.

"Aye," Bridie and Ailish agreed with eager nods. It was indeed *black*—crowded.

"Fag, hi?" Dymphna offered, brandishing her packet of unfiltered Rothman's. She looked sadly on as fag after fag slipped from her pack and into the lipstick-plastered mouths that surrounded her.

"Sure, am parched, so am are," Marie announced.

"Aye, am gasping and all," Bridie agreed.

"I've this round in," Dymphna sighed.

"Wile civil of ye, hi," Moire said, and the others nodded, their faces awash with relief.

"I'll help ye carry em, so," Bridie said.

"Right ye are," Dymphna said, grimly reaching into her handbag and unshackling a twenty pound note.

Bridie in tow, Dymphna pushed through the teeming teenaged masses, a hand flicking through her curls, searching for the appropriate father for her child. A big-boned battleaxe of a barmaid greeted them at the bar.

"Ye right there, love?"

"Aye, five pints of Smithwicks and a packet of pickled onion crisps."

Northern Ireland was the only province in the UK where abortion was still illegal. If Dymphna chose a termination, she would have to join the steady stream of abortion refugees—young Derry girls who took the bus down to Belfast, the ferry over to Birkenhead, a bus to Liverpool, and a taxi to the Powell Street Clinic. And then, of course, a taxi, a bus, the ferry, and the bus back.

Bridie had been through the shame the year before, and when she had whispered it all to her, Dymphna had been silently repulsed. Now she was grateful, knowing where to turn, knew from Bridie about an organization called Escort, the members of which were girls from the Women's Group at Liverpool University. They had met Bridie at the ferry terminal, brought her to the clinic and put her up in a B&B. They had visited her in the clinic after-wards and held her hand, and they had even given her a cup of tea! Even with the help of Escort, though, Dymphna would be hard-pressed to afford it. Half her pay packet was handed over to her mammy, and now approaching Ursula again—the only person she knew in Derry without an overdraft—was out of the question. Besides, the thought of murdering an innocent wee creature filled her with disgust.

Dymphna now mulled over a third option, suddenly happy she was amongst the crowd in the Craglooner. She could find an athletic and employed Catholic lad, entice him for a night of passion in some parking lot down the street and accuse him of being the father of her already-growing child. Then they would get wed at St. Moluag's.

She had seen it on a Jerry Springer episode devoted to paternity tests a few months earlier. If she blamed any of the four ... five? ... Catholic lads she had slept with in February, she had sense enough to realize it would end in tears as they were all useless. And as for a Proddy accompanying her down the altar ... the *altar*? What church would even have her and Rory Riddell?

"How's the talent in here the night?" Dymphna asked innocently.

"Ye see yer man over there?" Bridie asked.

"Him with the fine arse?"

"Aye, his cousin shifted me in the loos of the Pullman last week, so he did. And am hoping yer man there does the same to me the night."

"Ye dirty bitch, ye!" Dymphna said.

Bridie roared with laughter, and Dymphna peered at the lad in the Derry FC jersey and felt a slight tingle. She had to behave herself, though. She had to find a total stranger to be the new father of her child, an admittedly difficult task in Derry. And a lad her mate was itching to dig her claws into would not do.

The barmaid heaved the pints on the counter.

"And am away off to introduce meself!" Bridie said.

She grabbed her beer and teetered off. Dymphna hid her change firmly inside her coin purse, gathered up the remaining glasses and wormed her way back through the pulsating mob.

The girls were all roaring bawdily when Dymphna deposited the lager on the table. Gamely guzzling down, she tried to join in on their common chit-chat, but talk of the latest pop groups and which fit fella had popped into the bookies or Pricecutters irritated her senseless. She seemed to have matured years beyond her mates since the last time they had all sat here in the same pub one week earlier.

Dymphna sat silent and still, shredding a coaster under the table and keeping the grin of a simpleton plastered on her face.

He's too wee, and he's too aul, she thought, her eyes darting around the crowd, jumping from fella to fella, *too arsified, teeth too big, teeth too few ...*

Dymphna was the outcast, offering around the crisps, with a secret too sordid to reveal to even her best mates.

She didn't even trust herself to confide in Bridie as Bridie had confided in her. She still remembered thinking Bridie a filthy wee slapper, and Bridie's fella had been a Catholic! She had to tell somebody or she was going to go mental.

As her mates guffaws grew more sloppy, and she watched her brother flitting from table to table with a flash of pound notes, she remembered Eoin already knew half her secret. And she also knew that, unless she grassed him up to her parents—an unlikely scenario—that he would, quid pro quo, have to keep her secret to himself. And hadn't he served on the altar at St. Moluag's for years? If she could confess to anyone ...

"Am bursting for a wee, so am are," Dymphna suddenly announced. She grabbed her handbag and headed for the loos. After her business was done, she adjusted her bra straps staring at the point of the wall where a mirror should have been, then exited the toilet.

She scoured the crowd for her brother. He was laughing away by the dartboard. Dymphna waved him over. Eoin looked annoyed, but muttered something to his clientele and pushed towards her.

"Ye want some wingers for the night?" he asked her with a quick hug and manic grin. "I can give ye a special rate."

"C'mere you now," Dymphna whispered to him. "Am at me wit's end, Eoin. I gotta tell somewan about who yer man is, about—"

She gave a fleeting look at her stomach. Eoin's glassy eyes widened with sudden understanding and slight surprise.

"I kyanny tell the girls," Dymphna said. "I don't trust meself, sure. But ye're me broller."

Eoin was relieved. Anything more Dymphna told him, he knew his new career was just that bit more secret from their parents.

"Ye can count on me," he said, teasing her curls. "Ye know ye were always me favorite sister, Dymphna."

"He's ..." Her head swiveled to ensure nobody was listening in. "... a *Proddy!*"

Eoin jerked as if she had just smacked him. And even with the Ecstasy filling him with love, he bristled with a hatred older than his years, passed down from generation to generation, as if a barricade had just been erected between them.

"It's been sickening the heart out of me," Dymphna sniffled, grabbing his hand.

He thrust it off and glowered at her with a simmering apoplexy.

"*An Orange Bastard?*" he hissed through thin lips. "Merciful Jesus! Ye see you, Dymphna? Ye're on a fast road to Hell, so ye are."

"Now ye see why me mammy kyanny know."

She pleaded with her eyes.

"I'll give ye wan week to sort yerself out," Eoin said. "After that, all of Derry's gonny know of yer filthy secret!"

He fled, leaving her to her own misery.

Cold fear gripped her as Bridie staggered out of the ladies', pushing past a silly old fool in a purple track suit and a wide arrange of golden chains.

"Would ye look at the state of yer man?" Bridie giggled into Dymphna's shoulder. "Wearing gear fit for a wane! Wile lookin, so he is!"

"Aye."

"Let's get anoller round in," Bridie brayed.

"Aye, surely," Dymphna said, the grin plastered more firmly on her face. But there was nothing sure about anything anymore as she staggered towards the bar.

The man in the purple track suit looked hard at Eoin and scribbled discreetly in a black notebook, then picked up his pint glass and guzzled down with an air of triumph.

£ £ £ £

Ursula set her *True Crime* magazine to the side and glanced at Jed under the soft glow of the reading light. He *had* eventually arrived back home from the off-license, his face a curious pink, his eyes distracted with glee. There must have been some extraordinary sale on liquor, Ursula figured. He had raced upstairs and rummaged around, doing God alone knew what. When he finally returned downstairs, it had taken a bottle and a half of that white zinfandel to calm him down, but his deep snores now showed it had been worth it. Jed had even become a bit frisky when they slipped under the bedclothes half an hour earlier, but she had held him at bay with a giggle and a playful slap.

Ursula slid out of the covers, and her feet found her slippers. Casting glances at her comatose husband, she crouched slowly at the side of the bed and felt around for the tackle box.

Jed was right, of course; Fionnuala had some bold-faced cheek to ask her for more handouts. However, Jed didn't understand the strange pull of family. She knew there was no point in trying to make her husband see things from her point of view. Borrowing one simple savings bond was the only solution. It wouldn't have reached maturity, of course, so she was pissing money down the drain, but she could always buy another and slip it back into the box without Jed knowing. How she would scrounge up the funds for that, she'd worry about later.

She felt the cold steel, latched her fingers around the handle and tugged it across the carpet. She hauled herself up, then scurried off to the ensuite bathroom.

Ursula flicked on the light and stuffed a towel under the door. Settling herself on the toilet seat, she examined the combination lock hanging from the latch of the box. She set the combination at 00000 and tried to the lock. No such luck. She flicked to 00001 and tried the lock again. Nothing. Through the single digits, double digits and the beginning of the triple digits she trawled.

She caught her reflection in the polished sheen of the towel rack and realized she looked a right eejit—a woman her age in such a position! She only hoped Fionnuala would appreciate what she was doing for her.

With each click of the lock, each numerical advance, her frustration rose. Then, at 00146, she realized how simple it was. She flicked to 31567, the date of their marriage. Click!

Ursula flung the lock to the side, popped open the top and stuck her trembling fingers inside. She flipped through the children's birth certificates, the deed of the house, Jed's high school ring which would never again be able to fit on his finger, old medical records ... and chanced upon a bunch of letters from the '70s she had sent Jed when he had been in Vietnam.

Her face softened as she caressed the tattered envelopes with the Derry postmark. She had had no idea he had been so protective of them all this time. Out of one of the envelopes spilled saucy Polaroids of her younger self in various stages of undress, orchestrated for Jed's private entertainment while away on duty. As she inspected the photos, the years rolled back, and a wry smile sprung up as she recalled that Fionnuala's hands—*of all hands!*—had held that camera.

Ach, I was wile lovely looking back then! Ursula thought.

Although she was the object of the photographs, sneaking a look at them made her feel guilty. She had to find those savings bonds, and quickly. She stuffed the photos back into the envelope and dug deeper into the box.

She came across an envelope from the Foyle Travel Agency. Her brow furrowed. It was the only shred of paper in the box not yellowed with age.

What on earth—

The doorknob rattled.

"Ursula? Are you in there?"

A flash of irritation crossed her brow. She knew he was paralytic with drink, but was he simple in the head and all? Who else would be in their bathroom, for the love of God?

"Aye, am in here," Ursula called out. "Use you the loo in the Blue Room, sure!"

She sat frigid, envelope clutched in her hand, until she was sure he had wandered away from the door. She tossed back the envelope and scrabbled through the curling, cracked photos, their marriage certificate, and finally her fingernails scratched the bottom of the box.

Ursula was perplexed. She leaned back on the tank of the loo, considering. Perhaps Jed had moved the savings bonds to a safe deposit box she wasn't aware of? Perhaps he had, but her new post-lotto luxury mind wouldn't allow her to consider the obvious: that he had cashed them in. She plucked up his high school ring and wondered if she might pawn it and—

But, no.

Ursula slowly returned the ring and closed the tackle box of memories, slipped the lock back through the latch and clicked it shut. Then she settled to allow some time for Jed to come back from the loo and fall asleep again. All the while, she was mortified of having to break the bad news to Fionnuala.

3

The spuds had been peeled, and Fionnuala now stood before the cooker over the boiling pot, fag hanging from her lower lip, a row of Band-Aids across her forehead to hide the wounds from the poker. Tea that evening would be poundies: mashed spuds, egg and scallions. Fionnuala's wanes never went hungry; stuffed with cheap starch and carbohydrates, certainly, but never hungry.

Fionnuala couldn't care less that her wanes loathed poundies. *They'll just have to piggin well shovel them down their bloody cake-holes and savor every last fecking bite*, she thought.

The letterbox clanked. The sight of the aubergine bob shimmering though the misty glass of the front door caused her all manner of anticipation. Fionnuala tenderly touched the Band-Aids, turned down the latest Alice Deejay hit and called out: "Come you on in, Ursula. The door's open, sure."

Ursula entered the house with the usual strained attempt at friendliness.

"Right, Fionnuala."

Fionnuala's fox-like eyes darted towards the plastic Trendsetter's bag in Ursula's hand, then returned to the cooker. Ursula pressed the shopping bag with some embarrassment to her side.

"What's up with yer face?" Ursula asked in alarm.

"Walked into a door," Fionnuala shrugged off. "And what brings ye to the Bogside?"

Ursula thought grimly that her sister-in-law knew damn well what had brought her into her scullery. Fionnuala would grab the pounds from her, right enough, yet begrudged Ursula having a life which allowed her to move unhindered through the streets of Derry.

"I've brought some tights to give me mammy," Ursula explained with slight annoyance, unable to pull her eyes away from the Band-Aids. "And am gonny take her to the clinic to get her ears syringed in a wee while."

Fionnuala nodded silently as she stabbed her cigarette butt into an empty teacup. She thought that bag much too large to hold a solitary pair of tights.

Ursula remained a figure hovering on the threshold, not quite in the scullery or the front hallway. She looked over at the sink. Fionnuala followed her eyes. And started in shock at the plate *still* sitting on the counter.

"Dear God almighty! That's Eda's dinner, so it is. With all this palaver about me … walking into the door, like, it slipped me mind to take it round to her."

"Her *dinner*?" Ursula took a glance at her watch.

"Aye," Fionnuala grimaced, not a chance in hell of revealing it had been Eda's dinner from the day before. "I hope the poor aul soul's not perishing with hunger."

"Ye want me to take it round?"

"If ye could, aye."

Foam bubbled from the pot of spuds. Finally, Ursula spoke.

"Making the wanes' tea?"

"Aye."

"Poundies?"

"Aye."

Fionnuala was mortified. She couldn't let Ursula know she was subjecting her wanes to a meager tea of poundies.

"Aye, and …"

She reached into the fridge and revealed with a flourish a fillet of cod she had been freezing for Paddy's birthday in two weeks, tugged out a frying pan from the cupboard and threw the fillet on the pan. The scullery was soon ablaze with the pungent aroma of frying fish.

"I've come about that 400 quid," Ursula said.

Fionnuala's head shot up from the cooker, the spatula in her hand. Ursula appreciated the desperate hope she saw in those haggard eyes, but she wouldn't be the family's savior this time around.

"Am wile sorry, Jed says we can't afford it right now, but."

Fionnuala said much too quickly and brightly, "Ach, it's no odds, sure." She lit another fag. "There'll be some overtime going at the Sav-U-Mor."

She studied the boiling potatoes as though nothing had happened. Ursula's heart went out to her as much as it could.

"Fionnuala, love, ye've no idea how dear it is to keep up a house the likes of wer own. We've bills and all, ye know."

According to the look Fionnuala struggled to keep from her face, she didn't know at all.

"I really tried," Ursula continued. "I even suggested Jed cash in wan of his savings bonds to help ye out."

She reached out a weak hand, but Fionnuala recoiled from even the thought of her touch.

"Am after telling ye, it's no odds," she said through her teeth.

Ursula picked up Eda's dinner, uncertainly gathered together her shopping bag, purse, and car keys and prepared to take her leave.

"I've to get these tights to me mammy," she finally sighed.

"Aye, you do that, Ursula," Fionnuala snapped.

Dismissively? Ursula wondered as she hurried past the hallstand and clicked the latch on the door. She paused for a second at the threshold, plate in hand, the hiss from the frying pan in her ears.

Should she tell her? Should she let Fionnuala know she had spent the better part of half an hour perched on a toilet seat, rummaging through her husband's personal belongings, searching for a savings bonds she was prepared to lose money on just to loan her the money? Would Fionnuala even believe her?

She turned and just caught the tail end of Fionnuala's filthy look. It would have withered the less brazen. Ursula shook her head with a silent chuckle, then left the house.

As the latch clicked behind her, she wondered about Fionnuala walking into that door. When families were desperate for cash, the fists started flying. Could Paddy have possibly belted her one? But if they had enough money to afford a fancy fish fillet for their tea, they couldn't be that strapped for the money, sure.

Ursula headed around the corner to 5 Murphy, while in the scullery, Fionnuala quickly removed the thawing cod from the frying pan, swaddled it in plastic wrap and shoved it back in the freezer for another fortnight.

Their last hope, swanning out the door. Fionnuala stifled a hysterical cry of nervous exhaustion and felt the tears well. Where were they to get the money for the rates now? Her tears may have been directed towards the boiling pot of spuds but her anger, as usual, was aimed clearly at Ursula, and her finger was now on the trigger.

£ £ £ £

The young one chattered away on her mobile to her boyfriend, not paying her a blind bit of notice.

Ursula pressed herself against the customer service counter at the Bank of Ireland, clacking her nails impatiently and thinking grimly what a difference a few hundred thousand pounds made.

Four months earlier, right after the win, the manager of this very bank had greeted her and Jed's every entrance into his domain with a race from the inner sanctum and a smile and embrace. As they had gnawed steadily through the money, however, Mr. Bewley's delight had waned in stages, through cheery caution to slight disapproval to frank disbelief, until he couldn't even look them in the eye anymore. This distantiation hadn't begun until a few weeks ago, Ursula had noticed, and she calculated that their balance had been whittled away to a meager £100,000 by then. With the discovery of the missing savings bonds, however, she now wondered if Mr. Bewley had become a stranger when their balance had actually been even ... much ... less ...?

She stared out the window, ready to rip the mobile out of the girl's hand as she nattered on.

"Can I get some attention here?" Ursula finally boomed.

The girl eyed her indignantly as she whispered into her mobile, "Text ye later," then snapped the phone shut with a glimmer of irritation behind her pearly smile.

"Can I help ye there missus?" she asked.

"I've been stood before ye here for twenty flippin minutes without a glance of yers in me direction," Ursula said.

The girl appeared not to have heard.

"Can I help ye?"

"Am here for Mr. Bewley," Ursula said with a hope that never died.

"And yer name is?"

"Ursula Barnett."

They were even telling the interns the story of their fall from lotto grace, judging by the way the girl's face turned scarlet at the sound of her name, the way her eyes fell and her movements became less assured.

"M-Mr. Bewley ... he's ... is on holiday, him," she stammered. It was a good job she was studying finance as she made a terrible actress.

Ursula had seen the fat Protestant in his Armani suit moments earlier hovering around in the background next to the Motor Loans desk, but she didn't want to press the issue. She had resigned herself some time ago that nowadays she would have to take a number and wait in the queue like everybody else in the bank.

And what long waits they were. Was it any wonder that, years into the peace process, you still couldn't trust Proddy bastards? Ursula thought. They were all smiles and your best mates when you were rolling in it, but once you hit the bottom, they didn't know you from feck. Unlike the Catholics, who ... well ...

Ursula snapped a sigh.

"Ye don't say. Am here to see somewan about me account, then. Can ye get me somewan who'll help me?"

"Wan moment there, missus," the girl said before gratefully disappearing into the maze of desk panels.

After she figured out if and when and where and how Jed had abandoned them financially, Ursula would attempt some damage control on their bank accounts, if that were within the realm of possibility.

She heard harried whispering, saw heads pop up over panels, and finally a young bank clerk who looked like he was straight out of diapers approached her with a watery handshake and urged her to a desk festooned with little furry animals.

"How can I help ye the day, Mrs. Barnett?" he asked.

"I need some information on me husband's account. He's called Jed Barnett. I've the account number here," Ursula said, pulling out the hymnal and opening it to 'Nearer My God To Thee.' She had scribbled the account number on page 36 after secreting it from Jed's wallet the night before. "We won the lotto a few months back and—"

"So I've heard, aye."

"And he set up wan account for me, and anoller account for him, the main lotto account."

"Two separate accounts, non-joint?"

"Aye, and the interest from the lotto account is put directly into me own account, for the housekeeping, like. I don't know much about finances, ye see."

"That I can see, aye," he replied with a nervous tic, staring at the sorry state of affairs on his computer screen.

Ursula longed to grab the console and flip it in her direction.

"Me problem is, the past few months the amount going into me account has been getting smaller and smaller. I understand that every month the amount in the main account is smaller, but now am counting flimmin pence pieces every month. Could there be some mistake?"

"I kyanny give out that information," he said. "It's personal, like. The lotto account's in yer husband's name."

"And am his wife."

"Aye, and? A joint account I could help ye with."

"What about them savings bonds, then?" she asked. "Five thousand quids' worth he bought. Can ye tell me if they were cashed in?"

"Were ye listed as a beneficiary?"

"Naw."

"Then I kyanny, naw."

Ursula was getting nowhere. Although fighting the urge to clatter this jumped-up wee bastard across the face, she forced a smile and peered at his nametag: Ciaran O'Malley. She lit her face up.

"Are ye wan of them O'Malley's from the Bogside?" Ursula asked sweetly. "Am yer grandmoller's OsteoCare caretaker. Lovely aul wan, yer granny. She used to have the only phone in the neighborhood, so she did."

"Naw, am from Strabane. And personal information's personal information even if you be's changing me auntie's diapers."

"Ach, things is done a different way here in Derry," Ursula said. *Or they used to be at least* she thought with a slight fond ache.

Ciaran just shrugged and kept a firm hand on the computer screen, eyes telling her nothing. Ursula squirmed with frustration.

"I wanny speak to Mr. Bewley!" she finally seethed, fist pounding on the desk. "And don't ye be letting on to me he's on his holidays. I just seen him twenty minutes since back by the motor loans desk with a cuppa in his hand!"

"He's in a meeting," Ciaran said with a poker face.

"Just tell me if that bloody eejit of a husband of mines has put a second mortgage on wer home, for the love of Christ almighty!"

Eyes peered from around panels. Ciaran sat stonefaced and still, a mild panic in his eyes.

"In oller words, ye kyanny tell me a flimmin thing," she snapped.

"Right ye are," he said with a nod.

"Bleeding flimmin useless wanes working at jobs they're not fit for!" Ursula snarled. She snatched up her hymnal and handbag and stormed out of the bank.

The girl at customer service whispered into her mobile, "That miserable aul skegrat that lost all her lotto money's just leaving now, thank feck! I was about to ring security!"

£ £ £ £

Fionnuala was up to her elbows in dirty dishwater when the front door opened and Paddy lurched home from the night shift and the Bogside Inn, blotto with drink. His overalls were fetid, the sickly stench of dead sea creatures rose from him, and his black hair was slicked back. He planted a sloppy kiss on his wife's cheek, then attempted to focus on the row of Band-Aids on her forehead.

"Did ye walk into a door, hi?" he asked.

"What a carry-on there was yesterday!" Fionnuala snarled, Brillo pad in hand. "That flimmin Declan McDaid came at me with an aul poker! The bad wee brute roped Padraig into making petrol bombs in the back garden, for the love of God!"

Her husband gave a shrug and a chuckle, eyebrows raised with mirth.

"Ach, wanes'll be wanes, sure," he said.

"I've half a mind to report the incident to the peelers."

Paddy threw back his head and guffawed. There was no way in hell a Bogside Catholic would ever grass up one of their own to the police of the Royal Ulster Constabulary, staunchly Protestant as the RUC was.

"Ye want me to knock Padraig around a bit?" he asked.

"I already clattered him. If ye're up for dishing out a few more whacks, go you right ahead."

Paddy nodded absentmindedly, then got down to business. "Did Ursula call round?"

"She did indeed, aye," Fionnuala said, wiping her hands on a slimy dishrag. "Swanned into the scullery here yesterday, struggling under the weight of twenty shopping bags and fancy parcels, like."

"And?" Paddy asked, eyes flashing. "How did ye get on?"

Fionnuala shook her head.

"No joy?" Paddy asked warily.

"Naw. She had the bold-faced nerve to tell me they kyanny afford it! As if am flippin daft!"

Paddy stared open-mouthed.

"The hateful bitch!" he exploded. "Five hundred fecking thousand pounds they won! Five hundred thousand! She's always been quare and mangy with the purse strings, that wan. The effin cunt!"

"Ye don't think Jed put her up to it?" Fionnuala asked half-heartedly.

"Me hole!" Paddy seethed boozily. "She only did it outta pure badness! Jed's dead sound."

"Aye, a lovely man."

"That Ursula, but. Sleekit, narky ..." He had always thought his sister crafty and irritable, especially after 1973. "I've half a mind to ring her now and have it out with her over the phone!"

"If ye had've thought, ye could've asked Jed for the money," Fionnuala said.

As Jed had only been part of their clan for thirty years, he was still an outsider, what with his American accent and cowboy hats.

"What're we to do now?" Fionnuala cried. "Them rates is due the morrow!"

"What about Roisin? Kyanny she help us out? She's gonny be in town the morrow."

"I already thought of her. Her plane touches down in the evening, but, after wer electricity's already to be turned off. And she's on her holidays, anyroad. I don't wanny boller her."

"Call you the wanes down," Paddy instructed.

"What for?"

"Am gonny turn their flippin pockets inside out. It's about time they started to pay their way."

"Seamus and Siofra? Them has no source of income, but. And Eoin's out. And as for Padraig—"

"Call you Dymphna and Padraig down," Paddy instructed.

Fionnuala knew the drink was to blame for her husband making a show of himself and he would regret it in the morning, but she also knew that slipping a few more fivers out of her register and into her handbag at the Sav-U-Mor wasn't going to help them now. She wiped her hands on her smock, heaved a sigh and, slightly mortified, stepped into the hallway. Hand on her hip, she hollered with uncharacteristic uncertainty up the landing: "Dymphna! Padraig! Yer daddy wants a wee word!"

By the time they lumbered down the stairs, Paddy was dozing before the telly, lit fag hanging from his fingers, a gardening program blaring. He jerked to life as the offspring lined up before him and Fionnuala turned the telly down. She hovered in the background, passing back and forth before the Bleeding Heart of Jesus above the mantelpiece. Leaves from Palm Sunday—the last time they had all stepped foot into St. Moluag's together as a family—still poked out from the frame, curled and yellowed with age.

"What do ye want, Daddy?" Dymphna whinged. "I've still me hair to wash."

"And am knackered," Padraig said.

Whack! Whack! Whack!

Padraig screamed as Paddy clipped him around the ear.

"That's for messing with petrol bombs in the back garden and getting yer moller hurt, ye clarty wee bastard, ye!" he explained to the cowering child. "If I see ye with Declan McDaid again, there's more where that came from! Now if we don't get 300 quid round to the NIE and Fuel Services, we're not to be having the luxury of central heating nor electricity. Spuds'll be baking in the fireplace for wer tea."

Their impatience dissolved into nervousness. Parents without money? Who had heard of such a thing?

"Yer moller and me is skint," Paddy said, "and yer moller's after asking yer auntie Ursula for some money. The scaldy gee-bag refused."

Dymphna felt foolish; no wonder Ursula thought she had come to Xpressions to raid her handbag.

"We'll be grand in a week," Paddy conceded. "That doesn't help us now as youse are well aware the electric and gas companies is run by Proddies who has no mercy."

"What do ye expect us to do?" Dymphna asked.

"Pay wer effin electric and gas!" Paddy bellowed.

"Daddy! Am but eleven!" Padraig sniffled.

"If ye're aul enough to fling petrol bombs around the town, ye're aul enough to pay yer way!"

"That's me money, but!"

"Aye, and who gave it to ye?"

"You—"

"Get you back up them stairs then and find twenty quid before I clatter ye so'se you be's talking outta yer arsehole," Paddy warned.

Padraig scurried off.

"And you, Dymphna, is living the life of Riley, what with them flash wages the Top-Yer-Trolly dishes out!"

"Am earning bloody minimum wage," she huffed. "And half me pay packet is handed over to you lot anyroad."

"I wish I had the income when I was yer age to afford a mobile phone and glossy magazines and a trendy new top from Warehouse every week!" Paddy said.

Dymphna's face screwed with frustration. Eoin was strangely absent from the house, she noticed, probably stuffing more fifties into his pocket that night than she earned in a month.

"If ye've any complaints, ring yer auntie Ursula and spew yer filthy venom down the line!" Paddy barreled on, and, knowing his wanes, they would probably do just that.

"I hate me auntie Ursula!" Padraig seethed as he stomped down the stairs and tossed a handful of five pound notes at his father.

"Aye, don't we all, son," Paddy replied, snatching up the bills. "Now get you back up them stairs and think about all the boller ye've put yer poor aul moller through."

Off Padraig raced.

"And give us wan hundred, you," Paddy instructed Dymphna.

"I … I've only fifty, like."

"Me hole!"

Dymphna stole into the front hall, grabbed her handbag and reluctantly reached into it, realizing with a sinking heart the moment she handed over the £100, a termination—were she to choose it—would be that much further from her reach. She counted out the twenties with a sob.

"That reminds me," Fionnuala said with a nod at Dymphna's handbag. "Ye got the sausingers for yer faller's tea the night?"

"Aye," Dymphna said, the tears still fresh on her face as she delved dutifully into her handbag again. "And them bog rolls from the staff jacks ye was asking for and all."

Ignoring Dymphna's grief, Fionnuala snatched the toilet paper her daughter had lifted from the staff toilets and plopped them on the hall stand. As Dymphna tugged out the sausages, Fionnuala glared down, a twitch of irritation in her left eye.

"Am wile sorry, Mammy," Dymphna said apologetically. "The sausingers is skinless budget, just. That aul bitch Fidelma wouldn't leave me a moment's peace. I had to lift what I could."

"Ye think ye can dredge up the intelligence somewhere within that thick skull of yours to pinch some of them wile dear French cheeses from the counter the morrow?" Fionnuala asked. "To serve Roisin for her arrival? I'd be mortified to have to serve her up a packet of pickled onion crisps."

"I'll see what I can do, aye," Dymphna said through her tears. "What about Eoin?"

"Ach, sure, he doesn't be interested in boggin aul cheeses," her mother said.

"Naw, what I meant was, is he to give up some money as well, like?"

"Yer broller's drawing the brew, ye daft wee bitch."

How her dullard of a daughter expected Eoin to have money when he was collecting unemployment, Fionnuala was at a loss to comprehend. Dymphna could take it no longer.

"Eoin's dealing wingers down the Craglooner, sure!" she wailed. "He must be raking in loads!"

Dymphna actually gasped after she blurt it out and clasped both hands over her open mouth. Common sense had never been one of her stronger traits.

Now it was time for the parents to stare.

"Ach ..." Fionnuala began, a sneer and scorn ready. But it all made sense, she suddenly thought, Eoin's new mobile, his trainers, his good moods and bleary eyes, the shifty mates in hooded tops she had seen him with down the town.

And, as if the Virgin Mary herself were damning Dymphna for being a right old slapper, the front door opened, and who staggered in but the man himself—Eoin. Dymphna shrank against the mantelpiece, terrified Eoin would reveal her sordid secret, feeling the shame of every Orange ounce of embryonic fluid blatant in her womb.

Fionnuala gave Eoin the once over as if she were seeing him for the first time. She would never feel the same way about her second oldest boy again.

"What's the craic, hi?" he asked, staring in some concern at the odd way they were all looking at him.

"I hear ye've been dealing wingers in the Craglooner," Paddy roared.

Eoin glared daggers over at Dymphna, who pleaded "naw, naw, naw" with her eyes.

"A-aye," he admitted.

He flinched as his father's massive palms swooped through the air—

—and grabbed him by the shoulders, hugging him tight, pride aglow.

"Right man ye are!" Paddy said.

"Aye, good on ye, like," Fionnuala twittered around him, a pat on the head. Their son, the resourceful entrepreneur.

"If only I'd had the chance to deal drugs when I was yer age!" Paddy sighed. "Dealers was steering clear of Derry twenty years ago, but, with all the bombs and Brit soldiers crawling through the streets and all."

"And mind, Paddy, Ecstasy wasn't even invented back in them days," Fionnuala nodded.

Eoin and Dymphna regarded their parents in a new light.

"We need 180 quid for the gas and electric," Paddy said. "Could ye help us out there, son?"

All sorts of relief crossed Eoin's face.

"Aye, surely," he said, reaching into his pocket and counting out the notes on the coffee table, problem solved.

Paddy added them to the quickly growing pile.

"Thank bleeding feck," Fionnuala said, snatching the notes up and fondling them. "Ye don't know what this means to us, lad."

Eoin beamed proudly while Dymphna scowled. She didn't recall one word of thanks when she had handed over the equivalent of forty hours of slicing black pudding and stacking gorgonzola with a silly grin glued on her face.

"Just watch ye don't get yerself caught, Eoin," Paddy said. "Now the Peace Process has calmed things down, the Special Branch of the RUC the day has nothing to do with their time but go after enterprising spirits like yerself."

"Ach, it's no boller," Eoin said. "A spastic could steer clear of the Special Branch. Is that it, then? Am shattered and ready for bed."

"Aye, that's it, son," Fionnuala said fondly. "Night night."

"Night."

Dymphna followed the prodigal son out of the sitting room like an afterthought. His head whipped around and, with every step, he inflicted her with an ever more menacing glare.

"Am wile sorry, Eoin," she whispered meekly. "They forced it outta me. I had to tell em ye were flush. They needed the money, like. I had to hand over 100 quid as well, and that was meant to be me termination money. Still, they took the news about your drug sales well enough."

She smiled with a tense eagerness at his drug-addled face in the light of the landing.

"Aye, right enough. Ye've still only wan week to sort yerself out, but," he hissed.

As Dymphna snuggled in next to Siofra's sleeping limbs, she realized finding a lad to claim as the father was useless. She would have to take that ferry. Where would she get the money for the termination, though?

£ £ £ £

David the shelf stacker slunk up the meat and cheese counter with a sneer aimed at Dymphna.

"O'Toole wants a word with ye," he said. "In his office, like."

Fidelma sniggered at the summons—never a good sign for any employee—as David slouched off. Dymphna checked out David's arse as she suspected Mr. O'Toole had done minutes earlier. David was well fit. She wondered if he lived in the Waterside.

"Wipe that smirk offa yer face," Dymphna warned Fidelma. "Or am gonny wipe it off meself when I come back from the aul poofter's lair."

"*If* ye come back," her co-worker sang.

Dymphna plodded down the battery and lightbulb aisle, up past the staff lounge and loos, and paused at Mr. O'Toole's door. She pulled her nametag out of her pocket and pinned it on, thankful she still didn't have the Doux de Montagne, Crème de St. Agur and the Cheese and Pineapple Halo in her smock; they had been safely hidden in her locker. She rapped on the door.

"Come in."

She always envisioned Mr. O'Toole in his office busy at work on his finger-nails, emery board flying, sighing over glossy photos of Keanu Reeves, but there he was, sat at a desk, pecking away on his computer. Her stomach turned at the sight of the outstretched pinkie finger hovering over the key-board.

His beady eyes, normally frisky when a stock boy was in the area, seemed to be dulled as they suffered the sight of her scowling femininity.

"Ye wanted to see me?" she asked.

"I did, aye."

Dymphna examined her nails and straightened her smock. Finally he looked up at her, and he wasn't happy. When was he ever, Dymphna thought grimly; a strange disposition for one of them they called gay.

"This," he said, reaching into a file, "was discovered by the cleaner on the wall of the ladies' staff jacks above the soap dispenser."

He produced a Polaroid of a vulgarity scrawled in bright pink lipstick: MR. HENRY O'TOLLE IS A FUCKIN NANCY-BOY POOF!

Dymphna curled her lips inward and struggled to hide her lipstick and her guffaws. She could almost feel her wane tittering along with her. Mr. O'Toole stared pointedly at her mouth.

"The shade of lipstick used for this message seems remarkably similar to the wan ye've on ye now," he said.

When the merriment finally quelled, she trusted herself to ask, "A-are ye accusing me, like?"

"It's yer shade, if am not mistaken. *Sheer Temptation* from Boots the Chemist, is it not? If it weren't for wer admission into the EU and all their touchy-feely liberal shite, I could accuse ye of all sorts. Now I kyanny, more's the pity."

"What do ye expect me to do with that photo, then? Pin it on the bulletin board in the staff lounge so'se all the stock fellas can read it and get ye a date?"

Mr. O'Toole did not dignify this comment with a response. He reached into his drawer, pulled out a dog-eared file and swiftly shifted into third gear.

"Ye were twenty minutes late for yer shift the day."

"Aye, I—"

"—and ye took seventy-five minutes for yer lunch break—"

"The queue at the ChipKebab was flimmin desp—"

"—and ye were half an hour late yesterday and all."

"Me broller was pelting rocks at pensioners! I had to protect em."

"The likes of common Bogside muck like you coming to the aid of aul wans? That's likely, aye," he said with a roll of the eye. He heaved up the hefty folder and flipped through it, scanning the many incident sheets written up about Dymphna Flood.

"According to these, ye be stroppy with the customers, yer fag breaks stretch for hours, ye never lift a finger to help with the deliveries, ye slipped some budget pork into Mrs. Laughlin's order when ye knew she's the only Jew who's living in Derry. Ye almost had us in court over that wan, you."

He placed down the folder and glowered frankly at her.

"Have ye anything to say for yerself?"

She stood naked under his gaze, simmering, as her tongue revved up for a lashing.

"C'mere till I tell ye! Ye see you, O'Toole? Ye sit on yer fat arse in this boggin office week in and week out, dreaming up grievances to throw in wer faces like the fanny-hating arse-bandit ye are! How many grievances does that David from the stockroom have in his file? Not a wan, am betting, for you be's hungering to bugger the arse offa him!"

Mr. O'Toole's eyes devoured her with disbelief. He snatched up a pencil and scribbled furiously in her file.

"That's yer first written warning," he said.

"Shove yer written warning up yer hole, ye fecking aul poofter!"

Scribble.

"And that's yer second."

"But …!"

"Wan more grievance, and then ye're outta here, drawing the brew."

If she lost her job, how would she ever get together enough for the ferry to Liverpool? She fumed at him for a few seconds, her hands curled into fists, nails biting into her flesh. Gradually she relented and, shockingly, willed a smile to her lips.

"Was there anything more ye wanted to say?" Mr. O'Toole wondered.

Dymphna took a deep breath.

"Aye," she admitted.

Mr. O'Toole looked up wearily.

"Go on and advance us some of next week's wages, aye? Am skint."

His eyes widened. Then he said with a reluctant chuckle and a shake of the head, "Ye've a bold-faced cheek. You wee girls from the Bogside always have, but. I had this girlfriend from the Lecky Road wance, Magella Feeney ye called her, and I mind wan day she asked …"

The laughter within Dymphna pleaded to be set free. Did he really expect her to believe he was heterosexual? *Oh, the hilarity!*

She let on she was all ears and politeness as he blathered on. She just wanted to grab £50 and escape from the office, her two written warnings under her belt, and race to the ferry pier.

"Would ye go on and sub me the fifty quid or not?" she finally asked through her grin-arranged teeth.

"Am under no obligation, even under the laws of the EU."

He leaned back and took stock of her, his eyes drinking her in.

"I kyanny help but admire ye," he said. "Fair play to ye, Dymphna. Bold-faced cheek deserves to be rewarded. Not to the customers, mind, but between us …"

Dymphna's brain struggled in confusion. Was he being sarcastic? She found sarcasm so difficult to detect. Mr. Toole reached into a drawer and pulled out a little metal box.

"Here's yer sub," he said, tugging out a fifty pound note.

She snatched the money. Was it her imagination, or did his manicured fingers rest a second too long on her own? Was that beady little glare in her direction one of … could it be …?

She shoved the money into her smock, flustered.

"Am I free to go?" she asked.

"Aye, get you back to work. I've taken up enough of yer time. The good Lord knows ye spend little enough of it behind that meat and cheese counter as it is."

She closed the office door, lost in thought. She had seen the swanky car he drove. As area manager, he was sure to be raking in the cash! And she had noticed the impressive package in the crotch of those skintight slacks he favored; how could anyone not? She and the checkout girls had made themselves ill over the thought of that thing poking at boys' arses. But if it were for her own pleasure ...? A greedy smile graced her lips, and she was magically a woman reborn.

Would Mr. O'Toole be the father of her wee unborn nadger?

CARETAKER'S ALLOWANCE

4

"Put you some clean socks on fer yer auntie Roisin's visit! The almighty stench offa themmuns ye've on ye now is causin me grief of all sorts!"

Siofra blinked up in surprise at her mother. Hadn't Fionnuala battered the shite out of Padraig the week before for dumping his socks in the laundry pile before they were due, screaming something about washing powder not growing on trees? She feared her mother was turning into a right headcase, and perhaps this fear is what made her turn obediently.

As her daughter skirted out of the scullery, Fionnuala reflected that Siofra was indeed a wee angel when the mood hit her. It was a shame Roisin hadn't planned her trip to coincide with the First Holy Communion celebration the next month, she thought while arranging the French shite around the cheese and pineapple halo on a platter.

She should've told Dymphna to lift some crackers as well. Ach, well, Fionnuala thought, Roisin would have to piggin well make do with some crusty loaf or a stale roll.

She moved from the platter to the Flood Holy Communion gown she had dredged up to show Roisin. Moira had proudly marched down the aisle of St. Moluag's Chapel in that gown in 1991. Two years later, her younger sister Dymphna had followed down the same aisle in the same gown (much less proudly).

It was a wee bit stiff and colored a dingy yellow, Fionnuala noticed, but a quick spin in the Hotpoint and a few strokes on the ironing board and it would be right as rain for wee Siofra.

Fionnuala was removing some dried egg yolk from the collar with a thumbnail when she noticed Siofra at the threshold of the scullery, eyes on the gown. Fionnuala beamed down fondly at the family heirloom.

"Aye, it's grand and lovely, right enough," she said.

"Where did ye unearth that from?" Siofra demanded to know, hands on hips.

Fionnuala's smile dissolved into a threat. Her daughter glared with eight-year-old hatred at the unsightly mass of stained polyester blend.

"Naw, Mammy!" Siofra wailed. "Ye're off yer bleeding head if ye think I'd disgrace meself in that mingin frock! I'll be the laughing stock of all the Bog-side!"

While Fionnuala convulsed, Siofra raced off and returned seconds later, thrusting the catalog of princess dreams into her mother's face.

"This is what am gonny wear!" she insisted. "The Maria Theresa gown imported from Italy with the matching Andromeda veil on page forty-wan!"

Fionnuala snatched up the catalog, scanned the print, her eyes blazing in disbelief.

"Taffeta? Tulle? Slip and crinoline petticoat? Matching satin gloves, me hole! Wise up, wane!"

"But—"

"Wan hundred and sixty-seven pounds?! Ye're off yer bleeding head!"

"Me auntie—"

"And it's not just the fecking frock!" Fionnuala said, flipping dismissively through the gloss. "There's the bleeding tiara, the shoes, the missal, the sparkly bag—"

"Mammy!"

"The parasol, the rosary beads, the jewelry, the piggin tights—"

"Auntie Ursula tole me Grainne's mammy's taking her on a trip to Spain to get her a suntan for the day. And she's getting her the Royal Princess Gown on page thirty-two."

"So yer auntie Ursula forced this pile of shite into yer grabby wee paws?"

Siofra nodded haltingly.

"That woman!" Fionnuala quietly seethed. "That's the end of them fecking lessons! Me and yer faller is working all the hours God sends to put a bloody fish finger in yer piggin mouth every Friday, and we still kyanny keep wer heads above water! Ye're living a fecking dreamworld if ye think we're throwing away 200 quid on a frock ye're gonny have on yer flippin bones ten flimmin minutes outta yer life!"

"But Auntie—"

"Yer auntie's giving ye ideas above yer station! She's swimming in cash and hasn't a clue. Yer da's no famous footballer, and am no ex-Spice Girl. We've not the money nor the simple minds to waste 500 quid on yer communion.

Sure, it's a holy sacrament, wee girl, not a bloody beauty pageant! Ye're gonny wear the gown yer sisters wore. It was fine for Dymphna and Moira, so it was, and it's gonny be fine for you and all."

Fionnuala marched to the press under the sink, flung open the door and tossed the catalog into a trashcan overflowing with festering potato peels.

"The bin's the only place for overpriced shite!" she bellowed at Siofra's whimpering face.

Siofra's eyes finally welled with tears.

"That manky dress is a pile of shite!" she wailed, racing from the scullery into the front hallway.

Fionnuala was in hot pursuit. She clutched a handful of brown envelopes from the hallstand and shoved them into the wane's face.

"Ye see themmuns?" Fionnuala asked. Siofra recoiled against the wallpaper from her mother's wrath. "Ye know what themmuns is? Bills, ye silly wee gack! Bills and bills and bills! Am just after forcing yer brollers and sister to empty their pockets to pay the last round, and now here's anoller round of em demanding to be paid! Catch! Yerself! On! Wee girl! Naw means naw!"'

Siofra blinked, uncomprehending.

"Bills?" she asked, wide-eyed innocence. "I thought wer Auntie Ursula bought wer house, but!"

Fionnuala's outstretched palm shot into her face.

Stunned, Siofra's eyes bulged as her hand shot to her cheek. And then the tears flowed.

"See if I ever, *ever* catch ye saying that again," Fionnuala seethed into her tender face, index finger menacingly close to her nose. "I'll clatter the living shite outta ye, ye jumped-up wee bitch!"

"Just wait till me daddy comes home, so!" Siofra sobbed, turning and fleeing up the stairs to safety.

"Aye, and maybe he'll clatter some sense into yer gacky skull!" Fionnuala yelled up the landing. "Am warning ye, ye stay away from that madwoman! And don't ye be trying anything on! Any harm comes to that gown, and ye'll be marching down the aisle of St. Moluag's in a bloody fecking bin liner!"

After a moment's seething, she stepped back to the bin under the sink, flicked aside some potato peels and gingerly removed the catalog. She needed it handy to fling at Ursula's face the next time she saw the bitch.

£ £ £ £

The jewel on the Foyle was preparing for another sickly summer with vague pockets of sunshine and the barest hint of heat. Roisin Doyle, however, was delighted for a reprieve from the humidity of Hawaii.

Skin oddly taut and bronze, the brightly colored beads of her Bo Derek-style cornrows clanking, she sailed into town with all the fanfare of an old war-horse galloping triumphantly back to its stables. She peered with a frantic intensity out the windscreen of the taxi she had taken all the way from Belfast International Airport, marveling at the transformation of her beloved town on the River Foyle.

The brassy-green spire of the twice-bombed Guildhall now towered with pride over the fiercely-scrubbed cobblestones. Derry City had arisen like a luxury liner from the ocean depths, splendor restored thanks to millions of Euros from the EU.

The overabundance of new red brick threatened to mar Roisin's optical nerves, but she cooed at the sight of the new Ulster Bank, the new library, the new bus depot, and her credit cards squirmed in anticipation of the new shopping center, Foyleside. Gone were the trails of razor wire and the paratroopers, the checkpoints and the pram searches. Even a spanking new McDonald's had arisen from the grimy ashes of the past.

Derry had become a most handsome city, marred perhaps only by the menacing gangs of hooded teens who loitered on every corner. The taxi pulled into the smattering of historical political graffiti that gave the Bogside its tourist charm, and Roisin started the rabble-rousing at 5 Murphy Crescent even before her bags were unpacked.

"What's all this bloody caper about that bitch Ursula snatching the house from under wer noses?" she berated her mother, revving up to spread home truths that were nothing but a pack of lies. "It sickens the heart outta me!"

Eda wrapped her cardigan around her.

"Am wile cold. Stoke the fire, would ye, love? I think the damper's out."

Roisin stared at the blazing electric fire, and her heart went out to the pensioner, Eda's head of platinum curls perfectly coiffed and colored, her mind a madhouse.

Changes had been made to 5 Murphy since Roisin's last visit. After the lotto win, Ursula had had the heating switched over to oil, redone the bay windows and installed a chairlift for Eda.

The scabby bitch hadn't seen fit to change the furniture, though, Roisin thought, the same she remembered from the '70s: purple carpeting now frayed with scuff marks, white pleather sofa and matching loveseat peppered with fag burns, once bright orange cushions now dulled with the passage of the years and sagging from the weight of a thousand arses, all at odds with the old world charm of the lace doilies Eda had strewn on every vertical surface in a vain attempt at claiming the décor as her own.

"Have the Floods round the corner been taking good care of ye?" Roisin asked softly, taking her mother's frail claws into her hands.

"Ursula's been looking after me. She's a wee dote, her. Got me a new flat screen telly just the oller day."

"Mammy, ye mean Fionnuala, surely?"

"Naw. Ursula."

"Hasn't Ursula been torturing the life outta ye?" Roisin prompted. "Making yer time left here on Earth a misery?"

Eda seemed to consider, then her eyes flashed at some past annoyance, and Roisin pressed her fingers, urging her on.

"Aye, Mammy? Aye?"

"Now that ye mention it, Ursula forgot to give me me dinner the oller day. Weak with hunger, so I was, and all she finally brought yesterday was two skinless budget sausingers and a dollop of hardened turnips. I think she had them sitting out for days!"

Roisin nodded, satisfied. Just the ammunition she had been searching for.

"Don't ye worry anymore," Roisin said. "Am here to save ye."

As the stranger before her continued chattering away, Eda eyed her waveringly, wondering who she was.

Half an hour later, the letterbox clacked, and Fionnuala and her two youngest filed in. She had scrubbed them well, and had even forced clean socks onto Seamus.

"Ach, Roisin, it's lovely to see ye, sure," Fionnuala twittered, fairly ripping the carton of duty free fags from her sister-in-law's fingers and shoving Seamus and Siofra towards her. "Say hello to yer auntie," she demanded.

Roisin beamed down at her niece and nephew. Siofra shoved the platter of cheeses up, while Seamus cowered behind his plate of stale baps. Roisin grimaced at the meager spread, her eyes unable to avoid the car-accident pull of the cheese and pineapple halo.

"Themmuns looks wile lovely," she managed.

"Ach, just a wee something to welcome ye back to Derry."

"Ye shouldn't have, Fionnuala," Roisin said, and she meant it.

She took a nibble out of common civility, then made to hand over the Smirnoff she had bought for Paddy, but Fionnuala already had it sitting at her feet. Roisin reached into a bag and shoved gifts at the wanes. Siofra dubiously inspected some cheap bauble her aunt had snatched up from the newsstand at Honolulu International.

The swank new McDonalds on the Strand has better gifts in their Happy Meals, sure! Siofra thought. *Auntie Ursula's gifts is always wile clever and wile dear. This strange new aunt is a wile scaldy cunt!*

Seamus tossed his trinket aside and began to play with his shoelaces.

"So how does it feel, lodging here in the servants' quarters of her majesty's holdings?" Fionnuala began, with a nod over at the framed photo of Ursula and Jed grudgingly displayed on a remote corner of an end table.

"That Ursula!" Roisin grunted, revving herself up for a go. Siofra's and Seamus's heads shot up. Fionnuala noticed the attentiveness shining in their little eyes.

"You wanes! Go and play with yer granny!" she ordered.

Even Siofra seemed slightly fearful of this prospect, but they obediently left the sitting room and left the adults to their private natter.

"Ursula's been off her head ever since she won the lotto," Fionnuala fumed.

"Aye, only thinking of herself, the self-centered cow! Ye know she gave me mammy her dinner late yesterday? The poor aul wan was perishing for days!"

Fionnuala wasn't sure where to look. Roisin set her lips and prepared to let loose a string of insults when Seamus padded back into the sitting room.

"Where's me granny?" he asked.

Roisin and Fionnuala's eyes swiveled around the room in bewilderment.

"Where's Eda?" Fionnuala wondered.

"I kyanny for the life of me mind where I left her!" Roisin said.

Fionnuala pressed Roisin's arm as they leaned in together and stifled their giggles.

"Not in front of the wanes," Fionnuala admonished.

They had half-raised their arses from the cushions to go search when they heard the sound of a key in the front door. They froze, sharing a grimace. Although conventional Flood wisdom was that, her being a lotto million-airess, the dreary neighborhood of Ursula's childhood was somehow beneath a journey in her new Lexus, in reality Ursula visited her mother with a frequency that bordered on stalking. It could only be the lady of leisure herself.

"Roisin?" they heard Ursula warble. Then—

"God bless us and save us! What's me moller doing stuck on the stairs?"

They all rushed out to see Ursula halfway up the stairs, Eda clutching at the banister with a whimper, struggling to pry herself from the chairlift stalled at the top of the landing.

The silly aul bitch! Roisin thought as she climbed the stairs after Ursula. *Where the feck had the aul eejit been on her way to in the first place?* Roisin had waited an intercontinental jet flight to tell Ursula off, let her sister know what a hard-faced bitch she was, but she could hardly do that now, when it looked like she and Fionnuala had just left Eda to roam the house, unhinged and unattended.

"I've tole ye time and time again, Mammy," Ursula admonished. "The *green* button means go, the *red* means stop."

They inserted Eda back into her chair lift and calmed her down with pats and coos. Ursula pressed the appropriate button, and they waited at the bottom of the stairs for her journey to complete, exchanging gruff hellos.

"Long time no see, Roisin," Ursula said.

"Aye."

The trio guided Eda into the living room, each vying to be the most caring, gentle relative.

"Watch yer step."

"There ye go, Mammy."

Once in the living room, Eda settled on the settee under the portrait of the Blessed Virgin, and Siofra scampered up to Ursula as if she loved her and fit her little arms around as much of her waist as she could, just to annoy her mother. Fionnuala could put up with the charade of happy families no longer.

"Away from that woman, you!" she warned Siofra.

"What—?" Ursula gasped.

Siofra scampered out of the sitting room with a cackle, Seamus in tow. Roisin's eyes danced at the shock on Ursula's face. She settled happily into a white and orange armchair and let the commotion unfold.

"A wee word, Ursula?" Fionnuala's smile was chilling. She reached into her handbag and pulled out the catalog. "What in the name of feck's this pile of shite ye've been shoveling down wer Siofra's throat?"

Ursula blinked.

"It's for her communion gown, sure."

"Ye've spent the last three months splashing yer money around like ye was Richard flippin Branson! And now ye're poisoning the mind of a wee wan too young to know the difference, turning her into a jumped-up start like yerself!"

"There's budget gowns in the back pages, sure!"

"I'll budget gowns ye!" Fionnuala seethed. "Ye fancy yerself as the lady of the manor, better than the likes of us, prancing around with yer nose so high in the air ye'd drown in the flimmin rain. C'mere till I tell ye, Ursula, ye kyanny take the Bogside rowdie outta ye, no matter how many lottos ye win, ye fecking cunt!"

Ursula was affronted, hearing language like that under the eyes of the Blessed Virgin, Eda inspecting them in thin-lipped silence.

"That's just the kind of talk I expect from a Heggarty! Youse Heggartys have always been a scourge on the good name of Creggan, and why wer Paddy married wan of you lot I'll never know!"

Roisin guffawed silently. It was a common Bogside row, the likes of which she never saw in Hawaii. How she loved Derry City!

"Me great-uncle is a bishop!" Fionnuala pointed out.

A bitter laugh shot out of Ursula. Fionnuala was always pulling this none-too-hidden ace out of the sleeve of her bargain bin jumper. Ursula knew better.

"Yer uncle kyanny make up for the sins of the rest of youse. In and outta the jails for torching post boxes and slashings and bottlings in pub brawls! The men hard, the weemin harder. C'mere till I tell ye, Fionnuala, thank the Lord am looking out for that wee Siofra of yers, for she'd be well on her way to the gates of hell with only a moller the likes of you to show her the way! The best thing ye ever did in yer miserable life was to make me that wan's godmoller. That poor wane needs all the help she can get from—"

"Siofra's not to get yer 'help' any longer!"

Ursula twitched. "Am gonny teach her about the church and—" she said.

"Naw, ye're to teach her sweet feck all!"

"But—"

"Ye see if ye so much as whisper wan prayer into her ear, ye'll get the heel of me shoe up the crack of yer arse, mark me words!"

"Am her godmoller!" Ursula gasped.

Ursula was raging, but still had the presence of mind to wonder why her mother wasn't jumping to her defense. Roisin she could understand, but why was Eda just sitting there like she was, not a thought of her own in her head?

"Mammy! Help me!"

Eda appeared to be either considering or dozing. Finally, she whispered, "Well, she *is* Fionnuala's daughter, ye know."

Fionnuala grinned her triumph, but Eda wasn't finished. Her head trundled on its neck and faced Ursula's square on.

"… and ye know I haven't been able to trust ye since that night during the Troubles," she said, milky eyes straining with condemnation.

Even Fionnuala flinched. This was the family secret that dared not speak its name. Even when the Floods were arsified with drink, they never mentioned Ursula's shameful indiscretion of decades earlier, yet here Eda was, trumpeting it from the rooftops while stone cold sober and with a cruelty that only encroaching senility could account for.

"Ye mind that carry-on with you and that Francine O'Dowd?" Eda barreled on. "The shame ye dragged wer family name through?"

"That was 1973!" Ursula begged. "Ancient history!"

"Even now I kyanny hold me head up in the street," Eda said, a black hole where her heart should be. "Mortified, we was, absolutely mortified!"

"It's them new angina tablets making her say such things!" Ursula appealed to Roisin and Fionnuala. Although her sister and sister-in-law felt for her, Eda's comment well below the belt, they remained silent, arms firmly folded.

"And," Eda continued, "now ye've got them millions bulging outta yer handbag ye think ye own the whole piggin lot of us. Well ye don't."

"Mammy!" Ursula implored, tears welling. "Why are ye being so mean to me?"

Eda cast Ursula a look of dismissal. She made for her daughter-in-law's side and stopped just short of wrapping her arm around Fionnuala's waist.

"I've had me say," Eda concluded. "And that wane's better off without yer interference."

"Aye, don't ye be laying a finger on wer Siofra," Fionnuala said, although without the gloating one might have expected, her coup now upstaged.

Gutted, Ursula silently made her way to the hall. They heard the front door squeak shut.

"Good on ye, Eda," Fionnuala said, but half-heartedly, while Roisin looked at her mother sideways and wondered what actually *was* in those new angina tablets.

£ £ £ £

1973 (PART II)

Lance Corporals Ian Simms and Teddy Platt had spent the week sweating in their riot gear, searching through prams and dodging rocks flung at them by schoolchildren, but now the weekend had come and they were sweating with lust. They had hooked two Derry grots in the Quonset hut that was the Yank Enlisted Men's Club on the US Military Base, plied them with endless gin and tonics, and victory was soon to be theirs, under the sheets of a rented room in some hotel across the border. Gracie and Una their names were, and the mindless bitches had leaped up as the relentless disco of "Rock The Boat" suddenly blared from the DJ's speakers.

"Just look at those tarts writhing against each other," Simms said, nudging his barracks roomie. "Filthy Fenian grots. You think they'd put on a little show for us and the Polaroid?"

"It'll be brilliant for the grot board!" Platt said, attempting conviction. He felt ashamed about what they were going to do later that evening, but the commander had ordered the men of the barracks to pull the most hideous civilian girls they could—grots—snap photos of them in the most lurid sexual act possible, and hang them on the barracks "grot board." During a lager-fuelled off-duty party every Sunday night, the soldiers voted (Platt and a few others reluctantly) on the most depraved Polaroid, and the most disgusting photographer won a case of lager. Gracie and Una weren't really in the grot category, but Catholics received triple votes, and if the soldiers could further entice the Fenian bitches into some woman-on-woman action, maybe with a Union Jack draped over their naked Green bodies and some playful use of a lightbulb, the case of lager was sure to be theirs.

"You know what these repressed Catholic tarts are like," Simms said, already feeling the lager. "A lifetime of confessions and communion wafers and they're up for any bit of perv action, secretly gagging for a stiff Protestant tadger."

Platt ordered the girls another round of gin and tonics from the bartender.

"All this pansy disco and twangin country Yank shite!" Simms spat. He had been hoping for T-Rex and Slade, fine British groups.

Simms kept his eyes on Una and Gracie through the flailing arms of the dance floor, perverse visions dancing through his mind.

"We've to get our hands on their handbags, of course," Simms said after a while.

Platt sighed inwardly.

"Of course," he said flatly.

After ravaging the local slappers, after asserting the superiority of their religion or nationality, the soldiers always left them passed out in their drunken Irish stupors, defecated into their handbags, then stole away back to the safety of the barracks. It was the same game with every grot they pulled, Protestant or Catholic.

Those handbags were now on the dance floor, purple velour platforms stomping around them, as Francine and Ursula roared as best they could with boozy faux-laughter. They had been putting on a right show of two young Derry girls up for a night of craic for the lance corporals, flashing the young pink flesh below their sequined hot pants. Their minds were heavy with the gravity of their mission, however, as their feminine delights had hit their mark, having baited two young, randy and, most importantly, British *soldiers far from their hometown of Manchester. Flaunt a bit of cleavage at a soldier cooped up for months in the barracks in a hostile land, and you soon had his undivided attention; that's how easy the honey trap was.*

"Rock The Boat" ended and Ursula and Francine grimaced as the DJ put the needle on a Buck Owens classic. They scooped up their handbags and swiftly abandoned the floor, making a bee-line for the victims and gin and tonics which awaited them at the bar.

They saw Platt and Simms squint at their approach, hateful Proddy lips curled into smirks of lust. Ursula jumped as Master Chief Jungsten suddenly towered above her, arms outstretched in delighted surprise, a rum and coke planted in his right fist.

"Ain't you Petty Officer Barnett's wife? Ursula?" he said through his cigar. "Didn't I meet you at the fourth of July bar-b-que last year? You sure know how to eat a hotdog, if I recollect rightly."

Ursula was rigid with fear. If it ever got back to Jed that she had been caught with British soldiers at the Yank club bar, fighting for gin and tonics while he fought for democracy in Saigon …

"Me name's Gracie," she snapped up at him in alarm, "and am off to the loo."

She clutched Francine's elbow and turned abruptly from Master Chief Jungsten's startled face. With a wink at the Brit soldiers and a finger pointing urgently in the direction of the toilets, Ursula disappeared with Francine into the frugging masses.

"Me heart fairly stopped thumping!" Ursula gasped as she collapsed into the stall. "We've to get them Brits outta the club and into Tommy's cab dead quick. I kyanny risk been recognized by any more of me husband's mates!"

She glanced at her watch.

"Half ten he said he'd be outside the gate waiting for us. Twenty minutes, so."

"Them soldiers," Francine said, "must think we're off wer heads. Catholic girls teaming up with Proddy paratroopers."

"If only yer men knew."

Ursula flushed and left the stall, heading on unsteady feet for the mirror. She pursed her lips, then attacked them with lipstick.

"C'mere till I tell ye, am fear-hearted with all wer antics the night," Francine revealed, joining her girlfriend at the mirror and running the mascara over her false eyelashes. "Snogging the faces offa British soldiers! Wee girls in Belfast have been tarred and feallered for far less."

"*Ach, them girls wasn't fighting for the Cause,*" *Ursula said.* "*They had the cheek to wanny marry Orange soldier cunts! Ye've no need to be afeared; Tommy's gonny be looking after us. Mind yer mouth, but. Ye don't know who's listening in.*"

She motioned towards the stall doors. Francine was suitably silenced for them to spend a few moments making themselves more alluring as the twang of Tammy Wynette crept into the ladies room.

"*Platt and Simms seem terrible nice, but,*" *Francine said wistfully.* "*I kyanny fathom them raging with hatred as Tommy went on about. Are ye sure we're meant to be doing this?*"

Ursula put down her compact. Francine shrank from her filthy look. Such was the power Ursula had over her girlfriends.

"*Don't ye be backing out on me now. Ye kyanny think of them fellas as human beings. Ye gotta think of em as flimmin Orange beasts, responsible for gunning down wer brollers and sisters and wanes in wer streets!*"

Ursula rouged her cheeks with conviction.

"*Right ye are,*" *Francine said, but her eyes showed her doubt.*

"*Have you yer knock-out drops ready?*" *Ursula asked.*

Francine fiddled through the tissues and matchboxes in her handbag and tugged out the vial filled with colorless liquid Tommy had handed her in the taxi before he dropped them off outside the security hut of the Yank Naval base.

"*Two drops, mind, just to make em woozy. We kyanny drag them into the taxi all on wer lonesome if themmuns pass out.*"

Ursula extracted a similar vial from her own handbag and hid it in her palm. They adjusted their halter tops one last time, made their way out of the loo and towards their destiny.

Francine gratefully grabbed the drink Platt proffered as she pecked his cheek and wrapped her arm around his shoulder.

"*We was bursting for a slash,*" *Francine said, her voice high with the forced frivolity of it all.* "*Terrible sorry, like.*"

Ursula perched herself on Simms's lap and giggled into his neck, repulsed at the feel of his Proddy aggressor flesh as she covered it in tiny kisses.

"*The sight of you two birds on the floor got us thinking what it might be like if …*" *Simms raised his eyebrows suggestively.*

"*Ye filthy perv, ye!*" *Francine squealed with laughter, all the while her stomach churning.*

"*We're good Catholic girls, us!*" *Ursula said through a tight smile. She squirmed her buttocks well away from an alarming protrusion that was blossoming in Simms's lap.*

"We'll see about that!" Simms said, his lips assailing the cringing skin of Ursula's neck. He grappled his lager and made to guzzle it down.

Ursula grabbed the glass and held it fast. She let her fingers creep over his thigh towards the warmth of his crotch.

"Why don't youse take one last trip to the gents?" Ursula whispered into his ear, with a quick nip on his earlobe. "Then we'll be on wer way?"

She winked at his hateful Proddy face, her stomach lurching.

Simms and Platt exchanged a glance, adjusted themselves and beat it to the toilets. Francine gnawed on her lower lip as her eyes met Ursula's over the two empty barstools. The soldiers' almost empty pint glasses awaited their treachery. Ursula gazed around the crowd to be sure the shrieking Yanks and off duty Brits were oblivious to them. Master Chief Jungsten was nowhere in sight. Francine pleaded silently with her eyes. Are we doing the right thing? Ursula nodded barely perceptibly. Her hand reached towards Simms's pint glass, her thumb and forefingers trembling as they twisted off the top of the vial. Francine made similar moves towards Platt's glass. As a team, they slipped two droplets of chloral hydrate into the dregs of beer as "Knock Three Times" broke out around them.

Ursula's heart thumped against her ribcage as Simms and Platt swaggered towards them, slapping each other on the back.

"Drink up, lads!" Ursula urged. "And let's hit the sheets!"

Simms and Platt guzzled down. They collected their jackets and were out the door, the girls clutching the men's arms for support, staggering and giggling with girlish glee as they stumbled past the rows of Quonset huts. Ursula waved goodnight to the guard at the security hut.

"Ach, here's a taxi, sure!" Francine said, hoping her voice sounded sufficiently delighted.

"Ach, luck's with us the night, fellas!" Ursula said. "The Lord must be all for the mixing of the religions."

"Yeah, right," Simms snorted, shoving Ursula forcefully into the back seat. Ursula was grateful Tommy was at the wheel, all denim and white-man afro and lamb chop sideburns.

"Right, lads?" Tommy said from the front seat.

"None of your gob," Simms snapped. "Just do what we're paying you for and drive."

Francine and Platt shoved into the leather beside them. Francine and Ursula's thighs pressed against each other, their platform heels tight in collusion. Simms flashed Platt a sly smile over the bangs of Francine's shag wig, his finger kneading *the Polaroid camera in his jacket pocket. Ursula and Francine were exchanging the same glance, if only in their minds. Platt stifled a sudden yawn.*

"Where was that hotel?" Simms barked into Ursula's face even as his eyes drooped.

"We're for Muff," Ursula said to Tommy in the front seat, as if he didn't know. "The Starlight Hotel."

"Right youse are," Tommy said, revving up the car with a secret smile. "The Starlight Hotel it is."

The little town of Muff, one mile across the border into the Republic, had no Starlight Hotel. It did, however, have an IRA safe house with a sagging thatched roof and boarded windows, and three soldiers for the Nationalist Cause waiting for the lance corporals with ski masks and AK–47s, ready to tie their drugged bodies to chairs, beat them awake, engage in some playful torture and taunting, and blast away their hateful Brit faces.

Ursula and Francine squealed with forced laughter as the taxi sped off into the night.

£ £ £ £

As expected, Jed wasn't home when Ursula arrived at her empty trophy house, so she sat alone with her handbag at the dining room table, grieving.

She had nobody to turn to. Molly and Francine were busy at work. Ursula herself had Mrs. Feeney from OsteoCare to visit in half an hour, but she couldn't face it. Home visits were supposed to be cheery affairs, and she couldn't plaster a smile on her face as Mrs. Feeney babbled on about the price of Brussels sprouts when Ursula's own mother had just all but disowned her. The OsteoCare client only used her as a glorified taxi service every week, anyway, forcing Ursula to drive her down the town so she could collect her frozen steak and kidney pies from the Top-Yer-Trolly.

Ursula turned to the phone and dialed, guilty at leaving the old woman wanting. Then again, Mrs. Feeney always seemed to be wanting. Always.

"Mrs. Feeney? It's Ursula."

"Aye, love, I've me list of needs already written out. Am sitting here waiting for ye now."

In the front hall with her duffle coat already on, doubtlessly.

"Could I see ye the morrow instead?" Ursula asked.

There was a martyred exhalation of breath on the end of the line.

"Am rationing me spuds as it is," Mrs. Feeney said.

"Am terrible sorry; something came up," Ursula said. "If ye're low on food, ye can always go to the Sav-U-Mor round the corner, sure. I'll see ye the morrow at half three."

There was a silence. Mrs. Feeney finally spat out: "If ye must."

The moment Ursula hung up, the phone rang, and she eyed it with fear, dreading who might be on the other end, roaring abuse at her. But eager to not miss a call from Jed—as unlikely as him phoning her might be—she picked up.

"Ye know I kyanny abide ye," Roisin began. "That with me moller wasn't on, but. I felt for ye, Ursula, I truly did. That palaver with you and Francine O'Dowd's the buried past, as well it should be. And, ye know, Fionnuala's after telling me that that Francine's working now at the Foyleside Churches Advice Center. If ye want, ye can take me there the morrow and help me see about me pension. As you two is mates, who knows, maybe she can tack on a few extra quid for me. Then maybe after we can have a cappuccino and a wee natter at that new café on Shipquay Street."

Gratefully snatching any tidbit of kindness, not caring that Roisin was using her as a complimentary taxi service the way Mrs. Feeney did, Ursula eagerly agreed.

"Ach, Roisin," she said. "That's wile civil of ye."

"Me moller wants a word with ye now."

"Naw!" Ursula begged. "I kyanny speak to her! She'll have anoller mouthful of abuse for me!"

"It's alright," Roisin said. "I've spoken to her, and she's sorry for what she said."

Ursula froze as Roisin handed over the receiver.

"Am affronted, Ursula," Eda said down the line, "I haven't a clue what came over me. Pay me no mind, sure. Ye know I love ye as only a moller can."

Ursula's heart ballooned.

"Ye've been cooped up in that house for too long now," Ursula said. "When was the last time ye saw the sunshine? Ye wanny come with me and Roisin to the Waterside Churches the morrow? A wee outing would do ye the world of good."

"Sounds right lovely."

Ursula hung up a new woman, dismissing her heartache as completely as it had consumed her one phone call earlier, and suddenly realizing with tight lips that Roisin would probably expect her to splash out for the cappuccinos. For once Ursula wouldn't care.

£ £ £ £

Siofra stood outside the Craglooner in a brattish strop, stewing under the
cheap headphones of her cassette Walkman as S Club 7 blared into her ear
canals. It was the third pub Eoin had dragged her to so far that afternoon,
ostensibly to talk to his mates. He either had very many mates or loads to discuss, given the length of time she had been stood outside bored out of her
skull. She was sick of examining the pavements for cracks as her mammy
demanded she always do when walking around town, something to do with
orchestrating a fall and collecting loads from the city council.

Eoin finally emerged from the pub, and Siofra whinged, "Why've ye
dragged me down to the city center with ye anyroad?"

"Because ye're me sister, and I love ye," he said. "Only wan more pub, and
then we'll head back to the Bogside."

His little sister, in her pink dance skirt and denim jacket embroidered with
flowers, the purple Power Puff Girls handbag sauntering at her side, was, Eoin
hoped, a clever decoy to put off any meandering members of the undercover
narcotic squad and the Special Branch.

They turned off Magazine Street and into the makeshift market in the
damp shadows of the city walls and O'Doherty Tower. Eoin nodded to the
shifty-eyed fellas who sold bootleg CDs and DVDs, knock-off football scarves
and nicked perfumes from their stalls. He stopped for a pack of fags smuggled
in from Romania, and Siofra pretended not to notice the bag bulging with
sweets he pulled out of his hooded top and delved into, tossing a few sweeties
over as payment. She was biding her time.

"Eoin, I need to take a slash!" she announced, squirming on the cobblestones, as he handed a few sweets to the bootlegger in exchange for the fags.
"Take me to the ChipKebab. And I want some TakkoChips and all."

It was the least he could do. He held her hand as they crossed the square to
the fast food joint next to the Top-Yer-Trolly.

Under her purple and green striped cap embroidered with tiny camels, Bridie's eyes lit up as Dymphna's wee brother approached her cash register.

"Right, Bridie."

"Right ye are, Eoin, what can I get for ye?"

He leaned across the counter, avoiding the smeared garlic sauce and stray
chip, and whispered:

"Give us some TakkoChips, and me sister needs the use of yer loos. Me and all, for that matter. I scoffed down a chicken vindaloo last night that—"

Bridie's eyes danced with knowing.

"Vindaloo, me arse! Ye must think I came up the Foyle in a bubble. I know what the likes of youse does in public jacks."

"Am dead serious, am not here to shoot up or scoff down bangers," he said, shooting a look over at Siofra. "Ye've no idea the pain she's in!"

Bridie's face was like stone above the register keys.

"Them jacks is for the staff only, like," she announced.

"She's a wane, just," he pleaded.

"If I could sneak youse in, what's in it for me?"

Eoin considered.

"Go and play with them ketchup packets for a wee while, you," he instructed Siofra.

The girl struggled down the counter to do as instructed, the despair rising in her little loins. But she kept a crisp ear on the discussion at the register.

"I'll give ye ten bangers for half price," Eoin whispered.

"Five for free, more like. Ye said yer Siofra was bleeding desperate."

Siofra was, her face misshapen and pink as she arranged the ketchup sachets into an upside down crucifix.

"Ach, ye're doing me head in, you," Eoin relented, reaching into his pocket.

Bridie eyed her manager at the chip vat.

"Make sure yer man over there doesn't see ye sneaking in," she said, snatching the tablets and slipping Eoin the key to the staff toilets.

"What's them?" Siofra finally asked. Every young adult in the flipping city seemed obsessed with Eoin's sweets. Maybe they were those things she had heard all about on the telly.

"Never you mind," Bridie sang, slipping one into her mouth to add a bit of spice to the shift.

"Is them Viagra?" Siofra asked. She was puzzled by their answering guffaws.

"Sweeties," Eoin replied. "For discos."

Siofra licked her lips as she gratefully tottered off to the loo. Eoin's sweeties didn't look as tasty as Jelly Babies or Wine Gums, but if the delight on Bridie's face was anything to go by, they must be magic. She knew better than to ask for one right then and there. When anything was "for adults," she knew it meant she had to wait until she was ten or eleven to experience it. She would have to sneak into the boys' bedroom when Eoin was passed out and pinch a few then.

Business done, they waved goodbye to a Bridie waiting impatiently for the chemicals to kick in and walked outside. Eoin still felt wheezy, and was about to race back in and borrow the key again when an RUC police cruiser rushed towards them over the cobblestones. The car squealed, almost collided with a post, the doors flew open, and two coppers headed towards him at a steady gait, their rifle green tunics freshly-pressed, faces beaming menacingly under the peaks of their matching caps.

"Take you them," Eoin hissed, tearing the drugs from his hooded top and stuffing them into Siofra's handbag. "And pretend ye don't know me."

"Ye're me broller, but," Siofra said. "Of course I know ye!"

"Do as ye're tole!" he demanded, pushing her towards the Top-Yer-Trolly display windows.

Siofra scuttled away, feigning interest in the pyramid of mouthwashes, scoffing down her TakkoChips, and all the while her beady eyes strained at the reflection in the window of the scene unfolding behind her.

Eoin made to saunter around the corner to the Strand Road, but the two RUC peelers stopped him: a skinny bastard and a fat cunt.

"Just a minute there, mate."

"Where are you on your way to, mate?"

They crowded closer.

"Am aren't yer mate," Eoin scowled, the green of their uniforms blinding him and forcing his eyes into the pink of their faces.

"None of the sarky lip," smirked one, stepping forward.

Eoin felt the cold expanse of the ChipKebab window against his shoulder blades. Their patent leather Oxfords were inches from his trainers.

"You don't want to assist the RUC with their enquiries?"

The police presence in the city were used to sarcastic, spotty rowdies proudly displaying the chips on their shoulders, but that had never been Eoin's nature.

"A-am after coming from the Richmond Center," he lied.

The fat cunt raised an eyebrow, then they exchanged a nodding glance between themselves as Siofra licked the spicy sauce off her fingers, eyes glued to the reflection.

"That's highly irregular," the fat cunt said, "as we've just received intelligence that you've come from the Craglooner."

"Empty your pockets," said the skinny bastard.

Bookended by their lime green shirts, Eoin hastened to obey. He pulled out a wad of notes from his right pocket. From his left pocket he pulled out the pack of fags, a box of matches. The skinny bastard grabbed the cigarettes.

"Themmun's is mines!" Eoin protested.

"Hmm … contraband here," the skinny bastard said, struggling to read the health warning in Romanian. "Very serious offense, buying fags smuggled in from Eastern Europe. I'm afraid a search is going to be necessary."

"Mate," added the fat cunt.

"Your wallet?"

Eoin hesitated until an extendable baton appeared from behind one back, and a pair of speedcuffs from the other. He did as instructed, and the skinny bastard flipped through his wallet.

"And I'll take this."

The fat cunt plucked the mobile phone out of Eoin's hand.

"Give us that back, you!" Eoin wailed.

The fat cunt wagged a bloated finger at him, pig eyes twinkling, baton twitching.

"Tsk, tsk, tsk!"

He inspected Eoin's mobile—the last number he had dialed was the McDaid's—flipped open a mobile of his own and pressed a number. The fat cunt moved off around the corner. Eoin heard him muttering to someone on the phone, but couldn't make anything out.

Siofra gasped into the window as a black car sped into the city square, shoppers scattering, and squealed to a halt inches from Eoin. Out came a hulking behemoth with cropped gray hair, who grabbed Eoin and hauled him into the car. The bastard inside forced his skull down into the seat as it bolted off for points unknown. The constables high-stepped back to their patrol car, whooping in celebration. The car roared away down the cobblestones.

At the mouthwash display, Siofra finally turned around, blinking through the cloud of dust. It had been straight from an episode of *Cops!* she thought excitedly.

She stared down in suspicion at the handbag clutched tightly in her sweaty palm. It bulged with Eoin's sweeties. She knew she should probably phone her parents and let them know what had happened, but her mammy had always said she was too young for a mobile, so they could rot in Hell. She briefly considered going back into the ChipKebab and asking Bridie what she should do, or at least cajoling another TakkoChips out of her. She looked across the square at the market beyond the city walls. Then her lips curled with sudden connivance, and she skipped towards Magazine Gate.

5

Roisin clung to the arm rests in mild terror as braches flung themselves at the window to her side.

"Mind where ye're going, Ursula!" she implored.

Although a ceasefire had been called the day before, for two women bound by a childhood of imagined slights, lies of omission, filthy looks and perennial fallouts, there was still an understandable tension in Ursula's Lexus that was exacerbated by both her driving skill and the showy display of the air conditioning. In the heat of Hawaii, air conditioning in the Doyle family car was a necessity. In the Derry joke of a summer, the hum of the AC was something else entirely.

Ursula pulled into the parking lot of Foyleside Churches Advice Center and flicked off the air conditioning with a touch of studied nonchalance. Roisin turned to the back seat. Eda sat there, strapped to the Coach leather in her seat belt.

"C'mere now, Mammy," Roisin said. "Let's get ye out of the car."

"Ach, sure, there's no need," Ursula said. "By the time we get her outta that safety belt and up them steps and back down again, ye'll have already been in yer grave for years and have no need for yer pension. She's grand sat there as she is."

Ursula flung open her door and stood on the asphalt, flicking her keys with slight impatience.

"Get yer legs in gear, Roisin. I've a pensioner from OsteoCare expecting me at half three."

"Are ye right there, moller?" Roisin wondered, hesitant. She searched for some sign of annoyance or discomfort amidst Eda's wrinkles. She saw no sign of any emotion at all.

"Aye, am grand, so am are," Eda said flatly.

Roisin reluctantly left the car.

"That's not on," she said as Ursula marched her through the parking lot. "Leaving me moller locked in the car like a manky aul dog."

"Aye, it's far worse than forgetting her in her chair lift, right enough," Ursula sniped. "I've been taking care of me moller for years now. Don't ye be telling me what's best for her. A wee outing in the car does her the world of good, so her doctor says. To force her to run a flimmin obstacle course is bad for her angina and her brittle bones."

Ursula led Roisin into the inner sanctum of the Foyleside Churches Advice Center. Francine O'Dowd sat before a computer, punctuating each peck of the keyboard with a crunch of tomato and sausage flavored crisps, a bargain bag of which sat on her desk. Ursula knocked on the door and greeted her partner in crime all those years ago.

"Right there, Francine."

"Ursula!" Francine O'Dowd beamed, wiping a crumb from her chin, her withered face creasing into a smile. "What about ye? Long time no see!"

She struggled to heave her poundage up from her chair and peck Ursula on the cheek, shooting the obviously well-cared-for stranger at her friend's side a glare of mistrust. Francine's eyes flashed from the gently swinging beads of Roisin's cornrows to her 18 carat wedding ring, up to the suspiciously over-sized breasts straining the palm leaf print of her halter top, back to the wedding ring, up to the erect eyebrows that screamed Botox, down to her pink leggings and virgin white Nikes and finally rested back on the symbol of wealth and Yankee imperialism wrapped around the carefree finger bronzed from luxuriant Hawaii sunshine. Everything about her roared privilege and devil-may-care and stomach stapling. A Yank, no doubt. How they plagued Francine. A sour smile fell across her face.

"I'd like for ye to meet me sister Roisin," Ursula said quickly.

"Yer *sister*?" Francine gaped.

Roisin grimaced and offered a half-hearted hand.

"She's over from America, aye," Ursula explained.

"Am here to see about the pension am owed," Roisin said, pushing herself up to the desk.

So that explained it. Francine had seen them troop into her office through the decades: Yankee brides living the life and still greedy for handouts from the British government. And although Francine was quite aware that, as part of the United Kingdom, the money was coming from Proddy bastards who deserved their coffers raided, she still felt protective.

"Ye look well-mended to me, but, woman," Francine admonished. "Ye kyanny tell me yer Yank husband's not provided well for ye?"

"That's not the point, sure," Roisin said with a snap of impatience. "Am an Irish citizen. I should be allowed me pension!"

Francine returned to her computer with a mutter.

"Let me look up yer case. Roisin Flood, aye?"

"Aye."

Roisin carefully spelled out her name as if Francine was touched in the head, then supplied her birth date with a twinge of embarrassment. Francine looked doubtfully through Roisin's files and shoveled another handful of crisps into her mouth.

"Ye haven't been back to town much since ye discovered America, missus," she said, accusation in her tone. "According to me records, ye worked as a seamstress at the Foyle shirt factory for two years when ye was a wane."

She could barely conceal the disbelief rising in her voice. She did a few quick calculations on a scrap of paper and finally looked up at Roisin, a glimmer of triumph on her face.

"Ye'll be getting £3.72 a week."

Roisin might have felt a part of Derry lingered forever in her soul, but Derry seemed to have cast her aside and was now treating her like the stranger to her hometown she really was. She was crestfallen.

"Might there be some mistake?" Roisin asked hopefully.

"Ach, catch yerself on, woman! Ye kyanny expect the government to subsidize ye for the rest of yer days lollygagging around in the sunshine of America for a few flimmin weeks ye spent playing with a bobbin and a needle clamp some thirty-odd years back!"

Francine selected a few forms and tossed them across her desk. "Fill themmuns out and post em, and ye'll get what ye're owed."

Roisin eyed the papers dubiously.

Ursula sidled eagerly up to the desk. She suddenly realized why, subconsciously, she had felt the pull of the town on the River Foyle all her adult life. Family, friends and subsidized health care, and a hefty pension to help her in her twilight years.

"I've been back living here for seven years now, so I have," she said in a breathless rush she could no longer contain. "And I've never had any pension stamps put on my account!"

Francine's eyes widened with interest, and Roisin flashed them both a foul glare.

"Sure, Ursula, I know ye've always been an upstanding member of wer community," Francine wittered on as she pounded on the keyboard and stole glances at Roisin to make sure her point was being driven home. "And I know ye take care of yer aul ailing moller, like."

"Aye, aye, ach aye," Ursula said.

Francine stared in puzzlement at her computer screen. Her hand snaked into the crisp packet.

"Sure, I've no record here of yer work for yer mammy. Ye shoulda been getting an Invalidity Carer's Allowance. How many hours a week do ye take care of the aul wan?"

"Twenty, thirty ..."

"Eda Flood?" Francine asked.

"That's her, aye," Ursula said with an eager nod.

Francine searched through the databank, and her brow creased.

"That's wile odd."

A few more clicks, then Francine asked, "Sure, nobody else takes care of yer mammy, do they?"

"Naw," Ursula said, suddenly uneasy.

There was always some aul stoke desperate to move in where handouts from the government were concerned. She remembered the weeks after her mammy and daddy got back from visiting her and Jed while they were stationed in Guam, and a mob of squatters had taken up residence at 5 Murphy Crescent. It had taken an injunction to rid the house of them, and the stench took weeks to clear. Ursula shuddered at the thought of the peeled wallpaper, the state of the fridge and the used condoms that had littered the bedroom floors.

"Ye know a Paddy and Fionnuala Flood?" Francine asked.

Ursula tensed at the sound of their names.

"It says here that a Paddy and Fionnuala Flood's been claiming the caretaker's allowance on yer mammy for the past five years! They get £35.80 a week."

Ursula turned to Roisin, jaw slack.

"I kyanny—I kyanny get me head around this!" Ursula said.

"Right!" Francine announced. "There's only one thing to do."

She pressed some forms into Ursula's hands.

"Ye've got to apply for the caretaker's allowance yerself," she said.

"But them—"

"Has been nicking money that's rightfully yers."

"Paddy and Fionnuala won't have the city council on their back for pinching the money?"

"If ye don't make a fuss, naw," Francine said. "Unless ye wanny claim all five years they already doled out. Then ye gotta take em to court to get the money that was yers."

She felt Roisin staring daggers, stone cold silent at her side, but Roisin needn't have worried; the mere thought of confronting Paddy and Fionnuala before a trio of magistrates filled Ursula with dread. Plus, she *had* lived the past few months in the lap of lotto luxury.

"Naw," Ursula said. "We'll let the past lie."

They gathered their respective forms and made to leave. Ursula and Francine exchanged a kiss on the cheek and, when Roisin was on her way out, the secret handshake that meant "never mention the shame of '73." Once on the gravel of the parking lot, Roisin whipped around and lashed into her sister with a fury.

"Ye flippin cow, ye! Ye know Fionnuala's taking care of me moller!"

"Wan dinner a week she makes the poor aul soul! And she's been collecting forty quid for the hassle! That's fine talk from wan whose been shacked up in Hawaii for the past thirty years. Ye see you, Roisin, ye ran screaming from Derry the minute ye got the ring on yer finger, and haven't been back since! Ye've not a clue what goes on in this flimmin town! Me fingers is bloody from all the messages I do for me mammy week in, week out!"

As they approached the car, Roisin clutched Ursula's arm with a gasp and pointed through the windshield.

"What's up with me moller?"

Eda's brittle form was splayed across the back seat, her eyes seething with agony, fingers clawing the glass.

"She's having a heart attack!" Roisin roared.

"It's a wee flimmin angina attack," Ursula corrected. "Had ye been here to see wan before, ye would know—"

"Moller! Moller!" Roisin wailed, tugging furiously on the car door handle.

"All she needs is her tablets," Ursula said too calmly for Roisin's liking. Two nitroglycerine pills, a sip of water and fifteen minutes of peace and Eda would be right as rain. The last thing she needed was Roisin roaring out of her like a thing possessed.

"Where's them tablets?"

"At the house."

Roisin gaped in disbelief at Ursula's face before screaming into it: "Let me in the fecking car! Let me in!"

"Roisin! Stop the roaring out of ye! Help me calm her down!"

Ursula fumbled with the keys as Roisin snapped open her mobile phone and dialed furiously.

"Me heart! Me poor aul heart!" Eda moaned through the glass with a dramatic clutch at her chest and a gyration of her head across the car seat.

"Who's that you're ringing?" Ursula asked, heaving open the door and patting Eda on the her fluffy head. "There, there, Mammy."

"The ambulance," Roisin said.

"Ach, don't be daft, there's no need, sure."

"Then get you behind that fecking wheel and get this car down to Altnagelvin Hospital now or am having ye sent down for piggin manslaughter!"

Roisin flashed Ursula another filthy look as they exchanged places and she slipped into the back seat of the car. She rolled her fingers uncertainly up and down Eda's arms and legs while Ursula got into the front seat.

"Ye right there, Mammy? We're gonny get ye a doctor," Roisin soothed.

"Me heart, me poor aul heart," was apparently the only English of which Eda was capable.

"Close that door," Ursula instructed, reluctantly revving up the engine.

The car lurched through the parking lot.

£ £ £ £

Fionnuala hummed grimly along to a sparkly Kylie Minogue single as she shelved the tins of mushy peas. She possessed all the joie de vivre of a newly-diagnosed mad-cow victim. How she wished she could join her second eldest son, prancing through the pubs of Derry, flinging out handfuls of drugs for pockets bulging with cash. The lottery scratch cards behind her cash register no longer breathed tantalizingly down her neck, however, as with the new source of income in the family, things were no longer as desperate as they had been. It was wild civil of Eoin to have bought her those curling tongs, she thought, and now she was wondering how much longer she should hold off before asking him for that pedicure at Xpressions.

The bell over the door tinkled, and Mrs. Feeney barged in, eyes narrowed with accusation.

"I'll have you know yer piggin wane was flinging rocks at me the oller day!" she roared. "Almost cracked me skull open, so he did!"

Fionnuala attacked a row of baked beans with the price gun as Mrs. Feeney staggered towards the turnips.

"That wan's on his way to Magilligan just like his older broller, and them turnips looks as if they've gone off, so they do! Yer Lorcan was sent down for Grievous Bodily Harm, if I mind rightly. That's where the lot of youse Heggartys belong, locked up where ye kyanny harm poor decent folk."

Fionnuala let her have her say. Mrs. Feeney was just another in a long line of pensioners, one slipper in the grave, who would tramp through the door of the Sav-U-Mor, roaring abuse at those who still had a life left worth living.

"The wanes the day live for nothing but malicious crimes, and them hooligans of yers is worse than the rest. Piggin desperate, so it is! Ye've no fresh cabbage here?"

"Not the day, naw," Fionnuala hissed, turning her attention to a case of tinned custard and hacking at the industrial-strength tape that bound it.

"Ye musta been barely outta diapers yerself when ye started popping out the wanes, just to let em roam wild in the streets waving broken bottles and iron bars."

"Have ye a reason for being here, missus?" Fionnuala finally asked. "Oller than to roar abuse at me, I mean."

"Now that ye mention it," Mrs. Feeney seethed, "I have, aye! Am raging at that Ursula of yers! Bleedin useless, so she is, and there I was singing her praises to yer wane the oller day. Outta me piggin head, I musta been. She cancelled me appointment for yesterday, then said she was to see me at half three the day to take me down the town for me messages. Me cupboards is piggin bare! I've been waiting for Ursula forty-five minutes, me stomach thinking me throat's been cut! So now I've had to tramp all the way to this manky tip of yers, the feet taking the legs off of me, to waste me pension on yer overpriced shite! Am gonny be ringing up OsteoCare and asking for anoller provider! Ye're bloody useless the lot of youse!"

Fionnuala attempted to hide her glee at Mrs. Feeney's condemnation of Saint Ursula. Nobody, apparently, was beyond reproach in the pensioner's cataracts.

"Nowan asked ye to step foot in here," Fionnuala managed. *Hack! Hack! Hack!*

"And they've them same fish fingers ye've got here for half the price at the Top-Yer-Trolly down the town," Mrs. Feeney accused.

Fionnuala banged tin after tin of beans on the shelf.

"Aye, and ye're quite welcome to traipse down the town to fetch them there yerself."

Bang! Bang! Bang!

"Ach, ye're off yer bleeding head, you, the cost of a taxi cab the day! And I wouldn't step a foot in them mini-buses if me life depended on it! Crawling with stokes and alkies, so they are! The smell of sick from them cushions would fairly turn yer stomach! C'mere till I tell ye, I've been putting a wee bit of me pension aside every month, saving up to buy meself a wee motor. Then I can do me messages when I please, go where the spirit takes me. I'll have no need for that Ursula wan anymore, and thank merciful Jesus for that."

Fionnuala's eyes flashed with sudden fear at the thought of Mrs. Feeney behind the wheel of 3,000 pounds of processed steel.

The pensioner struggled over to the cash register and plucked a packet of steak and onion crisps out of their box. A promotional square in the right bottom corner screamed *24 Pence!*

"Ach, sure, even the crisps is wild dear here," she said. "Why this manky tip is called the Sav-U-Mor I'll never know! I'll be on to Truth in Advertising about youse!"

"We've a special on the prawn cocktail crisps the day," Fionnuala said, moving behind the register. "Twelve pee, only."

"Months after their sell-by date, no doubt. Themmuns is the only thing here I can afford, but," Mrs. Feeney said. "I'll take em."

"That'll be twelve pee then," Fionnuala growled.

Her fingers tapped on the sticky conveyor belt as Mrs. Murphy fiddled with her change purse, counted out the copper and lined the one pence pieces before her. Fionnuala scooped them up and tossed them in the register drawer.

"And mind," Mrs. Feeney said, "you keep a lead on them hooligan wanes of yers. Any more boller, and me eldest Sean's to be paying em a visit. There'll be hell to pay."

"Aye, you do that," Fionnuala snarled as the bell tinkled and Mrs. Feeney exited the shop with her twelve pence packet of prawn cocktail crisps.

Hateful cunt.

Fionnuala snapped an unfiltered Rothman from her pack and thrust it between her teeth. She snapped off the radio and sat stewing in her misery in a silence surrounded by Wine Gums and Jelly Babies. The phone interrupted her self-pity. Fionnuala snatched the receiver up.

"Aye?"

"Fionnuala?" Paddy hollered over the whirr of some machinery on the other end. "Am after hearing from Roisin. Me moller's been taken to hospital. That jumped-up cow Ursula's after giving her a heart attack."

The alarm on Fionnuala's face swiftly dissolved into delight.

"Poor aul Eda," she cooed into the receiver for her husband's benefit. "That Ursula'll stoop to the lowest lows to get her claws into 5 Murphy."

"Ye're dead right there. Am on me way to Altnagelvin now."

"Aye, am are and all," Fionnuala resolved. "I'll ring Magella and have her take over me shift here. And the wanes?"

"Am rounding up as many of em as I can find and getting them up to the hospital," Paddy said. "We need all the help we can get."

Fionnuala slipped into her jacket as she punched her co-worker's number into her cell, the excitement mounting, already envisioning the move into the house around the corner and her first evening lounging on the settee in the front room with its central heating and flat-screen telly.

£ £ £ £

With Roisin blathering down her mobile to Hawaii and Eda groaning in the back seat, Ursula steered with weak hands and bleary eyes into the Accidents and Emergency parking lot of Altnagelvin Hospital.

Ten floors of modernist architecture loomed before them. Once Altnagelvin had overflowed with bell-bottomed lads bloody from rubber bullets, pensioners and primary school children wheezing from too much tear gas, the casualties of tar-and-featherings, kneecappings, skulls cracked from the force of a well-aimed rock. Now, during the Peace Process of the new, Free Derry, they were greeted with the victims of joyriding pileups, drug-related slashings and pub-brawl bottlings. And it was into this milieu that the overworked doctors of Altnagelvin were about to receive their latest patient: Eda Flood and her angina attack.

Gasping from the wheelchair the paramedics had lumbered her into, the family matriarch was ushered by a flank of orderlies through swinging doors beyond which Ursula and Roisin were forbidden to venture. For an electrocardiogram, they were told. Ursula paced up and down a grimy corridor that stank of antiseptic, clenching and unclenching her handbag. Roisin sat on an uncomfortable orange chair, alternatively blowing her sniffles into a tissue, bemoaning the state of the waiting room drapes and glaring with ill-concealed hatred in Ursula's direction.

The tiny telly in the corner was out of order. There was nothing for Ursula to do but dodge Roisin's eyes and worry. They jerked as sounds of children in agony echoed through the corridor, and Ursula turned in alarm, wondering if the IRA had exploded a bomb on a school bus, the young victims now being hustled by stretcher into the operating theater. But, no. Ursula gazed in disbelief as the doors flew open, and Paddy, Dymphna, Padraig and Seamus Flood thronged the corridor.

"Granny! Granny?! Where's me granny?"

Padraig and Seamus were tear-stained. Roisin jumped from her chair in sudden relief and scampered to the safety of their numbers, as if Ursula had held her enslaved the past half hour.

"Where's me moller?" Paddy boomed boozily with an unsteady lunge at Ursula. "Am raging! What the feck do ye think ye were playing at, ye bitch, ye!"

It was not the face of a brother at all.

"Ye've done it now, Ursula," Dymphna sneered with shameless glee and a flick of her curls.

"Is me granny dying?" Seamus sobbed at her sister's knee as Padraig glowered over at his aunt, fists balled.

"She's well on her way, aye, thanks to yer auntie," Dymphna said.

Seven steps behind the wanes, Fionnuala galloped calmly into the corridor and reclined against the coffee machine, not wanting to miss a word.

"Clawing at the car windows like a common animal, so she was," Roisin sobbed into a tissue to anybody who would listen. She had many takers, hands caressing her shoulders, wanes sniveling at her Nikes. "I never seen the likes of it in all me life."

"I'll murder ye with me own bare hands, Ursula," Padraig seethed, "if me granny doesn't pull through this."

With the troops summoned and surrounding her, fully armed with rage and resentment, Ursula was helpless to make them see sense. It was a simple angina attack, one of the many Eda had weathered over the years. Or so Ursula had thought.

"Sure, it's not me fault," she finally implored, one helpless hand to her bosom. "It could've happened anywhere. She could've keeled over alone at home and been laying there on the carpeting for days and none of us woulda been the wiser!"

Their faces hardened.

Fionnuala stood by the coffee machine, not a trace of anguish on her face—the old dottery cunt wasn't *her* mother, after all—but with pride aplenty prominent on her hardened features. She smirked with the knowledge she had raised her children right and they were responding in kind.

"Physical exertion and … extreme cold … *that* wan …" Roisin was muttering into her sopping tissue, glaring over at Ursula with regularity. "… air conditioner blaring … only seventy flippin degrees Celsius out … me mammy … hooked up to all manner of machines …"

A very attractive young orderly happened into the corridor, and Paddy hurled towards her, wrenching her arm and flipping her towards him.

"How's me moller?" he roared into her face, fingers piercing her arm. "*Where's* me moller?! Mrs. Flood?"

Flinching from the stench of drink erupting from the madman's throat, Lily McCracken glanced around at the gang of hooligans that suddenly surrounded her from all sides. She had seen the likes of these tramp into the A & E through the years: shifty best mates of bottling victims roaring drunken abuse at the receptionists, cousins of the victims of bloody slashings from drug deals gone bad, hardened slappers of girlfriends of overdoses roaring out of them through the corridors and sucking down fags in the no smoking sections, street thugs menacing the snack bar hoping for a chance to terrorize their kneecapping victims as they lie in their hospital beds.

Lily's eyes suddenly widened. This was the father of her first lesbian love, Moira Flood. Paddy's eyes lurched as well.

"Wait a wee moment! You're the filthy perv we caught sneaking outta wer Moira's bedroom that New Year's morning!"

The Floods recoiled from her as a unit. After that hungover morning, none of them had been able to look Moira in the eye again, with the exception of Seamus, who was too young to understand the sins of the flesh.

Glancing up to be sure the security cameras were blinking, poor Lily shook Paddy's hand free and scurried through the swinging doors.

Paddy sputtered after her, "Ye hardened bean flicker bruiser!"

"Am never checking meself in here!" Roisin said, wrapping her arms around her abundance of silicone. "Ye never know what palaver the staff'll be up to with me unconscious form!"

Ursula could contain her anger no longer.

"Of all the foolish carry-on! Dry yer eyes, the lot of youse!" she finally spat out. "This is wile daft, dragging the poor wanes all the way up to the hospital for a simple angina attack, making em heart-scared, terrorizing the poor hospital staff. Am pure red, so am are."

"Ye're a fine wan to talk, you!" Paddy said.

"And am sick, sore and tired of this constant persecution!" Ursula announced.

"Ye see you, Ursula," Dymphna snarled as Seamus sobbed at her side. "Ye deserve every ounce of persecution ye get, ye hateful aul slapper!"

Ursula whipped around to Paddy and Fionnuala. "She's a mouth on her, that wan! Kyanny keep a civil tongue in her head!"

Although Ursula was shaking, somewhere inside her she felt as hard as stone as she came out with it:

"If the two of youse only knew what yer precious daughter's been up to! Up the scoot, she is! She came begging to me for money for a termination, so she did!"

"Ye promised, Ursula!" Dymphna gasped sadly.

"Ye hateful—!" Fionnuala leaped from the coffee machine towards Ursula, and Roisin's eyes grew ablaze at the glorious drama of it all.

The doctor rounded the corner. His brow furrowed as he was suddenly besieged by a gang of school uniforms clutching at his legs. Shrieks demanding to know the condition of Eda Flood echoed down the corridor. The doctor pleaded for some semblance of civility.

"Well, as I'm sure you're *all* aware, if you've been looking after ..." He glanced down at his clipboard. "... Mrs. Flood for some time—"

"Aye, aye, we have," Roisin said. Ursula longed to smack her bobbing head.

"An angina attack is *not* a heart attack, and these episodes seldom cause permanent damage to the heart muscle."

"Aye, aye!" Roisin said breathlessly, lapping up the pearls of wisdom.

"Of course, because of her condition, Mrs. Flood is certainly more susceptible than the population at large to heart attacks. There is a danger that if the pattern of angina changes, if the episodes, for example, have become more frequent, have lasted longer, or have occurred without exercise, the risk of a heart attack in subsequent days or weeks is much higher. I gather Mrs. Flood was not exercising when the angina attack took place?"

"That evil cow there had her locked up in the car with the air conditioner blasting on her poor aul bones," Roisin said, pointing an accusing finger at Ursula.

The doctor shot Roisin an odd look, then turned back to Ursula.

"As I was saying, Mrs.?"

"Barnett," Ursula said, relieved she wasn't tainted with the Flood surname.

"Just to ensure her condition isn't worsening, we'd like to run a few more tests on her and keep her in the hospital for the time being, for observation," the doctor said.

"Can I have a wee peek at her?" Ursula asked hopefully.

"She's being transferred to a hospital room this very moment. Once she has settled in, you'll *all* be able to visit."

And off he escaped down the corridor.

"Ye see youse doctors?!" Paddy roared at the still-swinging doors. *"Fecking Paki bastards the lot of youse!* Feck this! Let's go to the gift shop."

Dymphna attempted to stay in the waiting room, but Fionnuala grabbed her arm and dragged her down the corridor with them. Roisin tagged along after, stifling her mirth. Ursula stood and watched them go.

"Ye've made me a granny at forty years of age!" Fionnuala lied, clattering Dymphna round the head.

"I've to pour the drink down me throat every night," Paddy snarled, "to get some peace and quiet in me skull. Youse wanes is making wer lives a misery. Pregnant outta wedlock at eighteen years of age. Ye're no better than yer auntie Ursula."

"Daddy!" Dymphna pleaded.

"It sickens the heart outta me!" Fionnuala put in. "Ye're a bloody disgrace to the family! And me great-uncle a bishop and all! How are we to hold wer heads up in St. Moluag's on Sunday with a sinner for a daughter?"

They all trooped into the gift shop, and Padraig and Seamus made for the bin of toys.

"And who's the faller meant to be, that's what I wanny know," Fionnuala demanded as her eyes inspected the gladiolas.

"I kyanny tell youse!" Dymphna implored.

"Ye mean ye don't wanny, or ye've not a flimmin clue who the faller is?"

"Daddy!" Dymphna protested.

"It's that Liam!" Fionnuala shot, browsing through the get well cards. "Shifty eyes, so he had. From the moment he stepped foot through wer door, I—"

"Naw, it's not Liam," Dymphna cried.

"Then who in the name of merciful Mary—" Fionnuala said, her memory racing through the many fellas Dymphna had trawled through the front door of the family home.

The get well cards were captivating, Fionnuala thought, with views of lilies of the valley and bedpans and clowns and when she saw the price of them she fled.

"A bloody *paratrooper?!*" Paddy finally snarled.

"Daddy! *Naw!*" Dymphna said, affronted and heart-scared. Rory Riddell wasn't a Brit solider, swaggering through their front garden at whim, proudly brandishing an M-16. But, as a Proddy, he might as well be as far as her parents were concerned.

Fionnuala dropped a bunch of grapes.

"Not ... yer *broller?*" she gasped in sudden horror. "Ye see if that Eoin has so much as laid a fecking finger on ye, I'll—"

"Mammy!" Dymphna wailed, mortified.

Who the flimmin feck could it be, Fionnuala wondered. She fought against a sudden wondering glance over at her husband hovering by the register. *Paddy would never have ... would he ...?*

"How much are ye asking for them flowers?" Paddy asked.

"Nine quid, just," sighed the beleaguered shop assistant.

"Highway robbery!"

Paddy held his hand out to Dymphna. She dutifully reached into her handbag for a tenner.

"Leave the wee critter be," Roisin said softly with a nod at her niece. "I've me credit card, sure. Let's shop around for a few more things for me mammy. Them might be the last gifts she ever lays eyes on."

If they were on her credit card, *brilliant!,* the Floods thought as one. They started looting the shelves, and in the melee Dymphna slipped out of the gift shop and down the corridor. She would rather finish her shift at the ChipKebab than hear further abuse hurled her way.

Over in the waiting room, the same wee orderly fearfully approached Ursula.

"Are ye with Mrs. Flood?" Lily asked.

Ursula's head shot up from her handkerchief.

"Aye."

"The doctor says ye can see her now. Down that corridor, room 25."

Ursula crept down the corridor and into the hospital room, then sidled up to the bed, a tentative touch on the rail. Eda's fluffy head propped atop the pillow greeted her with thin-lipped silence.

"Ye know it's not me fault ye had the attack, don't you?" Ursula asked hopefully and not a little defensively. Her fingers anxiously kneaded the railing.

No response.

"I did nothing but put ye in the car to get ye out of the house for a wee while," Ursula said. "Ye believe me, don't ye?"

Still no response. Tears welled in Ursula's eyes. "Well ..."

She slipped out the forms from her handbag and presented them to her mother. No time like the present, with the acrimony of the Floods simmering in every direction, to claim the money that was so rightfully hers.

"Mammy, am after learning that Paddy and Fionnuala's been nicking money that's rightfully mines," Ursula said, her voice shuddering. "I don't really need yer approval for what I'm to do, but I'm letting you know anyroad. They claim they've been taking care of ye all this time. Now, Mammy, ye know it's me that's always there for ye. Don't ye?"

Ursula searched her mother's milky eyes for any flicker of acquiescence.

"Mammy?" she implored.

A nod of the head, a simple up and down motion of the neck was all she was searching for. It was the story of her life; Ursula was a wee girl again, doing her best to please Mammy and Daddy but always getting it wrong somehow, the best intentions leading her down a miserable path to heartache, an unending disgrace to the Flood family name. She blinked away tears of frustration. Ursula sighed.

"Just you sign here, Mammy," she instructed, her voice hard.

She wrapped her mother's fingers around the pen and forced them to move around the paper. The moment the signature was complete, Ursula jumped as the door burst wide and the Floods poured into the hospital room, laden with tins of Quality Street chocolates and bunches of bruised grapes and bouquets of flowers and handfuls of those horrid metallic balloons shaped like hearts that Ursula hated so bouncing against the walls. How and if they had paid for them Ursula hadn't a clue. She slipped the form into her handbag.

"Granny! Granny!"

"Moller!"

They surrounded the bed, nudging Ursula from her mother's side. Fighting her way through the balloons, Ursula slipped out of the hospital room. She scuttled on trembling legs down the dingy corridor, dodging electrical wires, a firm grip on her handbag, a victorious if slightly guilty smile on her lips.

£ £ £ £

Bridie's eyes swam with chemical love, thanks to Eoin, as she swept up the fag ends and greasy kebab baguette wrappers from the front of the ChipKebab. She glanced across the city square, past where the public loos had once stood, toward some commotion under Magazine Gate. A new shipment of contraband pinched from the back of a passing lorry must be going cheap. Always up for a bargain, she leaned on the brush and peered beyond the ramparts. Siofra Flood stood under the arch next to the stalls, surrounded by a pack of raver teens who were passing fivers and tenners into her hands in exchange for Eoin's gear. Shocked that a pack of hooligans hadn't already knocked the child to the pavement and snatched the stash from her, Bridie dropped the brush and raced across the square.

"Disco sweeties! Fifty pee each, just!" Siofra sang out, displaying the tablets in her sticky hot child-palm as young mothers wheeled their prams of squealing wanes past.

"Go on and give us ten there, hi," said a dreadlocked youth.

"Right ye are," Siofra said. She looked up from her careful counting of the now gooey treats and eyed him warily. "I wanny see the money first."

"Away from that wee critter, you!" Bridie bellowed.

The youth slunk off down the cobblestones as Bridie barreled towards Siofra.

"What's up with ye, hi?" Bridie demanded to know. "Where the feck's yer broller?"

"The Filth hauled him off in a car, and he gave me these sweeties."

"To sell on the street like a silly wee gack?" Bridie asked.

"Trouble's on its way, youse'uns," interrupted the fag salesman (who had bought twenty), nodding up the alleyway.

They turned, and Bridie stiffened at the sight of the copper plodding towards them. She cursed herself for not having snatched a few freebies from Siofra's palm before he arrived, and she scuttled a few feet away from the tiny drug dealer.

"Well, well, well," said Police Constable McLaughlin, towering over Siofra. "And just what have we here?"

"Am selling disco sweeties," Siofra said. "Ye want some? Fifty pee, just. Wile tasty, so they are."

The cop inspected the tablets in Siofra's hand and his bemusement turned to alarm. He set his lips and faced Bridie. Gone was the dance in his eyes.

"Does she belong to you?" the cop asked.

"I don't know her from feck!" Bridie announced, sidling backwards through the gate. "And I wasn't gonny buy from her!"

The copper turned back to Siofra, his face hard.

"Who gave you these?"

She recalled the night her mammy had sat her and Seamus down on the settee and instructed them to never, ever tell the Filth the truth.

"Nowan. I found them in a bin over there," she said, gesturing vaguely in the direction the Guildhall where there was no bin.

"I'm afraid I have to take these from you, young lass," he said, reaching for her hand.

"Naw!" Siofra screamed, clamping her fingers around the drugs. "Them-muns is mines!"

He pried her fingers open and confiscated them.

"Have you any more?"

"Naw!" But Siofra had not yet learned how to lie with her eyes, and they flickered down to her Power Puff Girls handbag.

The constable secured the handbag and snapped open the little golden lock as Siofra kicked him in the shins and pummeled him with her little fists, her squeals echoing down the city walls. PC McLaughlin was alarmed at what he saw inside the handbag: an S Club 7 tape nestled between Pikachu and Wurmple, and a polythene bag bulging with Class A stimulants. He hadn't known they still made cassette singles. *This wee girl must come from a deprived family,* he thought.

"What's yer name? Where do you live?" he asked.

"Siofra Flood's that wan's name, from the Bogside," Bridie said helpfully, always eager to assist the RUC if it got her off the hook.

Siofra scowled over at her, then glared up at the copper, defiantly silent.

"Where's yer moller? If you don't tell me, she will," he said, nodding over to Bridie.

"She's working cleaning the jacks of all the pubs in town," Siofra finally conceded.

His heart went out to her. *A very deprived family indeed.*

"These are very dangerous tablets, lass. Have you taken any?"

"I was dying to. I couldn't, but, as I had to sell em all."

His eyes narrowed.

"Who told you you had to sell them? Is someone forcing you?" He looked over at the market sellers, who were all folding up their tables and stealing away.

"Naw, nobody tole me to sell em," she said, her lower lip trembling. "I gotta sell em, but."

"If nobody's forcing you, why do you need to sell them?"

"Because me communion gown's a pile of manky shite!" Siofra sniveled up at him. "I had to sell the disco sweeties to buy a new wan meself, as me mammy says we've too many bills for her to afford me wan of me own! Both me sisters wore that boggin frock already, and wan of them's a bean flicker and the oller's a filthy boggin trollop!"

PC McLaughlin debated his options. They could never prosecute a child so young for drug dealing, and her apparent motive seemed to prove nobody was coercing her to sell them on the street. Perhaps she really had found them after all.

"And if ye don't leave me be, am telling me mammy ye interfered with me private parts!" Siofra sobbed, quoting verbatim what Fionnuala had told her to say in such an eventuality.

His eyes widened.

"I'll take her home," Bridie quickly intervened. "Her sister's a mate of … a mate of mine."

PC McLaughlin wanted to race home and disinfect his hands.

"I-I'm letting you go with a caution," he decided. "You understand what that means?"

"Aye," Siofra said, "if ye catch me again, ye'll send me down to Magilligan Prison, which is grand by me, as me broller's already there for GBH and he can look after me, so."

The little stoke glared boldly up at him. Her revelation didn't surprise PC McLaughlin. They didn't do themselves any favors, these families infected with the criminal element.

"C'mere you with me now," Bridie said, taking Siofra's hand and hoping she could lick the residue of Ecstasy off the wee palms once they were safely back in the ChipKebab.

PC McLaughlin watched them storm off, heard the young one scream, "I hate that bloody frock, hate it, hate it, hate it!," and shook his head with sorrow.

£ £ £ £

Ursula peered in the mirror of the ensuite bathroom, giving her face a critical once over. The carefree child of her youth, loving and eager to please, called out to her reflected self: "Have you forgotten me?" Those times were not decades but parallel universes away.

She had sealed the form for the caretaker's allowance in an envelope and dropped it in a post box the moment she had left Altnagelvin. She had no doubt the National Health Service would switch the benefit from the Floods to herself, especially with Francine urging her case through the system. An extra £38.50 would be coming her way weekly, but Ursula suspected she had won the battle and lost the war.

She ran lipstick over her mouth, and thought it made her look wild hard. When her image became too painful to peruse any longer, she turned her attention to the toilet bowl.

That damn loo had been flushing and reflushing itself lately, and it was driving her off her head. A few months ago, Ursula would have blissfully called a plumber, but now they couldn't afford the extravagance, and she'd have to tackle the refill valve and flushing rod herself. Ursula wrenched open the top and peered inside the tank. A chill ran down her spine. Against the chain nestled a flask. It may as well have been a human head. She was about to pluck it out of the water and examine it when the phone on the nightstand rang. Fearing it might be bad news about Eda's condition, she hastened to answer, leaving the flask unstirred.

"Aye?" she asked feverishly into the receiver.

"And ye call yerself an OsteoCare provider?" Mrs. Feeney brayed. "That's a right laugh! Ye almost had me eating me own two feet for sustenance. Covered with blisters, so they are now, from all the traipsing up and down the town I had to do to fill me larder!"

They were coming at her from all angles.

"Please don't berate me, Mrs. Feeney," Ursula pleaded in a small voice. "Am sorry I forgot to ring ye; I had to take me moller to Altnagelvin."

"Likely story, that," Mrs. Feeney sniffed.

"I've tried me best to accommodate ye over the years."

"And them has been years of pure torture. I've no need for yer services anymore, ye lazy effin toerag, ye."

Ursula slammed down the receiver. Years, she had carted that woman around town, and this was the thanks she got? The way Ursula had been thinking of the human race lately, Mrs. Feeney's betrayal came as no surprise.

She trailed, shoulders slumped, back to the bathroom to inspect her discovery. She pulled the flask out of the water, unscrewed the top and took a tentative sniff. It smelled like nothing, which could only mean one thing: vodka! She hoped for Jed's sake it was at least a name brand.

He was obviously desperate. Ursula was pained that her husband hadn't come to her for help, resented that he had whittled away all their lotto winnings and was keeping it from her. Hadn't they married for better or for worse? Did he no longer trust her? Did living with her bring him to such measures?

She passed through the Queen Anne foyer in a tizzy, the symbol of Jed's desperation in her hand, and when she entered the lounge she immediately took in the heavy rings of sleeplessness and the faint whiff of alcohol from him. How had she not noticed them before?

"Jed!" she shouted, displaying the flask. "What for the love of God is this? Is it meant to tell me am driving ye to drink?"

"And I never had the courtesy to thank you?" Jed finished off, a flicker of mortified anger on his face. It was as if she had just stripped him down to his Fruit of the Looms there before the bulging eyes of the gargoyles. "What were you doing poking around in the attic anyway?"

Ursula set her lips.

"I found this in the tank of the ensuite loo," she clarified. "Ye've anoller in the attic, do ye?"

"If you must know."

"Do ye mind telling me exactly how many flasks of drink ye have scattered around wer house?"

He did mind.

"What do you want me to do?" Jed pleaded. "You dragged me off to this godforsaken hellhole where I can barely understand what anybody says, where the sun shines three days a year, where the city center is crawling with thugs wielding broken bottles after dark so I have to do all my drinking during the day, where the dollar's so weak against the pound my retirement checks disappear before they're even cashed. And after this crap with the lotto, there are the car payments, the mortgage … yeah, the *second* mortgage, to pay off, all those stupid taxes we have to pay and the stupid standard of living these people put up with. I'm an American, goddamn it, and I don't wanna throw away my money on basic human rights that are priced as luxuries in this lunatic country. The price of the heat in the winter, the AC in the summer, a tank full of gas and a pack of smokes is absurd!"

Ursula hung her head in shame. She had seen the bills.

"And you forced me to live here to be with your family, but, let's face it, they all hate you now. If they ever even liked you in the first place. And, Ursula, I can understand it. Since we won the lotto, I've barely been able to look at you myself without wanting to strangle your stupid neck. Is it any wonder I need to guzzle down the alcohol as quickly as I can?"

She couldn't look at him. She took a deep, shuddering breath and plunged ahead in a tiny voice.

"I've been trying me best to live me life as selflessly as I can, helping the aul wans at OsteoCare, singing in the choir, going to mass every Sunday, confession every Wednesday—"

(Jed had phased her out by this stage)

"—and all I've been expecting from you is a bit of human kindness. Me moller's breathing her last in hospital, Paddy and themmuns is blaming me, everywan in town's clambering to snatch the money out of me handbag, money, by the way, I already know is long gone, as I went to see yer man Bewley at the bank the oller day, and that wan was avoiding me as clearly as if the flesh was hanging from me bones from the leprosy! If ye were having money problems, don't ye know ye could've come to me? Haven't we helped wan anoller out throughout the years of wer marriage? All them problems with Gretchen and Egbert, and all during yer eye surgery, and then that uncle of yers who wanted a lend of the money to start his own kielbasa business and ye had to turn him down, wasn't I there for all of it for ye?"

"Yeah, screaming in my face," Jed said.

That's not how Ursula remembered it.

"Ye could show me a wee bit of support," she said quietly, her face taut.

"What do you want me to do?" he pleaded again, reaching for the flask and guzzling down.

Ursula set her lips again.

"I want ye to talk some sense into me broller Paddy," she said. "Youse play darts every Wednesday, aye? I want ye to tell him the next time ye see him to stop this crucifixion."

Jed stared. There was no bad blood between Jed and Paddy, his darts partner and drinking buddy, and why should there be? His brother-in-law made life in Derry tolerable for Jed, had shared his finger grip wax and pints for the better part of the decade Jed had been prisoner in Northern Ireland. Ursula should thank her lucky stars for her younger brother because, without him, Jed would have been on a flight to Wisconsin years ago.

That Ursula's relationship with her younger brother had been rather less than stellar Jed was well aware. But that hadn't affected the camaraderie foraged between two men stranded in the matriarchal world that was Irish society, where women were brash and opinionated, hardened sons shed tears for fear of causing their mothers grief, and husbands raced home after last orders to avoid all hell breaking loose.

"Look, Ursula, Paddy's the only friend I have here, and I'll be damned if I'm going to get into an argument with him just because you lack basic human social skills and nobody can stand you."

Ursula couldn't have felt more alone among the living if she were buried alive in a coffin. The Floods, Roisin, her mother—*Mrs. Feeney even!*—and now her husband: all were discarding her like a piece of toilet tissue they had just discovered on the heel of their shoe.

A lesser woman would have marched up the stairs and slit her wrists in the bathtub. Ursula, though, glared at Jed with a steely resolve even as the tears of despair and isolation welled in her eyes.

"Why can't ye be on me side?" she asked. The way she said it, he never was.

She stood up and silently made her way out of the lounge.

£ £ £ £

Mr. O'Toole flounced up to David with a worried brow and a cagey glance around the merchandise.

"Stop shelving them body sprays and get yerself down to aisle seven. I want ye to clear out all them pregnancy tests ASAP," he instructed surreptitiously. "Am after getting word from the manufacturer that the whole piggin shipment's gone off."

David stared up at him.

"Gone off? How do ye mean?"

"How would I know, ye silly boy!" Mr. O'Toole snapped. "Am not a pharmaceutical expert, thank feck! Past their sell-buy date or some such."

"Ye mean—"

"Aye, they tell weemin they're up the scoot when they're not, and the oller way around." Mr. O'Toole glanced nervously again up and down the aisle. "I can only hope we don't have the solicitors banging down wer door clutching handfuls of flimmin compensation lawsuits."

"I think the customers would be relieved as feck! Me Vera's after taking wan of them tests the oller week, and we were heading to Liverpool next Friday for the termination."

Mr. O'Toole squirmed, aghast.

"Less of the personal life, if ye please!" he tutted. "Clear that rubbish off them shelves, just!"

Mr. O'Toole minced off through the video games, feeling slightly soiled, equal parts repulsed and aroused at the thought of the sex lives of the hired help.

As general manager of the local branch of Top-Yer-Trolly, Henry O'Toole lorded over a revolving door of unskilled laborers. His flush management salary and university education were evident in the specially tailored suits from Next which he bought at full high street prices. He was well aware from the weekly inventory what the problems and concerns of those under his wardship were, as huge crateloads of evidence were unloaded into the stockroom every week. He knew of their weakness for cheap lager and discount crisps, foot creams and rolling papers, mobile phone top-up cards and yeast infection suppositories, of the fizzy minerals and curry chips that rotted their stomachs and their teeth, their meagre National Health dental schemes unable to keep up with the abuse.

As manager of the underprivileged masses, he was privy to every detail of their dreary working lives: their misguided arrogance, their lack of common manners or civility, their grubby fingernails and methadone, strong thighs and weak morals. The slutty shop floor girls and lumpen stock boys from pebble-dashed council houses, the checkout girls in their cheap scent and out of cheaper knickers. He thought long and hard in bed at night about those in his employ and the beastly, swaggering fellas they always paired off with, unhygienic and undereducated, breeding viciously and uncontrollably after Sunday mass between bouts of screeching rows and lager-fuelled beatings while the drawing for the National Lottery played on the telly in the background (or so his imagination went). Were he to succumb to the revolting allure of their class, it would be like, the good Lord forgive him, bedding down with a common beast. He adjusted himself as he walked down the corridor. *What man on earth could resist?* He was thinking of both this and the requisition forms he would have to complete when who did he spy, standing in the corridor before his office, her fingers coaxing the door handle, but the queen of the working class slappers herself, Dymphna Flood.

Mr. O'Toole set his jaw.

"Ye're after coming back from Altnagelvin?" he asked. "How's yer granny?"

"At death's door."

"Ye're not getting anoller advance," he warned, "dead granny or no."

"Naw. It's a question about me duties am here for."

O'Toole feigned shock.

"Duties? And here I was thinking ye had none except for giving the customers all sorts of grief and unease!"

Was it his filthy fancy, or had she been welcoming him with her eyes over the meat and cheese counter ever since he had given her that £50 advance? The shameless tart now seemed to be wearing nothing but a smirk and her Top-Yer-Trolly smock. How he wanted her poised over his bony, naked back, perhaps gripping a whip!

"Have ye nothing on under that smock of yers?" he said. "This is a family establishment, ye know. We've standards of dress, if ye wanny look em up in the staff manual. Not that I suppose ye've ever taken a glance at it, reading not being yer thing and all."

"Where might we have a wee word?"

"Where de ye think?" he asked, giving a testy nod at the door to his office. "That's what an office is for, like."

Dimwittedness was another trait quite common in the lower classes, he remembered. They paired off against each other in the corridor, the tension as thick as her brain.

"Naw," Dymphna said, for she knew the entire store was hooked up with video cameras that spied on their every move. The presumption of management that all shop floor chattel were a bunch of thieving stokes was quite insulting to Dymphna, but she also knew that David had cleverly rigged the cameras in the back stockroom to run on an old looped tape so that he could rifle through the inventory when he had spent all his wages on drink. "I've to show ye something in the back stockroom."

Mr. O'Toole's face blossomed with intrigue.

"And what might ye have to show me in the back stockroom?" he asked.

"Ye mind when ye gave me that advance the oller day? I could barely credit it. I wanny show ye how thankful am are."

Mr. O'Toole felt a twitching.

"And how thankful are ye?" he asked.

"Lemme show ye how," she replied, reaching for his hand and caressing his knobby knuckles. She guided him down the corridor and tugged open the door to the store room.

"This looks a nice wee sturdy surface," Dymphna said, patting a crate. "It'll hold. C'mere you beside me now."

There was a clank as his belt buckle hit the floor.

"Ye filthy, common cow!" he extolled with a pant. "I've wanted ye ever since ye filled out yer application with an 'aye' next to the *Sex* category!"

And he had her there in the back stockroom, right on the shipment of new pregnancy tests, filling her with revulsion, but also finally—*thank feck!*—soaking her Orange bastard fetus in hearty Green spermatozoa.

6

Roisin the savior paraded into the front room with three fish suppers, one sausage supper, one single fish, one single chips, a single sausage, a chicken and chips, and three curry and chips.

"Thank Christ wer Lord!" Fionnuala moaned, almost knocking Seamus to the carpeting to get her hands on the food.

"The queue at the chippy was wound clear up to Creggan!" Roisin said as Fionnuala grabbed at the greasy parcels. "Like the flippin Soviet Union, so it was!"

"Never you mind that, lemme at them chips, just!" Paddy panted.

And then it was the like the National Guard passing out rations to a mob of haggard evacuees as the Floods clambered and elbowed each other, snatching the bundles of rations from Roisin and gashing at the paper to get at the provisions within. If Roisin was startled at their feral behavior, she didn't let on. She heaved herself atop an ottoman in a sea of discarded wrappings and chomped into a battered sausage.

Eoin, looking unusually flush and skittish, entered the front room. "Any bars, hi? Fish and chips? Fecking brilliant! I could murder a portion!"

"Sit you down and get stuck in, son," Paddy said.

Roisin tossed him a fish supper, and the sitting room pulsed with their slurping and smacking, the air pungent with vinegar and batter.

"Magic! Am ravenous!" Dymphna said, home from her romp in the stockroom of the Top-Yer-Trolly and settling herself down on the hearth, curls tousled, eyes bright and smock askew.

"Skulking off from yer granny's deathbed!" Fionnuala greeted her daughter, teeth tearing at a chicken breast. "Ye've not an ounce of shame, have ye?"

"I had to get back to work!" Dymphna protested.

"Me granny died?" Eoin asked, startled. *Was I there to see it? What's the feck's them wingers doing to me brain?* "Brilliant, hi! When can we move werselves in and watch that flat screen telly?"

"She's in the hospital, just," Roisin clarified, passing Dymphna a sausage supper. "Yer auntie Ursula's after torturing the heart clear outta her ribcage."

Dymphna reached up expectantly for her sausage supper, but Fionnuala smacked Roisin's hand away.

"She's not to be getting any," she said. "There's a Pot Noodles in the larder for that shameless tart. Chicken Vindaloo flavored."

Dymphna tensed. Her mother knew she couldn't abide curry. She plodded her way into the scullery. Fionnuala chomped down on her daughter's battered sausage and turned brightly to her beloved son.

"I was wondering if ye can chip in to get me an appointment at Xpressions to get me nails done. Me hands and feet both, like."

Eoin squirmed uncomfortably on the settee as he scoffed down.

"There's a wee problem with me finances at the moment, like."

Siofra had finally whiffed the vinegar and chips and batter and scurried down from her lair. She shirked at the sight of Eoin, recoiling as if she had been scalded, and scuttered back into the front hall. Eoin slipped out of his chair into the hallway, hoping the family was too busy scoffing down to notice. But Fionnuala's nosy-parker eyes never missed a trick. She sidled towards the doorjamb, head cocked, ears perked, jowls churning. Siofra made for the stairs, but Eoin grabbed her by the ponytail.

"Where's me gear, you?" he hissed.

"Yer gear?" Siofra trembled up at him. "I went over to the market after the peelers hauled ye off and sold it."

"Ye ... *sold* it?"

She was suddenly defiant.

"I did indeed, aye," she said proudly. "Got fifty pee for each disco sweetie! It was effin lethal! Thirty-two pounds, I got! Now where's me fish and chips?"

She tugged away from him and scuttled into the safety of the sitting room as Eoin stared after her, horrified.

"Thirty two ...!" He did some quick math and raced into the sitting room, his panic rising. "Where's the rest? There was over two hundred wingers left in that bag!"

"Aye. The copper took the rest."

"Copper?" Eoin blanched. "Me suppliers'll be looking for 300 quid off of me for the sale of that gear!"

"That thirty-two pounds is for me communion gown," Siofra said through a mouth bulging with batter. "It's mines!"

"Ye better give it to me or ye'll be spending it on a frock for yer broller's funeral instead," he said.

"Me brain's struggling to comprehend what me fecking ears is hearing!" Fionnuala spit out through a few bones, clipping Eoin around the head. "Ye mean to say ye hauled yer wee sister onto the pavement to sell yer drugs? She's but eight, her!"

She didn't know what made her more angry: Eoin's lack of common sense, or her pedicure slipping away.

"And what's all this palaver about the fecking Filth?" Paddy boomed from his chair as Roisin looked on, enraptured and shaking some salt onto her curry and chips.

Eoin took a deep breath as he settled back down with his fish and finally took the plunge.

"I've meself a new job," he admitted to his family. "The Special Branch picked me up the day and hauled me off to that deserted woodland next to the mental institution. Never youse mind, as the quids'll still be rolling in. The Special Branch said I could earn up to £12,000 a year informing for the peelers. All I gotta do is keep me ears peeled for any mention of clandestine activates when am picking up me stash from me suppliers in Creggan. The McDaids is in with the Provos, ye understand? Effin magic, aye?"

All molars ceased in mid-chew, and all eyes stared. As Padraig's curry chips clattered to the carpeting, Eoin's grin faltered.

"God bless us!" Roisin twittered, hand to her bleeding heart.

"Mary moller of fecking God!" Paddy finally roared from his armchair. "Consorting with the enemy, you!"

Eoin jumped as his father wrenched the cod out of his lap. There was a limit to the gainful delinquency his parents' greed would condone after all, and Eoin suspected he would soon be sat in front of a Pot Noodles as well.

"Have ye not an ounce of shame in that fecking thick skull of yers?" Paddy said. "Have ye forgotten the Easter Rising of 1916? The blood of wer forefallers spilled on O'Connell Bridge to give us the basic human rights of the rest of the world? Bloody fecking Sunday? Ye mind that? Thirteen innocent victims marching for civil rights gunned down in the Bogside by rifle-toting Proddy paratrooping bastards? The same murderous Orange swine ye're licking the arses of now!"

"That slapper's been *sleeping* with Proddy bastards!" Eoin protested, pointing at Dymphna sitting on the hearth slurping obediently out of her Pot Noodle. "Her bastard's a manky, mingin Orange cow!"

"Naw!" Dymphna cried, fork poised in mid-air. "I had me dates all wrong! The faller of me wane doesn't be a Proddy after all. It's Mr. O'Toole."

"Ye mean that pansy outta the Top-Yer-Trolly?" Fionnuala snorted. "Ach, go on away a that!"

"He had me on the stockroom floor," Dymphna insisted. "Four weeks ago, it was."

Paddy put down his chips, nauseated.

"Yer fancy man's a fecking nancy boy?" he demanded to know.

"How did ye come to think her wane's a Proddy?" Roisin demanded of Eoin. She took a bite of cod, quite happy to stir up the trouble.

"She tole me!"

"I was outta me mind with drink and hadn't a clue what I was saying," Dymphna pleaded. "I never slept with Orange bastards!"

Fionnuala gawped down at her tainted offspring.

"Jesus, Mary and Joseph! What are youse like?" she wondered.

"Flippin disgraces, that's what!" Paddy decided. "Orange Proddy bastards has been stealing wer land, raping wer weemin, sending their wanes to the better schools, snatching the best paid jobs …!"

"We live with em in the same town, sure," Eoin attempted. "We gotta interact with em somehow, like."

"Aye, and since the advent of the rave culture in the early nineties, E's has been spreading love between the religious factions—" Dymphna began.

"Me eyes kyanny stomach the sight of youse!" Paddy roared. "I've half a mind to march yer traitorous bodies out to the back garden for a tar and feallerin! I want youse outta me house before I batter the Orange-loving shite outta yer bodies!"

"God bless us and save us!" Roisin finally bellowed. "Stop the roaring out of ye, the lot of youse! If youse'd pay me some mind, I've the solution to everything."

All heads turned. Any other ex-pat fresh from the tarmac of Belfast International would have kept their nose out. Not Roisin.

She motioned over to Eoin.

"I gather that wan's been supporting the family with money from drug sales?" Roisin said, then nodded to Dymphna. "And that slapper is pregnant outta wedlock?"

Paddy and Fionnuala confirmed with sharp nods.

"It sickens the heart outta me to tell ye this," Roisin lied, "but there's to be more boller on its way. I hear ye've been collecting a caretaker's allowance for Eda these past few years?"

Fionnuala jumped at this peculiar turn in the discussion.

"Aye," she said, confused. "But that has sweet feck all to do—"

"It clear escaped me mind with Eda's brush with death and all," Roisin said, "but that flippin Ursula's gone and applied to the council to have it taken away from youse. She's gonny be claiming it herself, thanks to that Francine O'Dowd at the Foyleside Churches. So ye're about to be earning £38.50 less a week."

Of all the disgraces Fionnuala had ever encountered, including Dymphna and Eoin, this latest abuse was the most revolting of all. Fionnuala had borne her wanes, so she was committed to forgiving them their trespasses, even if very belatedly on her deathbed. Ursula, on the other hand, hadn't an ounce of Heggarty blood in her.

"What's this fecking world coming to?" Fionnuala seethed. "Never a moment's peace! Ursula knew sure as feck we've been claiming that care allowance for five years! And her swanning round town in her flash car and fancy Warehouse gear! Grabby for thirty-eight fecking more quid a week!"

"Sure, it wasn't enough that she married a rich Yank," Paddy bellowed, "and it wasn't even enough that she won the lotto. She went and snatched 5 Murphy from under wer noses, and now she's nicking the food from wer mouths!"

Fionnuala barreled on: "How did the shameless cunt even get it into her simple mind she's entitled to wan pence piece when it's me that's been tortured daily with that dottery aul fool? I trawl round that flimmin corner to shove the Brussels sprouts into that piggin mouth of hers, listening to the aul eejit chuntering on and on about God only knows the feck what!"

"Ursula don't give a cold shite in hell about me granny!" Padraig wailed.

"Right ye are, son," Fionnuala said, beaming proudly.

"Me auntie better keep in good with themmuns from OsteoCare, cause after am finished with her, she'll be in need of wan of their wheelchairs!" Padraig vowed.

"Calm down, calm down the lot of youse!" Roisin finally roared. "As I said, I've the solution to all yer problems, three problems solved in wan, the disgrace of them two wanes and the airs and graces of the almighty Ursula."

They all looked over expectantly at the lady of wisdom with jangling corn-rows, battered sausage in her hand.

£ £ £ £

Eda was released with a relatively full bill of health for a woman her age. The angina attack had passed, but the doctors told her to lay off the ready salted crisps and pickled onions as her sodium levels were unhealthily high. Eda had barely settled her arse into the settee of 5 Murphy Crescent when the front door burst wide.

Like a flock of buzzards Paddy and Fionnuala descended, bundling Eda up into an old cardigan, forcing Wellingtons on her feet and shoving her into the pelting downpour without even the dignity of an umbrella. She hadn't the inclination nor time to protest. She found herself speckled with damp and perched on the leather seat of a minicab. Fear-hearted, Eda squinted around the interior of the back seat. Her rheumy eyes widened.

"Roisin, love? Ach, sure, it gladdens me heart to see ye, so it does. Is that you over from Hawaii, wee dote?"

Her gums registered delight and perhaps a shudder of hallucinogenic fear as she gripped her eldest daughter's wrist and verified her physical presence beside her.

"Aye, am are," Roisin replied with grim determination. "Am here to save ye moller."

Fionnuala clambered into the passenger seat up front and barked an address at the minicab driver. Paddy sidled into the back seat and slammed the door.

"That effin bitch Ursula," Fionnuala said, "wants to grab the house from under ye before yer body's even lukewarm in it's grave, let alone cold!"

"But *Ursula?*" Genuine shock registered on the lines of Eda's face. Her mind wavered. It was so difficult with the passage of time to tell the difference between events real and imagined. Her thinking was so muddled as of late. Perhaps Ursula *had* been giving her grief lately and she had forgotten. She had been forgetting many things lately. "She's never been a trouble to me."

"Me hole," Roisin muttered.

"Aye, she has," Paddy insisted.

"Where are we away off?" Eda wondered.

"The solicitor's," Roisin announced.

"The ...?"

"Don't ye worry yerself, Mammy," Fionnuala said, her head twisted at the neck in the front seat. "Everything's to be just grand."

Mammy? Had Fionnuala ever called her that before? Eda didn't think so.

"That Ursula's never been a daughter to ye," Paddy said. "She's been nothing but a disgrace to the Flood name since 1973."

It was then that Eda detected the faint odor of alcohol on her son's breath. It explained the wide look in his bloodshot eyes, the crudeness of the abduction from the comfort of her settee. Eda descended into a slightly disapproving silence.

It all passed in a blur, the dispersal from the taxi, being shuttled up the stairs and down endless corridors, the leather of the chairs in the solicitor's office, your man blathering on and on in strange jargon her mind couldn't catch, her fingers being urged around a pen. Eda was baffled as to why pens were constantly being forced into her fingers and pushed towards various official-looking documents as of late.

"Sure, I don't rightly know ..." she said in a thin voice, uncertainty and indecision in her hand.

Paddy grappled her fingers, Roisin gently shoved her hand towards the document. She would swan off that evening to Belfast International, damage done, and catch the red-eye to Honolulu International, leaving a legacy of divine vengeance in her wake.

In the corner, Fionnuala lorded over the proceedings with well-folded arms and a self-satisfied smirk of triumph.

£ £ £ £

Later the same day, Ursula was on her way to the Richmond Center on Shipquay Street, selling forget-me-nots for the St. Eugene's Cathedral fundraiser. She had been cast out of the choir, but wouldn't believe it until she heard it from Father Hogan's own lips.

She was alone, wrapped up against the dull drizzle and the cold wind, the box of flowers hanging from a strap around her neck. She trawled through a landscape of broken bottles, ancient IRA graffiti, trails of human piss and dogshit, prams stuffed with screaming brats and bored hooligans on the prowl. Jed waited for her in the car.

"Ferget-me-nots! Wan pound, just!" Ursula warbled to nobody who was interested, moving through the market at Magazine Gate. "Help us get wer new hymnals! Ferget-me-nots!"

The delinquents selling shifty gear eyed her from their stalls as she traveled over the cobblestones towards Shipquay Street. Ursula pulled her pink slicker around her and forced a spring into her step. Clearing the alley and emerging onto Shipquay Street, she deflated with relief, then felt a tap on her shoulder. She turned around, and it was Roisin, leering at her. Ursula felt as if she had been slapped.

"Yer moller wants a wee word with ye," Roisin announced.

"In her hospital room?" Ursula asked, confused.

"Ach, she's been out for days," Roisin snorted.

Nobody had informed Ursula. Panic stricken, she heaved her body after Roisin's careening cornrows up the street. Eda was clutching for dear life on a lopsided bench outside the swank new café, and pressed up against her side was Fionnuala, cool as one of the packages of frozen fish fingers she priced daily. The breath left Ursula at the sight of Eda's taut, haggard face.

"Could I have a wee moment alone with me moller?" Ursula demanded.

If only Roisin and Fionnuala would leave Eda's side, if only she could get her mother alone. If only she could hold her tightly and whisper into her ear how grateful she was she had her health, tell her how much her love for her had grown over the years.

"Naw," Fionnuala barked. "Am not leaving her alone with the likes of you!"

If only …

"Okay," Ursula said. "Cheerio."

Ursula made to leave. She wasn't about to pour her heart out to her mother while dodging the daggers Roisin and Fionnuala launched her way.

Fionnuala screamed into Eda's face, "Tell her! *Tell her now, Mammy!*"

Eda stirred uncomfortably on the bench, all eyes on her. It wasn't quite Sophie's Choice, but she had a decision to make: should she side with the Barnetts or the Floods? Although Ursula was the disgrace of the family, she had been terrible kind to her the past twenty years. There had been the three years she and her now deceased husband Patrick had spent with the Barnetts in Guam. And then, after the lotto win, Ursula had done up the house for her and installed that chair lift. Of course, Ursula also claimed that house as her own although they had joint ownership, and Ursula knew Eda wouldn't be on this earth much longer, so her daughter had really done it up for herself, hadn't she? Eda wasn't getting much use out of that new flat screen telly, for example, as she couldn't understand the programs of the day, and her cataracts made it impossible to focus on the massive screen for long, but Ursula never missed an episode of *Antiques Roadshow* on it. Then there was Paddy and his brood, hardened stokes certainly, but they had always lived around the corner, disrupting her life, but also helping out as best they could with their limited resources.

Sensing safety in numbers, Eda took a deep breath and finally replied.

"Well, Ursula dear, they *have* been getting that allowance for years, ye know."

It wasn't much, but more didn't need to be said; the words scalded Ursula as the forget-me-nots bristled under her chin. The way Fionnuala sat there, tilted, with her hand on her mother's back, it was as if Eda were the dummy and Fionnuala the ventriloquist, in charge of springing open and clamping shut Eda's jaw, forcing the words of Judas Iscariot from her mouth.

"For some reason, Mammy," Ursula said slowly and carefully, "ye kyanny get it into yer thick skull that ye've no say in the matter. It's for the government to decide. A Proddy government, aye, but a government all the same. It's a *carer's* allowance. Ye don't have to sign anything, ye just have to sit there in wer house and reap the benefits of me care."

There was a definitive silence during which Roisin flashed Fionnuala a look which clearly said *I tole ye so.* In her sister and sister-in-law's slight change, Ursula seemed to have breached a point, a singularity beyond which there was no return. It was as if, had Ursula suddenly relinquished the £38.50 a week, the entire extended family would have welcomed her back into the fold. As if, indeed.

"Ye never learn, do ye, Ursula?" Roisin said in wonder. "Ye kyanny stop torturing that family and me moller, can ye? Isn't them million ye won enough to support yer lifestyle, ye sanctimonious cow, ye?"

Sanctimonious, the only five syllable word Roisin used with any frequency.

Ursula hated her sister for the pleasure she was deriving from the situation. Roisin had just come back for a wee holiday after ten years away; she should have been seen as the one who had turned her back. Any decent person in her position would have struggled to work their way back in and earn the right to have an opinion. Any decent person.

"The lotto money's all gone," Ursula finally revealed.

"Aye, and am a Proddy bastard," Roisin sneered.

"Am turning in that piggin allowance book so'se were not hauled off to the court by the city council," Fionnuala said. "Ye can kiss yer moller cheerio, but."

"We thought ye'd be too pig-headed to listen to sense," Roisin said with menace, "so we've already put the wheels in motion to stop ye from persecuting me mammy any longer."

"What's that meant to mean?" Ursula asked.

"It's called making yer own bed and laying in it," Fionnuala said with a smile.

"Maybe the bed in yer ... what do ye call it?" Roisin flicked a petal of one of the forget-me-nots. "... yer *blue* room?"

She whipped her head away, Ursula ducking quickly to avoid an eye being taken out by the cornrows which sliced the air.

"We've no need to tell ye anything now," Fionnuala said, waving Ursula away dismissively. "Ye're to be finding out soon enough, like. Go on away off and sell yer flowers, like."

Ursula could stand there in the drizzle no longer, mortified and hurt and confused as she was. She stared at her mother as if it were the last look she would ever pass Eda's way, then turned and plummeted tearfully back through the passageway to Jed in his Lexus. At the archway to the gate she barreled into Mrs. Feeney. Mindful of her public reputation, Mrs. Feeney forced a delighted look onto her face.

"Ach, Ursula, lovely to see ye—"

"I kyanny speak now!" Ursula shrieked through her tears, pushing the old woman to the side.

She clomped down the cobblestones. Mrs. Feeney pulled her cardigan around her and sniffed after Ursula, "Ignorant, jumped-up pig!" She set her lips and wondered what could be done about that ostentatious bitch just to knock her down a few notches more.

£ £ £ £

Dymphna scoured the Top-Yer-Trolly staff manual for the benefits that would soon be hers. Maternity Allowance! Statutory Maternity Leave! Statutory Maternity Pay! Time Off For Antenatal Care!

Top-Yer-Trolly's fecking brilliant! she thought.

Fidelma cleared her throat, pulling Dymphna from her dreams.

"Ye're dressed to the nines," she said, eyeing Dymphna's skimpy outfit under her smock. "Have ye found yerself a new fancy man?"

"None of yer fecking business."

Dymphna snapped the manual shut and made a show of fiddling with the tubs of tuna and sweetcorn cottage cheese, all the while wondering when she should approach Mr. O'Toole for a raise. Now he was going to be revealed as the father of her wane, it was only fair he help move her up a tax bracket from abject poverty.

She was taken aback to see her wee brother Padraig struggling to their counter under the weight of an overflowing shopping basket.

"Could ye ring these up for us, hi?" he asked, heaving his spoils over the counter.

Dymphna glanced at his haul: three bottles of fizzy lemonade, a package of dishcloths, a gallon of rubbing alcohol and a box of Swan's matches.

Her eyes widened. Her mammy had told her Padraig had progressed from paint bombs, and here was evidence aplenty. Well, it was a free country. Dymphna had tried to defend Mrs. Feeney from his rocks, and where had it gotten her? A kick in the shins and a "ye Heggarty bitch!" in her face. If Padraig had the money, he could buy whatever he wanted at the Top-Yer-Trolly, and whatever he did with it after that was someone else's problem.

"We kyanny ring up household items here at the meat and cheese counter," Fidelma sniffed.

"Get stuffed, ye four-eyed gack!" Padraig said.

"Go on away off and play with yer acne, Fidelma," Dymphna said, plucking out the bottles and ringing them up.

"What's them matches for?" Fidelma said, voice laced with disapproval. "Ye've not taken up fags, have ye? Not at yer age?"

Dymphna heaved a sigh and turned to face her. "Would ye not unpack them Thai lemongrass and chili sausages and leave us heart's peace?"

"And we kyanny serve family members and all. It's all laid out in that staff manual ye're after having yer nose in."

"Never you mind."

"There'll be hell to pay for all these infractions of the guidelines."

"Really?" Dymphna trilled. "And I hear O'Toole's considering me for a promotion."

"That's likely, aye."

With Fidelma watching every click of her fingernails on the register, Dymphna couldn't give Padraig the staff discount she usually did, and she tried to tell him this with her eyes.

"That'll be £8.98," Dymphna recited.

"Where's me staff discount?" he demanded.

David from the stockroom approached.

"O'Toole wants a word with ye," David said. "In his office, like."

"I tole ye," Fidelma rejoiced. "He's after seeing ye on the CCTV ringing up household items at the meat and cheese counter for a family member. And selling matches to a wane and all."

"I'll household items yer arse!" Dymphna snapped, shoving the provisions in a plastic carrier bag and handing them over to Padraig.

She was thrilled at the summons. O'Toole must be a randy old git; he had to be after another go in the stockroom. He might behave like a mincing queen, but he sure knew how to spread the seed. And once she offered herself to him again, there was no way in hell he'd turn down her demand for a raise. Things were finally falling into place. That night of desperation in the Craglooner seemed lifetimes away. She was a Bogside girl, not used to getting what she wanted in her harsh world, so could hardly believe her continued good luck.

She marched through the housewares aisle, checking her lipstick in the shiny surface of a 28cm roasting dish and mulling over if she should ask for £1 or £1.50 more an hour.

Mr. O'Toole was waiting for her behind his desk. She wondered with a quick flick of the lips if he was trouserless beneath the prefab oak.

"Ye wanted to see me?" she asked, then clasped her hands in delight at a bouquet of posies next to his "in" box, knowing at the sight of them that she had reeled him in good and tight, even if she would have hoped for a more expensive display of his affection than six wilting posies.

"For me?" she twittered.

"They was meant to be, aye."

He was so stern it sent a thrill down her spine. How she wanted him to take masterful advantage of her, with perhaps a few sharp spanks on her behind thrown in for good measure. Well, she supposed, that's what desks were for. Those piles of requisition forms would have to be shoved to the floor first, though.

"What," Mr. O'Toole asked, "are these?"

He reached under the desk, tugged open a drawer and exposed a sodden package of half-thawed sausages. Dymphna tingled. Kinky old bugger! Well, she could play along with his little sex game, sultry stock floor girl versus masterful management.

"Ye know yerself, sure! Smartprice skinless budget pork sausingers, wan pound twenty six pee a kilogram," Dymphna rattled off, a come-hither smile playing on her lips. "Sir," she added, to give him a special little thrill.

"And where are they meant to be stocked?"

She had to give the old nancy boy credit, he was certainly playing his role to the hilt, not a trace of lechery on his face, all stern manager incarnate.

"Between the jumbo premium pork and the Aberdeen Angus beef," she said. *Get on with it, man! Just tell me where to stock them* now!

"Precisely," Mr. O'Toole said. "Imagine my shock, then, when I went to put some flowers in yer locker this morning, and instead of a pile of freshly-laundered work smocks, I was greeted with *these*?"

He brandished the sausages with a curious potpourri of rage, triumph and contempt. Dymphna faltered for a fraction of a second.

"That Fidelma!" she barked. "That wee bitch's always rummaging through me private staff locker! Nicking stock from the floor and hiding it away to feed her fat mouth at night."

"Ach, Fidelma's a vegan, sure," he tutted, squirming with impatience. "Do ye think am a bleedin eejit? It's quite plain to anywan with two flimmin brain cells to rub togeller the culprit's nowan but yerself. Ye kyanny take the Bogside outta youse thieving stokes!"

"There's bottomless stomachs to feed round ours, sure," Dymphna said with a shrug. "Surely ye didn't call me into yer office to slap me on the wrists for a wee thing like this?"

The shamelessness that had so enraptured him one sex act previously now rankled.

"Ye've already had yer final warning. Stroppiness, tardiness, slovenliness, them I can all handle in me staff. Thieving fingers, but! Behavior like this kyanny be tolerated by this establishment!"

"What about getting randy in the stockroom? Are ye not up for anoller shag?"

"Getting ..." he sputtered, his face pink with rage and pinched with disbelief. "I musta been outta me mind the oller day when I let me body be abused for yer personal pleasure. Ye kyanny get it through yer piggin thick skull, can ye? Ye're *sacked*, ye thieving, clarty cunt ye!"

And he did strip the smock off her.

"Unfair dismissal!" Dymphna brayed as she struggled out of the sleeves. "Am hauling ye off to Labor Relations! Ye took advantage of me innocence in the darkness of the stockroom!"

"Innocence? Ye've not a titter of innocence in them gammy bones of yers!"

"There'll be a tribunal!"

Tribunals! The last resort of the lumpen working classes unwilling to lift a finger in the workplace.

"Aye, you just **try it**," Mr. O'Toole said, his lip curling into an ugly sneer. "We've packs of solicitors chomping at the bit to fend off vultures the likes of youse!"

Dymphna turned to go, and reached down for her flowers.

"I think those would be better left on me desk," Mr. O'Toole said, straining to compose himself.

Confusion revealed itself on her face.

"Ye got em for me, but!"

"*Out!* Outta me sight and offa the premises before I call security on ye!"

Mary moller of God, Dymphna thought as she headed for the door, *arse bandits is wile narky!*

She stropped out of the office, wondering frenziedly if she had come across anything in the staff manual for Redundancy Pay For Recently-Terminated UnWed Mothers.

7

Eoin, raw with worry, stood behind a stoke in a bright red track suit with congested lungs. The McDaids were a pack of dead hard hooligans, and would be looking for upwards of £300 when he saw them later that day to pick up more pills.

He shot glances at the "jobseekers" around him, a sea of swallow tattoos, glazed eyes and three day growth shuffling forward in the queue of the Foyle Jobs and Benefits Office. The deadbeat ahead of him heaved a spluttering cough ripe with nicotine and early death. Eoin wondered if that was to be his own future.

Half an hour later, some smarmy git in a double breasted suit gave him a smile devoid of pleasure through the scratches of the Plexiglas.

"And how can I help ye?" the git asked with a frisson of contempt.

"I've to change me address," Eoin explained. "I've been kicked outta me home."

The smarmy git raised an eyebrow.

"Yer name?" he asked. "Aul address and new address?"

Eoin gave him the particulars, and the change was quickly made in the computer. The git perused the Eoin Flood file, then smirked up at him.

"Ye pick yer benefits up at the post office, sure, so ye had no need to tell us of yer change of address. What are ye really doing here, hi?"

Eoin squirmed.

"I was hoping I might be able to get an advance on me next week's benefits."

The git raised another eyebrow.

"Ye seem terrible certain ye won't be employed next week," he said. "Perhaps we can find ye employment as a psychic? From a glance at yer records, I see ye've been drawing the brew since yer last day of school. I kyanny fathom how ye've not yet found a job. As am sure ye're aware, compulsory steps are meant to be taken to try to get yerself a job if ye wanny continue drawing the brew. I don't suppose ye've darkened the doorway of the job center as of late? There's loads of jobs going, I saw em on the bulletin board meself not two days since."

Eoin tapped his hand impatiently. All of this carry-on to pocket £33.85 a week? Was it any wonder young lads turned to peddling drugs on the cobblestones?

"Aye, am never outta the place, like," Eoin said with a thin-lipped non-smile.

The git gave him the once over, taking in the haggard eyes, the unwashed football jersey. His eyes became slits.

"Haven't I seen ye at the Craglooner?"

Eoin wasn't about to fall for that trick. There was no way this overly coiffed nancy boy would step one polished Oxford in the Craglooner; a swank wine bar over on the Waterside was more likely his watering hole. Did he think he was thick?

"I've no money to waste on drink, like," Eoin said quickly. "Not when am meant to support meself on £33.85 a week."

"Well, ye must be spending yer free time somewhere," the git said, "and I doubt it's spent at the job center. Have ye considered registering for a training course to learn some special skills to finally join the national workforce, like?"

"I already took loads," Eoin snapped. "There was the Keyboard Skills, the Brickwork, the Beauty Skills, the Plastering, the Extended Childminding Practice, the Carpentry and Joinery, the Scullery Portering, and the Engineering Maintenance."

"Aye, and?"

"I failed em all."

The git stared at the computer screen to verify this sad truth, then turned back to Eoin with disbelief.

"We've stacks more to suit every taste. Have ye tried Preparation for Nursing?"

"Aye."

"Footwear Design?"

"Aye."

"The National Certificate for Floristry?"

"I have it, sure."

"The National Certificate for Door Supervisors?"

"I have that and all."

"And ye kyanny find employment with all that training and all them skills?"

"Me body's not big enough to be a door supervisor, sure!"

"C'mere till I tell ye, wee boy, am glad ye've stepped foot into wer office. Sometimes wans the likes of youse gets lost in the bureaucratic shuffle."

"The likes of me?"

"Aye, filthy druggy street scum without an ounce of sense in their brains, them what wanny lollygag around the town pumping the drugs and the drink into their bodies, them that's taking the mick outta the government. Ye have the bold-faced cheek to march into this office and demand an advance on yer allowance when it's obvious to all but a thick headed gack that ye're taking advantage—"

"Steady on!" Eoin said. "I've been trying to find a job, like! Am bleedin desperate for a few quid!"

"Ye're dead right there, lad, and ye're about to be even more desperate for a few quid, as I've just sanctioned ye!"

"What the bleedin feck does *sanctioned* mean?"

"Yer benefits is to be stopped for 26 weeks," the git said. "That'll teach ye to take the mick outta the jobseeker's allowance!"

Gone were all thoughts of taking a minicab up to Creggan to meet the thugs. He couldn't even afford the bus. He'd have to hoof it. And of course it started lashing down the moment he left the Jobs Office. Buying an umbrella was out of his budget.

£ £ £ £

Ursula took a tentative step into the rectory office at St. Eugene's Cathedral. It had taken her long enough, but she had finally found a window of opportunity in her busy schedule where she could confront Father Hogan for transferring her to St. Moluag's choir. The priest was poring over a pile of papers on his desk, still slightly pale from his encounters in the confessional that evening. Ursula cleared her throat.

"Faller?" she ventured.

He looked up, his impatience masked by a benign smile.

"Aye?" he managed. He peered further and saw all the signs of one mentally distraught, living hell on earth: the tautness of her lips, the searching eyes, the disheveled aubergine bob.

Your woman's long overdue a trip to the hair salon, Father Hogan thought. *Ach, aye!* It was the one they had all come into his office to complain about recently; the lotto winner who had generously aided the church a few months back.

"Ursula, isn't it? And how may I be of help?"

"Am here about the choir," Ursula explained. "Ye've had me transferred to St. Moluag's down in the Bogside?"

Father Hogan raised an eyelid and motioned to the plastic orange chair. Ursula perched, clutching and unclutching her handbag.

"Is it me singing that's the problem?" she asked. "I've tried to improve. That Mrs. Gee's terrible tone deaf, but, and am always stood next to her."

"Ye're a Bogside girl," he said. "I thought I was doing ye a favor."

Ursula nodded haltingly.

"I don't think am up for it, faller," she said. "And I need to tell ye why."

Father Hogan avoided a glance at his watch and settled in his chair for the duration.

"Aye?" he sighed.

"I grew up there, aye, and I don't think am better than the likes of them Bogside people down there now after me lotto win; I know that's what wans might think. Me family, but, them is never outta St. Moluag's Chapel on a Sunday, letting on they've decent Christian hearts, when all the while they troop down the aisle like the pack of right hard stokes they really is. I kyanny face em every week. Am fear-hearted they'll point up at me and roar with laughter. I'll be terrible persecuted every Sunday."

He passed her a tissue, his heart going out to her, but he could hide the sorry truth no longer. He hated saying every word.

"It saddens me heart to say it, Ursula. The ladies of the choir here don't want ye singing beside em no longer."

She had heard it from their own mouths, but was still hoping she had misunderstood.

"Themmuns is me friends," she attempted, the tissue crumpled in her fist.

Father Hogan regarded her with pity. The poor old soul was clueless.

"The choir ladies say ye've not been the same since yer lotto win."

Ursula's eyes widened.

"I've been nothing but wile kind and generous! I had em over to me house for tea, I ... I ..."

"Am on yer side. I kyanny keep ye here, but, with all the girls whinging and moaning about ye every week. Ye'll haveta forgive them their trespasses, and they'll haveta look deep in their hearts and realize what evil they've done."

Father Hogan opened his palms to her.

"The Lord works, Ursula, in—"

"Aye, in mysterious ways," she snapped in sudden anger. "So I've heard. I hadn't a clue that them ways is so torturous to those of us that never put a foot wrong in wer lives. Persecuted and crucified, we are, just like wer Lord hanging on the cross!"

She flashed him a narrow glance over the sopping tissue.

"And I gave a sizable contribution to the parish and all, if ye recall."

He sat silently in his chair, then finally leaned forward.

"If it's new friends ye're after, might I suggest wer new Alzheimer's Round Em Up program that's looking for volunteers? The afflicted have a terrible habit of wandering away from their homes, and fully half of em not rounded up within twenty-four hours is likely to suffer serious personal injury or even death."

Ursula gawped at him in disbelief.

"Ach, catch yerself on, faller! Years I worked for OsteoCare, years I tell ye, and am sick, sore and tired of that aul Mrs. Feeney! And now ye expect me to traipse round the town searching for aul wans outta their minds? Ye must think am a right eejit! I've spent all me life helping all and sundry, and nobody pays me wan blind bit of notice! Am through helping ollers!"

She wrenched open her handbag and tore clumsily though its contents.

"And here's the money I collected for the new hymnals, peddling them for-get-me-nots all round the town," Ursula said, bitterly tossing over three crisp twenties. She had binned the flowers and withdrawn the money out of her own ravaged bank account. "It's the last flimmin quid am gonny hand over without expecting something in return. Am through with the whole sorry lot of youse!"

And out she stomped of the rectory. Father Hogan watched her go with a twinge of relief and a quick shuffle of his papers.

£ £ £ £

Dymphna clutched Bridie's arm as they skirted through the trail of filthy syringes that led to the Health Clinic. It should have been her mother at her side, but Fionnuala had banished her daughter from the family home and forbidden her from uttering a word to any Flood or Heggarty she came into contact with (besides Eoin). It was all her auntie Ursula's fault. If the useless creature had just handed over the money for a termination, Dymphna could have made the journey to Liverpool and nobody would be the wiser. No need to scour the city for a fit Catholic lad, no need to entice a mincing old queen like O'Toole to take her in the stockroom, and no need to now visit the Health Clinic, with seven and a half months of torture ahead of her.

"I wouldn't mind being sacked," Dymphna confided in Bridie, "but them sausingers I nicked was for the family dinner, and am not even allowed the creature comforts of me own home anymore. Kicked out of the house like a right slapper I was, and am still expected to provide for the family."

"Never you mind," Bridie said with a pat on her arm. "Working behind the counter of the ChipKebab with me will be a laugh, so it will."

"It was wile civil of ye to recommend me for the job. Them staff lockers looks dead wee, but. Am wondering how the staff's meant to nick food for the family dinner."

"Ye just make like it's yer staff meal and pack it all into a takeaway bag at the end of yer shift. It's wile simple, I'll show ye how. I've been feeding me family for months on TofuDippers and Hot Dog Baguettes."

"Thanks for coming with me, Bridie," Dymphna said as she opened the door.

"Ach, sure, no boller a tall. Are ye up for paying yer broller Eoin a wee visit when we're through?"

Bridie was hungering for more E's.

"Easy enough done, as we be living togeller at the moment. Does the Chip-Kebab pay for wer holidays, then?"

After giving a name at the counter, Dymphna flipped through some dog-eared *Hello!* magazines while Bridie inspected the sign above the broken telly which threatened: *We are here to help you, but in no way will we tolerate drunkenness, verbal abuse, threatened or actual violence.*

"I see Brad Pitt's gone on holiday again," Dymphna said, pointing wistfully at a page.

"C'mere a wee moment, hi. Have ye no clue who the faller of this wane might be?"

"Aye," Dymphna said, bracing her lips to lie to her best mate. "Mr. O'Toole from the Top-Yer-Trolly."

Bridie threw back her head and roared with laughter.

"Attracta Ni Oigthierna!" called the girl at the counter through the fag in her mouth.

They stared around the waiting room, nosy, until Dymphna realized that that was the name she had given.

"Ach, that's me," she said, gratefully scuttling off beyond the swinging door.

Dymphna would've preferred the Pakistani nurse, as they were all shipped over from Manchester and didn't have a clue who in Derry was who. She was saddled instead with Nurse Sheila Bryant, whom she knew from the Top-Yer-Trolly. She had the tartan shopping cart and the type of face you longed to slap.

Dymphna suffering the indignity of much heavy-handed prodding and poking, then was left frittering away on the examination table for a full thirty minutes, gown untied at the back, as the tests were gone over. Finally, the door opened, and Nurse Bryant marched back in.

"Let's see what sort of boller ye've gotten yerself into," she sighed, the weight of the world on her shoulders, flipping through some charts on a clipboard.

Dymphna braced herself for the news she already knew.

"Give me strength dear Jesus," Nurse Bryant muttered, shaking her head. "Ye are indeed pregnant, aye. If youse wanes the day only had more respect for the laws of the Catholic Church! What I kyanny get me head around is that youse heathens demanded the disgrace of condom machines in all the pubs and clubs in wer town, and now that ye've got yer filthy pagan way, ye never make any use of em!"

"How far along am I?" Dymphna asked.

"Two weeks."

Dymphna's brain couldn't comprehend what her ears had just heard.

"Ye mean six weeks, surely?" she asked.

"Two weeks, I've tole ye."

Dymphna's face was vacant.

"But ..."

"Two weeks, a fortnight, fourteen days," Nurse Bryant said as though English weren't Dymphna's native tongue.

"I was pregnant six weeks ago, sure," Dymphna insisted.

"Naw, ye wasn't."

"Aye, I was."

Nurse Ratchett placed a hand on her hip and glared down as if she wanted to clatter the shameless beast one around the head.

"Are ye trying to tell me how to do me job?"

Dymphna kneaded the tissue in her hand.

"D-did ye maybe find two wanes in there?" Dymphna asked in desperation.

"Ye mean, are ye having twins? We kyanny tell so early, sure!"

"Naw, not twins. What I meant is, I think ... I think ..." Her brain cells struggled. "It must be that I have two wanes inside of me, then, wan two weeks aul and the oller six weeks. Could ye go on and have anoller wee look inside?"

"That's a biological impossibility!" Nurse Bryant barked with a crabbit short fuse. "Wance ye conceive, ye kyanny have anoller wane until the first wan comes outta ye, and thank the almighty Lord for that."

Dymphna couldn't shake a vision of Rory Riddell's Orange wane and Mr. O'Toole's Green wane growing side by side within her.

"Where's me oller wane gone, but?" Dymphna implored tearily. "C-could the aulder wane have died and a new wane be growing next to its wee cold body?"

"Are ye mental? Ye've only wan wane inside ye, and that wane's two weeks aul. Surely wan wane's disgrace enough?"

A sense of loss shuddered through Dymphna's sobbing body, Rory Riddell's Orange baby now mysteriously erased from her womb. The affront of a Proddy bastard wane had given her no end of grief, but it was a wane she had already resigned herself to loving. She briefly imagined a horrid scene of sectarian violence unfolding deep within her chasm, of O'Toole's ersatz wane suffocating the life out of the original wane, the final triumph of the Provos over the Nationalists.

"Am dead certain I was terrible pregnant six weeks ago," she insisted with a sniffle.

"Fer Jesus' sake!" Nurse Bryant spat. "Naw, ye wasn't! Did ye have the morning sickness? Spewing the moment ye rose from bed?"

Dymphna looked at her blankly.

"Was yer breasts tingly, was they tender and all swollen like a football?"

"Naw," Dymphna admitted. Her voice grew shrill. "I took the pregnancy test, but! It tole me I was up the scoot!"

Nurse Bryant inspected her over her spectacles, then nodded her head with sudden understanding.

"And ye got yer pregnancy test from that Top-Yer-Trolly down the town, did ye?"

"Aye, aisle 7A."

"Them bloody manufacturers!" she roared. "All them tests was pulled from the shelves weeks ago for being defective. The clinic's had streams of right wee slappers pouring through wer doors, tears bucketing down their faces, begging to know the way to Liverpool. A bit less drink and a bit more common Christian restraint would've saved the whole sorry lot of youse from blighting wer clinic!"

"Ye mean—"

"God bless us and save us, ye're bleedin thick! If ye thought ye were pregnant outta wedlock six weeks ago, what possessed ye to spread yer legs again four weeks after?"

If only the nurse knew. Nurse Bryant droned on about pre-natal care, appointments for this and that, but Dymphna couldn't hear.

"—And ye're to lay off the fags and the drink and the Ecstasy!" Nurse Bryant finished. "And the lads, if that's within yer realm of possibility."

"Aye, right ye are," Dymphna murmured with a nod as though she would.

She tenderly removed herself from the examination table, grieving for her Orange wane who had never been and clueless as to who the father of this new wane should be.

£ £ £ £

Eoin approached the McDaid house, tape player heavy in the pocket of his hooded jumper. Now that his benefits had been cut off, the only way he could pay back the McDaid brothers was if he kept his ears peeled for the casual mention of gunrunning, the trafficking of falsified documents and the like, run back to the Special Branch with the intelligence, collect their blood money and hand it over to the Ecstasy-dealing thugs. He would be a traitor to his country and his religion, of course, and if the McDaids ever found out, there was sure to be some quick headbutting and a slashing in a darkened archway of the city walls, but what else could he do? A spot of male prostitution was out of the question, as the only poofter in the city was Mr. O'Toole, and his sister had apparently already had him, which put into question his availability as a client.

Mrs. McDaids cracked the door an inch to him. Her eyes glinted with suspicion, and the door creaked less-than-graciously open.

"Right ye are," she said flatly.

She led him into the front room, where Eoin was confronted with a horseshoe of three scalped heads and football jerseys around the telly, tablets and polythene bags strewn across the coffee table.

"Yer man's here," Mrs. McDaid said. As if they had all been waiting for him. She closed the door. Eamonn, Caoilte and Fergal turned from the telly as Eoin slipped in and stood in indecision before the Bleeding Heart of Jesus portrait, finger playing atop the On button in his pocket. Pleased to see him they were not. Their hands curled into fists in unison.

"What's all this palaver about yer fecking cunt of a sister passing out wer wingers at discount prices round the town?" Eamonn roared. "Am fecking sickened, so am are!"

Eoin felt faint. Did each of the 83,699 inhabitants of that city know each other's business?

"Aye," Caoilte seethed. "And her getting the bleedin Filth involved and all!"

Their wiry hooligan frames were ready to pounce, daggers fulgurating from their eyes. Eoin briefly considered making a run for it, but Derry was a city with only so many hiding places.

"Out with it, man!" Fergal snarled. "What the feck have ye been playing at with wer gear?"

"Where's wer money?" Caoilte boomed, ricocheting from the settee and dwarfing Eoin inches from his face.

At one with the peeling wallpaper, Eoin took in the eyes that pined bloodshed, breath thick with drink. He begged the dear Lord for mercy as Caoilte dug his fingers into the polyester blend of his top and twisted.

"Where's wer money, ye thieving cunt?" he whispered with crisp fury.

"I-I ..." Eoin stammered, the neck of his top digging into his tendons, his breath deep pants.

Caoilte's nostrils fluctuated wildly, his grim mouth twitched at the ends. Then he threw back his scalped head and roared with furious laughter. Eoin shuddered, his life in the hands of a mad dog. Eamonn and Fergal roared along with their brother. *Is themmuns off their minds with drink and drugs?* Eoin wondered fearfully

"The look on yer man's face!" Fergal said.

"He was shiten his fecking pants, so he was!" Eamonn said.

Caoilte's fingers unraveled from Eoin's neck and slapped him on the back. Eoin deflated against the wallpaper, sweat lashing.

"Fecking brilliant!" Caoilte chortled. "Ye had me pissing meself with laughter! I couldn't keep up with the hard man act no longer!"

"We had ye going there, lad," Fergal said.

"Yer wee sister selling wer gear had the lot of us in stitches, so it did," Eamonn said. "Even me moller was wetting her knickers at the thought of it."

"We'll still be looking for wer money, mind," Fergal put in.

"Ye've a few weeks to pay it off, but," Caoilte said, resettling himself on the settee and taking a sip of his cuppa.

"Th-that's wile civil of ye," Eoin managed.

"Ye're a good wee earner, so ye are," Eamonn said. "We'd hate to take yer knees out, so we would. C'mere you over here."

Eoin clutched the wall as he walked so as not to wither to the floor. Fergal tossed a bag of tablets at him.

"There's yer stash," he said. "Get yerself on them streets and fill wer pockets."

"Ta, youse lot."

Eoin was giddy from his near brush with death, uncannily invincible, courageous with relief. He was finally part of the pack, in with the hardest cunts in the city. He could do no wrong in their eyes, so Eoin threw caution the way of his altar boy cassock. He slipped the gear into his pocket beside the tape player and clicked it on before slipping his hand out.

"A-am so grateful," Eoin said, "that I was wondering how I can repay ye. C-could I maybe give youse a hand with yer oller activities?"

This they greeted with confused sniggers that paled to their earlier hilarity.

"With wer messages?" Caoilte asked, an affected smile forced on his face. "Shopping at the Top-Yer-Trolly for wer bog roll, like?"

The brothers exchanged a look that excluded the employee they had just raved about seconds earlier. Still high, Eoin was clueless to this subtle change.

"Naw, with yer activities to do with the Cause, like."

The tape player waited gamely in his pocket. Each McDaid brother shifted an inch on the seats, their eyes alive with hard suspicion, as if Eoin had just revealed he was a first class arse-bandit.

"What are ye on about, ye headbin?"

"Are ye outta yer bleedin fecking head?"

"I thought—" Eoin stammered.

"There's to be no talk of the Cause in wer house," Caoilte warned. "We've nothing to do with the likes of that."

As three sets of eyes glared at him, Eoin stood there with the fixed grin of a silly gack. The clock on the wall ticked the time. Their McDaid eyes twitched with suspicion and kneecapping as their brain cells trundled, managing thought. Eoin inched towards the door with tiny sideways steps more befitting a crab than a drug dealer. Caoilte leaped from the settee again, suddenly seething, and this time for real.

"Wan wee moment there, hard man," he said, spittle spraying into Eoin's face. "Forget you what we're after laughing at. We want wer money sharpish or there'll be hell to pay. And two shattered kneecaps, no doubt!"

They roared with laughter at the thought of it, and Eoin slipped out of the house. He reached into his pocket and turned off the tape player. At the doorway, Mrs. McDaid stared after him. She closed the door firmly behind her.

£ £ £ £

When two Wednesday afternoons had come and gone, and Jed still hadn't received a phone call from Paddy, he seized his darts case and aluminum chalk holder and headed alone to the Bogside Inn to see if he couldn't get in a few throws at the board himself.

All around him flights and tips pierced the air, lager slopped onto the linoleum, and cheers and jeers broke out from teams of workmates. Jed stood alone on a team of one in the corner, doubles and singles slim on the board as he squinted through the fag smoke to get his aim. The strangers in the pub had been friendly enough, raising their pints in greeting and inviting him to join their team, but they were just that: strangers. Jed had only one friend in Derry.

The dart barrel flew from his fingers, the tip precariously clinging to the thin metal edge of the bull's-eye. Jed froze. If the dart held on for six seconds, the bull's-eye was his! He looked around, amazement on his face, and stopped dead at the sight of Paddy, clutching a pint of stout and swaggering towards the rows of dartboards with three of his mates from the factory.

Jed lifted his cowboy hat and waved through the smoke. He fashioned his lips into a smile and made to saunter over, arms outstretched, bygones be bygones, their problem not ours—

"Eff off, you!" Paddy spat across the room, two brazen fingers flipped in Jed's direction.

Jed quickly looked away. Stunned. Three little words, three letters each, was all it had taken to switch him from liaison officer between the warring factions to a sudden lone henchman for Ursula in that city. He knew better than to approach his brother-in-law and attempt to talk sense. As full of hatred and drink as Paddy probably was, Jed could only imagine scenarios where darts rained down again and again upon his protesting body.

He glanced at his board. The dart had clattered to the linoleum, one second shy of a bull's-eye. Jed gathered his case and chalk, removed his glove and headed out the door to the pub next door for a much-needed pint.

£ £ £ £

Many were the times Ursula's fingers reached for the phone, only to shrivel back away from the receiver. Finally, however, she figured fourteen days of fasting were enough to have tempered the rage of the Floods. She wanted to visit her mother.

Ursula pulled her Lexus up to 5 Murphy and scampered up the steps, mortified at the state of the narrow strip of vegetation that was the front garden.

With their lottery winnings having dwindled to almost nothing, the future sale of the house was quickly transforming from a luxury to a necessity. Ursula didn't begrudge her mother a tenacious hold on life, but her daddy Patrick had succumbed to heart failure more than a decade earlier.

Surely a woman of 85, Ursula thought, *who still sucked down thirty fags a day wasn't long for the grave?*

Keys in hand, she made to force her way into the house. She cursed as the key slipped from the keyhole. Ursula tried the key again, then she noticed the shiny silver of the lock. Her heart clenched with shock. Surely that wasn't a new lock? *Who in the name of God ...?*

Ursula glanced at her watch. Ten to three on a Tuesday. Before Eda had disowned her, Ursula had taken her to Xpressions for a shampoo and set every Tuesday at three. God alone knew what her mother's hair must looked like now, as Eda hadn't seen the inside of the hair salon since her release from the hospital three weeks earlier.

Ursula stood on the welcome mat, heart racing, a river of denial forcing her to try the key again. The lock most certainly was no longer a match for her key.

Ursula snatched the knocker and pounded with short, sharp strokes. The house of her childhood, normally so welcoming and sweet (if damp), seemed to mock her with every moment of silence that passed. Ursula stepped gingerly around a tree of nettles and peered through the net curtains at the darkened front room. A teacup sat atop a doily on the coffee table. Her eyes widened as they took in the halter tops and hooded jumpers flung over the settee, the glossy celebrity magazines strewn on the carpeting, the rolling papers and empty lager tins scattered across the end tables. Their presence screamed Dymphna and Eoin. Ursula winced as a throbbing in her temples threatened to overwhelm.

She heaved her body over, grasping the flap of the letterbox, and peered into the hallway.

"*Mammy!*" Ursula called through the letterbox. "*Mammy! Mammy!*"

She hauled out her mobile and punched in Eda's number.

"The British Telecom customer you are trying to call has had their number switched to ex-directory ..."

Unlisted! Ursula staggered down the steps towards her Lexus and sat in furious silence on the Coach leather, staring with dismay at her twisted features in the rear view mirror. Not a pretty sight, but a sight better than that face with which she was about to greet Eda in Xpressions. She revved up, and the car roared through the city walls.

£ £ £ £

It was as if his auntie Ursula had tiptoed into their front room, bent over the settee and snatched a fistful of notes from his mother's open handbag!

Padraig, still shuddering at the indignity of it all as only the very young can, banged on the McDaid letterbox and stood back, nervous on the front step. He hid the carrier bag demurely behind his back, the bottles banging against his calves. Mrs. McDaid pried the door open a crack, and her eyes hardened.

"What the feck are ye blackening wer doorstep for?" she barked, wiping away a stray hair.

"Is Declan in, hi? Can he come out?"

"Naw, he kyanny. He's after being picked up by the peelers and hauled off to the station for setting light to that post office on the Lecky Road. I don't suppose ye had a hand with that?" She glared at him with suspicion.

"N-naw," Padraig said. Mrs. McDaid seemed to believe him; even a Bogside wane couldn't lie that well.

"Yer broller Eoin," she said, "he's not with the Filth, is he? A bit of a Proddy lover?"

"N-naw," Padraig said, confused.

She seemed unconvinced, then sighed.

"Clear on off outta here, then, ye manky rowdie! Ye're making me late for me shift at the packing plant!"

Mrs. McDaid slammed the door in his startled face. Padraig stood alone amongst the overgrown front garden with his bag of petrol bombs. Whereas once he had been reluctant to cause harm to others, to go against the teachings of the Church, he now thanked Declan for giving him the method and means of retribution. The fact that his mate was at that moment helping the police with their enquiries didn't deter him from his plans at hand. His hatred for Ursula welled. Padraig turned, Top-Yer-Trolly bag swinging, and headed off alone to the Barnetts.

£ £ £ £

Ursula burst into Xpressions, catching sight of Dymphna on the bench at the window. The slapper was flicking through a *Woman's Weekly* with not a care in the world, Siofra chomping on a biscuit at her side. They smirked into their cups of tea as their aunt entered.

"Ursula!" Molly said with a turn, curling tongs in hand, slight annoyance in her smile.

"Where's me mammy?" Ursula demanded over the blare of Radio One and a lone blow-dryer.

The junior stylists all stiffened in their poses around the clientele. Pensioners in smocks and highlight caps and tinfoil wraps turned their heads. Dymphna leapt up and took a defiant step towards her aunt.

"Who's doing me moller's hair?" Ursula demanded.

The dryer was silenced. A junior stylist slunk guiltily against the relaxers.

"None of yer effin business!" Dymphna jumped in, pulling herself up to her full height and glowering over Ursula.

Molly scurried over, uttering a vaguely worried "Ursula ..."

"Tell me where she is!" Ursula roared into Dymphna's sneering face. "Or by God I'll clatter the—"

"She's in the loo," Molly hissed with a quick nod to the back of the salon. "Ursula, we don't want any boller—"

"Yer mammy put ye up to this!" Ursula tore into Dymphna. "Changing the locks on 5 Murphy, refusing me access to me own house, changing the phone number, confusing an aul pensioner 85 years of age who hasn't a clue what's going on in the world!"

"Ach, sure, don't get yer knickers in a twist, Ursula," Dymphna smirked. "Ye—"

"Me *knickers?!* I wear em at least, ye shameless slapper! Yers is around yer ankles in the car park of the Top-Yer-Trolly more times than not!"

"Eff off, ye boggin aul geebag, ye!"

Ursula rose her hand to clatter Dymphna, handbag swinging from her elbow.

"Calm you down now, Ursula," Molly said firmly, grabbing Ursula's arm and pulling her towards the manicure table.

Ursula shook Molly off and barreled into her niece.

"Moving ye into wer house—*my* house! Flimmin squatters! And the nerve of ye, kidnapping yer granny and dragging the poor aul wan *here*, to me very own hairdressers!"

Eda shuffled out of the loo, the roar of the toilet in her wake, hand clutching the wall for support. In her blue smock, heating cap still on her head, lips parting at the sight of Ursula scuffling with Molly, Eda bent her head in guilt. Ursula cast a withering look at the perm rods sticking out of her mother's skull and whipped around to Dymphna.

"Perming yer poor granny's head!" she gasped.

It had been increasingly difficult for a woman on the wrong side of middle age to maintain a sense of dignity simply struggling through the streets of Derry, overflowing as they were with pale faces screaming their youth out at her every waking hour. To put on a spectacle, however, in front of the young staff of Xpressions, and the bother she was giving Molly who was always so supportive of her, shamed Ursula to no end. But there stood Eda, not a loyal bone in her body, and she had to be confronted, had to be shown up for the traitor she was.

"Why didn't ye wait for me to take ye to get yer wash and set?" Ursula demanded of her mother. "Why did ye change the locks on wer house on me?

Why did ye change yer phone number? How could ye move the likes of them-muns into wer house?"

Eda gaped at her blankly. Ursula wanted to grab hold of those shoulders and shake Eda until she saw sense rise in those milky blue eyes.

"Am ringing 999!" wailed Dymphna, reaching for her mobile, but her battery was dead.

"Leave me granny be!" sobbed Siofra, scampering over and grabbing Ursula's leg.

"Get offa me, wane!" Ursula warned, kicking herself free. Siofra tumbled to the black and white tiles and burst into tears, her cassette walkman skirting across the floor.

Mouths gaped above smocks. Molly reached for the phone to finish off the job Dymphna had started. Ursula gasped.

They were all against her, the old ones in their blue rinses, the junior stylists with their crimpers, her rowdy nieces, her friend Molly, and even her mother. Especially her mother. That betrayal grieved her heart most of all.

Ursula sensed she had done enough damage for a lifetime. She was never to receive the answers to the many questions she had for her mother behaving as she was. She had to make her exit, and swiftly.

"Put you the phone down, Molly," Ursula sighed. "Am leaving."

Molly's index finger hesitated before the final "9," and just seeing that hesitation in her mate brought Ursula at last to her senses. She didn't even know what she had been planning on doing with Eda once she got her home anyway, her hair half permed. To have it out with her, she supposed, but what if Eda wouldn't even allow her into the house?

"Am leaving, I've said," Ursula insisted.

Molly placed the phone back into its cradle with obvious relief, and disappointed clucks rang out the length of the salon.

As the door slammed behind her and she breathed in the blustery Derry air, Ursula imagined she could hear the howls of cruel laughter directed at her back, the young ones with the hand held blowdryers sticking the boot in her gut when she was down. She stumbled on the pavement and gazed around wildly, unable to remember for the life of her where she had parked her car.

£ £ £ £

"Mingin aul wrinklie!"

Eoin's best mates Charlie and Sean had just terrorized a pensioner at the ATM next to the Top-Yer-Trolly, threatening his eyeballs with a sharpened screwdriver and snatching the twenty pound notes out of his hand. Charlie had given the pensioner a kick for good measure, then they were off, sniggering down the cobblestones with the cash for another round of chemical love.

"Ye think Eoin's at the Craglooner?" Sean asked, slipping the screwdriver in the pocket of his Umbro windbreaker.

"He's never out of it, sure," Charlie replied.

"Naw!" Sean said, gripping Charlie's arm and pointing up to the city walls. "There's yer man now!"

A tin of lager in his hand, Eoin slouched against a cannon with a man in a purple track suit and loads of gold chains around his neck. Charlie's eyes narrowed. What was their drug dealer doing nattering away with the most obvious undercover copper in the city?

Playing back the tape he had made in the McDaid's sitting room, that's what. Eoin clicked off the cassette player.

"That's worth a couple of tenners, hi?" Eoin asked, hope in his eyes.

"Fifty pee, more like!" the man in purple and gold said. "You've nothing on that tape but them denying any involvement in the Cause, sure!"

"At least ye know I've been doing the work am meant to do," Eoin said.

"It's specific information we're after, stockpiling locations, references to involvement in past bombings, assorted offences against the Kingdom and the like. I thought the Special Branch made this clear to you when they picked you up and hauled you off the oller week?" He peered more closely at Eoin's ruddy eyes. "Or are you too arsified on them drugs to comprehend? Or too bloody thick?"

"Ehm, urgh," Eoin replied, his mind racing.

"You've two weeks to supply us with some tidbits of intelligence, or you're to be hauled into the cop shop and sent down to Magilligan for drug dealing! You can get a cell next to your broller."

Eoin took a deep breath as a sudden idea entered in skull.

"Are youse interested in aul information as well?" he asked.

"What are you on about?"

"Would youse be satisfied with information on unsolved crimes from years back?"

"Aye!"

"Me auntie …"

Eoin had loved Ursula dearly as a wane, but she was now a changed woman, the scorn of all Derry. He couldn't pry anything out of the McDaids, but he could string up his auntie Ursula for her past sins, her involvement in the Cause. Maybe then his daddy would let him back into the family home.

"Back in '73, ye mind them two weemin who ..."

"Aye? Aye?!"

Eoin shook his head. It was too early to betray Ursula; she was still family, after all. He hadn't quite reached that level of desperation. Not quite.

"Naw, nothing," he said.

The undercover copper was staring at him as if he were off his head. Which maybe he was.

Off in the corner, Charlie and Sean's stomachs turned as they watched Eoin shake hands with Lucifer. They would be taking their business elsewhere, the fecking Orange-arse licking traitor!

£ £ £ £

Ursula flung her shaken self into the house, all set to unload on Jed a day's worth of betrayal and heartache, but his flushed and angry face immediately put her on guard. In his hand was a document, the formality of which filled her with dread.

"You'll never believe what those idiot Floods have gone and done!" he said, waving the paper.

Ursula settled her handbag and reached out. She scanned the print.

"What's this?" she asked, struggling to comprehend the legalese. "Prohibitive Steps Order?"

"A temporary injunction barring us—*you!*—from 5 Murphy Crescent."

"Five Murphy? That's me own house, but!"

Her eyes fluttered to the bottom of the page. *Sworn to me this day by Eda Flood* it stated quite clearly.

"Them squiggles at the bottom doesn't be me mammy's signature!"

She read on from the top nevertheless.

"Since her lotto win ... daughter ... lunatic ... forced me to sell house to her ... roaring abuse ... my own house ... prisoner ... angina ... weak heart ... forces herself through front door ... all hours of day and night ... osteoporosis ... frail bones ... terrible afeared at the sound of the key in the front door ...

husband Jed Barnet barges in at whim ... in my dressing gown.... the stench of drink off him ... touching me in an improper manner ..."

She put down the document, bewildered.

"Me mammy would never say such things!" she said.

"They couldn't even spell our last name correctly."

Ursula's eyes flashed with understanding.

"That Fionnuala and Paddy put her up to this! Am after coming from 5 Murphy now, and do ye know the flimmin lock's already changed, and me mammy's got a new phone number and all. Why are we only getting word of this now?"

"It's dated two weeks ago," Jed said. He nodded to the envelope. "They sent it to the wrong address."

Jed had braced himself for her roars of outrage. Ursula implored up at him instead with shattered eyes and defeated shoulders.

"What am I meant to do now?" she asked dimly.

"Maybe we should phone a solicitor? I know you have joint ownership of the house with Eda, but that was only a technicality because she's lived there for so long. I'm sure they can't forbid you from going into your own house. And I'm not even going to begin discussing a defamation of character suit! Touching her in an improper manner, my ass!"

Ursula sank to the refectory crate and cradled her head, the sobs rising through her fingers.

"Why did I fork out all them pound notes?" she cried.

"Yes, dear—"

"Why did I remodel the house?

"Honey—"

"I didn't do it for any recognition. I piggin well did it because I love her."

"Let me see if I can get a lawyer on the phone," Jed said, scuttling uncomfortably off to the phone.

She heard him babbling down the line in the foyer, then lifted her head. She got up to straighten out the Venetian blinds, and through the window she caught a glint of red fluttering across their driveway beside the wheelie bins Jed had left out for the next morning's rubbish collection.

Ursula hurried outside to investigate, and goggled down at Padraig, calm as you like, with three petrol bombs lined up on the pavement, flicking a match against the box.

"Mary moller of God!" Ursula gasped.

Flames poured from a dishrag, and Padraig threw his arm back to pelt the flaming bottle at their bay window.

"We hate ye, we hate ye, ye bitch!" he squealed.

"Clear on off outta here, ye bad wee brute, ye!"

"Get offa me Ursula!"

—there was a flash of speeding orange metal, the squeal of brakes, the shriek of rubber, the crunch of wee bones as Padraig's body flipped over the car hood and disappeared from view.

The car door flew open, and out clambered none other than Mrs. Feeney, safety belt snapping from her body, face ashen. She took an anxious step onto the gravel and a tentative peek over the hood of her Saab.

"Jesus, Mary and Joseph!" she whispered, finger kneading the crucifix that hung across a display of spidery veins.

"Mrs. Feeney! Am terrible sorry!"

Ursula rushed to her side. The fear in Mrs. Feeney dissolved. She set her jowls, eyes like sharpened blades.

"Ursula Barnett!" Mrs. Feeney harrumphed, wrapping her cardigan around her. "I mighta known you would've had a hand in this!"

"It's me nephew," Ursula explained. "He just ran out into the road."

"That bloody wee effin hooligan brute!" Mrs. Feeney roared. "For the love of God, how am I meant to drive responsibly with piggin stokes crawling up from hell and flinging themselves across the street? Darting in and outta the traffic like manky dogs without a home! Answer me that, will ye?"

Both were lingering on the passenger side of the car, putting off the inevitable: the sight of the carnage on the blacktop beyond.

"Padraig!" Ursula called fearfully over the hood, her legs unable to make the trip around the fender. "Are ye right there, love?"

Two little hands, blood-free, crept onto the hood. Then Padraig's scowling, hate-filled head popped into sight, spitting, "Feck you, Ursula!"

The two adversaries, relieved, rounded the car, Mrs. Feeney inspecting her car for damage. But Padraig was already away, not a bruise on him, the picture of health, roaring abuse and flipping them off.

"Are ye right, love, are ye right?" Ursula kept yelling tears welling, lower lip trembling, as the child raced off.

"It would appear so," Mrs. Feeney snorted. "The hood of me motor might not be so lucky, but."

"Ach, maybe it's right as rain," Ursula said, hopeful.

More would be the pity, Mrs. Feeney's face said.

£ £ £ £

Dymphna dismounted the mini-bus and crept through the city streets, mortified in her purple and brown uniform festooned with camels and wee pyramids. She was just passing the Top-Yer-Trolly with something approaching wistfulness when she collided with Mr. O'Toole. He stared her strange outfit up and down and couldn't control his glee.

"I see ye've found anoller employer fool enough to take ye on," Mr. O'Toole greeted her. "It beggars belief!"

"Piss off, ye narky toerag!"

Mr. O'Toole kept his ready smirk.

"Any bars, hi?" he asked brightly.

"Aye, stacks of bars. Am up the scoot, if ye must know!" Dymphna hissed. "And ye're the faller."

"Catch yerself on," he snorted, not missing a beat.

"It's the God's honest truth!"

"Ach, ye've spread yer legs for every shelf stacker of the Top-Yer-Trolly, and for three-quarters of the men under fifty in wer city and all. Ye must think am terrible daft. Ye kyanny saddle me with this. Them sausingers ye were nicking, mind, that's an offense worthy of getting the coppers involved. Wan flick of me mobile phone, and ye could be hauled away. You'd be hard-pressed to find a fella in this town willing to take ye down the aisle with a criminal record to yer name."

Dymphna snorted. What wee girl in that town *didn't* have a criminal record? Mr. O'Toole inspected his manicured nails.

"Denying yer responsibilities, then?" she asked. "And threatening me and all?"

Mr. O'Toole tutted sadly, then shooed her with his hand.

"On yer way, ye mingin slapper, ye!"

He skipped into the store.

Dymphna resisted the urge to spit on the back of his suit. She turned and flounced down the cobblestones, thoughts of revenge crowding her raging mind.

£ £ £ £

"What's that smell?" Jed asked once Ursula entered the lounge. "Did you have a problem putting gas in the car again? I told you to let the attendants do it for you!"

"That Padraig was here, trying to petrolbomb the house!"

Jed went to the window and peered through the big bands of vertical blinds. A plume of smoke still rolled from the wheelie bin. The bottles had clattered to the grating, the petrol having disappeared into Derry's sewage system.

Jed's shock slipped into quiet rage.

"Where's the little bastard now?" he demanded.

"I clattered him across the head and he ran off into the road and into Mrs. Feeney's front fender."

"What? We're calling the police," he decided.

"Naw, naw!" Ursula gasped, grabbing his hand that was already reaching for the phone. "We kyanny get the peelers involved!"

"Why not?" he asked, staring down at the receiver as if it were his only refuge from lunacy.

"Ye know bloody well why not! Am a Catholic from the Bogside. And Padraig's me nephew, family. I'll never hear the end of it if we involve the coppers, never be able to hold me head up. Fully nine-tenths of the coppers is Proddy bastards. It'll be the end of me life here in Derry."

"You've got to be joking," Jed replied. He suspected her life in that city had already ended the moment the lucky numbers had fallen. How could Ursula not see it herself?

"Am dead serious," Ursula said, glaring at him to both contradict and complete his phone call.

"This is ridiculous." And this from a man who thought little in the world was ridiculous. But he placed the phone back in its cradle.

He hadn't married lower in life; he had grown up in poverty. Ursula came from the same of the damaged poor, but the Floods were proving a different breed, the politics of poverty quickly degenerating into the politics of envy (and now it seemed the politics of envy were turning into the hooliganism of envy). In Jed's eye, almost anybody he came into contact with in Derry, from the barmaid down the pub to the lowlifes in the bookies were stuck in a society where every pence piece was duly accounted for, every pound coin envied.

"... and now she kyanny bear to look at me," Ursula was saying softly, sitting on the sofa and staring into space.

Jed came over to her.

"Ye're on me side, aren't ye?" Ursula asked, but this time there was an upward inflection to her question tag.

For once in her life, Ursula truly didn't know an answer to one of her own questions. Her eyes stared up at him, searching, beseeching support. She reached out to him with her hands, those same hands that had changed the diapers of his children, clutched his own proudly during his promotion ceremonies. The nails were now bitten to the quick, fingers worn with the passage of the years. Her slight frame might now be straining under the weight gained, yet those fingers still maintained their familiar gracefulness. The wedding band was now tarnished, the frail bones of the hand straining against flesh once so smooth.

Condescending, over-opinionated, headstrong, infuriatingly self-righteous, even: Ursula had been all those things and more since he had carried her over the threshold. He had learned how to put up with her nagging throughout the decades of marriage, but now those goddamned Floods were changing his wife. The feisty Ursula that had always been was now in danger of being obscured by a simpering mess unsure of her every move. Much to his own surprise, Jed realized he didn't want a kinder, gentler Ursula. He wanted the infuriating shrew he had married.

Jed felt his anger veer from his wife and barrel towards her family. He had been counting down the days until his departure, but he now realized circumstances had intervened, and he would never take that flight of fantasy to the creature comforts of Wisconsin. That evening he had arrived at a different world, a place where flight was no longer an option.

"Now," Jed said in a moment of sacrifice, his triumphant homecoming to Wisconsin fading into a pipedream, "I am."

COMPENSATION

8

Moira, the eldest Flood daughter, gawked at her father over the dinner table as if he had just demanded she prance stone bollocks naked before the Bleeding Heart of Jesus above the fireplace.

"Ye kyanny be serious!" she gawped. "Ye had me rushed over from Malta to help ye out, like, and haven't I been help enough? Filling out them compensation papers, getting ye Legal Aid for a case that surely would've been thrown out of court without me help? Ye've already a protective steps order in place, barring wer Ursula from entering a house she owns."

"Ach, what's the sense in having a sister win the lotto if we kyanny squeeze her for all she's worth?" Paddy roared through a mouth stuffed with cabbage. "She's minted, the bitch! Minted!"

The Floods were never in the habit of ringing Moira as it was a long-distance call and she was a filthy perv. But as Roisin was back in Hawaii, the man of the house had been at his wit's end as to how to proceed. As the first-born daughter, Moira was the only one blessed with an education, and although she had struggled to pass her finals and had barely qualified for her job as a health and safety inspector, she was the family intellectual, the only one of the lot who wouldn't spend their life ringing up steak and kidney pies or drawing the brew. So Paddy had demanded she race home.

Flanked in a leather peacoat and austere jumper, a pair of dour spectacles jammed on the bridge of her nose, Moira had been terrible handy, but now her daddy wanted more.

She had helped them batter Padraig around a bit to make his injuries worse than they were, and that had been bad enough—Moira hadn't been able to look the doctors at Altnagelvin in the eye—but now they were expecting her to cross the line even further. With Lily McCracken, of all people!

"Get you up to that hospital again and do as you're tole!" Paddy growled.

"The tears of joy should be fairly lashing down yer face," Fionnuala warned, "for the chance to help the family out. Ye should be grateful we can look ye in the eye, even, the disgrace ye've brought upon wer good name!"

"But—"

"Yer sins of the flesh have barred ye eternally from the pearly gates, but ye can still use em to help feed yer family!"

"What youse are asking me to do, but ..." Moira pleaded. "Haven't youse evidence enough? If the peelers were to find out, it'll be *me* that gets sent down! Have ye any clue what them in the nick do to health and safety inspectors?"

"As if the goings on in a weemin's prison cell block wouldn't be heaven on earth for the likes of you!" Fionnuala snarled.

Moira wilted.

"Am only stating the bleedin obvious here!" Fionnuala snapped, daring her daughter to contradict.

Moira helplessly inspected her plate of ham hocks.

"But me and Lily ... We've not been togeller since—"

All eyes looked up from their plates, including those of the youngest wanes gobbling down on the sitting room carpet before the telly.

"What's Moira on about, Mammy?" Seamus asked.

A throbbing lacerated Fionnuala's heaving brain. She brought a trembling hand to her forehead.

"Turn that flippin telly up now!" Fionnuala barked at her two youngest. "See if I haveta tell youse again, ye're gonny be eating that cabbage through bleedin arseholes!"

Seamus and Siofra stared up in alarm, Siofra struggling to recall when her mother had become riveted by Bob the Builder. But she did as instructed until the cartoon character's voice shuddered from the speakers. Fionnuala pointed accusingly at Siofra.

"And you, wee girl, learn that effin Act of Contrition by heart, or yer teeth are to be gnawing on yer small intestine! We're gonny be at the church in half an hour!"

Siofra turned to her My First Missal, the spine of which had yet to be cracked.

"Listen to me, wee girl" Paddy said finally to Moira. "If you don't get yer pervy arse up to Altnagelvin, am gonny be telling all me mates on the dart team what filthy deeds that Lily McCracken gets up to, and heaven help her any time wan of them chances upon her when they're wheeled into the A and E!"

He glared threateningly. Moira's mind, schooled for logic, spun at the madness of it all, but she finally gave a grudging nod.

"I'll do it, aye," she sighed.

Paddy and Fionnuala deflated with relief.

"Right girl ye are," Paddy said, stopping just short of touching her hand.

"Am clearing away the table," Fionnuala said as happily as she could, scraping her chair across the floor and marching in the scullery with a handful of plates.

There by the clotheshorse full of dripping athletic gear she attacked a fag and gobbled down some ibuprofen. Her wanes were all disgraces, she thought. Thank merciful Christ Moira had somehow persuaded the court to rush their case through the system; it was due before the magistrate in a mere three days. Then the family perv could feck off back to Malta and slurp twats to her heart's content.

Fionnuala glanced down at her pack of unfiltered Rothman's, where the government health warning screamed out at her: *Smoking Can Damage The Sperm And Decreases Fertility*. She thought of Dymphna and curled her lip. Such a pity a daughter who sucked down thirty a day hadn't been affected, nor the father, whoever in the Waterside that may be.

Fionnuala flipped over the pack and read: *Smoking When Pregnant Harms Your Baby*. She raised an eyebrow.

How to convince Dymphna to suck down forty a day …? she wondered. Well, at least that shameless tart was engaging in heterosexual activities.

Tiring of the fearful eyes inspecting her, Moira sighed and got up from the table.

"I'd best make me way up to Altnagelvin, then," she said.

"And no sins of the flesh in the labs, mind," Paddy said.

In the front hall, Moira fastened the buttons of her leather peacoat, dreading the thought of confronting Lily at the hospital and begging her former bed partner to do the madness her family demanded.

Moira dearly loved her hometown on the Foyle, but couldn't help feeling a quiet dread walking down its unenlightened streets, the same dread she felt when she thought of following her family into obscurity or notoriety. As a schoolgirl, once her lesbian tendencies had dawned on her, she knew that if she stayed in Derry, she'd be fecked, and certainly not literally. There were no gay men, let alone liberals or lesbians, in that hardened town, where every male purchase of a Kylie Minogue CD was greeted with a raised eyebrow by the shop assistant at the Top-Yer-Trolly. Moira finally realized one day she would be a shriveled old pensioner spinster before she might chance upon another lone bulldyke shuffling along to an unknown Melissa Etheridge b-side in the depths of the Craglooner. Moira had announced her plans to emigrate to university in Malta the next week. And here she was, back, dodging suspicion over plates of ham hocks and cabbage.

Moira flinched at the sudden sight of Siofra staring up at her, a startling gleam in her eyes. Siofra held up the spotless My First Missal.

"Mammy's taking me to that flash new church in Gleneagles to say me first confession. I need to cleanse me soul before I can take the body of Christ into me mouth."

"St Brigid's, ye mean? Why's she hauling ye all the way over to Gleneagles? St. Moluag's is only down the road, sure!"

"I haven't a clue. Anyroad ..." Siofra tossed aside the missal and shoved a well-worn catalog under Moira's nose. "I need this Maria Theresa gown from Italy, and this Andromeda veil on page forty-wan. Me communion's in two weeks, and ye're raking in loads over there in Malta. Mammy and Daddy are always going on about it. Ye kyanny expect me to mortify myself in that boggin frock ye had on ye years ago, sure! Ye can surely afford to get me a new outfit with all them quids ye have from been gainfully employed in a profession, like."

Moira gazed down in sudden alarm. What was her family like? Her parents had already raided her handbag the moment she had stepped off the plane.

"Moira? Four hundred quid only!" Siofra demanded.

Her weekly pay packet could be stretched only so far.

"Eoin's raking in loads from them drug deals of his," Moira said. "His pockets is bulging! Ask him, sure!"

"Aye, but ..."

Siofra felt silent. Nobody had thought to tell Moira she had handed over her big brother's stash to the coppers.

Moira buttoned her coat with finality. Siofra watched her final hope for upmarket communion gear plodding out the door with an unfurled umbrella. She threw the catalog on the floor and stomped atop it in a fit, bitter tablets being forced down her young throat at every turn where the gown was concerned. Padraig sauntered down the stairs.

"What's up with you, hi?" he asked.

"Where's yer mate Declan live?" Siofra suddenly wanted to know.

"Declan McDaid? Ye mean—?"

"Aye, the stoke who almost killed me mammy."

"Ye fancy him, do ye?"

Siofra shrugged; she'd admit to anything, no matter how grotesque. "Aye."

"It don't matter where he lives. He was hauled off to that Youthful Offenders Center in Belfast last week for torching a Post Office, sure."

"Just give us his address or am telling me mammy about them filthy websites ye visit when ye think we's all outta the house!"

Padraig dutifully recited the address. Siofra thanked him and skipped upstairs, pausing to scoop the catalog from the floor and glance lovingly at page forty one.

£ £ £ £

Was it the morning sickness or the six pints of Smithwicks she had guzzled with Bridie the night before?

Dymphna wrenched open the bog door and spewed down the toilet bowl. Her head hanging into the porcelain, Dymphna caught sight of the Rothman's still lodged in her fingers. She coughed and gulped and wiped tears from her eyes. The fag shot to her lips. She inhaled greedily.

Outside on the landing, Eda, swaddled in a pink bathrobe, floated regally down to the front hall in the luxury of her electronic chairlift. Initially she had been terrified of those journeys, but now they were the highlight of her day.

The Flood matriarch teetered under the strip lighting of the scullery for a cuppa, shuffling through the ChipKebab wrappers and staring around in dismay. Empty milk bottles littered the scullery table. Rusty tins of beans and peas, crusty socks, Boyzone fan magazines, moldy rolls and Rizla tobacco rolling papers darkened the table and its surrounding chairs. Eoin had recently begun rolling his own fags. *Them new fags of his smell wile odd*, Eda thought.

Atop the cooker splattered with chip grease and hardened cheese lumps sat pots piled up to the grill. Before the Hotpoint sat a damp pile of Eda's laundry, which Dymphna had unceremoniously tugged from the washer the night before. That had been before Eoin had burst in with tins of lager and a gang of his rowdy hooligan mates. All hours, they had been up to.

Eda lifted the countertop kettle to check the water level. Empty, of course. She hauled it over to the sink to fill it. Every piece of delft she possessed permanently resided there now, rank and fermenting and apparently awaiting the touch of her own hand to be washed. Eda maneuvered the edges of the plates to fill the tap.

The Flood matriarch sat—once again—alone in the scullery with only a cup of sweet tea and her slightly jumbled memories as company. Her lifelong home had been transformed into an after-hours honky-tonk for the stokes and the junkies of Derry City. She took a sip and shrank into herself. Fat droplets of rain shook the window.

The ceiling above her suddenly throbbed into life. The fringes of the scullery light jumped in time to the pounding bass. Eda sat in fear, a withered hand clasped to her brittle collarbone.

"Coz you're ride on time, ri-ri-ride on time! C-coz you're ride on time, ri-ri-ride on time!" screamed some colored woman from the boombox in Dymphna's bedroom.

The letterbox clanked, and Eda braced herself. She tottered uncertainly towards the door and squinted at the frosty pane. Shadowy figures lurked outside. Eda struggled to undo the locks and open the door.

"I'm a firestarter! Twisted firestarter!" roared a sudden devilish voice from the depths of Dymphna's room.

Five hardened youths clutching lager tins smirked in at her from the lashing rain. Their football jerseys and scalped heads and scarred faces revealed their profession: brew-drawing junkies. Eda set her lips. They showed up at the house at all hours of the day and night now, pushing past her and demanding their drugs. Eoin always left a stash in the calico cat on the china cabinet, and Eda had to dole them out and collect the money when her grandson wasn't home. She had already exhausted the supply Eoin had given her for the day. Eda wrapped her furry pink bathrobe around her exposed neck and peered out at them.

"Are ye right there, missus?" slurred one.

A trainer slipped into the jamb of the door. One of the lads cocked his head, mock shock on his face.

"Are ye listening to the *Prodigy*, woman?"

A reference, she supposed, to the harrowing noise that continued to blare from Dymphna's bedroom.

"At *yer* age?"

"Aye, in her early hundreds!"

"Dirty aul cunt!"

They erupted in laughter.

"Is Eoin in, hi?" asked another, teeth chattering in the driving rain.

"Youse can clear on off outta here; there's none of them filthy drugs left the day!"

"Let us in, woman!"

She was frozen in terror at her own front door, at a loss as to what to do.

"Naw! I'm not letting the likes of youse into me house!" she said, struggling to add an uncharacteristic edge to her voice.

"Sure, it's pelting down, woman!" cried one. "Ye're to let us in before we catch wer deaths!"

Eda knew the type: those who wouldn't take no for an answer. They would sully her doorstep until she filled their pockets with Ecstasy. Although she was hard pressed to recall what her name was, it came to her that there was an emergency stash hidden under the mountain of soiled undies in Eoin's bedroom.

"I'll go fetch youse some," Eda relented. "Youse're not to step wan foot in, or am gonny be calling 999!"

"Crabbit aul bitch!"

Filthy mingin rowdies.

Eda mounted her beloved chairlift with as much dignity as she could muster and located the *Up* button.

"Merciful Christ! The aul slapper has a bleedin fecking funfair in her house, so she does!" came from the crack of the door.

Eda fought back the tears as roars of laughter echoed up the stairs.

"Ye got a rollercoaster in there as well, missus?"

As she inched full of fraught towards the landing, a hand slipped through the door and smacked the rosary beads hanging on the hallway stand.

"Leave me rosary be, youse!" she implored.

Guffaws erupted anew.

"Dymphna! Dymphna!" she wailed, but the radio drowned her cries.

Captive halfway up the staircase, Eda pushed frantically at button after button to get some speed. Both the chairlift and her body shuddered, wheezed, then ground to a halt.

"Feck this for a game of soldiers. Am ravenous. Let's see what the aul cunt's got in the fridge."

The door flew open and in they trailed, dripping, through the front hall and into the scullery to rampage.

"Out! Outta me house, youse!" Eda squealed.

The old woman attacked the gadgety buttons with her claw, scraping and pounding at their confusing technology. A fuzzy slipper shot from her foot and pirouetted down the stairs. The chair lurched to life, mechanical malfunction spinning out of control, swiveling sharply to the right, pounding her into the wall again and again, Eda's heart rattling against her breastbone.

"Tins of Smithwick!" came from the kitchen. "Fecking dead on!"

"Mary moller of God! Help me, youse!" Eda screamed through clacking dentures, grappling the armrests and careening forward as she plowed into the wall in a jerking, ever increasing frenzy. Half her joints locked, the other half jittered. Clanking and crashing roared from the scullery.

"Help me, dear Lord! Help me!"

But the Lord was busy elsewhere.

£ £ £ £

"Don't get riled when you're up there in that dock, whatever you do," Ms. Murphy said in the offices of McMurphy & Hennessey. The solicitor flashed Ursula a look of warning.

Ursula was taken aback. This jumped-up wee start, fresh out of McGee University with a diploma under her arm and the attitude to match, telling her elders how to behave! As if she knew all about the world, and her with the spots still cluttering her face!

"That wee hooligan Padraig Flood tried to set me house ablaze, and am expected to keep calm?" Ursula snorted. "Can ye tell me how?"

"I don't know how, but just make sure you do. Roaring about the plaintiffs to the magistrates won't do you any favors."

"A fine lot of help you are," Ursula snorted. "For all the pounds we've thrown at ye, ye could at least give us some advice."

"I just have, Mrs ..." she quickly consulted a paper in her hand. "Barnett."

"I was wanting somewan with a bit more experience," Ursula announced with a harrumph. "Not some wane barely outta diapers. No offense, mind."

"I can assure you I am fully qualified to present yer case," Ms. Murphy said with prickly insistence.

"Honey," Jed said, gently touching Ursula's elbow.

Ursula shook it off and barreled into him: "It's not you that's to be mortified in the dock, strung up and made an example of for all the world to see! I wouldn't mind all this palaver, but I kyanny even reap the benefits of the money no more as ye've guzzled it all down yer throat and rammed it into slot machines!"

"Ursula!" Jed protested, shooting Ms. Murphy a mortified look.

Ms. Murphy was realizing well enough why the whole world seemd to have ganged up against her client. Ursula Barnett didn't do herself any favors, she thought. Prickly and defensive, a minefield of exposed nerves waiting for the unsuspecting to trod upon. She decided to let Ursula stew in her bitterness, and turned brightly to Jed.

"Now, then, Mr. Barnett, shall we not review the facts of the case?"

As they huddled over some documents, Ursula felt a buzzing against her thigh that made her shriek. It was her mobile, set to vibrate, and nagging out at her was Roisin's number.

Her heart jumped with hope eternal. Perhaps her sister was calling to apologize, to show support, to tell Ursula everything would work out for the best. She flipped open the phone. Jed cast a glance at his watch and motioned with his hands to wrap it up quickly. Ursula shot him a filthy look, then turned her attention to the phone, pipedreams dancing.

"Roisin?" Ursula whispered uncertainly.

"Ye hateful boggin clarty effin cunt ye!" Roisin roared. "What the feck do ye think ye're playing at? Am just after hearing ye tried to murder wer Padraig! Ye never learn, do ye? I've half a mind to take the next flight back to Derry and rip the bloody limbs from ye—"

Ursula snapped her phone shut with shuddering fingers.

Ms. Murphy studied Ursula anew. She had heard every word of the abuse; it would have been difficult not to.

"Ye see the persecution am expected to endure on a daily basis?" Ursula pleaded.

"Have you been receiving many such calls?" Ms. Murphy asked.

"Ach, their fingers is bloody from punching me number into their mobiles, sure. All hours of the day and night they call, me broller Stephen from New Zealand, me sister Cait from Gibraltar, I've even me nephew Lorcan phoning me from the nick, roaring abuse down the line at me!"

"Have they been threatening you in any way?"

"Ach, aye, crucified to no end, I've been," Ursula said. "C'mere till I tell ye the clever ways themmuns have tole me am meant to meet me end." She counted them out on her fingers. "Me head's to be shoved into a bubbling chip fryer, me body's to be drawn and quartered by four separate lorries on the Strand, tarred and feallered in the city square and me body tugged up on a pulley to the top of the Guildhall for all to see ... shall I go on?"

There was silence, and even Ms. Murphy seemed to blanch. Finally, Ms. Murphy spoke.

"Your extended family seems to have embarked on a well-orchestrated campaign of harassment. Might I suggest we lay a complaint? File a counter-suit?"

Ursula's shoulders showed her resignation.

"I'd never drag them through the courts they way they're doing me. We kyanny extradite me sister Roisin from Hawaii anyroad. Even when I found out me sister-in-law had been claiming me caretaker's allowance for ages, I kept a wide berth from the courts. Maybe they hate me; they're me family but. All am wanting is that damn injunction lifted so's I can visit me moller and be sure the aul wan's fine."

Her voice trembled, and her eyes welled with tears. Ms. Murphy felt her heart turning as she handed the poor woman a tissue.

"How did I know it would come to this," Ursula sobbed into the tissue. "With us at opposite ends of a courtroom, like?"

Jed looked down anxiously at his watch and tried to will Ursula's tears away. He knew the situation was difficult, but if only his wife could cry about it when they were out on the street; every extra minute in the solicitor's office was depleting their already ravaged bank account.

Ursula's mobile rang again, and they all jumped. Ursula regarded it with trepidation, thinking Roisin had speed-dialed for more abuse. It was an unknown number, however.

"I'll answer it if you want, dear," Jed said.

Ursula shook her head as she dried her eyes. "Ye never know, it might be Francine or Molly or Mrs. Gee or maybe even Faller Hogan calling to say they're to be character witnesses after all," she said. They had all declined, claiming a wide array of sudden illnesses.

She flipped open the phone and whispered into it:

"Aye?"

"Ursula?"

It was her niece Moira's voice. Ursula tensed, but she was now prepared. She wouldn't be made an idiot of again.

"And what do *you* want?" she growled.

"Am on me way to Altnagelvin now. Am only ringing to let ye know what me moller—"

"Have they shipped ye over from Malta to torture me heart?" Ursula roared down the line. "I caught ye outta the corner of me eye down the Richmond Center days ago!"

"Naw, Ursula!" Moira tried to interject, hurt. "Am on yer—"

"Ye mingin filthy perv, ye!"

"I just wanted to—"

"You and yer kind is a disgrace to the human race!" Ursula barreled on like a bulldog. "Get yerself back to Malta and give me head's peace!"

"Ye've got it wrong—"

"Ach, go and lap up some twats, you!"

Ms. Murphy reeled in her empathy with crisp professionalism and snapped a glance at her watch. Ursula slammed the mobile on the table with a high-pitched squeal. Jed massaged her shoulder helplessly. She knocked his hand away.

"Am a right aul eejit sure enough," Ursula sniffed. "Thinking it might be Francine or Molly. Themmuns have been steering clear of me ever since all this here foolish carry-on began."

Her circle of friends now numbered one, and that one was herself.

"We'd best be on our way," Ms. Murphy said briskly.

Jed was only too happy to vacate the premises.

"You're not gonna charge us for the full hour, are you?" he asked hopefully.

£ £ £ £

Fionnuala high-stepped through the nave door of St. Brigid's Church with a Jackie O-type wee veiled hat on her head, Siofra festooned in rosary beads trailing behind her. Fionnuala felt it her God-given right to sneak her wane into a neighboring parish to celebrate her First Penance. Going to Father Hogan at St. Moluag's was out of the question.

Sure, she thought grimly, he knew all their voices, and those latticed screens were no help at all in hiding her face, and what with her great-uncle being a bishop and all …

As Fionnuala stepped further into St. Brigid's luxurious depths, she felt a twitch of irritation. This flash new church was wild modern, designed by some postmodern architect twats for those who could afford to live in the area, while her desperate lot in the Bogside were saddled with the threadbare pews and leaking holy water fonts of St. Moluag's Chapel.

"Sit you there," she hissed at Siofra, pushing her into one of the many empty pews. "While yer mammy goes and cleanses her soul first."

Fionnuala adjusted the veil to shield her features, then disappeared into the darkness of the confessional.

Siofra sat alone in the hush, twisting at the strings of rosaries she had flung around her neck. Just like, she thought, that teetery old hag Madonna in some ancient video her mammy had forced her to watch on the telly. The rosaries, however, made her feel glamorous amongst the saints.

"Bless me faller, for I have sinned," Fionnuala hissed into the darkness and the vague face beyond. "It's been ... some time ... since me last confession. I've been busy with the wanes, like."

"Good on ye for coming back after all this time," the priest said in a soothing tone.

"C'mere till I tell ye, faller," she began. "I've such terrible sins to reveal, am in a right state, pure shattered."

His eyes flickered with interest beyond the latticework. Fionnuala thought it better to start out with a few inconsequential sins and work her way up.

"I've clattered the wanes, and I've taken the Lord's name in vain. And when me sister-in-law was over from Hawaii, I nicked fifty quid from her handbag. And am having impure thoughts about me oller sister-in-law's exotic Yank fella when me own husband's snoring away in a drunken stupor on the pillow next to me. It's been going on ever since yer man won the lotto. When we were going out celebrating all them nights, I found me fingers sneaking many times towards his thigh."

The priest's eyes widened with interest ...

"And I force me pregnant daughter to lift the family dinner from her place of work, and I've a lad dealing drugs in all the pubs of Derry—he's an informer for the peelers and all—and we've gone and banished themmuns to me moller-in-law's house. I only agreed to it as am certain me lad's the faller of me daughter's wane, and so I kyanny abide the sight of em, and am hoping the strain of living with the two useless pervs puts me moller-in-law in an early grave."

... and with shock.

"For months now I've been doing me best to kill me moller-in-law off, ye see, faller. At first it was so'se we could buy her house off the city council for a bomb, like. Then me sister-in-law went and bought the house for herself, the bitch. So now am trying to send me moller-in-law to a long overdue grave now purely as she does me head in, the blathering aul eejit. Am meant to make the tea for her every now and again; more times than not, I visit me sister Maire instead and leave the pensioner to fend for herself, gnawing away at her fingernails for sustenance and all the while am hoping against all hopes she'll perish from the starvation. When the guilt gets the better of me, I do rouse meself out of a notion of Christian kindness to stick two bread slices togeller for her with a slab of ham in between; I fairly pile on the salt, but, huge heaping mounds of it, for am hoping it'll clog her arteries and send her into anabolic shock."

Fionnuala stopped to catch her breath as she heard the priest wriggling on the other side, his lips puckered tightly to avoid an unchristian outburst. Fionnuala fiddled with her veil.

"I can see ye peering through them wee holes at me, faller, trying to make out the details of me face. Confessions is meant to be anonymous, ye know."

The eyes snapped away into the darkness. There was a pause as pregnant as Fionnuala's daughter.

"Have ye more sins to reveal, me child?" the priest asked almost fearfully.

Fionnuala searched her mind.

"Now that ye mention it, faller, aye I have. We're hauling me sister-in-law before the magistrates for a crime she didn't commit. And we're doing it just to reap the compensation money from her, tight-fisted cunt that she is. She won that lotto and gave us nothing but three Game Boys for seven wanes to share, a tanning booth, a padded loo seat and a bloody useless karaoke machine. And that's it faller, the extent of me sins."

She waited tersely for a response.

"And are ye sorry for these … many sins?"

"Aye, am are!" Fionnuala barked out mechanically.

"Then ye're absolved of all of em," he said.

Fionnuala deflated with relief.

"Considering the grievous nature of yer sins, but," he continued, "for yer penance, ye're to pray the Rosary."

"Steady on there, faller," Fionnuala protested. "Ye kyanny mean twenty times the ten Hail Marys and twenty Our Fallers and twenty Glory Bes?"

"I can mean just that," he said. "And more than that, I want ye to pray the Rosary at each of the fourteen Stations of the Cross in wer chapel."

"*At each of the …??!*" Her mind struggled to compute just how many prayers that would be, but soon gave up. "I'll be at it for piggin hours! Surely ye kyanny expect me to …?"

Silence reigned. He did, seemingly, expect her to do just that.

Fionnuala took a deep breath and rattled off with resignation: "Oh my God, I am heartily sorry for all me sins because they offend thee. Thou art so good and with Thy help I will not sin again. Amen."

"Go in peace and … sin no more," he said, like telling an alkie to lay off the drink.

"Right ye are, faller," Fionnuala snapped. "The next in's to be me wee girl who's making her first confession. Ye're not to be making that wan heart-scared, ye hear me?"

Fionnuala stomped from the confessional and shoved Siofra into the depths.

"Good luck to ye in there with that wan, wane," she said, and stomped off towards the First Station of the Cross, Jesus Is Condemned to Die, knowing exactly how He felt. She unearthed a string of rosaries from some unknown depth of her handbag, muttering expletives to herself.

"Good evening, me child," Father Bryant said to the wee girl, relieved to have an innocent soul after the hardened transgressor that was her mother.

"Bless me faller, for I have sinned," Siofra began tentatively. "It's me first confession."

"Aye?" Father Bryant said gently.

"I peeled away the wallpaper in the front room and …"

Siofra felt his eyes inspecting her in the darkness. She gripped the bottom of the cross dangling from her rosary and hacked into the polished veneer of the confessional: S

"… and I call me mammy a hateful bitch in me mind when she won't let me eat sweeties …"

"That's more like it, wane," urged the priest. "Go on and tell me every-thing."

C

"And I was picked up by the Filth for selling me broller's disco sweeties to all the junkies and stokes in the city. I was only selling em cause I hate me bloody communion gown and wanny look nice for the Lord, but!"

Father Bryant grunted. Siofra couldn't tell if this meant he understood that the ends justified the means, and that he would therefore subtract a few Hail Marys from her penance. She hacked away, more out of attention deficit dis-order than nerves.

L-U

"And I stole me sister's camera mobile phone wan day and took it up to the playground, where I clattered the shite outta Kate O'Riordan for telling me mammy I nicked her Pokemons, then I took photos of the narky bitch sobbing away all bloody on the roundabout and posted em on the Internet for all the world to see ...”

B

“... and then I did a poo into a bin liner and shoved the manky mess through the O'Riordan's letterbox ...”

7

“... and wan day me and me mates rang 999 and tole them aul Mrs. Feeney was after having a heart attack, and we hid in the hedges round her front garden, and when the paramedics came we pelted rocks at the eejits, and I hit wan in the head,” she said proudly.

R

There was no sound beyond the latticework. Siofra wondered impatiently if the old idiot had fallen asleep. She strained her ears and heard him mutter something that sounded suspiciously like “Get thee behind me, Satan.”

Finally, Father Bryant spoke aloud:

“That was yer moller am after having in the confessional before ye?”

U

Although her mammy had told her never to reveal family secrets to the priest, Siofra replied “Aye.”

“May the good Lord have mercy on yer souls.”

L

“Am finished with me sins,” Siofra announced, reaching for her My First Missal. “Can I recite me Art of Condition now?”

Father Bryant had heard worse sins revealed in the confessional from Provos, especially during the '70s and '80s, a litany of lurid tales of tar and featherings, kneecappings, midnight searches of innocent Protestant families, terrorizing them in the name of the Cause. But none of the defenders of Eire had been eight years old.

“Am I absolved of me sins?” Siofra demanded.

“Are ye sorry for em?”

Now it was indeed nervousness that made her hack away.

E-Z! she finished off with a flourish.

“What's that noise am hearing?” Father Bryant asked in sudden alarm. “What are ye playing at in the sanctity of the confessional, wee girl?”

“Nothing, faller,” Siofra said, butter wouldn't melt.

He peered through the latticework. She watched his eyes gape with disbelief.

"Ye're not after hacking away at the confessional with the sacred cross of yer rosary?!"

Fionnuala, her fingertips raw from rubbing the beads, jumped as the confessional door flew open. Father Bryant clutched Siofra's arm and hauled her from the darkness. She screamed as the confessional door smacked against her head.

"Compensation!" Siofra wailed, and down the aisle Fionnuala was thinking just the same.

"A bold faced lie tole to a man of the cloth!" Father Bryant bellowed. "Making a mockery outta the blessed sacrament of confession! What are ye like, wane? Are ye trying to merit eternal damnation? For yer penance ye're to say wan hundred Hail Mary's and fifty Our Fallers for vandalizing church property! Clear on off outta this confessional now, and may the good Lord steer ye away from the road to Hell!"

Father Bryant scuttled off down the hallway to the safety of the rectory office.

Much later, last Glory Be finally growled, absolved of her sins, Fionnuala pocketed her rosary and sprang away from Jesus Is Laid In The Tomb. The usual sneer twisted her face as she collected Siofra from her pew, clattered her across the skull and headed out to cast more judgment on the world.

£ £ £ £

Moira scurried past the *Free Derry* wall towards the family home in the Bogside. Before heading to the hospital, she had tried to warn Ursula of her family's duplicity, but Ursula had done herself no favors, roaring abuse at her on the phone and propelling Moira towards Altnagelvin with a new spring in her step. Lily had been alarmed at the request, but had come through, as evidenced by the X-rays which Moira now clutched tight to her chest. And there had been no sins of the flesh in the lab.

Moira noticed with some concern the front door of 5 Murphy slapping unattended against the jamb in the rain. She hurried through the ten inches of front garden and paused at the clattering door, hearing slurred male voices whooping with malicious triumph from the depths. Brandishing her umbrella as a weapon, she stepped inside.

And gasped at her sobbing granny crawling, headfirst and crablike, down the stairs. Eda babbled away as the empty chairlift pounded staccato beats above her bare feet. Down the hallway in the scullery a pack of hooligans guzzled down beer and pissed themselves with laughter, practicing their football kicks on a field of overturned chairs and scattered takeout cartons with one of Eda's rolled up girdles which they had plucked from the sopping laundry pile.

"Clear on off outta here, ye manky fecking stokes!" Moira roared.

"Bean flicker alert! Bean flicker alert!" they called out, knowing the truth when they saw it.

They scattered into the driving rain, and Moira ran to the stairs.

"Granny! Are ye right, there? It's me, Moira!"

She pried her granny's fingers from the step, flipped her bones around into an upright position and guided the slippers onto her feet.

"Eoin! Dymphna!" Moira crowed up the stairs.

Eda clamped Moira shoulder and held her tight.

"Moira, wee dote! It's been ages since I seen ye!" Eda said, struggling to rise from the stairs.

"This morning, actually."

Moira pursed her lips in anger as she guided her granny into the scullery.

"Where's wer Eoin?" she demanded.

"Out dealing his drugs."

"And Dymphna?"

"Have ye found yerself a man in Malta, then?"

Her granny peered at her with great suspicion.

"N-naw," Moira managed.

Eda sighed.

"Them lads over there is probably all Proddy bastards anyway. Living amongst them must be wile lonely for ye, love."

Moira didn't know where to look, so she hurried to the sink and slipped on some rubber gloves.

"I can at least do the washing up for ye," she said.

"Naw, leave them mingin dishes be," Eda said. "Sing me a wee song instead, Moira. Ye know how I love them rebel fighting songs of me youth."

Feeling both a sense of duty and like a right idiot, Moira warbled away as she burrowed into the mountain of dishes, while in the hall, Dymphna snuck out the lad she had picked up the night before, clicked the door shut behind him and smoothed her curls.

"Armored cars and tanks and guns!" Moira sang gamely, Brillo pad in hand.

Eda's dentures blossomed, and her foot tapped along to the ditty of solidarity for Republicans interned without trial by the Orange Proddy bastards.

"Came to take away wer sons!" Dymphna joined in, padding into the scullery for a tin of lager from the fridge.

They trilled as Moira scrubbed away, then finished the song with a flourish. Moira cast her sister a foul look.

"What do ye think ye're playing at," she griped, "leaving me granny at the mercy of a gang of druggies? And this house is a boggin tip! And get that fag outta yer mouth!"

"Ach, not you and all! I had the woman from Child Services by and she tole me the same flimmin thing. Is the world turning fecking Yank? Weemin who's up the scoot has been sucking down the fags and drink for centuries and popping out wanes that is right as rain."

"So!" Moira said brightly, swiftly changing tact as the plates clattered around her. "Have ye a clue who the faller of this wee critter might be?"

Dymphna seemed to struggle, then leaned forward.

"You been a journalist, I know ye had to study all them ethnics and such, so I know ye'll keep to yerself something if it's tole ye in confidence."

"Ethics, aye," Moira corrected, squirting more mild green Fairy liquid into the greasy water.

"He's Harry O'Toole."

Moira scrubbed away in silence as Dymphna unloaded the whole sorry story off on her.

"What I kyanny get me head round," she finished off, "is how I missed me time of month in the first place."

Moira shot a glance over at her granny, wondering if such a discussion should be unfolding in front of her. But Eda was still sipping her tea and beaming and tapping her foot along to the song that had ended seven plates, a roasting pan and four teacups earlier.

"There's hysterical pregnancies and such from stress," Moira explained. "I missed me time of the month when I was revising for me final exams, like. Ye haven't a clue what's going on in that womb of yers. What am concerned about is what role ye think this O'Toole's to have in the life of yer bastard wane. Am sure me daddy would be up for planning some sort of shotgun wedding. If ye were up for it, like."

"That woman from Child Services, a right narky specky four-eyed bean flicker, she was—" Dymphna clasped both hands to her mouth, while Moira pretended she hadn't heard. "Anyway, she sat too closely to me on me granny's settee and blathered on endlessly about the rights and dignity of the unwed moller and the responsibilities of the faller and here's a pamphlet for this and a pamphlet for that and this telephone number will come in wile handy and blah blah blah. *Bleedin feck off outta here, ye filthy specky gack!* I was dying to scream into her bleedin gacky face. Thank feck I kept me mouth shut, as then yer woman startled rattling on about Sure Start Maternity Grants, Statutory Maternity Pay, Lone Parents Allowance, child benefits and the like. It was bleedin effin magic, so it was, as if I had won the lotto meself!"

Moira finally hung up the dishrag and regarded her sorry sister.

"Have ye no clue the disgrace of an unwed moller in Derry?" she asked softly. "Ye know what it's like round here, Dymphna. When we was wanes, ye mind even we would toss rocks at that aul slapper Reeny McCarthy every time she passed wer front garden with her stomach hanging outta her, the proof of her shameful activates bared for all the world to see."

Dymphna threw her empty tin into the sink and marched to the fridge for another.

"Who needs a faller," she spat, "when me pockets are to be bulging with thousands from the Proddy government! Now I've no need for the likes of O'Toole and them Lyrca trousers that display every crevice of his bony wee arse for all the world to see. I've hatched a wee plan to get him back, ye see. Am all prepared and biding me time."

She marched over to her ChipKebab smock and delved into the pocket.

"Bridie tells me O'Toole has a TakkoKebab for his dinner every Wednesday at the ChipKebab," Dymphna explained, pulling out a polythene bag with what looked like large sugar crystals.

Moira peered in at the bag. Sea salt? Unrefined sugar? Then she gasped.

"Ye're not giving him some sorta … hallucinogenics?"

"Ye must think am terrible daft, you!"

Moira did, but that wasn't the issue of the moment.

"So ye're gonny add some, erm, sugar to his meal?" Moira asked with a sly smile and a nod of understanding. "Aye, that'll be a quare aul craic right enough."

Dymphna snorted.

"Sugar, me hole! These particles is ground glass!" she clarified. "Am gonny be roaring with glee behind me register as they drag him off to hospital!"

"Te his coffin, more like!" Moira gasped.

At the table, Eda's hand kept tapping her thigh. "That'll teach the aul poofter!" she said, causing them both to jump.

Moira turned to her sister, knowing too well the malice that could come from a stoke scorned. "What are ye like? They'll have ye marching up and down the courtyard of Magilligan next to wer Lorcan, so they will!"

"Naw, the female prisoners is let out at a different time, sure," Dymphna said, wiping a dribble of lager from her chin. "Am gonny be committing a crime of passion. Weemin is given special treatment if they kill the faller of an unwanted wane. I see it on the telly all the time."

"They'll still lock ye up."

"I've me plan and am sticking to it!" Dymphna insisted, her eyes daring Moira to intervene.

Moira sighed. Her sister would have to learn from her own mistakes. Dymphna lit another fag.

"Anoller wee song there, girls," Eda demanded. *"Anoller martyr for aul Ireland."*

"Anoller murder for the Crown," Dymphna and Moira grudgingly chirped.

As she sang, Moira thought of the sorry lot of stokes that was her family. Torturing their granny, trying to raid Ursula's bank account … Maybe it was living in the sophistication of Malta that did it, but she realized to her shock she was on her auntie Ursula's side. Before becoming a health and safety inspector, Moira had dabbled in journalism, and she had now decided Ursula Barnett would be the focus of the first investigative report she would do for the Living Large section of the *Malta Mail*. The readers always lapped up a lotto story, especially one with a tragic ending. If the editor accepted her story, she might even be able to supplement her income on a regular basis with more articles in the future. She would ring up her auntie Ursula, apologize for her family's behavior and attempt to squeeze a few quotes out of her, maybe even arrange a wee photo. Her family was sure to disown her but, sure, hadn't they done that already?

"Anoller martyr for aul Ireland, anoller murder for the Crown!"

9

Mrs. McDaid's haggard eyes widened in alarm at the two wee creatures on her doorstep, one with a Power Puff Girls handbag, the other sticky from head to toe from the lollipop he was sucking.

"Is Eamonn in, hi?" Siofra demanded, reeling Seamus in with a tug of the arm.

The hardened woman was taken aback.

"Surely ye mean wer Declan?" she asked. "He's banged up at the Youthful Offenders—"

"Naw. Caoilte, then. Or Fergal, I don't give a flying feck. Wan of them lads of yers who pushes them disco sweeties all over town."

"Disco …?"

Mrs. McDaid's eyes flickered with apprehension.

"Get yerselves away from wer door before the peelers catch sight of ye, for feck's sake!" she hissed, flinging open the door and dragging Siofra and Seamus by their twiglet arms into the drug den. She marched them into the front room.

"Ye've some visitors," Mrs. McDaid said, then closed the door on the sorry scene. She could always cry ignorance when the coppers hauled her in at some stage for aiding and abetting.

Fergal, Eamonn and Caoilte turned as a unit, slight alarm in their eyes. Seamus wobbled brightly to the table, eyes drinking in the sweeties displayed in mounds.

"Right, boys?" Siofra asked, hands on hips.

"What are youse here for, wanes?" Fergal asked.

"Am Eoin's sister," Siofra announced.

"Are you the wee girl who was selling wer stash all over town?" Eamonn asked.

179

"Aye, am are. Got picked up by the Filth and all," she said proudly. "Thirty eight quid I made! Me manky broller snatched it all back, but."

"C'mere a wee moment. Yer broller was here the oller day spouting all sorts of claptrap about the Cause. He wouldn't be trying to grass us up to the peelers, would he?"

"Ye must be joking!" Siofra scoffed.

"Me mammy says all peelers is right Orange bastards!" Seamus said.

This didn't seem to satisfy them, but they chuckled as Seamus held his hand out towards the coffee table strewn with polythene bags and Ecstasy tablets of all shapes and sizes.

"Ach, themmuns is for adults, wee fella," Caoilte said.

Seamus' lip trembled.

"What am here for, actually ..." Siofra announced, pushing Seamus into a corner. She hauled out the well-tattered catalog and spread it amongst the stimulants.

"... is to get youse to pay for me communion gown."

"And why in the name of flimmin feck would we do that?" Caoilte asked in shock.

"Me auntie Ursula who won the lotto's a tight-fisted cunt and won't buy it for me, and me mammy and daddy kyanny afford it, and me broller never lets up about how youse is rollin in it. Minted, he says youse are. Anyroad, I've me heart set on the Maria Theresa on page forty-wan—" She flipped furiously through the pages, her wee finger jabbing excitedly at the photos. "—and this Andromeda veil, and this sparkly handbag, and these effin brilliant white shoes with silver angel buckles, and these Heart of the Conception tights; they've a special red heart for the private part which only Jesus can see, like. This wee parasol's optional; Grainne's mammy's to be getting her wan, but, and I don't want that foul bitch showing me up at St. Moluag's Chapel. So if youse wouldn't mind ...?"

She eyed them expectantly, finger on the photo of the parasol. There was a startled silence broken only by Seamus sucking on his lollipop. A wide range of looks were exchanged between them. Then Caoilte threw back his head and roared with laughter, and his brothers joined in.

"Dead on!" Caoilte said. "Reach into yer pocket, Eamonn, and give the wane what she needs."

Siofra nodded righteously; she hadn't expected anything less. Eamonn pulled out a wad of banknotes. Siofra's eyes bulged as he counted them out. Never before in her young life had she seen so much money in one hand. And there were even those hundred pound notes, which she had long doubted the existence of, now revealed in all their glory inches from her trembling fingers.

"Six hundred quid do ye?" Eamonn asked. "Will that cover the parasol and all?"

"We kyanny have that foul bitch Grainne showing ye up, like," Caoilte said with an understanding nod and a nudge into Fergal's ribs.

Siofra tsked and stamped a foot. The brothers roared with laughter, and Caoilte motioned to Eamonn to dig into his pocket again.

"Ye're a right wee chancer, aren't ye?" Eamonn said. "Seven, then."

Siofra tore the note from his fingers.

"Wile civil of ye," she said. "Ta, like."

"That money's yers, but," Caoilte warned. "Ye're not to be giving yer broller any part of it."

Siofra snorted. "Am not fecking daft, sure!"

"Just you let that wee fella know we're keeping wer eyes peeled for that 300 quid he owes us."

"Right ye are," Siofra said, knowing she would do no such thing and stuffing the pound notes into her pink handbag.

£ £ £ £

The Greek Revival-style courthouse on Bishop Street had been largely destroyed by an IRA bomb in the late '80s. Perhaps the Derry Council was proud of the swank new renovation, but Ursula couldn't stand it. The ultramodern interior was more akin to a shopping mall, where people should be reveling in conspicuous consumption, not spitting out their sins to the public.

Intimidated by the luxury and authority of her surroundings, Ursula peered over the railing of the dock in her aqua pantsuit, the sick begging to be set free from her stomach. There the Floods were, thronging the courtroom and casting their foul looks into every corner. Only Dymphna seemed to be missing. A drug-addled Eoin was leading his granny to the public seats, Eda staring around as if unsure of her whereabouts. Moira's appearance grieved Ursula the most; she was the only one of the lot who had paid the price of an airline ticket to sit and gloat.

The Flood's solicitor—a hard-faced Protestant-looking bitch in a black pants suit Ursula had seen on the racks of Next for upwards of £100—scurried up to the family, looking professional with her Mark Cross briefcase. Padraig's eyes danced, and he beamed charmingly at her. They had that wane well-rehearsed, no doubt, Ursula thought, given him a personality transplant and prepared him to spew out a pack of lies by rote before the magistrates.

The magistrates filed into the courtroom in a flurry of dark robes, and Ursula braced herself.

As Miss O'Donnell cleared her throat, Ursula clung to the last vestiges of dignity.

"*My Lords!*"

They all flinched as Miss O'Donnell slammed her briefcase shut and impelled her thunderous voice through the courtroom. Her arms flailed with dramatic flourishes, lies transplanted from the Floods now accusations flying from her mouth, her eyes casting glares of outrage at the miscreant in the dock. Ursula was aware of the blood pumping though each of her many veins, her face ablaze with the mortification of the packs of lies posing as home truths. The magistrates leaned forward as a team, riveted.

Moira had sat herself emphatically on the press bench. She now flipped open her notebook and, after a moment's thought, scribbled *Woman Wronged*. She looked up and tried to illustrate to Ursula with her eyes that she felt sorry for her, that she was on her side and a traitor to her own family for it, and that she was even at that moment running through headline alternatives for the story which would vindicate her persecuted aunt. Her eyelids soon tired.

The peculiar foul looks Moira was shooting her across the courtroom, Ursula thought, and her checking out Ms. Murphy's legs while she was at it! Ursula had always held Moira to a higher standard as she was the only one of the Flood pack who could write in cursive. Now, though, with the press card displayed around her neck and the smarter-than-thou attitude that went with the pen poised over her notebook, her intelligence and lesbianism sickened Ursula's stomach. Ursula whipped her head around as Miss O'Donnell wrapped up her character assassination, and Ms. Murphy addressed the magistrates.

"Accidents," Ms. Murphy said with all the passion of a hooker turning her twelfth trick of the evening, "will happen. Have your honors never had an accident? Have you never left the iron on when you went on holiday?"

They all gave her a look that implied that, no, they never had.

"Similarly, my client can't help it that she was standing on the pavement at the precise moment the plaintiff went flying into the street. It's not her fault that Mrs. Feeney happened to be driving down the street at the same moment. Accidents, as I have said, will happen, and one happened to my client."

She smiled and returned to her seat, opening argument over. Ursula whipped around to Jed, her eyes bulging circles. Jed peeped back, his eyes vacant of hope.

Miss O'Donnell marched to the wide screen telly to the magistrate's left and flicked it on. Padraig's tearful face tugged at the strings of every mother's heart in the courtroom except Ursula's.

"I was collecting rubbish from the pavements to make the town nice," Padraig sniveled on the screen, "and I was placing some empty crisp bags in me auntie's wheelie bin when she burst out of her house screaming the odds. She said the likes of me had no business in her part of town, the posh part of town, now that she had won the lotto she hated me and I was a mingin stoke. She throttled me neck, then looked up and down the street until she saw a motor racing towards us, and she waited until it was inches away, then threw me into it. Me body fairly flipped over the hood of the car, and me shoulder cracked against the bumper and me head landed on the blacktop. Blood spurt everywhere. Heart-feared, so I was. I hauled meself up and limped all the way back to the Bogside."

The magistrates shifted in their robes and regarded Ursula with distaste. Fionnuala was proud, knowing she had raised Padraig right: how crocodile tears could stream down his wee face with such conviction!

"Mrs. Barnett has told me," Ms. Murphy's disembodied voice, apologetic and somewhat embarrassed, now said on the screen, "you were lighting, erm, petrol bombs to set her house ablaze?"

Padraig's eyes widened with hurt, then he winced and brought a tender hand to the bandage around his head.

Brilliant, so his act was, Fionnuala thought, pondering how she could ship him off to Hollywood and reap the rewards.

"Naw! I never!" he said, his pout indignant.

"Could you please explain to the court why your aunt would say this?"

"Cause she's a mad aul cow, hi!"

This seemed to satisfy the defense, and the cross-examination was at an end.

As the telly was snapped off and a pensioner struggled to make her way to the stand, Siofra sat in her usual fidgety, brattish strop. While it had been a right laugh watching her auntie Ursula squirming on the stand and her brother lying through his teeth on the telly, now her bag of Jelly Babies was close to empty, and she found herself thinking only of her new outfit, and imagining the scene when it would be delivered to her house with much fan-fare.

Mrs. Feeney raised her hand and righteously confirmed she would tell the truth, so help her God.

"Would you please tell the court what transpired the afternoon of May 23rd of this year?"

"I was motoring down the street," Mrs. Feeney said, "when I looked out me window and saw that flippin eejit of a woman roaring outta her like a mad beast and grappling that wee fella by the neck. The pure rage in Ursula put the fear of God into me. I saw her point at me car, and I saw the gleam in her eye. She bided her time until I was driving by, then she took careful aim and shoved the wee fella into me hood."

Siofra amused herself by clicking open her handbag and pawing through its sticky depths.

"I enter into evidence, my lords, the following photographs of the extensive damage Padraig Flood's innocent young body made to Mrs. Feeney's car."

"And mind," Mrs. Feeney said, "ye enter into evidence me bills and all. Am expecting compensation from that wan."

As Ms. Murphy approached Mrs. Feeney, the door opened, and Molly from Xpressions slipped into the courtroom. Ursula's heart lurched with joy, her faith in humanity restored. Molly would be a character witness for her after all! Molly settled herself in the front row of the public gallery, hand prim on a knee, eyes firmly turned from Ursula.

Ms. Murphy addressed the witness for the prosecution.

"Mrs. Feeney, did you not see this young man with a petrol bomb in his hand, and with three other such malicious weapons lining the pavement, ready for action?"

"Are ye fat in the forehead? Themmuns is desperate lies dreamed up by that aul cunt of a bitch! Padraig Flood's never touched a petrol bomb in his life! A wee dote, so he is. Always helps me carry me messages to me house."

The magistrates looked surprised.

"Is the court expected to believe that the story of this petrol bomb attack is the work of a delusional mind?" one of them intervened.

"I wouldn't put it past the sleekit aul minger," crabbit Mrs. Feeney har-rumphed.

"But Mrs. Barrett is," Ms. Murphy continued, "an upstanding member of the community. Can you explain why she would behave in such a manner?"

"That Ursula Barnett's always had it out for me!" Mrs. Feeney lied through her dentures. "She was meant to be me provider for OsteoCare; that wan provided me with nothing but bleedin misery. Am reduced to a bundle of nerves, ingesting tablets to calm me nerves and help me through the nightmares, after being forced to be the instrument of her hatred. And she always tole me she couldn't abide that Padraig, couldn't stomach the sight of him."

"I put it to you, Mrs. Feeney, that you are lying," Ms. Murphy intoned.

"Say what ye like. I want that wan to pay for me hood, but!"

She teetered off the stand with a smirk at Ursula.

"I now call Mrs. Fionnuala Flood," Miss O'Donnell said, to Ursula's great dread.

The air crackled with anticipation, the Floods beaming proudly, a deathly hush descending as Fionnuala commanded her place in the witness box, her face radiant with conviction, tissue at the ready.

£ £ £ £

"Are ye not due in court at some stage the day?" Bridie asked, a dripping chip basket swinging from her hand.

The Top-Yer-Trolly meat and cheese counter had never seemed so good. Dymphna had worked seven shifts at the ChipKebab and had already received two verbal warnings. She couldn't help it: the hoards of customers heaving though the doors were legless and stroppy and endless, and the one thing she couldn't abide at her register was rudeness. Her eyes were vacant of joy at the sight of the little brown camels which festooned her fat-splattered smock in vertical stripes, the daft cap she had to place on her head, and her stomach turned at the stench of the curry sauce.

"Yer man won't let me go until after the dinner break," Dymphna said, shooting the manager a foul look. She measured out some chips and dreamed of her next fag break, the likes of which were doled out with the precision of a Nazi work camp. "He's making me work a double the morrow to cover the time off. It's to be a quare aul craic, but, watching that hateful bitch Ursula squirming away in the dock. If only I can make it there on time."

"Ye'll be there soon enough, then," Bridie said with a nod at the door. "Dinner break rush is on its way now."

Dymphna turned and glared under her hairnet like the wage slave she was at the clamoring at her register.

"What do ye want?" she snapped at the first one fool enough to have chosen her register.

There followed a flurry of lurching to the sandwich bin, snapping open bags, snatching pound coins and shoving them inside her register drawer. The chaos was just dwindling down, and Dymphna was by then panting for a fag, when who did she see next in her queue but Mr. O'Toole, with Fidelma clutching his arm in a manner not befitting an employee. The three shot daggers at each other over the garlic sauces as if they had all been slapped. The bag of ground glass was heavy in the pocket of Dymphna's camel and pyramid smock.

Dymphna's head swiveled to ensure the manager wasn't in sight, then she bent over the register keys and hissed: "Get that sleekit minger away from me till before me fist lands in her gob."

Fidelma whispered into Mr. O'Toole's ear, shot Dymphna a foul look, then dismissed herself to a table cluttered with the remnants of past diners, where she perched herself as if she were guest of honor at a banquet.

If Dymphna had ever had any doubts about causing O'Toole harm, seeing him stepping out with Fidelma filled her with a steely resolve. Didn't people realize they brought their troubles on themselves? she wondered.

Aloud, she demanded, "What's yer order?"

"Give us a TakkoKebab, a ChipButtyKebab, Crispy TofuDippers—"

"Sauce?"

"Garlic. Curry chips twice and two small orange minerals."

Dymphna punched in the order in a surprisingly jealous strop; Mr. O'Toole had never taken *her* out for a meal. As he cooed over at Fidelma, Dymphna turned to the bin and selected a TakkoKebab with trembling fingers. Shuffling over to the deep fat fryer, she discreetly slipped the foil wrapper off and peered inside at the bubbling mince meat, wilting lettuce and onion, the stray tomato and some minging spicy sauces. Her hand slipped into the pocket of her smock and, head swiveling, she tugged out the polythene bag. As the grease splattered around her, she sprinkled the ground glass into the halves of pita bread, massaged them gently so the particles trickled unseen into the steaming depths, then tightly rewrapped the foil.

She considered adding some glass to Fidelma's ChipButtyKebab as well, just for taking up with the old pansy, but realized that Fidelma's face was punishment enough in her life.

Dymphna marched back to the register, a woman empowered, and shoved the lot onto a tray.

"Seven quid fifty-nine pee," she said brightly, forcing the tray across the counter.

"Good luck to ye," he said curtly as he collected the change.

"Ta, to you and all," Dymphna sneered, slamming the money drawer shut. "Now clear on off outta me sight and leave me head's peace."

He settled himself at the table, muttered something to Fidelma, and they both peered over at her and snickered. A rush of anticipation swept under Dymphna's greasy smock, revenge a dish best served in a steaming hot TakkoKebab.

As she made a show of busying herself over the next order, a new dance in her fingers, she shot glances at the two. Their hands met under the table, the toes of Fidelma's trainers fiddling with O'Toole's Oxfords through the sea of straw wrappers and dropped TofuDippers.

The sick almost shot from Dymphna's throat at Fidelma's giggling and cooing, one hand poised coyly under her chin, the pinkie raised, leering under her eyelashes across the table and allowing O'Toole to slip a chip dripping curry sauce into her mouth.

Mr. O'Toole whipped open a napkin and unfolded it carefully across the tightness of his lap. He aligned the straw to a 90 degree angle from his mouth, ranked his plastic fork and knife on a napkin and daintily unwrapped the deathly TakkoKebab, adjusting the foil just so, forming a perfect square plate of aluminum around the kebab. Dymphna shuddered as she stacked the minerals cup lids. Perhaps if Mr. O'Toole *had* married her, she would've been driven to an early grave.

He unwrapped his TakkoKebab and brought it up to his lips. Dymphna tensed, ripping a napkin into tiny shreds. Panic took her unawares, a cell in Magilligan in her near future. Then he lowered the pita bread from his mouth and spewed out more nonsense.

Their conversation was endless, so it was, Dymphna thought. What in the name of feck did they have to discuss, the new shipment of prawn cheese spread?

"Right, there, love? Wan BaconNCheeseDippers—"

Dymphna scowled into the eager face of a pensioner.

"Get yerself off to anoller till! Can ye not see am busy?!"

"Useless, more like," the pensioner muttered, stomping over to Bridie.

Dymphna fiddled with her register roll as if it were wonky, her eyes trailing her victim. Mr. O'Toole put the TakkoKebab inches from his relentlessly babbling mouth, then placed it back down again, not a bite taken.

"Get it down yer effin bake, ye hateful aul nancy boy!" she muttered into the concentric circles of the register roll.

She slipped out her mobile and glanced at the time. She was sure to miss her auntie's crucifixion at this rate. O'Toole nibbled on a TofuDipper, all the while talking a mile a minute, Fidelma's ears enraptured.

Would he never get that damn thing between his teeth and finally give her head's peace? Dymphna wondered.

Resisting the urge to march over and shove the TakkoKebab down his gullet herself, Dymphna snapped the roll dispenser shut and waited.

£ £ £ £

Fionnuala sniffled into a tissue for a few seconds, blinked bravely, and addressed the court in a reedy voice.

"I had just finished praying the teatime Angelus, yer honors, and was out hanging the washing on the line when I heard the clatter of wer front door, and the grievous roars of me wane in pain. Me heart was gripped with fear. I saw blood trailing all over the scullery linoleum. Stains, mind, that we kyanny remove no matter how hard we scrub. We're expecting compensation for some new linoleum and all. Anyroad, we rushed the poor wee nadger up to Altnagelvin, where they tole us his skull was fractured, his ribs was bruised, and he was clinging to life by a thread."

"I enter into evidence, my lords, the hospital records and X-rays of the extensive damage done to the young victim," Miss O'Donnell said.

Ursula craned her neck to catch a glimpse of the X-rays, confusion vying with shock on her face. The magistrates pawed them over, clucking and shaking their heads as they inspected the damning evidence, casting daggers over at Ursula.

"Why would she do this?" Miss O'Donnell barreled on. "What can you tell us about your family's relationship with the defendant?"

"A misery, it's been, since that lotto win. We was in need of fifty quid to pay off the rates. Pure desperate, we was. Down on me knees in the middle of the Saturday shoppers on Shipquay Street I was wan day, begging Ursula Barnett for a loan of the money. She fairly spat in me face. And then there was the carer's allowance for me poor aul moller-in-law, Eda Flood."

Eoin had been propping up his dozing granny, and he now nudged her at the mention of her name. Eda didn't budge. Eoin went back to jittering with post-E panic, sitting ringside at his aunt's crucifixion doing him no favors.

"Years, we've taken care of the frail aul pensioner, then Ursula steals the allowance from us. Shameless, so she is!"

Before coming to court, Eoin had taken a quick trip to the Craglooner, but he couldn't give his wingers away. Heads had whipped around, chatter faltering, eyes inspecting beermats. One week earlier his mobile had never stopped ringing, and 5 Murphy had been a revolving door of junkies.

At the stand, Ms. Murphy approached Fionnuala.

"Did Mrs. Barnett not pay off your mortgage for you after the lotto win?" Ms. Murphy asked.

"Aye," Fionnuala spat, wrapping her arms around herself.

Not the brightest bulb, Eoin couldn't understand what was up. That rumors were flowing about him grassing for the RUC never entered his mind. All he knew was that he was in desperate need of new clientele. He glanced over at Siofra, who had Pikachu wrapped up in a soiled handkerchief she had stolen from Paddy's pocket, and was marching him up and down her dozing granny's thigh.

"Was that not extremely magnanimous of her?" Ms. Murphy asked.

Confusion flickered on Fionnuala's face.

"If ye mean was that wile civil of her, naw!" she snarled. "Swanned into wer sitting room the moment the deal was done, barking out orders for me to change me drapes and the flimmin wallpaper! Just so's she could sell it for more money, like, and put us out on the street! She's turned us into squatters in wer own home! We live in mortal fear of hearing them hammering the For Sale sign into wer front garden, scoffing down wer baked beans under a cloud of guilt!"

Siofra shoved her last Jelly Baby against Pikachu's painted mouth. "Body of Christ, Body of Christ ..." she whispered into Pikachu's ear. A slow smile now began to play on Eoin's lips, and connivance glinted fleetingly in his vein-speckled eyes. He now realized who his new clientele would be. *The younger they got hooked, the better,* he thought.

"Why did you not contact the authorities when you were in hospital?" Ms. Murphy asked.

"Ach, we're Catholic, so we are!" Fionnuala spat.

The magistrates nodded in understanding.

"And you did not smell petrol on Padraig when you were rushing him to the hospital?"

"Grieving, we were. We hadn't the time nor the presence of mind to go sniffing around his hoodie and trainers! Them petrol bombs is a pack of lies, anyroad! Ye can scour them hospital records until the cows come home, and ye'll not find a mention of flimmin effin petrol in any of em."

Fionnuala turned and addressed the magistrates, her voice ringing with conviction.

"Yer honors, Ursula Barnett is a sleekit, conniving bitch who hates her life and is taking out her hatred on all of us. I kyanny wait to see that wan sent down for the misery she's put wer family through!"

"That's quite enough, Mrs. Flood," Ms. Murphy said sternly. "One could say, actually, that your only reason for bringing this case against my client was to receive the compensation money."

"Ach, we've no need of the money. We've stacks of wanes working all the hours God sends to pay off wer bills, sure!"

"I put it to you, Mrs. Flood, that everything you have said under oath has been a lie."

"Aye, you would and all!" Fionnuala snapped her arms around her and glared with eyes that insinuated Ms. Murphy was a Proddy cunt she would be happy to kneecap. "Ye kyanny prove me wrong, but."

"I am through with this witness," Ms. Murphy, at a loss, said.

Fionnuala triumphantly dismounted the stand.

"My last witness, your honors," Miss O'Donnell said, "is Molly Harris."

Ursula's brow rimpled with bewilderment. Surely Molly should be her own character witness? She tried to get Ms. Murphy's attention, but her solicitor was busy fiddling with a paper clip. Molly plodded to the stand, her face burning with shame.

"Could you state your occupation for the court?" Miss O'Donnell asked.

Molly steered her eyes well away from Ursula's.

"I own Xpressions hair salon."

"How long have you known Mrs. Barnett?"

"Ages, we've been mates," Molly said as if revealing some hideous and mortifying secret.

"She is a regular customer of yours, is she not?"

"Every Wednesday at two, aye; wash and set."

"Could you tell us something about her character?"

Molly felt her stomach lurch. She was certain she felt lasers of hatred beaming from Ursula and frantically wondered about witness protection schemes. Perhaps they could hide her away in some Proddy village. She had to force the words out of her mouth.

"First I wanny say am here under extreme duress, me lords. It grieves me to say it, but," and here her voice grew even more conspiratorial, and the magistrates all leaned towards her, "I think Ursula's going through the *change*. Am wile heart-scared when she steps foot into the salon. We've to lock away the curling tongs for fear she'll have a go at wan of the clients with em!"

"When did you notice this change in her personality?" Miss O'Donnell asked.

"Ursula's been a wee bit touched in the head ever since that lotto win."

"Could you give us some specifics?"

"Wan week she'll tip me fifty pee, anoller week fifty quid. She marched into the salon with a card and chocolates, like, on the tenth of April when everywan in Derry knows me birthday's November 12th."

Molly chanced a glance at Ursula out of the corner of her eye, but instead of the rage she expected, Molly saw a woman struck dumb with betrayal, Ursula's eyes pleading up at her in confusion, like those of an innocent child beaten senseless by a loving and trusted mother.

"And was there ever a time when the defendant became violent?"

"I kyanny … I kyanny …" Molly heaved huge gasps. "I kyanny continue, yer worships."

"May I remind you you are under oath," Miss O'Donnell warned. "You have sworn to tell the truth."

"Am terrible sorry, Ursula," Molly pleaded. "They had me subpoenaed!"

"Do not address the defendant!" Miss O'Donnell barked.

Molly bowed her head in silent shame, then confessed haltingly.

"A few weeks back, Ursula stormed into the salon in a right rage. Her two nieces had taken their granny, Ursula's moller, in to get her hair done. Ursula was pure spitting when she laid eyes on em. Berated themmuns something terrible. She knocked that wee girl Siofra there to the tiles, and grappled her moller by the arm and made to drag the poor aul soul out the door. We were all afeared for the aul wan's life. Anyroad, I made to ring 999, and Ursula finally saw sense. She fled the salon and I've not set eyes on her since. And it was only a wee demi-perm, yer honors."

Molly face was stippled with affliction, her fingernails lacerating the polished oak of the stand.

"Your witness," Miss O'Donnell smirked.

Ms. Murphy jumped up, shuffling some papers in desperation.

"You told the court you've been a friend of Mrs. Barnett's for many years, did you not?"

"I did, aye," Molly admitted.

"Yet you sit here today and sully her good name. Is betrayal one of the attributes Mrs. Barnett cherishes most in your friendship?"

Molly burst into tears.

"Am under oath," she sobbed, clutching at a tissue one of the magistrates proffered and harrumphing into it.

"I have no more questions for this *witness*," Ms. Murphy sneered.

Molly scampered out of the courtroom to spew up in the nearest available loo and Ursula watched her go, firmly resolved from then on to get her washes and sets at NuStyles.

"Your honors, I rest my case," Miss O'Donnell said.

As the court deflated and Moira scribbled furiously in her notepad, Ms. Murphy quickly took center stage.

"For my first witness, your lordships, I call to the stand Jed Barnett."

Jed pledged, as the Lord was his witness, to tell the truth.

"Please inform the court what you observed on the day in question."

"I was on the phone with a solicitor," Jed said, "when I saw my wife run out of the house. I heard some yelling outside, then the screech of a car, then my wife ran back into the house and told me she had caught Padraig with four fire bombs. He had lit one and was aiming it at our house. She knocked it out of his hand, then he slapped her and when she went to slap him back, he ran into the street and into a car—"

"Hearsay!" shrieked Miss O'Donnell.

Jed looked sheepish, and Ms. Murphy shuffled through some papers.

"What was your wife's demeanor?" she finally asked.

The memory of Ursula's face twisted in rage still haunted him, but what use was a husband if he couldn't lie for his wife in court?

"Disappointed, I guess."

"And why did you not contact the authorities?"

"Ursula said her family would hate her if she did."

"Thank you. Your witness."

Miss O'Donnell approached the stand like a vulture sniffing fresh carrion.

"You told the court you were conversing on the phone during the incident?"

"Yeah."

"How was it possible that you heard all the yelling and crashing while chatting away?"

"I was on hold," Jed said.

"There was no music blaring into your ear while you were on hold?"

Jed blinked.

"There was music, I guess. Something classical. But it wasn't blaring. Besides, I had moved the phone from my ear."

"And did you move your eyes to the door?"

"What do you mean?"

"I mean, did you not see anything?"

"No, but—"

"And this yelling you talk about before the sound of the crash you allegedly heard. Was it your wife's enraged voice, or the terrified squeals of a child being beaten senseless?"

Jed squirmed.

"It ... it seemed like Padraig yelling angrily at my wife."

"And this you could discern while classical music was bellowing down your ear?" Miss O'Donnell said, disbelief lacerating her voice.

"I told you—"

"You've told me many things," Miss O'Donnell said. "Except what actually happened outside your front door, as you don't have a clue, now do you?"

"Well, I—"

"Did you see the petrol bombs?"

"No, but—"

"Did you see Padraig slap your wife?"

"No, but I told you—"

"In other words, you can tell us absolutely nothing," Miss O'Donnell said.

"No, I—"

"You may leave the stand." She waved her hand as if shoeing away an irritating fly.

"But ..." Jed said weakly.

Miss O'Donnell fixed him with a steely glare. Jed shrank back and slunk to his seat.

"If it please the court, I now call Ursula Barnett herself to the stand."

Fionnuala would never had credited it, but as Ursula stepped up to the dock, she realized she no longer gave a cold shite in hell in seeing her being sent down. All she wanted was that compensation money.

Ursula stared out at the rows of sneers in the public gallery and braced herself for the persecution.

£ £ £ £

Fidelma and Mr. O'Toole had scoffed down most of their curry chips and every last one of the TofuDippers. Fidelma's ChipButtyKebab had three bites taken out of it, but still the TakkoKebab remained untouched. Bridie and Dymphna huddled together by the minerals dispenser, the clank of ice cubes cloaking their conversation from the milling staff. Dymphna, tetchy with anticipation, kept a rag flapping to simulate labor.

"Ye see that slapper Fidelma's here with Mr. O'Toole?" she said.

"Aren't ye after telling me he's the faller of yer wane?" Bridie asked. "Got himself a new fancy woman quick enough, like. How can ye stand the sight of the two of themmuns practically snogging the faces offa each oller before ye like that? Disgraceful, so it is! Especially as yer man's meant to be an arse bandit!"

"It's no odds, sure," Dymphna said nonchalantly.

Bridie stared, suspicion gleaming. Dymphna seemed to consider, then leaned over to whisper.

"I kyanny keep it to meself no longer, Bridie!" she said, eyes glinting. "Am after filling yer man's TakkoKebab with ground glass!"

Bridie's eyes bulged, then her shock became anger.

"Ach, wise up, you! Ye're gonny get the fecking sack!"

"Chance'd be a fine thing!"

"And am gonny be sacked right along with ye for recommending ye in the first place! If yer man keels over, have ye any notion how long were to be holed up here, what with the paramedics barging in and the Filth with their eternal interrogations? Am on me ninth hour in this manky tip as it is! Get yerself over to that table and snatch it away from him now or am off to the management!"

"I kyanny do that! What am I meant to tell him?"

"I don't give a piggin feck!"

Dymphna stamped a petulant foot.

"Naw," she said.

Bridie set her lips and launched a hand to her hip.

"If you don't get yerself over there, I'll do it meself! And don't boller punching yer time card here the morrow, for this'll be the last ye clamp eyes on the back end of this counter!"

Dymphna pleaded at her silently; she was spoiling everything. Bridie shoved a TakkoKebab into Dymphna's hand and pushed her around the counter. Dymphna flashed her mate a look of betrayal and reluctantly wallowed towards the dining lovers, right as Mr. O'Toole was finally inching the pita between his gaping teeth. He flinched at the sight of her approach from the corner of his eye, but chomped down just as Dymphna screamed, "Get that outta yer mouth, hi!"

She whipped the deathly TakkoKebab from his gob and froze as he kept chewing the lone bite.

"That's a HotDogKebab!" she said with an approximation of urgency, tossing down the untainted TakkoKebab. "I gave to it ye by mistake."

Mr. O'Toole smirked as his jaws worked. Dymphna peered curiously, searching his eyes for signs of pain, the soft flesh of his lips for traces of red.

"A slapper *and* useless behind a counter and all!" he said through his full mouth. "What a winning combination!"

Fidelma sniggered into the remnants of her curry chips. Dymphna wanted to smack the silly smile off the cunt's face, but felt Bridie's eyes boring into the back of her smock.

Mr. O'Toole suddenly lurched up from the table, his face contorted, eyes bulging.

"Mary moller of God!" he mumbled through the pita and lettuce and glass, fingers flying to his lips. "What the flimmin feck?"

Fidelma backed off in confusion, Mr. O'Toole squirmed in his tight slacks. Dymphna stood rooted to the spot, fascinated. He spat out the spiky mouthful. It shot through the air and spattered across Dymphna's face. She yelped, and a hand shot to her eye, sharp white pain in a chunk of mince meat slitting the flesh of her eyelid, blood and garlic sauce dribbling down her cheek. O'Toole gasped in mortification and reached for a napkin as Fidelma pushed away her curry chips with a grimace.

"Am wile sorry, Dymphna," Mr. O'Toole said, reaching out and gently wiping the mess off her cheek. "Christ almighty, but! What in the name of feck's in them HotDogKebabs?! Feckin revolting!"

"Get yer manky paws offa me!" Dymphna wailed with eye clamped shut, smacking his napkin away and skittering like the wounded beast she was toward the counter, unable to look Bridie in the eye, pushing away her helping hand as the slivers of pain shot through her speared eyelid. Dymphna maneuvered herself to the staff loos, squealing as her hip cracked into the chip fryer, and Bridie trailed in after her.

"Have ye some tweezers in yer handbag?" Dymphna demanded with feverish hysteria, plopping the tainted TakkoKebab on the edge of the sink and peering through her one eye at her bloody self in the mirror. She was terrified of moving her injured eyeball one iota in its socket. "Am feckin blinded!"

"Serves ye bleedin right!" Bridie sniffed. "Ach, let's have a look at ye."

Furious pounding shook the bog door.

"What the feck are youse playing at in there?" roared the manager.

They froze before the mirror, tiny drops of blood spattering into the sink. Bridie grabbed the TakkoKebab and shoved the evidence of malice into the bin.

"We … have a wee problem here," Bridie called out. "Go on and grab us the first aid kit? We're in need of some tweezers and a Band-Aid, like."

"The pain, the pain!" Dymphna squealed, stamping her foot as agony shot through her eyelid.

The door inched open. Dymphna turned and faced a row of prying eyes under camel caps peering in. The entire crew was assembled outside the loo door.

"Clear off outta here!" Bridie roared, snatching the first aid kit from the manager's hand. "Can ye not see the poor wee girl needs some privacy?"

Bridie slammed shut the door. She grabbed Dymphna's face with both her hands and inspected the eyelid. Dymphna whimpered and squirmed.

"Ach, blinded me arse!" Bridie snorted. "Wan tiny sliver of glass's lodged in yer eyelid, just, half the size of me wee toenail. Yer eyeball's grand, so it is."

Fifteen minutes later, shard of glass plucked from the tender flesh, retina rinsed clean of blood and spicy sauce, plaster affixed and Dymphna was feeling right as rain. Six paracetamol had helped. She reluctantly scribbled out an incident report, then lurched for her time card.

"I've to get meself to the courthouse," she explained as she clocked off. As she hurried through the dining area, glaring at O'Toole's TakkoKebab still sat on their empty table, untouched, she glanced at her mobile, but instead of the time, a text message flashed out at her. *i no all about it u cant hide my uncles a copper! Rory*

Rory? Surely not Rory Riddell? He must have seen her by the chip fryer, maybe lurking by the rubbish bins, as she was shaking the glass into the TakkoKebab! Gnawing at her lip, the pain in her eyelid suddenly throbbing, she heaved her handbag over her shoulder and headed out of the ChipKebab, heavy with new grief.

£ £ £ £

"We've all heard what your husband said happened on the day in question. I've no doubt you concur with him in every detail?"

"Aye," Ursula nodded.

"We've no need, then, to repeat the story," Ms. Murphy said. "Let's concentrate on the details. Do you swear by almighty God that Padraig Flood slapped you first?"

"I do, aye."

"And this was because he was angry that you had quashed his plans to petrolbomb your house?"

"Aye."

"And that, without provocation on your part, he ran into the street on his own accord?"

Ursula nodded eagerly. "Aye, aye," she breathed.

For the first time, Ursula felt as if the case might be going her way, now she was being given the chance to tell her own part of the story.

"Thank you. Your witness."

Ursula jumped—that was *it?*—as did the magistrates. In the public seats, Jed wondered briefly if they could put a stop on Ms. Murphy's check.

Miss O'Donnell sidled up to Ursula.

"Why have you no evidence of these alleged petrol bombs?"

Ursula composed herself as best she could.

"If only I had've thought to keep em as proof. I threw them into the wheelie bin, and I kyanny help it that it happened on a Wednesday, and that's the day, me lords, when they come to collect the rubbish."

Miss O'Donnell snorted as if she thought Ursula story was nothing but rubbish.

"Why is there no police record of this 'attack?' Why did you not contact the authorities?"

"I wish to the Lord Almighty above I would've done it now. I relented out of common Christian decency, not wanting to see members of me own family dragged through the courts. Not that that stopped themmuns from doing the same to me."

She glared pointedly in the public seats. Miss O'Donnell gave the assembled masses a look which said "likely story."

"You've heard much evidence weighing against your own version of the events. I wonder what you could possibly have to say in your defense, Mrs. Barnett?"

Ms. Murphy flashed her a look of warning. Ursula ignored the useless cow.

"There's no justification whatsoever for dragging me into court like a common hooligan!"

Miss O'Donnell started. "No justification?"

"Yer honors, anywan with an ounce of common sense can see them stokes has piled into the court to try to claw the money outta anywan in their path that has it."

Eyebrows were raised all around the magistrate's bench, and as Ursula's voice grew, Fionnuala gave a little prayer of thanks to the Lord that Ursula had been born with red hair, her temper unable to control itself.

"Are you implying this is all a fabrication?" one of them asked, leaning forward with great interest.

"Aye, am are! A wee glance at them X-rays and ye can see that skull there's too big for a wee nadger like Padraig! And if them damages ye see done to the ribs would've been his, he'd be in a body cast for life!"

"How could this simple working class family have procured these X-rays if—"

"Two spastics with wan brain cell between em can figure out they got them documents bought off some shady site on the flimmin Internet!"

"But these hospital reports—"

Ursula spat her disgust and singled out Moira with a trembling finger.

"Ach, that wan's got a bean flicker lover working at Altnagelvin, sure! Wile simple, it would be, for the filthy perv to nick some letterhead and scribble down some maladies!"

Moira set her lips and scratched out *Wronged Woman* on her notepad.

"If that wane's damages is so extensive, why for the love of God is there not wan single photo of em? When Padraig left the side of the car, he was the picture of health, flipping me off and language not fit for even a sailor spewing from his mouth."

"There are extremely serious allegations you are making, madam," a magistrate said over his pince-nez.

"I put it to the court," Ms. Murphy swiftly intervened. "Why would this upstanding member of St. Moluag's choir invent a pack of lies?"

The magistrates on the bench exchanged glances, seemingly thinking of many reasons why she should. The Floods all looked startled at the news Ursula was singing at their neighborhood church.

"Am a decent Christian woman, me," Ursula insisted, "never tole a lie in me life and am saddled with sinners and heathens and hooligans for family. Mortified, am are, to call the likes of themmuns family! Their moller's a Heggarty, and youse all know what that means!"

Her accusing finger pointed down the front row of the public seats which the Floods had annexed.

"That wan's pushing drugs all over town! And they've a wee slapper who's pregnant outta wedlock with a Proddy at eighteen years of age! And they've anoller broller, the pride of the family, locked up in Magilligan for GBH!"

"Madam—"

"Thieving beasts!" Ursula bellowed into the magistrates' alarmed faces. "Themmuns isn't human beings!"

"Madam!"

"Hardened, filthy stokes!" Ursula screamed as security raced at her from all sides.

"Exercise control over yourself, or you will be ejected from the courtroom!" blared a scarlet-faced magistrate.

Ursula shrank from the uniforms which girdled her, and Ms. Murphy's voice rang out.

"I apologize profusely for my client's behavior."

"I should hope so," muttered one.

"We'll adjourn the court whilst we arrive at our verdict," another said.

"Your worships, may I at this time request bail for my client?" Ms. Murphy asked.

They exchanged a look at her impudence, but finally one harrumphed, "Bail is granted, but I really don't feel we'll be very long in coming to our verdict."

"All rise!"

And, once Eda had been kicked awake, they all did.

10

On her way to the Craglooner, Dymphna selected a broken brick and placed it in her handbag between her lipsticks. She would use it as a last resort if her wits couldn't keep up with the mind games. She knew well enough the conniving ways used by Proddy brains to extract information, the same tricks used by the Special Branch to extract confessions from, for example, Bridie's father, an upstanding IRA member who never did anybody any harm. They asked leading questions and used the innocent answers as ammunition in a circular, insidious way of circumstantial proof you had strung yourself up in a web of lies. Rory had caught her trying to cause O'Toole harm. Any self-respecting Catholic would have marched up and confronted her directly; Rory had sent her a cryptic text. So like a Proddy bastard.

Entering the pub, she saw him at the video game, blasting away the aliens, not a care in his Orange world. The wane curdled in her womb. Dymphna's eyes flicked through the wide array of old alkies and druggies on stools; she'd never hear the end of it if somebody she knew eyed her chatting to an Orange bastard while stone-cold sober. Relieved she saw only strangers, she plodded towards Judas with a steady gait and a flick of her curls, the brick heavy in her handbag.

"Right, Rory," Dymphna said guardedly.

"Dymphna!" Rory said, forgetting the aliens, his face breaking into a smile that put Dymphna on red alert. "Let me get the first pint in."

Dymphna's confusion rose, but no way in hell would she refuse a free pint. She plodded after him to the bar, stealing glances at all the nooks.

"Where's all them mates of yers hiding away?" she asked.

What could have been mistaken for actual shame flashed in Rory's eyes as he leaned forward to order.

"Ach, am wile sorry about that day at the Top-Yer-Trolly. Me mates was winding me up something awful for sleeping with a Fenian. I had to defend meself. At yer expense, I now see. Ye know yerself what this sectarian shite is like, like. Some people is too thick to see the way of the future, the mixing of the religions. If it's any consolation, them is me mates no more."

His copper uncle had obviously taught him a thing or two. If Dymphna hadn't spent a lifetime listening to her elders rabbiting on about the duplicity of Proddies, she would have thought him genuine. He was spewing forth the lies to gain her confidence so she would incriminate herself, then he would race to the peelers, and there would be a fierce banging on the front door later that evening, handcuffs clanking.

"This has nothing to do with me mates, anyroad," Rory said. "This has to do with you and O'Toole."

He stared at her pointedly.

"Double scotch, actually …" Dymphna reconsidered.

"Right ye are." He ordered and paid, and Dymphna guzzled down.

"Why I brought ye here—"

"I never laid a finger on that poofter O'Toole!" Dymphna hissed.

"It's all over town!"

Already?!

"As God's me witness, I never laid a finger on him!" Dymphna ventured in increasing desperation, feeling the cage tightening around her.

"If I know, if me *moller*'s heard tell of it, surely ye must realize the whole town's in on it! It's foolish to deny it!"

Dymphna's jaw dropped, the brick in her handbag growing steadily more useless.

"Yer *moller*?" she snorted. "Ye must think am quare and soft!"

"Am telling ye the God's honest truth!"

He steered her to a seat and placed her gently on the edge. Her head swam, the thoughts struggling to connect in her brain. Perhaps she shouldn't have guzzled down that double scotch.

"Ye might not believe it," Rory said, "am here to lend me support, but!"

She eyed him warily, searching his eyes for a flicker of connivance. She found none. No Proddy could be that well trained, even a copper's nephew.

"I swear am are!" Rory insisted, reaching out and touching her with kindness.

Dymphna startled herself by believing him, the waterworks abruptly spewing down her face, genuine or to gain his sympathy or from the double scotch she hadn't a clue.

"I kyanny keep it secret no longer!" she sobbed.

"So ye're finally letting on ye did it?"

Dymphna nodded gently into a tissue. Rory lips disappeared with an air of finality. So she *had* given herself to Henry O'Toole while pregnant with his wane after all! He quelled his rage, the pride of his impending fatherhood overwhelming his anger.

"Why did ye do it, Dymphna?" he pleaded to know.

She shifted gingerly, the sniffles disappearing into her tissue as she thought back to the scene at the ChipKebab.

"It was a harrowing experience, if ye must know," she admitted in a barely audible whisper.

He nodded with quick understanding and not a little anger, knowing how traumatic sexual relations between the floor staff and upper management could be.

"It's revolting, so it is!" Rory spat. "A full grown man taking advantage like that!"

Dymphna nodded bravely as the tears continued to flow.

"I was shameless, but," she revealed with a mournful wail. "I just didn't give a flying feck about meself nor anywan else! I gave it to him right there at the counter, bold as brass, with all the customers looking on!"

Rory started, his eyes ballooning with shock. His fingers slipped weakly from her curls. Dymphna turned to Rory and revealed in a conspiratorial whisper: "At first, I had terrible trouble fitting it all in. It took flimmin ages."

Rory blinked, and Dymphna grasped his knuckles and peered into his eyes, the tearful need to reveal her sordid deed all too evident.

"I had to try to shove it in a few times on the sly, as yer man from the chip vat kept giving us the eye. Wance it was finally all in, but, and tightly wrapped, ach, the power I felt! Nothing could stop me! Not the customers, not fear of reprisals, not even fear of the sack! I knew it was something I needed to do right then and there!"

Rory attempted a nod.

"And after it was done and over with," Dymphna continued, "Bridie tole me to go over and get it from him again. I really wasn't up for it, but the silly cow forced me!"

He tried to locate a vestige of sympathy.

"So I just marched out from behind the counter and did as she demanded right there at the table in the middle of the ChipKebab dinner rush!"

Rory scrutinized her with renewed horror.

"Ach, Bridie was egging me on, practically panting down me back! And that Fidelma shoulda kept her nose well out, but she couldn't help it, the nosy effin parker! Couldn't keep her eyes off the silly thing clutched in O'Toole's hands with the mess oozing outta it! Well, she *was* staring at us from the very same table ...!"

Rory no longer clung to a hope. Heaven help him, he knew the creature sat beside him was nothing but a filthy fecking slapper.

"I was mortified, right enough, when O'Toole couldn't hack it no more and spat up all over me. I kyanny blame yer man, but. It was a right manky mess by that stage."

Rory regarded her sadly. He was silent for much longer than a while, trying to get his head around the whole sorry event.

"I'll tell ye my only regret," Dymphna sniffed.

"Aye?" Rory asked with eager hope. "And what was that?"

"I just raced out for the courtroom afterwards, like, and left poor Bridie to clean up the mess. Splattered all over the floor and the table, it was. And all down me work smock, I might add. Some I just licked off. I quite like the taste of it, ye know."

Rory inspected a beer mat, feeling cheap, vulgar and soiled for having had her himself. What base perversions could be hidden behind a slash of lipstick from Boots the Chemist and a few barrettes!

"Wait just wan minute!" Dymphna said, her tear-strained eyes flashing with suspicion. "I thought ye saw it all yerself!"

And here Rory's rage finally made itself known.

"Naw," he said through tight lips. "I didn't see it. But from what am hearing, if I had been looking on with all the ollers, that woulda gotten ye even more randy. And I think ye're having a right laugh at me by revealing all this filth to me. Ye've some cheek, blathering on about yer sick-making pervy sexual exploits with anoller man when ye know full well am the faller of that wane ye're carrying! And making a show of yerself in the ChipKebab in yer state, making a mockery of the sacred institution of mollerhood, fairly makes me wanny spew! I invited ye here today to offer to make an honest woman outta ye, but after all this revolting palaver, I kyanny even bear to look ye in the eye! Am mortified to have ye as the moller of me first wane! There's many a name for what ye are, Dymphna Flood. The most civil that comes to mind, but, is a desperate mingin exhibitionist slapper!"

Dymphna slowly took in his purple-veined rage, his lancelike contempt, with a horrified disbelief. Then she threw back her head and exploded with mirth, the empty glasses jingling as she pounded the table. Rory shuddered with the agony of restraint, his nails lacerating his balled palms, resisting every urge to dislocate her eyeballs.

"Ye headbin!" Dymphna finally managed, her stomach weak with laughter. "I was talking about the ground glass I put in O'Toole's TakkoKebab to cause him harm! And all the time, ye thought, ye thought …!"

Her roars heaved anew. Rory lurched back, aghast. And then she saw the realization dawn, and he looked up at her with a sheepish grimace.

"Ach, I've made a right show of meself, aye?" he asked.

Dymphna's brow wrinkled.

"What was all this palaver, then, about yer uncle been a copper?" she asked. "Ye had me shitein meself with fear!"

"Just to let ye know what a good family ye'd be marrying into, like," Rory said, cheeks ablaze.

"*Marrying* into?!?"

Dymphna's merriment swiftly dissolved, while Rory's face settled into seriousness.

"Am here to do the civil thing and ask for yer hand in holy matrimony. Marry me, Dymphna!" Rory begged.

Her arms were a fortress, and her eyes glared with the hatred of centuries of oppression. Her curls shimmered.

"Are ye a fecking gee-eyed eejit?! Me set up home in the effin Waterside?! With the likes of you and yer whole clan of fecking Orange-loving bastards?! Ye can take that hand and shove it up yer filthy Proddy arse!"

"Are ye still denying am the faller of that wane growing in yer stomach?"

"*Why* do ye keep harping on about being the faller? Youse Proddies don't own everything, ye know!"

Rory cleared his throat delicately.

"Me auntie works at the Health Clinic. She tole me all about you thinking ye had two wanes of different ages growing inside ye, wan six weeks aul and the oller two weeks aul. I just put two and two togeller."

Nurse Sheila Bryant! Rory's auntie!

"That flimmin cunt—!" Dymphna seethed.

The glasses jangled as she thrust herself up from the table. "I was mistaken! Henry O'Toole's the faller of this wane! This *Green Bogside wane!*"

Rory jumped up and reached for her stomach.

"Lemme have a quick feel, hi!"

"Get yer hands offa me wane!" Dymphna screamed, smacking him in the shoulder with her handbag.

Rory yelped as the brick cracked against his shoulder blade, and Dymphna beat a retreat with shuddering knees. Outside the pub, she heaved against the brick wall, her limbs trembling, tears welling anew.

Henry O'Toole couldn't give a toss about her; to him she was just a pathetic laugh. Someone had just begged her to marry him, happy to claim the bastard as his own, and she had just turned him down.

Was it the hormones making her a raving lunatic? What the feck had she just done?

£ £ £ £

"The defendant will stand."

Ursula did as instructed, her heart giddy with hope. She suspected the magistrates would realize only someone wrongly accused would descend into such desperate displays of outrage. She adjusted the collar of her pantsuit and smiled down at Ms. Murphy. When all was said and done and the ludicrous charges dropped, Ursula wouldn't hold her solicitor's uselessness against her.

Some doubt niggled Ursula, to be sure, but the magistrates seemed to be beaming at her, secretly revealing with their eyes that her innocence was assured, that, once she was vindicated, she would be free to file her counter-claim for wrongful prosecution in an office on the next floor. Jed nodded his support. A magistrate cleared his throat.

"Mrs. Barnett, ladies and gentlemen of the court, we have given careful consideration to the evidence and sworn witness testimony presented before us today. After reviewing the facts of the case, it did not take us long to reach a unanimous verdict. We find the case proved ..."—and here he actually winked at Ursula and flashed her a kindly smile—"... not guilty!"

Ursula squealed in triumph as she bounded from the dock and flung her arms around a gasping Ms. Murphy. The solicitor almost crashed against her desk. Knees shuddering, Ursula made her way to Jed, his strong hands shielding her from the Floods' glares, his lips caressing her eyelids with kisses. She tore from him and sidestepped towards Fionnuala. Fionnuala flinched at her approach, but she needn't have.

"Don't ye worry yerself, Fionnuala," Ursula said with neighborly grace. "I forgive ye. I'll even help ye pay them hospital bills if ye want!"

Fionnuala couldn't meet the eye of one who was so much her moral superior, but she made her gratefulness known with an imperceptible nod.

"Th-that's terrible civil of ye, Ursula," Fionnuala said. She eventually forced her eyes into those of her wronged sister-in-law. "It makes me almost sick to me stomach to say it, but am sorry for all the persecution we've tortured ye with. Ye were nothing but wile civil to us all them years."

"Ach, go on away a that," Ursula waved her off kindly, so relieved of her win in court that she could forgive her sister-in-law, her mother, her brother, indeed even Molly, any trespasses, no matter how malicious. "Kiss and make up, shall we?"

The wanes horseshoed the two old backbiters, cheering and pointing in delighted shock as Fionnuala and Ursula did indeed wrap their arms around their suddenly unburdened shoulders and exchanged a wee kiss.

Paddy marched up to Jed and extended a greasy hand. They shook in a manly fashion.

"The best man won, hi," Paddy said, wrapping his arm around Jed's back. "Am no sore loser, me. Darts next week?"

And even the magistrates approached and surrounded the happy party, clapping in their gowns and beaming proudly at the power of reconciliation of the Northern Irish justice system.

Then Ursula stirred with a jolt. What in the name of all that was sacred was she doing still enslaved in the dock, with the magistrates glaring their reproof from above? She'd have to lay off those tablets to calm her nerves she gobbled as of late, she thought, plummeting back from her flight of fancy, registering the sniggers that had been coming from the gallery, the look of concern that clouded Ms. Murphy's face at her side.

"Mrs. Barnett?" a magistrate repeated. "Are you listening?"

Ursula stared in confusion.

"Wh-what are ye after saying?" she asked.

"I said we have found your case proved *guilty.*"

Ursula collapsed against the railing as the magistrate rabbited on.

"In view of your hitherto unblemished record and, indeed, your age, we don't believe there is any necessity for a custodial sentence. However, the court takes a dim view of maliciously abusing children, in addition to the fact that your obvious perjury must be discouraged. Therefore, we have come to the decision that you must pay the court a fine of £500, and you are ordered to pay compensation to your victim in the sum of £3000, the award of which shall be lodged in court, invested and managed by the Court Funds Office and released to the minor at the appropriate time. Do you wish to ask for time to pay these amounts?"

Still reeling, Ursula hadn't a clue exactly what he was blathering on about, let alone how she and Jed were meant to propagate £3500, but she shook her head vehemently. She wasn't going to give Fionnuala the satisfaction of hearing her plead poverty.

"No, I don't," she said. Then an edge crept into her voice as she peered up at them, her lips disappearing, anger simmering. "But what I *do* wish is that *youse* lot sat up there would catch yerselves on! Youse are away in the head, so youse are—"

"I'd advise you to think carefully about your comments, madam!" Magistrate Hope warned.

"Advise me hole! Youse sit up there laying down the law and ye've not an ounce of common sense between the three of youse!"

"I won't stand this impudence any longer!"

"It's flimmin pathetic, so it is!" Ursula slammed the railing of the dock.

"Ms. Murphy, would you please exercise control over your client this moment!"

"Sitting up there all high and mighty," she shrieked, veins bulging, "swallowing a pack of lies any simpleton can see through! If youse had any judgment at all, you would've seen that. And *am* accused of perjury?! Bloody useless, so youse are!"

She turned to the public gallery.

"Youse want me money? Torturing me when am trying to peddle ferget-me-nots for the good of St. Eugene's, yet ye've enough cash for a flippin fish fillet for tea?"

The magistrates gawped at the unstable woman in the dock. What on earth was she on about? they wondered.

"Mrs. Barnett! Do not address the public gallery!"

"Am selling that flimmin 5 Murphy, so!" she roared. "Am unsaddling meself of that milestone around me neck and kicking that hateful aul woman out into the street! Then youse can collect all the carer's allowance ye want! Air conditioning, me arse!"

"Mrs. Barnett, I am holding you in contempt of court! Prison officer!"

Jed leaped up in alarm as the dock officer marched over to his wife. The magistrate turned to the lumpen masses in their uniforms.

"Security! Remove this woman!"

Jed sat back down as prison officers circled her.

"Right ye are," said one, grabbing Ursula's arm.

Ursula shook him off.

"Don't ye lay a flimmin finger on me, ye stoke!" she seethed.

"Take this ... deranged creature! ... *down to the holding cell!*" Magistrate Hope barked.

They dragged the mother of three down into the darkened pit.

£ £ £ £

"Feckin brilliant!" Fionnuala brayed into her wanes faces. "Justice was done! That slapper got shown up for what she is!"

Paddy had sent Eoin on a quick trip to the off-license across the street, and they were guzzling tins of lager in the court car park amongst the solicitors' BMWs. The pinstripes passed by, shooting them nervous glances. Paddy had propped Eda against a bumper and shoved a fag between her lips to keep her content. Nobody noticed Siofra teaching Seamus how to pelt pebbles at the windows of the courthouse.

"And banged up in the cells and all!" Paddy roared, wiping the lager foam from his upper lip. "Fairly split me sides at the sight of Ursula struggling down them steps, clawing and kicking at the security!"

"Mammy," Seamus wondered, "will Auntie Ursula be visiting wer Lorcan?"

"We can but hope, wane," Fionnuala laughed, hugging her youngest against her leggings.

"We're minted now, so we are!" Paddy said.

"What was all that shite about the money being lodged in court, hi?" Eoin wanted to know. They all turned to Moira for clarification.

"They said it would be lodged in the court until the appropriate time," Moira recited from her notebook.

The joy was snatched from Fionnuala's eyes.

"Ye kyanny trust them Proddy bastards where money's concerned," she said.

"When's the appropriate time?" Paddy wondered.

"Now!" Fionnuala decided. "With all them bills to be paid! Am away off to see about getting that check in me mitts."

"Mammy," Moira warned weakly. "Go on and let me come with ye."

But it wasn't common sense Fionnuala needed. She knew well the power of a shrieking working class mother.

"Naw!" Fionnuala insisted, selecting instead Siofra, Seamus and Padraig to accompany her; if their malnourished faces couldn't turn the stone heart of a court official, nothing could.

She marched off towards the Information Booth, the wanes trailing behind. The girl behind the counter warily eyed the approaching crew.

"Me wane's after winning damages of 3000 quid," Fionnuala announced. "Flood Versus Barnett. We'd like it now, ta."

"I've ... we've *all* heard of the case, aye," the girl said, pecking her keyboard, eyes unable to meet Fionnuala's. "What age is the wane?"

"The poor wee soul's but eleven," Fionnuala said, pushing Padraig forward so the woman could verify his pain, suffering and youth.

"Looks like when all is said and done, you'll be getting about £6000," the girl said, her gaze frozen five inches over Fionnuala's right ear.

No fool her, Fionnuala wasn't about to let on that her money had magically doubled due to some clerical error. Her eyes jigged, all her Christmases having come at once, the money already spent.

"Ach, that's grand, sure!" Fionnuala warbled, wrapping a squirming Padraig into her bosom. "Go on and give it to us now!"

The girl faltered, her lips straining to maintain a smile.

"Erm, Mrs ... Flood, right now it's only £3000."

"Don't ye be taking the mick outta me, ye sleekit minger!" Fionnuala said, swiftly incensed. "Ye're after telling me I was to be receiving six thousand!"

"I was including the interest."

"The *interest?!*" Fionnuala's eyes glinted with just that, then she gave an easy shrug. "Ach, ye can pay us that later, sure. Go on and give us the three thousand the day! When are we to get wer hands on the rest?"

The girl fought to contain a smile, and Fionnuala fought to contain a fist in her overbite.

"Well, you see, Mrs. Flood," she said in a tone best reserved for spastics, "you'll get it all in one lump sum. Actually, if I have all the facts straight, which I believe I do, you're not to be receiving the money at all. Your son is.

And we will be keeping the money—*all* the money—in a special fund until he turns of age."

"And what age's that?"

"Eighteen."

"Ye kyanny mean ..." Fionnuala calculated the years on her fingers, then her eyes bulged. "Seven years? *Seven flippin years* we're meant to wait?"

She fumed for a second.

"*Naw!*" Fionnuala decided, refusing point blank to accept what her ears had heard. "I want a wee word with yer superior!"

"They'll tell you the same thing, I'm afraid."

"Aye, ye're right to be afraid!" Fionnuala snarled. "What about this £500 Ursula Barnett is meant to pay the court? Do ye expect me to believe youse are to put up with waiting seven years for yer own money as well?"

"That, actually, is none of your business."

Fionnuala inspected her face with a mounting suspicion, and the girl shrunk from the drunken glare.

"And could ye tell me exactly what part of the Waterside you be's from?" Fionnuala demanded.

"Excuse me?"

"What do ye call wer town?" Fionnuala pressed.

"Sorry?"

"What do ye call the town we is living in?!"

"L—"

"I knew it!" Fionnuala shrieked. "*London*derry! Ye're nothing but a thieving Proddy bitch, so ye are! I can see it in yer eyes and yer Sephora mascara! Youse Orange bastards make sure yer own pockets is lined with quids while the likes of us, hard working Catholic families, is expected to make do with a pot of spuds and rummaging through the bargain bins of the January sales for ladder-ridden tights! Same as it ever was!"

"I can assure you, ma'am—"

"Ach, assure me arse!" Fionnuala raged. "We're all to be dead of hunger in seven flippin years! Let *that* be on yer cunty Orange conscience!"

And as Fionnuala marched away, dragging Padraig, Siofra and a wailing Seamus behind her, she realized it really wasn't the Proddy bitch's fault; it was Ursula's, promising them money and yet again not able to make good on it. Another windfall snatched from her claws, Fionnuala stomped back into the car park, the weight of the world on her shoulders.

£ £ £ £

Ursula cast a wary eye at the scraggly deadbeat, her arms peppered with weeping sores, passed out on the only available loo.

"What for the love of God am I doing here," Ursula sobbed through the bars at her solicitor, "banged up with the common hooligans of Derry City?"

"That, madam, should be painfully obvious," Ms. Murphy sighed.

The solicitor searched Ursula's tortured face, then finally asked with a surprising undertone of sympathy, "Would you like me to locate you a cup of tea?"

"Ach, go on away a that with yer cuppa!" Ursula spat with contempt. "Them wardens has been pumping me full of tea since I stepped foot in here! Am bursting for a wee, if ye must know, but don't trust meself to lift that junkie offa the loo! This cell's flimmin boggin, dreary and damp and them pipes keep clanking until I kyanny hear meself think and am dead starving with cold! Why is me bed expected to be that concrete slab, how long am I expected to be holed up here, and why won't themmuns let me husband in to visit me?"

"You're not serving a life sentence. You should be spending your time here reflecting on your inappropriate behavior in the courtroom, not chatting with your husband."

Atop the seatless loo, the druggie stirred and Ursula let out a mournful wail.

"Deloused, am gonny haveta be! A good Christian woman like me! Would ye credit it?"

Ms. Murphy inspected the disheveled woman in her aqua pantsuit with a sympathy that tightened Ursula's throat.

"Do you not see that you could have spared yerself this indignity—and I daresay many more in yer life besides—had you only been able to control these outbursts of yours?"

"Ye cheeky wee …!" Ursula began halfheartedly.

Ms. Murphy hesitated, then, hoping she wouldn't live to regret it, reached between the bars and stroked Ursula's aubergine bob.

"Do you not understand," Ms. Murphy said softly, "that when you react with anger—no matter how justified—*you* look the fool? With the glinty eyes and bulging veins in the neck and the roars pouring out of your mouth? There's something to be said for keeping a civil tongue in your head, for maintaining a shred of self-respect befitting your age when those you love and who have loved you have turned their backs."

Ursula couldn't believe she was being lectured in anger management by a Proddy one-third her age, but considering the wads of cash they had lavished upon her, she supposed it was only right.

"You may find this difficult to believe," Ms. Murphy continued, "but my heart goes out to you. I understand how difficult it is to control yourself. If you must know," and here she glanced over at the junkie and lowered her voice, "my own family disowned me when I married a Catholic lad, and I felt all the anger and betrayal you displayed in court. There was flying crockery and slamming doors for months round ours. I understand, I really do. But the closing arguments of a personal injury case in Her Majesty's Court is neither the time nor the place to unburden yerself."

Ms. Murphy turned gratefully at the sound of keys clanking down the damp corridor.

"Here comes the warden now. For the sake of us both—don't forget I've just lost a case because of you—you must keep your anger in check. You must go back into the court and you must apologize to the magistrates," Ms. Murphy begged. "Say you're sorry for abusing the court, or you won't be going home! Do you promise me?"

"A-aye," Ursula agreed.

As they led her through the cells, Ursula, still reeling from her discovery that Ms. Murphy possessed a history and a heart, cast reproving glances at the stokes within and adjusted the buttons of her pantsuit. She was so much better than all of them.

They entered the courtroom. Ms. Murphy read Ursula's face as her client marched past the assembled Floods. Ursula paid Fionnuala no mind. Ms. Murphy was relieved.

The magistrates filed in and sat down, seemingly enduring a second glance at the guilty woman in the dock purely out of their best graces.

"As magistrates," the worst of them said, "we feel it is vital to protect and foster a basic respect for the authority of the law."

"My client wishes to apologize unreservedly for her outburst," Ms. Murphy quickly ventured. "Now if your honors would be so kind as—"

"With the greatest of respect, we'd prefer to hear all this from Mrs. Barnett herself."

They eyed Ursula expectantly. Ursula clasped her hands together in a close approximation of demureness, but her fingernails bit into the brass. She counted to ten as Ms. Murphy had instructed, then spoke.

"When I think, me lords," Ursula began in a reedy voice that soon picked up speed, "about why I behaved as I did, all I could see in me mind's eye was me family prancing outta the court with 3000 quid of mines clutched in their grabby fists. I haven't a clue where we're meant to conjure up such a sum from. It sickens me heart to say it, but we've no money left in that piggin bank account of wer's! I kyanny blame me family for their pig ignorance; they've never stepped foot outta the Bogside in their lives and doesn't know no better. Falsifying hospital records and cajoling Mrs. Feeney to spew out lies to further their own agenda—"

"We are not here to retry your case, Mrs. Barnett!"

Ursula jumped, and the magistrates watched a variety of emotions cross her face. Then her lips curled with contempt as she singled them out with one trembling finger.

"Youse, but, have years of training and have yer licenses and such, allowing youse to tell truth from fiction. If yer reaction to me case is anything to go by, youse need to get yerself down to the job center for some retraining, the whole sorry lot of youse!"

Ms. Murphy hurried over to Ursula's side and tugged her sleeve in alarm, all her personal revelations for naught.

"When yer man there called out guilty," Ursula seethed, "I just couldn't contain meself! Youse've landed me with a criminal record, youse've had me banged up in the cell with a druggie who couldn't keep her eyes offa me cleavage. I kyanny blame me family for their greed; the wans at fault is the three pig-ignorant simpletons wearing daft robes!"

The magistrates exchanged looks of abject disbelief.

"We've given you a fair hearing, madam! We went over the evidence and—"

"Fair hearing, me arse! I was on oath when I tole youse about that wane and his petrol bombs—"

"Not these fantasy petrol bombs yet again!" sputtered one.

"Ach, lemme get a word in edgewise! Are youse not sick of the sounds of yer own judgmental whinging?!"

"Madam, we are giving you final warning!"

"Ye know well enough where ye can shove yer effin mingin final warning, ye clarty wee gee-bag!"

"You are in contempt of court *again!*" one sputtered with barely concealed rage.

"Me solicitor tole me raging people make fools of themselves, and wan look at yer purple face and I can see she was dead right! A right aul eejit ye look! All three of youse!"

"You will be remanded in custody for five days!" he barked. "Security! Take this woman down *again!*"

Fionnuala actually felt sorry for Ursula as the guards dragged her, howling, into the pit. She was raging they wouldn't be receiving the compensation money for seven years, but she also was of no doubt the court would demand the Barnetts write the check before sundown. Between Ursula or the laws of the oppressors, Fionnuala knew which her hatred was greater for. She did her best to mask her pity behind a grin of triumph as Ursula's shrieks were smothered; she didn't want her family to see her weak.

As the masses rose with a smattering of applause, all Jed could think of, heaven help him, was five days of unrestricted access to all the bookies and off-licenses in town. Little did he realize, however, that Ursula would be much safer in that cell than he would be alone in their dream house.

SIOFRA'S FIRST HOLY COMMUNION

11

Siofra beamed proudly into the mirror between the curling S Club 7 posters at the gown of her dreams, purchased with IRA gun-running, drug-pushing, midnight-house search, kneecapping, headjob bullet-in-the-skull money.

The bodice of her Princess Royal gown caressed her undeveloped chest as the layers of tulle skimmed sleekly over her bony hips and rippled to the floor. Her mother had relented and gotten her the battery-operated flashing tiara. It jagged into her scalp, but twinkling atop her brow, it transformed her life from one of raw spuds and cheese and onion crisps into her very own wonderworld. She did a wee shimmy at her reflection and giggled.

"It's effin class, aye, Eoin?"

On his sister's Power Puff Girls bedspread, Eoin opened the sparkly white handbag which held *My First Missal*, twenty pence and a strawberry lipgloss. He shoved 100 tablets of Ecstasy inside and nodded with a grimace.

"Effin class woulda been had them McDaid brollers cancelled me debt instead of handing it over to you," he sighed. "That's life, but."

Eoin understood how the shining eyes of a wee bride of Jesus hungering for her first communion wafer had softened a trio of concrete McDaid hearts. It didn't matter, as soon he would have the £300 he owed anyway. The wanes in their communion best would be banging on all the doors of the Bogside, scrubbed palms outstretched for hard cash. They'd be minted, and would gladly hand over a fiver for a winger. Even after giving Siofra her ten percent, he'd still have £100 left over after he paid the McDaid brothers off. Then he could continue his surveillance to be sure he wouldn't have to grass on his auntie Ursula, and could get himself a new video game into the bargain.

"Ye know what you're to do?" Eoin asked his sister.

"Aye," she hummed vaguely, adjusting some frill on her hem. "Do ye think Mammy'll be up for me wearing me frock to school the morrow?"

"Ye headbin!"

"Grainne's sure to go effin mad when she latches eyes on me. The silly spastic passed out from the strength of the sun on the beach in Spain, and her face's covered with wile ugly blisters. Am gonny be princess of St. Moluag's after all!"

Eoin grabbed her and twirled her from the mirror, her head a searchlight.

"How much are ye to ask for them wingers?"

Siofra heaved a sigh.

"Am gonny go no lower than five quid," she recited. "No pence pieces. And I kyanny let on to the Faller am selling in the church. Am aren't an eejit, Eoin! Now am away off to ask me mammy!"

She raced down the stairs, beams pulsating from her skull.

"Mammy! Mammy!"

Fionnuala was in the front hall, clutching the phone, a look of horror in her eyes. She waved the wane away, but some corner of her subconscious mind brightened at the sight of the girl in the gown; Siofra would have to fast before her first communion; that would be one less mouth to feed. Siofra skipped into the sitting room to wake her daddy.

"What do ye mean," Fionnuala hissed down the line, "ye've not a clue where them hooligans live?"

"Somewhere in Creggan Estate, just," Lorcan said from the pay phone at Magilligan.

"Yer auntie's banged up in the cell now. She made a wile eejit of herself in the court and was ordered to pay us 3000 quid. Them Proddy bastards of the court won't give it to us for anoller seven years, but I kyanny blame yer auntie for that. Ye'll never credit it, son; me heart goes out to her."

"I never thought I'd live to see the day," Lorcan smirked.

"Ye're dead certain ye kyanny call them hooligans off?"

"Liam and Finbar was released two days ago. I gave em Ursula's name and address, and that was me done with it. If ye're up for it, ye could go banging from door to door up Creggan asking for em. Them is both called Doherty, but."

"God bless us and save us! Fully three quarters of the people living in Creggan is called Doherty! I've not enough get-go in me feet to go ferreting em out. Ach, well."

She gave a gentle shrug. Perhaps it served aul bitch Ursula right, anyroad, she thought.

"I kyanny visit ye this Sunday. Ye know it's yer sister's First Holy Communion. I wish ye could be sitting with us in the church."

"Ach, I'll be out in time for Seamus' first, so."

"I don't half miss ye."

"Aye, and me you. Cheerio, mam."

"Keep yer arse to the wall, son."

Fionnuala hung up just as Eoin was slinking down the stairs.

"C'mere a wee moment, you," she said. "Could ye not loan us anoller hundred quid there? We've credit card bills spewing outta wer ears."

"There's a problem with me money at the moment," Eoin admitted. "Next week, but."

"Ach, ye're useless, you! Get yerself round to yer granny's and don't ye come back!"

The door slammed and she was glad to see the back of him. If she could only figure out a way to keep the credit card companies at bay for seven years. Fionnuala sat down with a pencil and began to calculate just how many days there were until Padraig's eighteenth birthday.

£ £ £ £

Even arsified, Jed realized something was wrong with the front garden the moment he pulled into the driveway. After wringing Ursula's hands through the bars of her cell for an hour or so, he had headed for the nearest pub to melt the fear which had frozen him since the verdict had been called. The fear was for himself, not Ursula. He had guzzled four pints and wondered which financial acrobatics he might perform to conjure up the £3500 they now owed the court.

Jed swiveled out of his Lexus, barely succeeded in closing the door and lurched to the front gate of their dream house, liquor bottles clinking in an off-license carrier bag. Almost tripping over the garden hose, he peered through the approaching dusk at the shabby lawn; they had let the landscaper go months before.

"What the ...?!"

Someone had gone crazy with the weed killer, scrawling out the epitaph FUCKIN MINTED CUNTS! into the decaying grass, fully three feet wide. It would take weeks to grow out. They were destined to be known in the neighborhood as the Fuckin Minted Cunts now. How ironic, Jed snorted, thinking of their bank balance. The garden gnomes, he noticed, had been spared.

He tried three times to place his key in the front door, then squinted at the window. CUNTS! CUNTS! CUNTS! was scratched into the glass.

Jed peered at the lettering in fascination, trying to deduce how it had been executed. If it had been made with a box cutter, which he finally decided it had, it could only be removed with fire polishing, which they hadn't the funds to afford. Well, he thought, as long as the perpetrators kept the blades to their windows.

He heard a rustling in the hedges, and turned with a shiver, hoping the thugs weren't still lying in wait.

Once upon a time, fresh from the battlefields of DaNang, Jed might've played the have-a-go hero, grappling a golf iron and lurking amongst the gnomes, ready to launch a counter-offensive. But lately he had given up hope of wanting his life to continue.

After a quick glance at the hedges revealed no sign of track suits or hooded tops, Jed scuttled into the house and reached for the phone; he needed the cops there. Fast. He punched 999 with unsteady fingers. Then a vision of Ursula's twisted face shrieking abuse at him rose in his mind. He could only imagine the roars out of her if she heard he had contacted the hated Protestant oppressors. Deferring to the higher authority of Ursula, he let the receiver slip back onto the cradle.

He double-bolted the doors with a look over his shoulder.

£ £ £ £

Charlie and Seamus lolled against a car parked on Shipquay Street outside the thatched cottages of the Craft Village, the only place in the city reminiscent of flaxen mills and pan pipes and open turf fires, and therefore likely to attract a tourist. They were lying in wait for the handbag of a just such a victim to nick at screwdriver point. The travelers checks would have them in wingers for weeks.

One nudged the other at the sight of Dymphna impelling her body down the slope past them in her ChipKebab smock, ten minutes late for her shift. It wasn't so much the glow from her that betrayed her unwanted pregnancy, more the glower.

"Filthy Orange-loving slapper!" Seamus hollered.

Dymphna cast him daggers, the disdain turning to alarm as he fired a rock at her stomach. She was stunned to see her hands shoot out to protect the beast within. The rock cracked against her knuckles, and Dymphna seethed, all but concussed with rage.

"I'll claw the eyes offa yer fecking gacky faces if ye fling anoller rock at me wane!" she roared, knuckles biting.

"Fecking Orange beast, ye mean!"

"Me wee nadger's a *living being*, Orange or no! I'll have youse up for attempted murder!"

They guffawed as her spiked heels galumphed over the cobbles, her aching hands flapping, the curses muttering out of her, for once in her life her step uncertain.

"Aye, run to the peelers!" Charlie yelled. "Just like yer pansy broller Eoin! We've seen him consorting with the coppers, licking them sweaty Brit arses! Yer family's a disgrace to the good Catholics of Derry!"

"Ach, go and feck yerselves," she spat over her shoulder, but the abuse was halfhearted. Somewhere in her muddled brain she knew they had every right to slag her off as she *was*, after all, a slapper.

Dymphna arrived, heaving for breath, at the ChipKebab door and paused to examine the damage to her knuckles. They were red but unfortunately not mangled enough to qualify for sick leave. She tousled her curls and appraised her appearance in the side view mirror of a parked florist van. A gash of lipstick, and she'd be fine. But what was that look in her eyes? She hauled open the door and stropped towards her timecard. She was serving her fifth Chip-ButtyKebab when she realized the look was, another first for her, shame.

£ £ £ £

Ursula, slouching on her slab of a cot, had just circled 'R-E-J-O-I-C-E' in the word search puzzle when the wee hole in the door snapped back.

"Ye've a visitor here to see ye," the guard said beyond the eyehole.

Ursula cast the puzzle book aside as her heart leapt. Jed? Francine? Ms. Murphy to finally deliver her from that hellhole? The door was unlocked, and she wilted at the sight of Father Hogan, looking as if he were there to perform her Last Rites before she approached the gallows. She wrapped her arms around herself and flashed the traitor the look he deserved. They faced off in the cell.

"Missing me packet for the church collection, are ye?" she asked. "More fool you, as themmuns've locked me handbag away with me shoelaces."

"Ursula," he said, deeply sorrowed. "Am here to support ye in yer time of need."

He attempted a step toward her and she shrank, a touch of the shoulder out of the question.

"Christian compassion doled out for a price, more like," she sniffed. "Am only too well aware of it. Now."

Father Hogan reached into his pocket and revealed a bouquet of roses he had just bought at the corner shop.

"I smuggled these in past the security for ye. The girls of the choir had a whip-round for ye, ye see. They heard about yer plight and their hearts went out to ye. Maybe ye can hide em under yer wee cot there so the guards kyanny lay eyes on em?"

"Does the girls want me back singing in the choir?" Ursula asked.

The naked hope on her face, the persistent innocence at odds with her years, gnawed at Father Hogan's heart.

"A-aye," he lied, heaven help him. "Wer church, but, is in the posh section of town, and the bishop kyanny allow themmuns what've been banged up to participate in church organizations. I pleaded with the bishop and all, like, to no avail. Faller Kilpatrick, mind, over at St. Moluag's, he's certain to welcome ye with open arms. Fully two thirds of the congregation there has been in and out of Magilligan and various other prisons dotting the countryside, as ye well know."

"Hardened stokes," Ursula muttered. "Gangs of sinners."

"Ye're to be released in time for their First Holy Communion mass, but. And did ye not tell me yer wee goddaughter's to be Receiving for the first time there?"

Ursula seemed to be struggling with some inner torment. She finally said in a voice that was barely a whisper, "Faller, I kyanny go back to the Bogside! I kyanny step foot inside St. Moluag's! All me life I tried to rid meself of the likes of them wee-minded gacks. Me mammy forced me to leave school at the age of fifteen to work in the shirt factory. That was me sorted for the rest of me life, I thought. When I married me husband, but, and spent all them years traveling round the world with me wanes in tow, I set eyes on things the likes of which no Bogside wane would've ever credited. Still, me heart was aching something terrible, hungering for the green pastures of the Foyle, the loving arms of me mammy and daddy and me brollers and sisters. Me husband was sent away to Vietnam, and I wasn't slow in trailing me wanes here to Derry to live in 1973."

Ursula leaned towards the slightly mortified priest and raised a conspiratorial eyebrow.

"Being banged up in this cell now," she said, "it puts me in mind of what mighta happened if ..."

She took a deep breath.

"Do ye not mind me revealing all in the confessional to ye a while back? The disgrace I engaged in in 1973? The shame I brought upon wer family name?"

Father Hogan's eyes widened at the sudden memory. He stared at her as if she had just announced she was a post-op transsexual.

"Ye kyanny be saying," he gasped. "Ye mean that was *you*?"

"Aye, faller, it was," Ursula said. She leaned back and moved her eyes over his body. "Now ye understand me problem. When me husband retired, I forced him to come back to the hometown I loved, desperate to make amends for me sins of 1973. Me family wasn't having none of it, no matter how much I begged and cajoled. When we won the lotto, I fairly threw the pound notes at em, but I was persecuted and tortured for that, and now here am are, banged up in this cell with no loo roll, and me family is to blame. I've made me own peace with the Lord, but, and that's all that matters."

Father Hogan was silent for quite a while. He finally trusted himself to speak.

"If me memory serves, yer husband's a Yank. Have ye never given thought to moving away from Derry? Living with his relations over in America? There ye might find somewan to welcome ye with open arms."

"Aye, surely," Ursula said with a shrug, "when hell freezes over."

Father Hogan had nothing else to say to this woman.

"Shall we not sit down," he finally acquiesced, "and say a wee rosary togeller for yer speedy release?"

"More practical might be for ye to use yer influence to locate me some bog roll instead."

He perched beside her next to the seatless loo and began to pray.

£ £ £ £

1973 (PART III)

Ursula plodded down the hill to Murphy Crescent, arches aching in her platforms, shag wig swinging at her side. She had been walking for hours. Mascara cascaded down her face from the agony of it all.

As she passed the barricade of burnt-out cars, the shame of what she and Francine had done finally overwhelmed her. Down the pavement swaggered paratroopers. Considering what she had just been through, the sight of them made her even more sick to her stomach than usual. She avoided the creepy little eyes peering out at her from the boot polish on their faces. She hurried past the barricade, almost tripping on a charred gas pedal.

Through the drizzle, she could see the lights blazing in the front room of 5 Murphy, the shadows of a gyrating crowd in the bay window. She cringed as she made out boozy voices raised in a song of rebellion:

"Armored cars and tanks and guns, came to take away wer sons!"

She paused at the front door, head hanging. There was a flickering of the net curtain, a hissed "She's back! She's here!" and the door flew open.

They were all there, their faces ablaze with anticipation, their skulls adorned with little paper hats from last Christmas that someone had crawled up to the loft to unearth. She made out bits of her mammy and daddy Patrick and Eda, her brothers and sisters Roisin and her man Eric, Paddy and his fiancé Fionnuala, Stewart and his wife Frannie, Cait and her husband Steve, the neighbors from the right the Hughes and from the left the Sheenys, even her wanes Gretchen, Egbert and Vaughn in their jimjams, the last people she wanted to lay eyes on, all struggling to be the proud one to drag her over the threshold.

"Ursula, love!"

"Welcome home!"

Ursula's head swiveled, but she couldn't locate a smidgen of sobriety in any of their eyes (except the wanes). Fingers clamped onto her limbs and maneuvered her into the sitting room. Over the Bleeding Heart of Jesus had been strung a hastily-scrawled banner Ursula Go Bragh! Eire's Savior! *Ursula forever! Ireland's savior!*

"Anoller martyr for aul Ireland, anoller martyr for the crown!" *blared from the transistor atop the china cabinet.*

"At long last, ye've finally done something to make us proud of ye!" her daddy Patrick said.

Roisin grabbed her and tugged her to the best seat in the house—the chair closest to the fireplace. Paddy shoved a lager in her hand, Stewart a fag in the other. Had they been able to afford them, Ursula was sure there would've been cigars.

"*Tell us all about it, hi!*" *Fionnuala breathed, curling herself at Ursula's feet and staring up awe-struck at her heroine in the flesh.* "*I never liked ye much, I must admit. Now, but …!*" *Her eyes glistened with pride.* "*When Paddy and me gets married, I'll be wile proud to have ye as me sister-in-law! Please, Ursula, be me maid of honor!*"

"*Get them wanes into bed now!*" *Ursula hissed.*

The children scuttled upstairs, and Ursula stared in rising horror as Cait grabbed Stewart's hips, who grabbed Eda's hips and so on, and an impromptu Conga line broke out before her disbelieving eyes. Ursula's head was splitting. They can-canned around her in the cramped sitting room, lager spilling from their tins, the floorboards creaking, the fringes of the overhead lamp jumping, the few precious items in the china cabinet lurching from side to side. As they burst into song,

"*Olé, olé, olé,* hey!" Kick!

Ursula burst into tears.

"*Olé, olé, olé,* hey!" Kick!

"*Stop it! Stop all this flimmin foolish carry-on now!*" *Ursula begged.* "*Am not worthy, so am aren't!*"

They collapsed on any available horizontal surface, the fireguard banging into the smoldering embers, the poker knocked to the side, as their lager-fuelled laughter and love for their savior poured down the wallpaper.

"*Ye've not a clue what me and Francine's after doing!*" *Ursula sobbed.*

"*Aye, we know right enough!*" *Paddy said.*

"*Ye've snuffed the life outta two Brit bastards!*" *Eda rejoiced, smothering her favorite daughter in kisses and hugs.*

"*Naw! Naw! Youse've got it all wrong!*"

It all came back to her as she struggled to remove Eda's arms from her neck: just outside Muff, the taxi stalled for ages while they waited for a flock of sheep to cross the road, the hedgerows high on either side, rain clattering down on the roof of the car, the doubt suddenly rising within her, the live human warmth of Simms's hateful face nuzzled against her neck, his hand weak on her thigh, and across the vinyl Francine struggling to remove Platt's hand clamped around her elbow. The look of greedy vengeance on Tommy's face, the hatred she saw in his eyes through the rear view mirror, the composite sketch of herself and Francine in their shag wigs plastered over the daily newspapers, the inevitable knock on the family home door, and the coppers flinging on the handcuffs, the vision of herself banged up in Magilligan, her wanes being raised by her mammy and daddy, Jed rushing to Derry from Saigon.

She flashed Tommy's eyes in the rear view mirror a look of apology as her fingers inched across Simms's legs towards the door knob.

She roused the Brit bastard out of his wooziness and shoved open the door.

"Out! Outta this car!" Ursula had wailed.

"You mad cow!" Simms slurred, life flickering in his droopy eyes as he struggled to comprehend.

"What the feck?!" Tommy roared. "Una! Are ye off yer bleedin head?!"

"I kyanny do it! I just kyanny!"

The flash of relief on Francine's face as she followed suit, her hand clicking open the door and heaving Platt onto the rain, the sheep scattering as his body rolled under their hooves.

"Bitches! Filthy Fenian grot bitches!" Simms spat into the car, on his knees on the blacktop, the farm animals braying around him.

"Thank the Lord I came to me senses just in time," Ursula whispered.

The relief dissolved from Francine's face: "Themmuns is trying to climb back into the car! On wer way, Tommy!"

She kicked away Platt's creeping fingers. Simms rose and staggered towards them, his face puce with rage.

"You Green slags!" Simms snarled as Ursula slammed the door into his face.

The taxi lurched across the gravel, Francine's door slapping against Platt's skull. Ursula turned and saw them crawling through the sheep, fists raised, faces twisted with anger. Francine gave Ursula a little squeeze as they raced through the rain, then the taxi ground to a halt. Tommy whipped around, glaring through his teeth.

"Traitors to the Cause!" he snarled. "Get yer hateful arses outta this car!"

Francine and Ursula blinked at the dark and the rain and the hedges beyond the windows.

"Ye kyanny drop us off here in the middle of Bogs End! We're nowhere, sure!" Ursula said.

"Youse'd be nowhere right enough if I had an ounce of sense and pumped a round of bullets into yer gacky skulls! Aborting a mission midway through ..." Tommy sputtered with incomprehension. "I've never seen the likes of it in me life! Get yer-selves outta this car before I kyanny control meself no longer!"

Ursula and Francine pursed their lips, piqued, then reluctantly reached for their handbags. Two hours later, a lorry hauling spuds picked up the bedraggled duo and dropped them back off on the outskirts of Derry.

In the sitting room, Ursula squinted through her tears at the horseshoe of slack jaws, everyone eyeing her like a stranger. Fionnuala had since recoiled from her platforms.

"... I was afeared of the RUC coming and dragging me away," Ursula explained through her sobs. "And me wanes been raised without their moller."

Her father Patrick stood in his straining suspenders and sooty hands, a resigned look on his face. Ursula would've preferred a flushed face of anger. He tore across the net curtains and pointed out at the street, where there was never a shortage of British soldiers.

"Would ye have a wee gander out that window?" he said. "There yer men are, patrolling wer streets with guns and dogs and hatred. Ye think a few hijacked cars can keep em out? We needed ye to do this for us, to free us from their shackles."

Ursula reached out to coddle his left hand, but her daddy flinched. Her fingers slipped back as if they had been bitten.

"I saw the life shining in their eyes," she tried to explain in a hoarse voice. "They was living beings. Flesh and blood like us—"

"Murdering Brit bastard pigs, more like!" roared Paddy.

"Ye silly bitch, ye!" Roisin snarled. "Why are ye such an unending disgrace to the family? Ye were given an opportunity the likes of us never had to rid wer homeland of two of them limey Orange scum, and ye spat in its face!"

Ursula squirmed, the roaring fire cooler than her face.

"Am pure sickened at the sight of ye!" Paddy roared. "Have ye not a clue what madness ye've brought upon us all? We'll have the Provos banging down wer door in the middle of the night, kneecapping all us men and tarring and feallerin all the weemin! Tainting the entire lot of us for being traitors to the cause!"

Sudden fear crept into the eyes of the assembled masses. The neighbors inched out of the sitting room, the door sidling shut behind them.

"For the sake of yer own peace of mind, ye've put all of us in the line of fire!" Fionnuala brayed. "I've half a mind to haul ye into the back garden and tar and fealler ye meself!"

Patrick's quiet voice shuddered with smoldering rage.

"Ye were given a chance to redeem yerself for all the filth ye've brought into wer lives!"

"Daddy, naw!" Ursula begged as the tears welled.

"—Entering that beauty pageant when the priest tole ye not to, up the scoot without a ring on yer finger at eighteen. Now we kyanny go to sleep at night for fear we won't wake up the next morning!"

Eda had stood in silent reproof throughout it all, arms a fortress. She finally could hold her tongue no longer.

"This honey trap of yers" Eda began, "I've always had me suspicions. The whole slew of fancy men ye paraded up and down them stairs when ye was a wane. Knowing the tarty, slapperish likes of you, I've half a mind that honey trap was but an

excuse for ye to bed down with an effin Brit soldier instead of murdering the blessed spirit outta him!"

"Mammy! Naw!" Ursula implored. "How can ye say such things?"

"Dressed like a painted trollop, ye've always been," Eda continued, "the knockers hanging outta yer halter top and yer knickers on display! Mortified, am are, to have ye sitting beside me in the pew at St. Moluag's more Sundays than not, a right aul tramp reciting the prayers of the Lord without a second thought of the blasphemy of it all!"

"Stop it, Mammy! Please stop it!"

Far from it, Eda hauled Ursula's protesting body up from the chair and dragged it towards the hallway, the others trailing after.

"Get you out that door and kill them Brit soldiers, ye silly bitch ye!" Eda seethed into her daughter's face as the others all roared their agreement.

"They're already away off!" Ursula sobbed. "I kyanny kill em now!"

"Ach, there's stacks of Brit bastards to choose from out there!" Eda seethed. "Out wer door!"

She clutched the knob and wrenched the door open, heaving Ursula's struggling body towards the bucketing rain. Ursula scrabbled at the jamb and slammed the door shut, knocking her mother into the hallstand, brollies and rosary beads flying. Roisin and Paddy caught Eda and propped her upright.

"Clattering yer own moller to the floor!" Patrick gasped. "What are ye like, wee girl?"

"Ye see you, Ursula!" Eda heaved, a finger wagging, eyes flashing. "Ye're a right nasty piece of work! When am gasping me last on me deathbed, aul and lonely and begging for a bit of human kindness, ye're to let me rot in peace, ye filthy bitch!"

"Don't say such mean things to me, Mammy!" Ursula begged against the door-frame.

"Ach, go on away and shite, you!" Eda winced as she rubbed an elbow.

"Am sickened pure and simple," Patrick said to Ursula. "I kyanny bear to stare ye in the face no longer. Am away off to bed."

"Aye, me and all," agreed the others.

And, their hopes for a new, Free Derry dashed, they clomped up the stairs to lick their wounds under their bedclothes, all except Fionnuala, who was by Catholic law forbidden from spending the night with Paddy. She slipped out the door with a giggle. Ursula watched their backs parade up to the landing. She clutched the bottom banister and hauled her weary self up the first step. Eda turned, eyes flaring.

"Ye've some nerve, wee girl! Ye think any of yer brollers and sisters is up for sharing their space under the bedclothes with the likes of ye?! Ye're to get yer sniveling

arse into the cupboard for the cleaning supplies and clear up that mingin tip of a sitting room!"

As above her hot water bottles were filled and muffled curses were hurled her way, Ursula sobbed, collecting the saucers piled high with fag ends, scrubbing away the sick all down the back of the settee and knowing she would never be maid of honor at Paddy and Fionnuala's wedding.

12

She slammed the car door and strode up the path to the Barnett's dream house as purposefully as her orthopedic shoes would allow. Hidden in the hedges, Liam eyeballed her course and nudged Finbar with a grunt.

"Is that yer woman, hi?" he asked, grappling the tire iron.

Finbar hadn't a clue; Lorcan hadn't shown them photos, for the love of God.

"Looks like a right crabbit aul bitch," Finbar said. "Am up for causing her a bit of misery, anyroad."

"Aye, me and all."

When the recent parolees had visited the house the night before, there hadn't been any cars to demolish. They had had to make do with the weed killer and scratchitti. This was child's play for two hard hooligans, but they owed Lorcan for the months in the nick he had poured the Vicodin down their needy throats.

Mrs. Feeney cast a look of disgust at the letters razed in the front garden and rapped on the door, a document clutched in her talons. She set her lips at the filthy words etched into the window. Did the silly beggars not realize Ursula was banged up? she wondered. Not that she didn't agree with every letter.

There was a hesitation beyond the door, then Jed opened up.

"I can see ye've some problems here," Mrs. Feeney said, with a nod at the front garden and a flinch at the stench of drink from him.

Jed's lips parted, his brain unable to comprehend what possible reason this woman had for blackening his doorstep.

"Uh ..."

"And am only here to add to em, mind," she said, waving the paper under his nose. "Though it grieves me heart to say it."

Right, Jed thought.

"I've the invoice here for the cost to fix me battered car hood, for the pounds me grandson had to lay out. Am a pensioner on a miserly state pension, and I kyanny afford to splash the quids around as if *I* had won the flimmin lotto. And, as yer front garden clearly states, youse is minted."

Jed sighed, his hangover heavy.

"You'd better come in," he said, but Mrs. Feeney hadn't expected anything less and was already halfway down the foyer.

"It was terrible dear to fix me hood. Six hundred quid. Ye've not the cash handy, I suppose?"

She scanned the lounge, sniffing out suitable hiding places for money.

"I'm sorry, but I'll have to give you a check," Jed said, reaching sorrowfully for his battered checkbook.

The expectation in Mrs. Feeney's eyes expired. Her claw shot out, however, insatiable, as pen touched paper.

"Could you do me a favor?" Jed asked mid-scribble.

"What's that?" she asked, brimming with suspicion.

"Don't deposit it until the third of next month."

That was when his military pension, his only financial solace, would be wired into his account. He tore out the check.

Mrs. Feeney's look of disbelief was cut short by the thundering screech of metal on metal, the shattering of glass.

"What the ...?" Jed gasped.

He raced down the hallway, Mrs. Feeney staggering behind. He wrenched open the door and caught the backs of two shaved skulls slipping around the corner. Mrs. Feeney's car was a wreck, battered and windshield cracked, and she herself was apparently a DAFT OLD BICTH, if the message sprayed across the body was to be believed.

"Me auto! Me wile dear auto!" she sobbed, as Jed stifled a smile.

"Well, there's £600 to tide you over at least," he said, handing over the check more graciously than he would have two minutes earlier.

£ £ £ £

Dymphna stared down her queue and stiffened at the sight of Rory Riddell at the end. She eyed Bridie at the adjacent register, and Bridie swiveled her eyes. Dymphna's fingers pounded the register keys with increasing fury as Rory inched customer after customer closer to her register until he was finally before her, his smirk over the counter filling her with rage and confusion. She threw a stuffed bag at a hapless customer and glared down her nose.

"What's yer order?" she snarled.

"Am not here to order," he said, pulling a ChipKebab container out of a wrinkled bag festooned with pyramids. "Am here to lodge a complaint,"

"Ye can lodge yer complaint up yer hole!"

Dymphna peered past his shoulder and motioned to the next customer in line to come hither.

"You, there, wee girl! What's yer order?"

Rory nudged the girl to Bridie's line and barreled on regardless, flipping open the container and displaying the congealing mess between the pita.

"Last week I bought this ChipKebab here," he said, "and me stomach turned at the foreign object I found in it."

"I'll foreign object ye, ye mingin—!"

"Would ye have a wee look at what the foreign object is?" he demanded.

The sharpness in his voice compelled her to look down. Among the wilting lettuce, the tomato chunks slick with garlic sauce, wedged between two fat and greasy chips twinkled a diamond engagement ring.

"Ach, would ye catch yerself—" Dymphna began scornfully.

Her scorn was clipped by Bridie's gasp of delight. She sidled up to Dymphna in her grubby smock, cooing and preening.

"Ye know it makes sense, hi," Rory said, falling to Dymphna's horror on bended knee amongst the ketchup packets and trodden chips. "Marry me, Dymphna."

She peered over her register at the crown of his head as around her the customers and chipfryers and kebab makers cheered and chanted.

"Say ye will, aye?" he asked.

"Aye, aye, aye!" Bridie roared. "Ye daft cunt, Dymphna! Of course ye're saying aye! If ye don't, I'll grab the ring offa him!"

"Merciful Jesus!" yelled a man at the back of the queue. "Nod yer fecking head, would ye, before the hunger gnaws a hole in me stomach!"

A finger scooped up the welling tear in the corner of her eye. She thought of the rock bouncing against her stomach, and the many more it would receive when she started to show. Rory's uncle was a copper; he could protect her and her wane.

Her mammy would be black with rage if she raced to the altar with an Orange bastard, but feck her mammy, she thought. Fionnuala didn't give a cold shite in hell about her. Her mother still had her nicking curry chips and BaconNCheese Dippers for the family tea, for the love of God. Dymphna suddenly understood why Moira had fled to Malta.

She thought she felt her wane leap eagerly in her womb, egging her on to a halting nod of a face which burned with equal parts mortification and excitement. She plucked the ring out and gave it a quick wipe with a napkin before plunging it on her finger.

"Aye, Rory," she agreed. "Aye, surely!"

£ £ £ £

There was much unlocking and relocking of doors as Ursula was led to freedom. She had only been banged up five days but had aged a decade, her bob a fright.

"I'll bet ye kyanny wait to put yer feet up with a wee cuppa and an Agatha Christie back at yers," the warden said over the jangle of his keys as he led her through a perplexing maze of corridors.

She had thought of nothing but, dreaming of the two shower heads in their ensuite bathroom blazing full-force on her flesh. They finally reached a counter lorded over by a hard-faced cow, and upon which were splayed Ursula's belongings: her handbag, car keys and plastic rain cap. How she had missed them. Ursula reached out a hand, which was smacked lightly by the cow, who apparently wore her RUC epaulets with pride.

"I hope to high heaven you've now learned yer lesson," sniffed the cow. "The magistrates is to be treated with the respect their years of education has earned em."

Ursula did Meryl Streep proud as she managed a docile nod and smile and signed for her belongings.

Beyond a glass pane she saw Jed under his cowboy hat, holding out one of those reflective thermal blankets in which to wrap her, as if she were suffering from hypothermia. Which, she supposed, she was: hypothermia of the heart.

Ursula pecked the warden on the cheek, collected her belongings and found herself enveloped in Jed's arms. That was what husbands were for.

"Are you okay?" he asked.

Jed seemed to have aged ten years as well, and Ursula was saddened when she saw he couldn't meet her eye. Had her custodial sentence brought him so much shame?

"Aye, their cavity searches is thankfully far and few between," she said.

Jed swaddled Ursula in the tinfoil-looking wrap and led her down the steps, dreading her first sight of their dream house. She was sweltering inside the cape, the sweat lashing down her, but couldn't let on. She was so relieved to be let free, to sniff the exhaust fumes from the Ford Escorts, hear the muttered obscenities of the passing wanes and feel the horizontal rain lacerating her flesh. All that and the kindness of a human touch.

Through the thundering downpour, Ursula's Lexus was barely visible in the court car park. Jed stared at it forlornly through the bouncing raindrops. It was still as resplendent as the day after the lotto. He couldn't bring himself to tell her about the damage that had been done to his own car, to their house. He didn't want her racing back to the holding cell for safety; she would see it all soon enough herself.

"I'll drive you home," Jed said. "You got your car keys?"

Ursula blinked.

"In me own auto? Where's yer car, but?"

Sitting before the garage, its tires slashed, its locks glued and labeling him a HATFUL BICTH, that's where.

"I took a cab," Jed said.

Ursula opened her mouth to jammer that they didn't have the money to throw away on wild dear luxuries like cabs, not with £3500 owed the court, but stifled herself. Jed guided her into the passenger seat, and she had to duck so the automatic seatbelt didn't slice her head off.

Jed steered through the bucketing rain and the scattering prams, his fingers digging into the wheel with a sense of impending doom. He had expected her to have plenty to say, and none of it cheery, but Ursula was strangely subdued.

"The prison serves a wile lovely chicken curry roll on a Thursday," she said. "I asked yer man the warden for the recipe; they get them sent in, but."

Jed prayed to God almighty Ursula would be unable to see the damage done to their house in the lashing rain and the approaching dusk; Lord knew he could barely make out the curves of the blacktop before him. But as they pulled up to the house, he saw with a glance and a sinking heart the blight was only too evident in the sodium glow of the streetlamps.

"Ach, ye've not a clue how I've longed for this moment," Ursula sighed, her head assuming a position of safety as she clicked her seatbelt open. It whipped toward the ceiling with the precision of a guillotine. "Be it ever so humble."

The wind had knocked over the gnomes which had anchored the hastily-scrawled *Welcome Home Ursula!* banner Jed had hoped would hide the ravaged front garden. The banner was probably halfway to Muff by now, and they were instead greeted with FUCKIN MINTED CUNTS! Jed got out of the car and clamped a hand down on his shuddering cowboy hat. Ursula slammed shut her door and rounded the car, her feet unsteady on real ground. Jed clutched her elbow. She was set to sprint up the path with him when she stopped short at the gate. She threw off his hand.

"What's that on wer front garden?"

Then she cast her eyes towards the house, the rain splattering on her sopping bob. She let out a yelp. The tinfoil cape slipped from her shoulders, and she almost fell to the pavement after it, one hand clutching her chest. Signs of Jed's hurried scrubbing from the evening before couldn't hide the great swaths of red, white and blue splattered across the eaves, trickling down the pebble-dash, blackening the windows.

"Wer lovely wee house! Somewan's gone and covered it with paint, with—" She choked on the words "—the piggin colors of the Union Jack! What will themmuns next door think of us? Sympathizers to wer hateful Brit oppressors! Themmuns'll think we're Proddy bastards!"

"Wait until you see the foyer," Jed mumbled, urging her down the path.

"Ach, am pure affronted!" Ursula wailed, "I kyanny hold me head up in wer front garden."

He placed the key in the lock and revealed the devastation.

He remembered the night before, freezing at the clank of the letterbox, feverish it would be more final notices for bills he would have to hide from Ursula. He had thudded with a heavy heart to the Queen Anne foyer and stared in confusion at a metal-tipped rubber tube snaking its way through the open letterbox. He recalled the realization as the water started flowing that it was the garden hose, the shock of the gloved hand slipping through the letterbox at its side and shaking orange dye into the flow, the bubbling, flowing orange mess, the hours of mopping and scrubbing and bucketsful of orange water dumped down the scullery sink, the sink now orange as well.

"And what's up with wer carpeting?" Ursula wondered.

Her shoes squelched down the foyer as she made her way to the scullery.

"Wer self-heating tiles!" she wailed, angry tears flowing down her already haggard face. "And the legs of all wer chairs! And the bottoms of the dishwasher and *me Gaggenau fridge!* Dyed Proddy orange! Did ye not try to stop em?"

Jed was ashamed of the sight of himself in his memory now, frozen half-way up the stairs, watching the orange water rise, wondering how many of them were out there, how many drug-addled hooligans with shaved heads and black hearts, a third his age and three times as strong, the phone useless in his hand, unable to dial that final 9.

His shoulders slumped in defeat.

"When did all this caper start?" Ursula asked.

"The day you were locked up."

She placed a hand on her hip as the tears disappeared and pure rage took over.

"Did ye not think of ringing the coppers?"

"I thought Catholics never wanted to get the police involved?" Jed said, his voice cracking.

"Ye wile daft—!"

Ursula caught herself. Her stay in the nick had been like an entire anger management course shoved into five days. She reeled in her fury and squelched back down the carpeting. Her eyes flickered with sudden under-standing.

"Would ye mind telling me what state yer auto's in?" she suddenly asked.

"Uh ... well ..."

"Keyed?"

"Yeah. They wrote 'hateful bitch' on it."

"Locks glued?"

"That too."

"Tires slashed?"

"Twice."

"Right!" Ursula said, and although fresh from the hell of being accused unjustly, her mind was made up as to where to point her finger with the con-viction of a born again Christian. "That Fionnuala's to blame, with that hooli-gan Heggarty blood flowing through her veins. Car keying, lock gluing, carving insults into windows, garden hose through the letterbox, them is all textbook malicious crimes them wanes down the Bogside get up to when they've run outta post offices and phone booths to torch, ambulances and fire engines to fling rocks at. She's rounded up her wile hard Heggarty neph-ews—and some nieces and all, I've no doubt—to put the fear of the Lord into us. The politics of envy, so it is! Themmuns kyanny abide the likes of us with two pound coins to rub togeller—not that we've many left, mind—all in the hopes we're gonny be heart-scared to walk outta wer home. Shall I let ye in on a wee secret there, Jed?"

He was too terrified to nod.

"I was mortified at the thought of attending wer Siofra's first holy communion the morrow, afeared of making a show of meself as I sang along in the choir. After all this palaver, if they think they can keep me out, they've anoller thing coming, especially after all them lessons and them hours I spent shoving Jelly Babies into wer Siofra's wee skull. Am gonny be right up there, warbling proudly away to me heart's content!"

Jed had long ago given up trying to understand the inner workings of the female mind. He gawked at his wife, and jerked as she suddenly reached out and grappled his wrists with the determination of the Hillside Strangler. She bored into him, a woman renewed, with eyes so frightening he didn't know where to look.

"I kyanny do it on me own, but," she hissed. "If ye do wan thing for me, wan thing for all the torture, persecution and heartache me family's put me through ..."

Jed stood frozen, fearful of what ominous task he would be obliged to perform.

"Will ye for the love of God accompany me to St. Moluag's the morrow?"

Jed's heart welled for his battered wife. Something so small could bring her so much joy. This is what her family had reduced her to. He struggled to contain the lump inching up his windpipe.

"I'll do it for the love of you," he said, his hand on hers.

As Ursula lingered in the shower, humming "We Shall Overcome" while lathering up, she began to feel guilty about her defiant outburst, no matter how well-deserved. Aye, her family had dragged her through the seven circles of hell and beyond, she thought, but they were ignorant and didn't know any better. That wouldn't stop her from making a grand entrance at St. Moluag's, though. She scrubbed her armpits with conviction.

Downstairs, Jed guzzled down the rest of the Absolut from the fridge. He squelched his way into the sitting room, plucked the flask of Jim Beam from behind the third gargoyle to the left, and soon saw the bottom of that. He didn't know how much more of life in Derry he could take. He thought of his ticket to Wisconsin. His one way ticket. He sat at the empty dining table for eight and pulled out his battered checkbook.

Struggling with written English in his drink-fuelled stupor, he wrote out a check for £3000 and another for £500, knowing fully well they would bounce even after this navy pension was added to the account.

Unless …

There was always that huge life insurance policy he had taken out, the one whose monthly payments he could now barely afford to make.

His bleary eyes flickered with understanding, his head nodded with the certainty of it: he was worth more dead than alive. He placed the checks in their envelopes and scribbled out the addresses. They had return address stickers with a shamrock on the left hand side. He cast the shamrock a look of disdain, then peeled off two stickers and affixed them to the envelopes. He stuck a second class stamp on each, not only to save a few pence, but also to buy him the extra time he needed to put his plan into action before the checks arrived. As he sealed the envelopes, he realized he was also sealing his fate.

13

Dymphna felt the guilt gnaw at her as she dipped her fingers into the holy water fountain, and as well it might, entering the frigid depths of St. Moluag's with a Proddy bastard on her arm!

Inches behind her stepped Fionnuala in a grand shipwreck of a hat festooned with exotic bird feathers, which she had draped creatively around her face to hide her shame. As her wee brothers groped at the font for free holy water, Dymphna blessed herself, then froze at the sniggers from the usual hooligans slouched against the back wall next to the bulletin boards. Nothing save an E trip gone bad or a stint in Magilligan could make them miss this most holy of family celebrations. Under their shaved heads, glares of menace met Rory. Dymphna clawed the arm of his suit, and Rory cleared his throat and tried to hide his Protestantness by offering an awkward curtsy towards the likeness of the Virgin Mary which glowered over him.

"Sarky Orange fecker!" a rowdy called out.

Fionnuala's eyes glowered behind the finery, and the plumes flared from the force of her bark. "Youse'uns!" she threatened, a finger still dripping the blessed water. "Away from the faller of me grandchild or ye're to have the tip of me stiletto up the cracks of yer arses!"

The hard men's roars of laughter echoed through the nave. Brylcreemed heads turned, including that of PC McLaughlin in the last pew. His wife, fiddling with her disposable camera, dealt him a swift kick in the shin.

"Can ye not be off duty for wan second of yer life?" she snarled. "Let them stokes be. Wer wee Catherine's what's important the day. Whip yer head round to the altar and give her a wave."

He could look now at the gang of hooligans only if he were demonically possessed. He located his daughter in the front pew, but instead of a fatherly beam, his brow furrowed.

"That wee girl beside wer Catherine …"

"The wan with the flashing tiara?"

"Aye. I know the wee stoke. I kyanny mind from where, but."

Fionnuala elbowed Paddy in the stomach of his ill-fitting suit, shoved her disgrace of a daughter a pew further down the aisles, clutched the heads of as many of her wanes as she could and forced them down the nave.

"Shove you yer granny into that pew there," she instructed Eoin the third pew in. "And sit you beside her. Am not heaving that dottery aul wan up the length of the church just to haul her right back down at the end of the cere-mony!"

Eoin stopped, frigid at the sight of Caoilte, Fergal and Eamonn McDaid. Fresh from craning their necks and appraising Siofra's choice of trimmings, they greeted Eoin with eyebrows that demanded to know the where and when of their £300. Eoin ran his tongue across the lips of a suddenly parched mouth.

"Don't you worry yerself, mam. I'll guide me granny down the aisle meself. We'll catch youse up in a wee while."

Fionnuala flashed him a look fit for a simpleton and pressed further on down the aisle after Dymphna.

Next to the confessionals, Mr. O'Toole, sitting sheepishly with Fidelma's family, looked away from the car crash that was Dymphna and her Proddy fancy man plodding past. Fidelma tapped one of the three hunched backs in front of her.

"Would ye have a look at that?" she marveled with a smirk and a nod at the shameless pair. "Up the scoot by a Proddy!"

Mrs. Feeney, Mrs. Gee and Mrs. O'Hara thrust their heads up from their rosaries.

"Disgraceful, so it is!"

"Aye, shocking!"

"Effin Orange-loving bitch!"

—then returned to their Hail Mary's with renewed vigilance.

Fidelma slipped her twigish arm around Mr. O'Toole's bicep and hugged it tight. She grinned. Mr. O'Toole grimaced and jerked as an elbow cracked him in the back of his head.

"Sorry," muttered Jed, drunkenly clutching the back of their pew for sup-port.

"Ach, no problem a tall," Mr. O'Toole said, wincing as he rubbed his head.

"Hiya, ladies," Jed said, lurching past Molly and a selection of her off-spring. The hairdresser's smile deflated at the stench of cheap drink from him as he dissolved into the seat beside them, hymnals clattering to the kneeler. Molly reached out and moved her youngest away, far away.

"Ursula's singing in the choir, you know," Jed said in a close approximation of English, his face beaming with what might have been pride.

Molly's eyes stung as she forced a nod and an upward curl of the lips.

"I gave up on the church years ago," Jed droned on.

"I'm only here to support my wife."

Molly nodded wildly and her eyes couldn't meet his, whether from pity or the smell, she didn't know.

Fionnuala faced the Lord suffering on the cross and completed a theatrical genuflection, and the Floods thronged into the second pew from the altar.

"Shove yer Orange fancy man in the corner there, outta view!" Fionnuala instructed Dymphna.

Fionnuala plopped herself directly behind Siofra, then whipped around to inspect the heads in the pews, making sure that bitch Ursula hadn't seen fit to skulk her way into her daughter's most holy of days. She tapped Siofra on a frilly shoulder. The wee girl turned around, and Fionnuala squinted through the staccato beams discharging from her daughter's head.

"No sign of yer auntie?" she asked.

"No, Mammy," Siofra said, affronted her mammy was right behind her. She kicked a sniggering Grainne in the shin and twirled her parasol menac-ingly at her.

Fionnuala gasped at the sight of Siofra's mate's face, then flipped open her prayer book with a smug nod. Ursula hadn't dared poke her nose inside St. Moluag's; Fionnuala hadn't expected anything less.

Then the sacristy door flew open and the choir members filed in, resplen-dent in their robes, Ursula Barnett in the lead.

Ursula stared down at the congregation spread out before her like a road-map, the wanes' heads the wee villages and towns, their elders' the cities. She wondered briefly if this is what it felt to be like the Lord himself, staring down at his creations and, she thought as she caught sight of the Floods splayed across the second pew, his miscreants.

The choirmaster nodded to the organist, and the congregation jumped as the air jangled with discordance.

She shouldn't judge them too harshly, Ursula thought, there in the house of the Lord. Compassion and forgiveness welled as she parted her lips and began to sing along:

"Holy God, We Praise Thy Name,"

Fionnuala's annoyance subsided slightly at the disheveled sight of Ursula, haggard and frail, deep circles under the eyes, trying her best to smile.

"Lord of All, We Bow Before Thee,"

Ursula's hair was a fright, the gray roots showing under the Aubergine Exotica haircoloring, but Fionnuala couldn't fault Ursula for not having her hair done, considering what Molly had said about her in court.

"All On Earth Thy Scepter Claim,"

Fionnuala hoped Lorcan's mates hadn't been too hard on the Barnett's house,

"All In Heaven Above Adore Thee,"

then chastised herself for being a soft touch.

"Infinite Thy Vast Domain,"

She mouthed along to the hymn, snapped to the next page, and firmly resolved to never entertain such thoughts again.

"Everlasting is thy name!"

Father Kilpatrick and the eucharistic minister and the altar boys swiftly overtook Eoin and Eda—still making their way up the aisle—then took their places on the altar. As the organ was silenced and the choir members settled themselves, Eoin finally guided Eda into the overstuffed pew. He took a seat behind her.

All except Rory followed the priest in making the sign of the cross, and the Act of Penitence had barely exited Father Kilpatrick's mouth before Eda turned to Dymphna and hissed, "I expect that wee girl's here for her exorcism, aye?"

The foundation Grainne's mother had splattered across her face had been a vain attempt at concealing the sun blisters and weeping sores.

"Am bored outta me skull," Eda said. "Am away off for a fag."

She extracted herself from her seat.

"Am coming with ye, granny," Dymphna said, not to assist the aul wan down the aisle but to chat to Bridie on her mobile. She patted Rory on the arm. "You'll be alright there, aye?" Rory gave a grudging nod.

Clutching her hymnal, Ursula saw Siofra whisper into her mate's ear. Grainne's ravaged face lit up with delighted surprise, and she quickly nodded. Siofra whispered again and Grainne nudged the wee girl next to her and hissed something, heads bent. Ursula took a deep breath and flipped a page. She watched the babble, whatever it was, rippling down the first pew, and over to where the boys were sitting.

Ursula warbled along with the choir, tens of untrained voices raised in song, Ursula's especially defiant:

"Praise God from whom all blessings flow—"

As Father Kilpatrick held aloft the gleaming paten laden with the most holy Lord's body and the deacon the chalice brimming with His blood, Ursula watched sweeties appear from Siofra's handbag and pass through a succession of sticky hands, passing the aisle to the wee boys with parts in their hair. Ursula started in shocked pride. The wee stoke, she thought, had taken heed of her lessons about the Christian virture of sharing after all! Ursula smiled into her hymnal and concentrated on transforming the flats and sharps on the pages before her into some semblance of song, so she didn't see—

"Praise Him, all creatures here below—"

—the crumpled fivers and the odd tenner making their way back down the pew—

"Praise him above, ye Heavenly Host—"

—and into Siofra's sparkly white handbag.

"Praise Father, Son and Holy Ghost."

The paten and chalice were lowered and the congregation trudged through a Lord's Prayer peppered with hacking coughs, while in the front pew wee hands slipped before mouths and Ecstasy pills disappeared down throats, gobbled down as if they were indeed sweeties.

Ursula frowned. Sharing was praiseworth, but surely the wanes knew they had to receive the Body of Christ on an empty stomach? Hadn't they all fasted? She briefly wondered if she should tap the priest on his shoulder, but … hadn't she caused enough grief? She settled back to listen to the liturgy instead.

"Deliver us, Lord, from every evil, and grant us peace in our day," Father Kilpatrick intoned.

Under satin and tulle petticoats, under starched button down shirts and clip-on ties, heartbeats galloped,

"In yer mercy keep us free from sin and protect us from all anxiety."

blood pounding though wee veins,

"As we wait in joyful hope for the coming of our Savior, Jesus Christ."

speckles of sweat breaking out on bright young foreheads.

"**For the kingdom, the power, and the glory are yers, now and forever,**" recited the congregation.

Siofra's stomach lurched.

"Lord Jesus Christ, you said to yer apostles: 'I leave you peace, my peace I give you,'"

Grainne clutched at her racing heart, the blood pumping deep in her eardrums, her pulsating blisters aching.

"Look not on our sins, but on the faith of yer Church,"

Wee boys wriggled in their creased polyester slacks, their buckled shoes scraping against the flagstones, chests suddenly swelling, feeling they were the hardest, boldest men of all Derry City,

"and grant us the peace and unity of yer kingdom where you live for ever and ever."

Jaws clenching and molars grinding, sweat now lashing down their bulging faces, sopping their Sunday finery.

"The peace of the Lord be with you always."

Fionnuala heaved a sigh.

"**And also with ye.**"

This was the part of mass she loathed. Like an automaton, she turned to Rory and grappled his hand, grinning from ear to ear with Christian compassion.

"Peace be with ye," she managed.

"Aye, and with you," Rory mumbled in return.

Siofra grabbed a bulging-eyed Grainne, woozy grin on her face, and hugged her tight.

"I love ye!" Siofra squealed. "Yer me best effin mate in the world," while around them their schoolmates squeezed and clutched and cuddled one another and swore lifelong friendships, tears of affection welling in glazed eyes.

Ursula cleared her throat and roared out of her through the voices on either side vying for attention:

"Lamb of God, who takes away the sins of the world, have mercy on us,"

"Am floating! Am floating on a heavenly cloud!" whispered Christine McLaughlin. "Weeee!"

"Lamb of God, who takes away the sins of the world, have mercy on us,"

Siofra's cheeks ballooned like a chipmunk's, her porcelein face suddenly violet.

"Lamb of God, who takes away the sins of the world, grant us peace."

She clicked open her sparkly handbag and retched into it. Then she snapped it shut.

"This is the Lamb of God who takes away the sin of the world. Happy are those who are called to his supper."

"Am flying! Am flying!" Christine hissed.

"Lord, I am not worthy to receive ye, but only say the word and I shall be healed."

Christine started flapping her hands and then zoomed down the sacristy and out the front door. There was a mortified shuffling as her mother extracted herself from the congregation.

"Christine! Ye daft eejit, ye!" she hissed down the pew. Her heels clacked along the flagstones and out the door, PC McLaughlin following close behind.

Father Kilpatrick's perplexed face softened. It wasn't the first time a child had lost their nerve at the prospect of being filled with the body of the Lord. He beamed down at the remaining first communion takers. They seemed to be a remarkably eager lot, chomping at the bit, eyes blazing hungrily at the paten and chalice. He understood well, remembering as a lad when he became one with Jesus for the first time.

Ursula smiled over at the priest, encouraging. The silence was broken only by an assortment of phlegmy coughs and the snickering from the bulletin boards. His parishioners stared up, awaiting his words of wisdom.

"Youse is what youse eat!" Father Kilpatrick boomed to the eaves, even the McDaids jumping in alarm. He pointed a trembling finger at the front row. "You wanes have all learned that when youse scoff down something, whether fish and chips on a Friday or a packet of crisps for yer after school snack, yer body changes the things ye've eaten. Today, but, a miracle's about to happen to youse for the first time. Today, when ye eat, it's to be the oller way around. Yer bodies is to become the body of Christ itself! Ye've joined many a club in the school, or maybe even a gang, in yer young lives. But ye're to join the most blessed gang in yer lives the day. The gang of them what've become the body of Christ himself! Dead on, aye?"

Grainne grimaced as she massaged her stomach.

"I've no appetite," she whispered, "for the body of Christ just now."

Perhaps she shouldn't have gobbled down three disco sweeties, but they were so cute with their wee dolphins on them.

Siofra glumly regarded her soggy handbag and knew just how Grainne felt. She wondered if she could make it to the loos, but her legs felt terrible bandy, and the toilets were far away at the entrance of the church. Perhaps she could use her parasol as a crutch of some sort and—

But all of a sudden the first row was ushered up from the pews and forced towards the kneeling rail, boys on one side, girls the other, the crowds craning their necks for a glimpse, Polaroids flashing up and down the aisles.

Fionnuala nudged Paddy.

"Get yourself up there and snap a wee photo of wer Siofra with her tongue hanging out, waiting for the body of Christ," she hissed.

Paddy did as instructed, hunched over and scuttering sheepishly up the aisle to join the other fathers snapping away.

Outside in the car park, Dymphna tried to make out what Bridie was saying over the laughing and shrieking erupting from the side of a Capri, and Eda, puffing away at her side, nudged her granddaughter.

"Simple in the head, that wee girl over there," Eda pointed out.

The wee girl in question was propped against the bumper of the car, blubbering and sobs pouring from her lolling head, her eyes like two raisins, as her parents hovered over her.

"Who gave it to ye? Who gave it to ye?" PC McLaughlin demanded, shaking Christine so that her eyeballs fairly clattered in their sockets.

"Siofra Flood gave it to me!" Christine sobbed. "Siofra Flood gave us all loads of wingers to celebrate wer first holy communion!"

"The feck—!"

As Mrs. Laughlin's hysterical wails filled the car park, PC McLaughlin whipped out his radio and barked into it.

Dymphna snapped her mobile shut in alarm. *What the bleedin feck is me wee sister playing at?* she wondered.

"Stay you put, granny, I've to alert the ollers."

As Dymphna skittered down the aisle, however, she realized she was too late. The exorcist-girl, wee palms forming a chapel, tongue tip pointed up at Father Kilpatrick, suddenly let out a wail. Her fingers unclasped and clawed the air.

"Me veins! Me veins!" Grainne wailed as the congregation gasped in unison.

Father Kilpatrick, wafer in hand, recoiled at the convulsing mass of frilly tulle, and Grainne collapsed to the flagstones, eyeballs rolling, limbs jittering. The wanes next to her, their own hearts streaking, their brains about to erupt, gasped and sobbed and guffawed and pointed. Siofra felt the wafer catch in her throat as she jumped up from the kneeling rail and inspected her mate in wonder, her fingers firmly clutched in prayer, the dainty handbag swinging from her elbow. The wee boys milled around, yammering and roaring. The chalice fell from the minister's hand, and wine splattered in a huge pool across the sacristy.

"Feck! Feck! Fecking Feck!" Eoin hissed, racing from the pew and pushing through a hip-high tangle of taffeta and contorting limbs. He slid across the splattered wine and tugged at Siofra's handbag.

"Naw!" Siofra wailed, clutching it tight. "Them pounds is mines!"

The handbag burst, sending pound coins, E's, tenners and the meager contents of Siofra's stomach scattering across the hallowed ground. Grainne's mammy burst through the yapping youngsters and crunched across the pill-strewn blood of Christ, tears streaming.

"Call the fecking ambulance, will somewan?!" she roared into Father Kilpatrick's startled face, bounding down and scooping her daughter's jittery limbs into her breast.

Ursula threw down her hymnal and clawed her way past the choir members and pointed an accusing finger.

"Me niece Siofra's been shoving the drugs down themmuns' throats!" Ursula roared. "That's her mate Grainne with an overdose!"

"Keep yer fecking bake shut, ye hateful bitch!" Fionnuala roared, scrambling to make her way out of the pew, Rory dragging her back down. She knocked Rory's hands from her. "Get yer Proddy mitts offa me!"

"Me broller gave em to me!" Siofra wailed.

"Where's the fecking ambulance?!" screamed Grainne's mammy above the palaver.

The McDaid brothers bolted like the hammers of hell out of their pew, suddenly retreating as the doors flew open, and PC McLaughlin galloped up the aisle.

"Filthy, hardened stokes!" Ursula roared as the copper pushed through the horde of swarming, squealing wanes. "Dealing drugs in the house of the Lord! I shoulda known! Themmuns sent hooligans to terrorize me! All to get their grabby paws on 5 Murphy Crescent!"

Eoin made to race up the altar and out the back door, but PC McLaughlin was swift, knocking him to the floor, shoving his arms behind his back and clanking on the handcuffs. He hauled Eoin up and grappled Siofra with his free hand. Siofra squealed and kicked and bit, the tiara sailing off her head and clattering to the apse. Paddy kept snapping away the photos, and Rory watched it all with shining eyes, thinking the Protestant services at St. Columbines had never been as exciting as this! The McDaid brothers slunk out the doors seconds before they banged open again, and a stream of police and paramedics raced down the aisle.

In minutes, Eoin and Siofra were being led through the gasping congregation, ringed by coppers, with the Floods trailing behind, Fionnuala roaring abuse. As they all passed Jed, he realized with a sobering nod that he had made the right decision; these people were lunatics, and he wanted nothing more to do with them.

Fionnuala paused at the door, allowed the contorted wane on the stretcher and the paramedics and the sobbing mother pass, then her voice rent the air in an awful blast that boomed down the narthex: "You're never to hear the end of this, Ursula Barnett! It's the depths of hell for ye, ye mingin geebag! 1973 me arse! Now ye've a greater disgrace on yer soul, mark me words!"

Ursula made her way with ginger steps over the spilled wine, her face shuddering with conviction and rage.

"Ach, shut yer cake hole, miseryguts! Am free of the whole flimmin lot of youse now!"

Outside, Eda stared with disbelieving eyes at the sight of her granddaughter and grandson being paraded around the car park, heavy with handcuffs and fury and shame, flanked by peelers and shoved into a waiting copper car. She puffed furiously on her fag and felt her heart jolt within her ribcage. She clutched at her breast as Fionnuala knocked her to the side.

"Outta me way, aul woman!" Fionnuala bleated, racing to free her wanes from the peelers' grasp.

"Me heart!" Eda gasped under the cacophony of wailing sirens, her ancient limbs all quivers and tremors, her lungs begging for breaths of air. "Where's me angina tablets?"

Her body toppled against the wall. Her knees buckled, and she crumpled to the ground.

"Keep youse that ambulance there, hi!" someone called out. "This pensioner's collapsed!"

The ambulance was revving up, heading for Altnagelvin under a hail of rocks from Seamus and Padraig's hands. Halfway to the copper car, Fionnuala whipped around, saw the calamity that was her mother-in-law, cursed under her breath and ran up to the ambulance, banging on the door.

Appearing through the church doors, Ursula stared agog at the crowd around her mother.

"*Mammy!*" she wailed.

Ursula pushed though a throng of bodies and raced to wrap her arms around her mother's shuddering body, stopping only to unplug the fag lodged between Eda's lips. The ambulance backed up through the parked cars, and Paddy emerged from the church.

"Mam!" he gasped. "What's up with ye?"

Ursula held him at bay with a hand, then turned to Eda. "Mammy! It's me, Ursula! Don't leave me, mammy, don't leave me yet!"

"Ursula ..." Eda moaned. "Ursula ... I always ...!"

As her mother's body heaved and Ursula motioned for the paramedics, Eda muttered something incomprehensible.

"What is it, Mammy?" Ursula held the trembling limbs tight and pressed her ear close to Eda's mouth. "Wan moment!" she warned the paramedics.

"Ursula, I always...." Eda grunted.

Through the tremors, through the spittle, Ursula couldn't understand.

"What are ye after saying?" Ursula said, her voice now laced with impatience.

Eda's eyes rolled, guttural sounds gurgling up her throat and spilling out her mouth.

"Tell me, Mammy!" Ursula wailed. "Tell me again!"

Eda sputtered and was dead. Ursula shook the lifeless body, willing her mammy back to life. The paramedics tried to pry her hands from Eda's limbs. Ursula knocked them away and whipped her head around, appealing to the thugs and peelers and wee brides of Christ towering over her.

"What's she after saying?" Ursula begged to know.

Fionnuala pushed through the crowd as if it were the first hour of the Top-Yer-Trolly January sale.

"Are youse all after hearing me mammy's last words?" Ursula begged the assembled masses. Her eyes stared at those which hadn't turned away in pity and tried to read them. She played and replayed the muttered sounds in her head, and it finally came to her. Her ravaged face lit up.

"She loves me!" Ursula proclaimed triumphantly. "Me moller's after telling me she always loved me!"

"Ye daft bitch, ye!" Fionnuala snapped. "Ye kyanny hear yer ears, sure! She's after saying Ursula I always *loathed* ye! And now that the aul wan's finally gone and met her maker, when are ye signing 5 Murphy over to us as ye promised in the court?"

And all this while Eda's body was still warm, Fionnuala eyeing her mother-in-law's fags. The paramedics placed her body on the stretcher as Ursula collapsed on the ground in a pool of tears. Jed and Molly rushed to her side with pained expressions and not much else.

Useless, Ursula thought, the two of them were. As usual.

The copper car had slipped out in the melee, and Fionnuala cursed her mother-in-law's death.

"Had that aul wan not kicked it, I mighta been able to talk some sense into them peelers," she said to Paddy. "Stop them wanes from flinging rocks at the ambulance, would ye, now that their granny's inside it."

Paddy, still shell-shocked at the sight of his mother passing, just stood there thinking of Ursula's hoarding Eda's death for her own. He was still Ursula's wee brother, sitting on the sidelines as the family dramas unfolded before him. Well, that was one funeral invite that wouldn't make it into the post, he decided.

Fionnuala gasped in horror.

"Wer Siofra's tiara! The gacky cunt left it in the chapel."

"It's no odds, sure," Paddy said. "We can retrieve it later."

"Retrieve it me arse!" she raged. "Twenty-five quid that tiara cost! The silly bitch had it on her head ten bloody minutes!"

In she marched through the church and down the aisle.

"You! Wee stoke!" she roared through the church. "Hands offa me wane's property!"

The altar boy jumped in alarm and dropped the now rayless tiara. At the sight of the enraged creature bearing down on him, pound signs dancing in her eyes, he scuttled off into the sacristy. Fionnuala ran to collect her property and clutched it to her breast, right beside the pocket which held Eda's last pack of fags.

"Get a move on, woman!" Paddy called to her from the holy water font.

"Right ye are," Fionnuala said.

If she didn't have to use the money to bail her simpleton eejit wanes out of the nick, she would buy herself—

She screamed as her stiletto heels skid on the blood of Christ spattered on the slick flagstones. The feathered nightmare jumped from her head as she toppled over, her skull cracking against the baptismal font. Dim, dimmer, dimmer yet …

Her body shuddered and was still.

"Hi, call that ambulance back, youse!" Paddy yelled out in alarm to the crowd in the car park. It was to be a very full ride back to Altnagelvin.

£ £ £ £

Having ensured Ursula was safely tucked in bed and properly sedated, Jed reached under the bed and dredged up his tackle box. Years in the Navy had given him a dark view of humanity. Not that he had actually stepped a boot on a battlefield, but while at his desk in a Quonset hut on the outskirts of DaNang he had heard over the clacking of his typewriter keys acts of depravity and cruelty; base, desperate tales that had laid bare a grotesqueness of human nature. None of it had prepared him for Ursula's family.

When word of Eda's passing spread to the four corners of the globe, those who had decades before run screaming from Derry for a quick buck had charged back into Belfast International Airport, hankies brandished, the dutiful sons and daughters only when it suited them, Stephen from New Zealand, Cait from Gibraltar, Moira from Malta and, of course, Roisin and her architect husband and their four wanes from Hawaii, all with vowels stretched or clipped in their odd adopted accents, marveling at the transformation of their beloved hometown on the Foyle, dressed to the nines in strange foreign finery that Paddy and Fionnuala couldn't understand, and all happy to point an outraged finger at Ursula for Eda's fatal heart attack. Roisin had even had the bold faced nerve to ring Ursula and inform her of the sad fact: Ursula would be allowed to attend the funeral of the woman who had given birth to them all and who she had just murdered when hell froze over.

Jed had to park his HATFUL BICTH Lexus just outside the cemetery gates, forcing Ursula to make do with catching a glimpse of the proceedings through the railings and a veil of tears. After Father Hogan shuffled away, prayers for salvation over, trailed by the black-suited undertakers who had lowered the casket into the gorge, Ursula stifled a moan, teeth clenched into the back of her fist, as she watched Roisin, Cait, Stephen and Paddy sneer at the card on the wreath she had gotten delivered. *To Mammy: I hope you do love me* she had written. They spat out a few words of contempt, chucked the flowers to the adjoining grave and gently placed their own ostentatious bouquets in its place. She glumly regarded the abundance of lilies Fionnuala bestowed with grand self-importance upon the mound of upturned earth and wondered how much they had set the Floods back and how long it would take them to ask her for help paying the bill.

But, no. As Ursula peered through the bars, Jed massaging her shoulders and cooing words of comfort that were anything but, Ursula realized a line had been crossed. They would never approach her again, even for money. She had wasted seven years of her life, coming back to that godforsaken town and trying time after time to ingratiate herself to people who hated her. From that moment on, she and Jed would live alone in their upmarket house, surrounded by their Jamie Oliver roasting pans, brushed aluminum and a row of gargoyles. She had turned to Jed in the driver's seat and told him as much.

In your dreams, Jed had thought, grimly asphyxiating the steering wheel. He loved his wife dearly, but enough was enough.

He had opened the tackle box and now scrabbled through the yellowed documents and black and white photos until he came upon the envelope from the Foyle Travel Agency.

He took a quick inventory of Ursula with his eyes, his wife swaddled in the bedclothes, her face graced with something approaching a smile. It had been such a long time since he had seen her smile without the aid of pharmaceuticals. He hated himself for what he was about to do—abandon her to the vultures—but when she awoke, she would want for nothing. Except, perhaps, love and affection. Brandishing the ticket, he leaned over and kissed the harsh lines around her lips. Ursula murmured and rolled over.

The hidden airline ticket showed that Ursula was a part of his past. Finding the right time had always been the difficult part, when he hadn't had the nerve, hadn't had the heart, was too decent a man to pack his bags and head back to Belfast International. He had deserted her mentally months ago, and now it was time to desert her physically.

14

Jed squinted through lager-riddled eyes, shards of sleet lacerating the wind-screen. His destination: Belfast International Airport.

Dead Slow! warned the road sign. Jed didn't give a damn.

In his beleaguered mind, he repeated like a deranged mantra: 7, 9, 12, 20, 24, 29 Bonus: 36, 7, 9, 12, 20, 24, 29 Bonus 36.

And, in the murky arena between suicide and accident, somewhere between Ballykelly and Limavady and in the pelting spring sleet, Jed's new Lexus squealed on black ice and collided with a telephone pole. It was three hours before the paramedics hauled his body out of the wreckage.

£ £ £ £

Ursula was imagining Jed's funeral: in her mind's eye, it was a dour affair, attended only by the occasional golf partner, his bookie and the woman from the corner off-license. And Ursula, of course. His wake was another matter: Ursula's OsteoCare patients and the members of her old choir and neighbors she hadn't clamped eyes on since paratroopers had swanned through their front garden crawling out of the woodwork and elbowing their way into a sitting room already black with beings and fag smoke. And not a Flood in sight.

Ursula could hear the pensioners clucking in sorrow, their rosaries jostling for position around the coffin and their curious eyes gazing down at the stranger in the suit within, cowboy hat on his chest. They wouldn't have known the Yank very well, but they were always up for a grieving, and where better than at the funeral of the husband of a woman who had already suffered so much. Her family casting her out, the affront of the court case, the harass-ment of the rowdies, the whispers of mental instability, her mammy's death just the week before, and now this. They would be hard pressed to find somebody more deserving of their tears. And, after that lotto win of hers, they were all of no doubt Ursula would splash out, stocking the sideboard and fridge with wild dear drink and finger foods much more elaborate than sausage rolls.

Their kind words paired with the wringing of hands:

"Yer man's lovely looking in his coffin."

"The undertaker's gone and done a quare grand job."

And to Ursula herself—

"Am wile sorry about yer trouble."

"C'mere, it was dead sudden, aye?"

"It musta been a terrible shock, like."

—Ursula nodding and turning away, her eyes still raw from the tears, her feet squelching through the still-damp orange-tinted carpeting as she shoved her way through the masses, balancing a tray of crab canapés on a silver tray. The odd bleeping sound in her ears, casting the canapés a look of suspicion.

"Ach, Ursula's quare and cut up."

"God luck to her."

Ursula watching them raid her drink out of the corner of her eye, clawing their way to get at the stuffed shitake and the crudités and the Thai dipping sauce and realizing she was alone in the world as all the while the bleeping grew more insistent. A party of one raging against a town of stokes which had turned its back against her, banished from the choir, her mother growing cold in her grave ... wondering did Eda love her or loathe her, she would never know, the sight of Fionnuala's rabid face barking at her without end, Dymphna's smirk as she eyed her handbag, Padraig's wee hand clutching a petrol bomb, hooligans from Magilligan poised to attack her frail body and mind and where in the name of the merciful Lord was that bleeping coming from?!

Ursula jerked, thinking she was in a video arcade, what with all the flashing and blinking and bleeping around her, the machines alive with some change in Jed's condition, her fingers stuck in his clutching hand, barely able to make out his features beyond the bandages and tubes, the plaster casts bulky on his limbs. Ursula moaned against his leg brace, the tears rolling down her face. She squeezed and squeezed, wringing his hand and willing him to health.

"Nurse! Nurse!" she wailed. "Something's up with them machines! Me fella's dying!"

A pack of orderlies and doctors burst into the room and booted her out as they set to work on his sputtering body. Ursula fretted at the threshold for a minute until the door was slammed in her face.

She stared down at the curious one way ticket in her hand. The paramedics had pried if from Jed's fist in the ambulance enroute to the hospital, and the police had handed it over to her. That and £4000 in cash.

"Ach, Jed, Jed, Jed ..."

He had always been hovering in the background, shuffling alone to his daily pleasures of the off-license and betting track and darts club, bull's-eyes celebrated alone, always to be relied on, and never a loving word did she have for his ears. If Jed died, Ursula would never know if he had been planning on deserting her, just as she had never demanded to know of her mother if she loved her. She would phone the Foyle Travel Agency and insist on knowing when he had purchased the ticket to see if she could figure it all out.

She glanced into the room. They were still toiling away on Jed's spasmodic body, the machines bleeping, and she couldn't tell because of the doctors' face masks if they were smiling or not. She didn't know if Jed would make it.

She hurried over to the payphone and dropped a coin in the slot.

"Foyle Travel Agency—"

"C—"

"—One moment."

Ursula stood before the apparatus, tongue poised, "S Club Party" blaring in her ear. She tapped her fingers impatiently on the wall, then whipped around at a commotion erupting from down the corridor.

"We want her moved to a private room!"

"Ye kyanny have a woman of her standing lying there with the druggies and alkies from the next bed pawing through her grapes!"

"If ye want to pay for a separate room—"

"—all her privates spread out for the world to see—"

"—kyanny take a comfort break without the—"

"Have ye the funds—"

A glimpse of Roisin's flailing arms, the curls of Dymphna's hair and the spittle from Paddy's mouth spraying into the face of a beleaguered orderly. Ursula crouched behind the payphone as she fought to contain the alarm, seeing her family for the first time as a clinical psychologist might.

"Funds me hole!"

"Private rooms is only for Orange bastards now? Is that what you're trying to say?"

"Ye see you, ye mingin wee bean flicker—"

"I've had it up to here with the likes of youse!" Lily screamed. "Security! Security! Fling these stokes into the car park now!"

Straining the telephone cord, receiver still clamped to her ear, Ursula skulked, gorilla-like, toward Jed's room and glanced inside. They were still toiling away on Jed's convulsing body, the machines bleeping. It was still impossible to tell if Jed would survive. A human voice finally broke through the Europop.

"Foyle Travel Agency? May I help you?"

"I've a wan way ticket to Wisconsin here," Ursula said, struggling to make herself heard over the scuffling and elbowing and effin and blinding echoing down the corridor. "I was just wondering if you could tell me ..."

She couldn't shake from her mind the vision of rage and desperation and unjust entitlement that her family inflicted upon the world.

"If you could tell me ..."

It was suddenly all so dead easy to understand. She had had enough of them and all. A decisiveness steeled her tongue.

"Could ye tell me how I can go about adding anoller passenger to the ticket?"

As Ursula wittered off her details and dragged out her weary credit card, the plans poured through her brain and the heavy load of a lifetime's worth of persecution slipped from her shoulders. She would creep around the corner to the Floods and silently slip the keys to 5 Murphy through the letterbox. They could have her new dream house as well; she just wanted rid of it, the sight of her orange Gaggenau fridge making her sick.

"So that's two passengers confirmed for flight 608."

"Aye, aye, that's right," Ursula said when all the particulars had been rattled off.

As she hung up, she wondered briefly where in the continental US Wisconsin might actually be, what vegetation it had, and what its exports were.

Would Jed survive his ordeal? she wondered. Would the doctors work their magic so she would be able to cover him in kisses, tell him he had always been—

Father Hogan rounded the corner, almost knocking her to her feet. He had been called to read Jed his Last Rites, but had been in the car park for a fag break. The stench of tobacco from him had Ursula retching, but she managed a grin.

"Yer services might not be required no more," she said.

Father Hogan didn't know where to look.

"Mind when I was banged in the cell, faller," Ursula said, "and ye asked me if I might not clear outta town? Am on me way to a new world called Wisconsin, no thanks to the likes of you. And I don't mind telling ye am handing over the ill-gotten gains from wer lotto win to them shameless pack of sinners I used to call me family. Not an ounce of Christian compassion in any of their bones. Me dream house, including me Jamie Oliver roasting pans, 5 Murphy Crescent, they are to have em all. Probably put em on the market and sell all me gear down the market stalls at Magazine Gate with all them drug dealers, I don't give a rat's behind. Mark me words, their lives'll change!"

She knew well Fionnuala, if she ever woke from her coma, wouldn't offer a word of thanks. That would give Ursula something to smile about on the flight to Wisconsin. The flight home.

She left Father Hogan and went to wrap her arms around her loving husband. She prayed he was still living.

Ursula opened the door and stepped inside.

SOME TIME LATER

Deep within the chipped-paint corridors of the intensive care ward of Alt-nagelvin, Fionnuala's lids flickered and slowly peeled from her eyeballs. She winced in confusion at the unfamiliar light. The fog lifted from the outskirts, and her eyes twitched in puzzlement at an outstretched arm with a catheter snaking up to an IV and life support machines which whirred away inches from her bedridden form. As Fionnuala's brain cells struggled to comprehend, her eyes took a wider tour of the environs: the wilted flowers on the bedside table, the half-deflated heart-shaped balloons moored against the enclosing curtains, the get well cards curling at the corners and yellowed with age. Her body suddenly lurched up with fear.

Fionnuala spied the nurses' call button and hauled her long-dormant limbs the length of the mattress, struggling, the bed clothes sliding to the floor, her mind racing.

She reached a trembling hand forward, alarm registering as she took in the frail, claw-like nature of her flesh, the bulging blue veins and spidery wrinkles. Tendrils of terror prickled up and down her spine. She stifled a hysterical moan and jabbed away at the call button like a thing possessed. An *elderly* thing possessed. She had become a pensioner and hadn't had the state of mind to see it.

How many years had passed? She feverishly wondered how Magella had coped without her at the Sav-U-Mor, who had gone to Eda's funeral, what Dymphna had worn to her wedding, and how many times over she and her Orange fancy man had made her a grandmother. She even wondered if the North had at long last been reunited with the South. And then she wondered about Ursula. Had the greedy bitch finally got her comeuppance? Was she suffering for her tight-fisted sins? Paying her penance for ... *paying* ...?! A sudden thought came to Fionnuala, hope glittering in her eyes. Her finger jabbed frenetically at the button, impatience dissolving into fury.

"Ach, would ye hurry yerselves up," she muttered, "ye flimmin lazy-arsed—!"

A young one in white tights and cap rushed into the room, the look on her face as if the Virgin Mary had just planted herself astride one of the sagging balloons.

"Mrs. Flood!" she gasped. "Ye've come to yer senses! At long last! Lemme seek out the head nurse!"

"Wait! Just wait you there a wee minute!" Fionnuala croaked.

Already halfway out of the room, the nurse turned back.

"H-How many years have I been laid here, me body wasting away, like?"

The orderly stared at her, her brow furrowing with concern and not a little confusion. At the very bottom of the list of emotions a recently awoken coma patient might experience was excitement, yet there it was, staring out eagerly from Fionnuala Flood's face. Sometimes, the orderly thought, these patients were a wee bit simple in the head for the rest of their lives, the coma having eaten away at those brain cells which contained common sense.

She took a timid step toward the bed.

"We'd best get the nurse," the orderly said. "We kyanny—"

"It's a question any simpleton would have no boller spewing out the answer to!" Fionnuala barked.

The orderly chewed her lower lip.

"What year does it be?" Fionnuala demanded feverishly, clutching the nurse's lapels and dragging her into her face. "What age's me Padraig? *What age is me Padraig?*"

A bevy of hospital employees now crowded the threshold in wonder. Such a selfless woman, this Mrs. Flood, they marveled, wrenched from a coma and unconcerned about her own traumas, a caring mother, worried sick only about the welfare of her wanes. This Padraig she kept mentioning must be her favorite wee dote.

"Is he eighteen?" Fionnuala begged to know, staring wildly around the room. She caught the fleeting silhouette of a tall orderly, broad shoulders, sauntering down the corridor. The hope blossomed on her ravaged features.

Her Padraig, she marveled, finally of age!

"Is that me Padraig?" she insisted on knowing.

"Calm you down, Mrs. Flood," the head sister, finally arriving, cooed, wiping her brow. "Ye've not been out long, sure."

The feverish excitement lunged into despair, Fionnuala's lips curled with scorn.

"Ach, catch yerself on, ye headbin!" she spat. "Not been out long, me arse! Would ye look at the state of me body!"

The head sister looked Fionnuala's body up and down and pursed her lips, thinking, *That's the way it came in, sure.* She spread a copy of the latest *Derry Journal* on the nightstand.

"Go on and have a look at the date, love," she said.

Suspicious, Fionnuala willed herself to cast a look at the newspaper. Her eyes widened. Her body shuddered, incensed.

"Nine bloody days?" she gasped, clutching at her heart. "Ye kyanny be telling me I've still *seven flippin years* to wait? *Seven flippin years* for that fecking compensation money?!"

"Code blue! Code blue!" wailed the head nurse. "A cardiac arrest, so it is!"

They wheeled Fionnuala off to surgery.

Anderson Publishing
324 Fleet Street
London W1
UK

Dear Ms. Moira Flood:

We are pleased to inform you that we have decided to take on your novel, *An Embarrassment of Riches*. Might we suggest, however, that you work with our editor to change the first-person narrative to third person?

Paul McMurphy will be in touch with you in the near future regarding this matter.

Congratulations!

Best,

Lucretia Neff
Editor-In-Chief

978-0-595-44759-6
0-595-44759-7

Printed in the United States
127424LV00009B/95/A